ABOUT THE AUTHOR

Mandy Magro lives in Cairns, Far North Queensland, with her fiance, Des, their daughter, Chloe Rose, and their two adorable pooches, Sophie and Sherlock. With pristine aqua-blue coastline in one direction and sweeping rural landscapes in the other, she describes her home as heaven on earth. A passionate woman and a romantic at heart, Mandy loves writing about soul-deep love, the Australian way of life, and the wonderful characters who call the country home.

www.facebook.com/mandymagroauthor
www.mandymagro.com

Also by Mandy Magro

MANDY MAGRO

The Stockman's Secret

First Published 2020
Second Australian Paperback Edition 2023
ISBN 9781867287285

THE STOCKMAN'S SECRET
© 2020 by Mandy Magro
Australian Copyright 2020
New Zealand Copyright 2020

This is a work of fiction. Names, characters, places, and incidents are either the product of the author's imagination or are used fictitiously, and any resemblance to actual persons, living or dead, business establishments, events, or locales is entirely coincidental.

Published by
HQ Fiction
An imprint of Harlequin Enterprises (Australia) Pty Limited (ABN 47 001 180 918), a subsidiary of HarperCollins Publishers Australia Pty Limited (ABN 36 009 913 517)
Level 19, 201 Elizabeth St
SYDNEY NSW 2000
AUSTRALIA

A catalogue record for this book is available from the National Library of Australia
www.librariesaustralia.nla.gov.au

Printed and bound in Australia by McPherson's Printing Group

Some secrets are so extremely powerful that, when uncovered, they can unite, or they can divide

Dropping to her knees
She clasped her hands tight
While staring into the eyes of the devil
She did as she was told, and prayed for all her sins
Although, she did not understand
How he could be speaking of heaven
When all he brought to her life was hell

PROLOGUE

Little Heart, Far North Queensland

Twelve-year-old Joel Hunter listened as the wild wind lashed the branches of the towering Bowen mango tree he loved to climb against the side of the house. A distant curlew called out, the lone bird's song eerie, and Joel was grateful to be tucked up inside, safe and sound.

Making the sign of the cross, he tightly folded his hands, closed his eyes, and drew comfort from his hero – his father – kneeling close beside him. Soft lamplight cast shadows across the bottom bunk bed, and over Joel's cheeks, grazed in the attack. The Muller boys had started bullying him when he became an altar boy at Little Heart Church – a role he was extremely proud of. Trying to ignore the relentless sting in his knees, hands and arms from when they'd dragged him from his pushbike and across the gravel, along with the horrible ache in his heart caused by the humiliation, he joined his dad in their usual nightly bedtime prayer. He watched as his father drew in a steady breath, his big chest rising, before sighing it away as his eyelids closed. Only then did Joel squeeze his eyes shut.

'Lord, I pray for my son, and that you would comfort him in this hard time. Please grant him the strength to forgive the three boys who've bullied him for being a loyal child of yours and protect him from any further harm. I trust you'll help the culprits to see the injustices of their ways, and hope that, in time, they and their parents will come to believe in the teachings of the Bible, so they can live a wholesome life devoted to you, as we do in this house that you have blessed us with. Amen.'

His father finished, Joel quickly added, 'Yes, please, Lord, to everything Dad just said. Thank you for everything you do for me. Amen.' Then, swallowing hard, he blinked back another onslaught of tears. He didn't want to cry again. He wanted to be big and strong, like his dad.

A reassuring pat on Joel's back brought his gaze to that of his father's. 'Proud of you, son.'

'Thanks, Dad, and thanks for going and talking to Principal Edwards, and the Muller boys' parents too. I just hope it doesn't make things worse.' Joel frowned. 'You know how much of a grump their father can be when he gets mad.' The time he'd watched Mr Muller yell at the lady who worked in the grocery store because she'd given him the wrong change flashed before his eyes.

'It won't, my boy. I promise.' With a groan his father rose from his knees, as did Joel. 'Their father needs to take a long hard look at himself, teaching his boys that violence is okay. Champion boxer or not, Michael Muller should know better than that.'

Shaking his head, his father heaved another gentle, weary sigh as he sat on the edge of the bed. 'I think after being suspended from school for a week, as well as having to attend the anti-bullying classes your mum is running down at the church with Mrs Kern, the three of them will've learnt their lesson, hopefully.'

Nodding, Joel sniffled, gruffly wiping the tears from his sore cheeks. He hated being a big sook, hated the fact he was all lanky arms and legs without an aggressive bone in his body. Hated the fact it was a girl – *the* girl, the one he'd had a crush on for the past year – the very pretty and very nice Juliette Kern, who had saved him from the bullies. He wanted nothing more than to impress her, to make her see he was big and tough, a match to her gutsy spirit and tomboy persona, but try as he might, he just couldn't fake it. 'I'm sorry I was too afraid to stand up to them and Juliette had to chase them off by throwing rocks at them. I feel silly, having a girl do that for me.'

'Don't you dare feel silly, my boy.' Patting Joel's arm, William half-chuckled, shaking his head. 'She's certainly a little firecracker, that girl. I think she'd scare most boys with how fiercely she can yell.'

Remembering Juliette's stern face as she'd protected him so fearlessly, hands on her hips while telling the three Muller brothers to rack off, Joel chuckled. 'She sure is a little firecracker.' And right then and there, he decided that would be her nickname – if she didn't mind it. 'I wish I was more like her.' His smile faded with the declaration.

Reaching out and pulling his son to him, his father ruffled his hair. 'Don't beat yourself up. You're a good boy, Joel, and you did the right thing by not stooping to their level. God wouldn't take kindly to you throwing punches just because they are.' He unfolded his towering frame and stood. Then, with a warm smile, he peeled back the doona and patted the animal-printed flannel sheet. 'Now, come on, it's time for bed, so in you hop.' He glanced to the top bunk. 'Zoe's already fast asleep, the sweet child.'

'Yeah, I thought she was just trying to get out of eating her peas and carrots at dinner …' Joel peeped up at his baby sister. '… but she must have been telling the truth about being super-duper tired.' His cotton pyjamas askew, he straightened them before climbing beneath the sheets.

A flood of reassurance filled him as his father tucked him in and kissed his forehead. 'I love you, son, and I want you to know how proud your mother and I are of you for always telling the truth, and not resorting to violence.'

'Thank you, Dad.' His tears and fears all but forgotten, Joel smiled. 'And I love you too, to the moon and back, and beyond.'

'Now that's a whole lot of love, my boy.' His father's smile widened as he chuckled. 'I'm one lucky father, having a wonderful, kind and very clever son like you.'

Joel grinned proudly as his dad's tender chuckle warmed him from the inside out. 'Night, Dad.'

'Night, Joel. Sweet dreams, son.' Leaving the lamp on, his dad padded to the doorway, paused momentarily as he offered a final reassuring smile and, leaving the door half-open, disappeared down the hallway.

Joel rolled onto his side, squeezing his eyes shut. He was even more tired than the days he'd help his dad train the horses. Hovering in between realms, it wasn't going to take him long to drift into dreamland, the shelter of his home and the unconditional love of his family giving him all the comfort he needed to let the horror of the day go. As his mum had said while gently tending to his scrapes and bruises, her frown deep and her blue-green eyes filled with compassion, he would live to tell another tale. He just hoped it was going to be a good one.

CHAPTER

1

Six years later

Juliette Kern fought to keep her eyes from the door to the cupboard tucked in beneath the spiral staircase, her heart racing a million miles a minute. The little area terrified her, the enclosed space so velvety black she couldn't see anything once locked away in there – as she had been more times than she cared to remember. But the fear of that room wouldn't stop her now, although she had to be extremely careful. Being caught wasn't an option.

Stepping into the lounge room, she sucked in a shaky breath. 'I've finished my Bible study assignment, so I'm off to bed,' she said as casually as she could, then forced a yawn.

Brows furrowed, her stepfather barely acknowledged her, his steel-grey eyes glued to his weekly dose of the ABC's *Australian Story*. Juliette was glad for his distraction. She glanced to where he'd hung his belt and tie over the back of a chair, and icy fingers travelled up her spine.

Leaning over the back of the lounge chair, she brushed a kiss over her mother's cheek. 'Night, Mum. I love you.'

'Night, love.' Cradling her cup of tea, her mum looked up, smiling. 'Don't forget to say your prayers before you go to sleep.'

'Of course I won't,' Juliette replied before turning and treading back down the hallway.

After shutting her bedroom door, she rearranged her pillows and doona to make it look like she was in the bed and, just in case, turned off her lamp. Satisfied she'd done all she could, she grabbed her torch and thongs and quietly slid her window open. Balmy air mingled with that of her air-conditioner, and the scent of her mother's frangipani and jasmine blossoms hung heavily. Cattle bellowed in the distance and from the paddock down the driveway, her horse whinnied. Holding her breath, she hitched up her dress and glided out, one long leg after the other, then slid her window shut and slipped on her favourite diamante-studded Havaianas. Sticking to the shadows while moving fast across the back lawn, she vanished into the night, waiting until she was safely surrounded by the scrublands of Crystal National Park before she flicked her torch on. She couldn't wait to see Joel, or for the day she didn't have to live beneath her parents' roof.

* * *

Summer had arrived in Little Heart with typical Far North Queensland vengeance, with the balmy temperature still hovering in the high twenties hours after the fiery orb of the sun had slunk behind the distant mountain ranges. Switching the outside light on, Joel Hunter watched hundreds of insects swarming towards the sudden brightness, like soldiers into battle. A loud ding from his back pocket almost made him jump. He grabbed his mobile phone, flipping it open.

I'm down by the river, hiding behind a clump of bushes. Video camera at the ready. I'll make sure I stay quiet. See you soon buddy.

Smiling, Joel punched back, *Thanks Ben, I owe you one.*

He couldn't believe this day had finally come. It was the day after his eighteenth birthday, he was officially an adult, and this was the first day of the rest of his life. Now his high-school years were done and dusted, he had moved from beneath his parents' roof into the renovated ex-tobacco barn and become his father's right-hand man on the farm. It was an absolute dream come true. Now, all he needed was for her to say yes and his life would be perfect.

He heard her hurried footsteps just before she appeared from the trail that led to her place. Right on time, she had a torch in hand, and her long, dark hair was loose and swaying around her back.

'Hey there, beautiful,' he said, his heart careening at the mere sight of her. 'I've missed you.'

'Hey there, handsome.' Juliette ran into his open arms and wrapped hers around him. 'We only saw each other seven hours ago. But I missed you too,' she said, a smile playing on her glossy lips as she pulled back a little, rose up on her toes and kissed him.

'So, did you tell your parents you were meeting me tonight?' he asked cheekily.

'Yeah, right.' Her radiant smile faded as she shook her head. 'I wish I could tell them the truth, but Dad would kill me if he knew I was sneaking out, meeting some boy ... doing god-only-knows what.' She mimicked her stepfather's booming voice while rolling her eyes. She tried to force a smile – he could tell she was faking it because her lips trembled.

'I'm not just "some boy", Jules.' Her words cut, but he shook it off. Malcolm Kern, Juliette's stepfather and the town's pastor, was very strict about Juliette doing anything outside of school or church. Joel had high regard for the man, who'd always proven himself to be a devout Christian, and he always felt a little guilty breaking Malcolm's rules, even if he didn't know about it. 'I'm your boyfriend. We've been together for almost a year now, even if it's on the quiet, and our families know each other so well. Surely your parents would be happy about our love when you find the right time to tell them?'

'All in good time, my gorgeous man.' She gently touched his cheek and studied him with her dark eyes. 'I know you think you know my dad. Heck, the whole town thinks they know him because they see him up on his pulpit every Sunday, giving his sermons. But trust me – I know him the most, and he won't like me being with *any* guy, especially before I've turned eighteen.'

'You're only five days off it, though.' Not that Joel needed to remind her of her birthday, a date easy for him to remember when they were only a week apart.

'Yeah, I know.' She sighed with a half-shrug. 'Stupid, but I live beneath his roof, and I have to abide by his rules. Or at least do my very best to make sure he doesn't find out I'm breaking them.' She grimaced. 'Because if he did, I'd be in big trouble.'

'He's only so strict because he loves you and wants the best for you, I'm sure,' he said, gently tucking stray hair from her face and over her ears, which were donned with the dangly heart-shaped earrings he'd bought her for Valentine's Day.

Sadness splashed across her face as she cuddled into him, slicing at his heart – he hated seeing her upset. Ignoring his burning urge to do what he so longed to do and go around to ask Malcolm Kern for his stepdaughter's hand in marriage – not something easily done when Malcolm thought he and Juliette were just friends – he did his best to focus on Juliette.

He turned his face into her ear, whispering, 'I love you.'

'I love you too, Joel. So much.' She pulled back a little and smiled now. 'So, tell me, what was so important that I needed to sneak out to meet you?'

Feeling on top of the world, though a little nervous, he unravelled his arms from around her and grabbed her hand, savouring the sensation of his fingers interlaced with hers. 'Come on and I'll show you.' She allowed him to lead her, their footfalls softened by the blanket of leaves along the path leading from Hunter Farmstead to the burbles of Little Heart River.

'Where are we going?' she asked, her sweet voice hushed.

'To our special place.' He fleetingly remembered their very first kiss by the river and his heart quickened.

'I only have an hour or so before I have to be back, Joel.' She hesitated a little. 'The longer I'm gone, the more chance of Mum or Dad sticking their head in to check on me.'

'All good, Firecracker.' He flashed her a grin. 'This won't take too long, I promise.'

Juliette regarded him and then nodded. 'Then let's get there, quick smart.'

The weight of the ring in his back pocket only added to Joel's nervousness. He couldn't get to the bank of the river quick enough. He'd been waiting for this day to arrive ever since he'd locked eyes with her across the packed Sunday church seven years ago. Tonight was the night he'd make an honest woman of her – if she said yes.

Juliette's soft voice broke his satisfying train of thought. 'Joel, there's something I have to tell you.' She seemed apprehensive to speak what was on her mind, so much so his heart skidded to an almighty stop.

Trying to act nonchalant, he looked at her. 'Sure, Jules. Shoot.'

She bit her lip and then released a sigh. 'Remember I told you I'd applied to James Cook University to do my Bachelor of Education?'

'Yeah …' He held his breath.

'Well, I got a letter back from them this afternoon,' she said in a rush. 'I've been accepted.' She gave his hand a squeeze.

'Holy heck.' His thoughts took off like spooked wild horses, and his heart sank to his boots like lead. She'd have to move. The university was in Cairns, only two hours away but still too far. With the course going for four years, they wouldn't be living together anytime soon. He couldn't move with her. It meant too much to his father that Joel had taken the job by his side, and Joel was proud and keen to follow in his footsteps.

Her pained expression pulled him to a stop. 'Joel, please say something.'

He swallowed down his bitter disappointment – this meant a lot to her. 'Sorry. Wow, that's wonderful news! I'm so happy for you.' And he genuinely was – just not so much for himself. Not wanting her to glimpse his deep sorrow, he picked her up and spun her around until she laughed, just long enough to pull himself together.

She pulled back a little, her smile wide, warm and relieved. 'So, you're okay with it?'

'Of course, Firecracker,' he lied. 'You've always wanted to be a teacher, so who am I to stop you from reaching your dream?' He placed a lingering kiss on her lips as he eased her back to the ground. 'We'll be right. Long distance won't matter a bit.'

Her hands slipped from his shoulders. 'It's not really long distance,' she offered with a little shrug. 'I can drive here, and you can come visit me. Any time, day or night.'

'When we're not studying, or working, or …' At the hurt flashing in her eyes, he stopped himself from going further into the negative, a habit that frustrated her at times. 'But yeah, of course we can, all the time. What's four years anyway? We've got this.'

'You're the best boyfriend ever, Joel Hunter. Thank you for being so awesome.'

'I do my best.' He puffed out his chest and forced a gallant grin. 'And you are the most awesome girlfriend ever.' He wrapped his arms around her tiny waist, imagining her as his wife and himself as her husband.

'Naw. I love you, so much.'

'I love you, too, Jules, always and forever.' It hit him that he didn't need to curb his plans, just tweak them a little. Their love would get them through the next few years. God was just testing them. The new awareness buoyed him.

Juliette pushed up on her tippy toes and pressed another strawberry-glossed kiss upon his lips. When she sank back down to the earth, she flashed him a familiar challenging grin. 'How about the first one to our secret spot scores a foot rub?'

'Even though I'm always giving you foot rubs.' His swooning heart skipping beats, Joel matched her grin. 'You're on like Donkey Kong, Jules.'

'On like Donkey Kong?' She chuckled. 'My goodness, Joel Hunter, you're so darn *groovy*, I can't handle it.' With a wide smile, she lingered for a moment before clapping her hands. 'Right then, race ya to the finishing line!' Competitiveness flashed in her eyes as she spun in her thongs and took off, long black hair swishing around her waist, her turquoise boho-style dress floating at her ankles.

'Oi, no fair! You got a head start,' Joel called after her playfully.

'Come on and catch up, you slow coach,' she teased, her laughter hanging heavily on the air.

Joel chuckled at her exuberance. She always made him feel acutely alive, and so very loved. She was beautiful, ethereal – his very own gift from the heavens. With beads of sweat trickling down his back, he trailed her swiftly, weaving through the thicket of trees and scrub towards the gurgles of Little Heart River. The river bordered and divided three properties – Hunter Farmstead, all of two hundred acres, the opulent Davis Horse Stud, close to nine hundred acres with a sprawling homestead and classy stables to boot, and Juliette's parents' house on a humble five acres. Juliette and her parents had moved there six years ago, when she was almost twelve, from a cramped flat behind the church. Word was the property had been a bribe from Ron and Margery Davis, but for what, Joel had never bothered to ask. He didn't believe the tale. Gossip was the devil's tongue, his mother always said. He just thanked his lucky stars that they were virtually neighbours and they got to see each other a lot more than when she lived in town.

A full moon shimmered against the velvet black of night, spilling silvery light over the worn path they'd taken many times before. Clearing a fallen tree trunk just in the nick of time, he patted his back pockets, making sure the ring and the key were still safe and secure. He was still going to offer both to her – it was her choice what happened after that. His heart flip-flopped at the thought of her walking down the aisle to him, and then afterwards, to the very first time he and Juliette would make love, both waiting until fully committed.

Juliette's squeals of laughter carried from up ahead, bringing him back to the present. In the thick of the shadows, the path turned sharply, and he cornered it perfectly, the thicket of native trees finally giving way to a small clearing that was home to their small part of Little Heart River – their special spot. It always would be. One day, they'd bring their children here, to share it as a family. Just up ahead, Juliette was kneeling at the edge of the river, scooping up handfuls of the water lazily travelling over the rocky riverbed. She and the stream were lit up, dreamlike, by the silvery moonlight.

Hearing him approach, she looked over her shoulder, grinning. 'About time you showed up. I thought you'd gone and got yourself lost.'

'Oh, hardy-ha-ha, Little Miss Comedian.' Beaming from ear to ear, Joel fought to catch his breath as he looked to where Ben would most probably be hiding, ready to film the special moment with his video camera. A quick thumbs up from the shadows let him know they were good to go. 'You're lucky to have a boyfriend like me, who gives you a head start and then lets you win,' he said a little less breathlessly.

'Pull the other one, Hunter. I beat you, fair and square.' She gave him the forks and he grinned wickedly. 'Now you owe me an even longer foot rub than I usually get.'

'Talk about a bloody slave driver.' Joel playfully groaned. 'But if I have to …' He loved being able to touch her soft skin, so it was no chore to rub her feet.

Somewhere in the line-up of the huge paperbark trees that hugged the river's banks, a barn owl screeched. Seconds later, its mate replied.

Joel glanced upwards. 'Man, oh man, they sound eerie.'

'They do, huh.' Standing, Juliette joined him in trying to spot the birds. 'But I love how they mate for life.' She looked back at him. 'So romantic, don't you think?'

'Damn straight it's romantic.' His passion stirred by the privacy granted by the bushlands surrounding them, he grabbed the perfect moment to do what he came here for.

Offering him a delicate smile filled with love, Juliette regarded the trees once more.

Lightheaded with anticipation, Joel dropped to his knees.

Turning her attention back to him, Juliette tilted her head, bewildered. 'What are you doing?' She looked to the ground. 'Did you drop something?' She fell to her knees, ready to help him.

Unable to get a word out for the lump of emotion stuck in his throat, Joel just shook his head. He'd practised a huge speech at length, one filled with sentiment, but now, in the heat of the moment, he was finding it hard to string a sentence together. *Come on, pull it together, Hunter.*

Juliette took his hand, her gaze deeply concerned. 'Joel, is everything okay?'

'Uh-huh.' He fleetingly glanced to the blanket of stars, glittering like millions of crystals, before bringing his teary gaze

back to the love of his life. Then, with a deep inhalation, he
went to his back pocket, plucked out his grandmother's ring, and
flicked the box open. 'Juliette Kern, will you do me the absolute
honour of marrying me?' He held his breath.

'Oh my goodness! Joel ...' Juliette's lips quivered into a happy
smile, but before she could answer, heavy footfalls sounded.

They appeared out of nowhere.

CHAPTER
2

A split-second's notice was all that Joel got, yet it felt like everything was moving in slow motion. Helpless to the brute force of the three burly Muller brothers, he didn't have time to pull Juliette to safety, or throw his arms up in defence. He watched in horror as a hand went across Juliette's mouth as she was yanked to her feet, eyes wide with fear. As he rose to save her, a sharp blow to the back of his head sent him hurtling to the ground like a ragdoll, the thud knocking the wind right out of him. Juliette cried out. The ring and the velvet box went flying. The world spun nauseatingly as everything around him went in and out of focus.

In a world of pain, and with something dripping into his eyes, Joel grabbed the side of his head and pulled his hand away to find it covered in blood – *his* blood. Woozy as hell, he fought to stand but strong hands gripped him, flipped him, and dragged him backwards, away from Juliette. The strong stench of rum and marijuana haze was exhaled into his face. Dazed and terrified, he tried to get up again, but he was held down. Through the ringing in his ears, he heard someone was laughing. He knew that malicious laugh, could pick it out a mile away – he'd been the target of it many a time.

The steel-cap toe of a boot met his ribs, hard, three times, and an elbow crushed down upon his chest. Then a blade came to his throat, the very point of it piercing his flesh.

His ribs felt broken and he needed to cough but Joel stayed stock-still, meeting the steely eyes of Desmond Muller, the second oldest of the brothers. Desmond had bullied him for as long as he could remember – a school suspension and the anti-bullying classes they'd been forced to attend had done nothing but fuel their fire and cause a massive rift between their fathers. Near him but out of reach, Juliette's pleading was tearing shreds from his heart.

His heart was trying to bash its way out of his chest, but the blade pressed forebodingly into his throat, trapping him. Joel prayed to god they didn't discover Ben hiding in the bushes, if he was still there. Ben was a computer geek from way back – a lover, not a fighter – without a hope in hell of saving himself if they got their hands on him.

'Have you all lost your damn minds?' Joel growled through gritted teeth. 'What the hell do you think you're doing, Des?'

'Move an inch, Hunter, and I'll slit your damn throat and send you to heaven nice and early. Your pretty little girlfriend can watch.' Desmond Muller gestured to Juliette with a tip of his head. Joel watched in horror as Levi Muller – the oldest brother and the spitting image of his hostile father – man-handled Juliette.

The fear and humiliation Joel had felt the day he was dragged off his pushbike all came crashing back. Pain shot through his body. He knew he needed to be the man he felt he'd become and save Juliette, like she'd saved him that awful day, but with the knife holding him to ransom and a stout Muller boy on either side, he couldn't get to her. And if he tried, he was afraid they'd hurt her even more.

As he weighed up his limited options, his focus wavering as if beneath water, his arms were grabbed and twisted at awkward angles behind his back. Zip ties were wrapped around his wrists and ankles, excruciatingly tight, and he watched as the same was done to Juliette.

He shouted, 'It's me you want to hurt, and I'm all yours. Let her go, Levi.'

The red-headed giant glared in his direction, his lips curled into a sickening smirk. 'Come on over here and make me, Hunter.'

'I bloody well would if I wasn't tied up with a knife to my throat. You need your brothers to protect you from me?' Joel knew he didn't stand a chance in hell going up against these three bullies, but he'd damn well die trying if it meant protecting Juliette.

With a smug smirk, Levi shoved Juliette into his younger brother. 'Take care of her for a minute, would you? And shut her up while you're at it.'

Jackson Muller jumped to his brother's command, and Levi stepped towards Joel, stopping just short of him.

With Jackson's hand clamped tightly over her mouth, Juliette's cries were muffled, but they still tore at Joel's heart. He tried to see her, but Levi's bulk blocked his line of vision. 'I'm so sorry, Jules.' He should have been able to stop them, to protect her.

'Did you hear that, Juliette?' Levi sneered. 'Your hero boyfriend here is sorry he's a big wuss and can't help you.'

'How in the hell did you know we were down here?' Joel demanded. The only people who knew were his mum and dad, Ben and Zoe.

Levi picked at something beneath his fingernails as he sucked air through his teeth. 'Your little sister told someone, who told someone else, who came and told us.' He threw his arms up, his smile unnervingly wide. 'And voila. Here we all are.'

'Why are you doing this, Muller?'

Levi's eyes narrowed as he squatted and shoved his face a mere inch from Joel's. 'For years, I've watched you get everything you want without even trying.' He jabbed him in the chest with a stubby finger. 'Enough's enough.'

Joel was gobsmacked. 'I don't know what you're on about. I've worked hard for everything I have.' None of this made any sense. He strained to catch a glimpse of Juliette before Levi grabbed his jaw and squeezed it tight.

'Shut your damn trap, Hunter,' he snarled. 'You nabbed the one girl I've fancied ever since I knew what the yearnings in my jocks were about, and all because butter wouldn't melt in your saintly little mouth.'

Joel huffed, almost laughed in his face. 'Like you'd ever have a shot with her. Juliette and I love each other. Get over yourself, Muller.'

'What a load of shit.' Levi half-laughed. 'Juliette just doesn't know what's good for her. She's not sickly sweet and boring like you religious lot, even though that's what she tries to make people believe. *I* see the fire in her belly and that wicked spark in her eyes. She's got a wild child begging to be brought out and I'm not gonna sit back and let you bore her to fucking tears with that picket-fence lifestyle.'

'You're insane,' Joel heard Juliette spit. 'I'd never fall for a scumbag like you. Stop wasting our bloody time and let us go.'

'Is that so?' Levi looked over his shoulder to where Jackson had his arm clamped around Juliette's throat. She glared back at him, dark eyes wild. 'What do you think, Hunter? Maybe I should give her a little taste of what she's going to miss out on by choosing the likes of you over a real man.'

Red rage washed over Joel, the pure fury surging through him an overwhelming sensation he'd never felt before. 'What in the hell do you mean? Don't you touch her!'

Levi snickered, standing and looking between his younger brothers. 'You two keep him quiet. If he makes a noise or pulls any funny business, shut him the hell up and teach him a damn good lesson.'

Pushing Juliette to Levi, Jackson grinned. 'Gladly.'

'We got your back, bro,' Desmond added.

Levi sent Juliette to the ground with one backhand slap.

The sound of her body slamming against the earth, and the loud whoosh of her breath, seemed to ricochet around Joel. Panic seized him and he desperately tried to free his hands from the zip ties. 'Get away from her, you son of a bitch.'

With a sneer, Jackson slammed his boot into Joel's ribs. 'Shut the hell up, Hunter.'

Standing over him, arms folded, Desmond planted his feet wide apart, his smirk unholy. 'Hey, altar boy, do you think god's going to swoop in and miraculously save you both?'

'Go to hell, you sick bastards.' Believing with all his might that god *would* somehow save them from this, Joel silently prayed harder than he'd ever prayed before while Levi pinned Juliette to the ground beneath his bear-like weight, her struggling ceasing with the glint of the knife.

'Hey there, sweetness.' Straddling her, Levi opened his pocketknife with a sneer, flipped his cap backwards and leant into her, his massive bulk shielding the moonlight from her face. 'So, tell me. Am I right? Are you made of sugar and spice and all things nice, or is there a little bit of the devil inside of you?'

Her eyes clamped shut, Juliette turned her face away from him, whimpering.

'You're gonna pay big time if you hurt her, Levi.' Joel struggled against the two sets of hands pinning him down, the blade of the knife nicking his throat again in the process. It felt deeper this time, though the pain from it was the least of his problems.

'I won't be paying for anything.' His meaty fist forming a pistol – thumb cocked and index finger pointed at Joel – Levi snorted cynically. 'So shut your damn mouth, Hunter, or I'm going to hurt her *real* bad.'

Juliette whimpered, her lips clamped shut.

Joel eyed his enemy as if he wanted to kill him with his bare hands. And he was afraid that if he wasn't tied up, he very possibly would. His wits were all he had right now, so he had to take the risk and play to Levi's bluff. 'Oh come on, Levi. You're not going to do anything more stupid than you already have. We all know that.'

'Do we, Hunter?' Levi spat.

'Yeah, we do,' Joel ploughed on. 'Because there's not a hope in hell of you becoming a doctor if you have a criminal record.'

'Just let us go now,' Juliette put in. His brave girl looked dazed but suddenly determined. 'We can forget about the whole thing.'

Levi's evil expression turned all the more menacing. 'And just how am I going to get a criminal record if none of you are going to be able to blab to the coppers?'

Joel remained silent as his heart sank. That threat had been his trump card and it had failed.

'Don't say I didn't warn you.' The atmosphere thickened as Levi clamped Juliette to the ground. He unzipped his jeans, the tautness of his underpants revealing just how much he was enjoying all of this.

Mortified, terrified for her, Joel cried out something incomprehensible.

Juliette bucked against Levi as he sliced at her dress. Joel froze as she screamed out. 'You've cut me, you bastard.'

'That'll teach you to stay still, Juliette,' Levi shot back.

'Enough, bro.' Desmond took a step forwards. 'This shit ain't funny anymore.'

'Yeah, Levi. Don't do it.' Jackson's voice quavered, although he held the knife steadfast against Joel's throat. 'We don't want any trouble with the cops. Dad will have our heads if the pigs turn up at his door.'

'I fucking know that, and I also know they fucking won't.' Levi shot them both a warning glint. 'Back off, little brothers.'

Like obedient mongrels, Desmond and Jackson did as they were told, but their fear was tangible. It gave Joel a smidgen of hope that there was some way out of this.

Levi opened the top half of Juliette's dress. 'Nice red bra, sugarplum.' He licked his lips, running his fingers beneath the lace. 'I might just have to have a little taste of those beauties.' Levi's free hand muffled Juliette's sobs as she continued to buck beneath the weight of him. Levi just laughed as he wrestled her into submission.

Cold fear seeped beneath Joel's skin. 'Please, Levi, stop, please, she doesn't deserve this.' The hoarse voice didn't sound like his own.

'Shut up, shut up, shut up!' Jackson bellowed, clearly starting to lose it, the hand holding the knife shaking. Convinced his throat would be slit, along with Juliette's, Joel clamped his mouth shut.

Juliette's soft whimpers were all that could be heard over Levi's grunts and groans as he tried to tug his jeans down fully.

Revolted to his very core, Joel squeezed his eyes shut, feeling the sting of tears behind his lids. Shudders filled him. He didn't want to watch, didn't want to witness the love of his life, the one woman he felt compelled to protect, being sexually assaulted by a man as immoral and repellent as Levi Muller. He had to do something. Anything. Now. Or forever hold himself accountable for what happened next. He'd never be able to live with himself if things got even worse. He prayed for god to give him the strength to do what he had to, and to forgive him now for what might happen if he somehow got his hands around Levi's throat.

A violent rush filled Joel, the longing to hurt another something he'd never felt before. The urge to do whatever it took, even if it meant losing his own life to do it, overcame him. He sucked in a deep breath, readying himself to push to his feet and somehow get to Juliette before it was too late. He was primed to fight until his very last breath.

Suddenly, crashing out of the bushes, a huge rock in his hands, Ben sprang for Levi. 'Nooo,' he cried. 'Leave her alone!'

Before Desmond or Jackson could react, Ben brought the rock down on Levi's skull with an almighty crack. The loud thump seemed to echo as Levi collapsed atop Juliette, blood spilling from him. Pinned down, probably suffocating beneath his weight, Juliette fought to roll free. Ben took one last look at Joel, petrified, before vanishing back into the scrub – he was running for his life.

Jackson and Desmond dove in to help their brother, now in a heap beside Juliette. Desmond slapped his brother's face, desperately trying to wake him, but to no avail. Joel kept one eye on them as he wriggled to where Jackson had dropped his knife and, grabbing hold of it, frantically cut through the zip ties at his feet. His hands would have to remain bound.

So much happened, yet it all went down in a matter of seconds. So fast that Joel's head was spinning. And then, as his and Jules's eyes met, just like that, it was as if a switch had been flicked and time seemed to slow, falter, stop. Struggling to stand, he stumbled over to Juliette and fell to his knees beside her. She reached for him, sobbing.

With hands too steady for the situation, Joel tugged her dress down and then pulled the top of it closed as best he could. 'We have to get out of here,' he whispered into her ear.

She nodded, lips trembling. She looked so vulnerable, so broken. If Levi survived, Joel was going to make it his mission to make him pay for what he'd done tonight, along with his bastard brothers. Slipping the knife beneath the zip ties around her ankles, he freed her feet so they could make a run for it. Helping her up, he watched cautiously as Desmond heaved a limp Levi over his shoulder. Unmoving, his hair and face covered in blood, Joel couldn't be sure that Levi wasn't dead. Part of him hoped he was.

But he wasn't about to wait to find out.

He pulled Juliette into the shadows and they took off down the worn path that led to home, with Jackson Muller yelling out something incomprehensible behind them. Joel made sure to keep Juliette in front of him, constantly looking over his shoulder. If they came for them, he would be the barricade that kept her out of harm's way. Looking at what had been his favourite white T-shirt, he shuddered. There was so much blood. Was it his? Was it Juliette's? A wave of dizziness almost sent him crashing to the ground, but he fought it off. Juliette needed him. He needed to be strong. His heart hammered. His ribs hurt. His head pounded. The world around him blurred, twisted and spun. He pushed through all of it. For her.

It didn't take them long, although it felt like forever, to reach the outhouses of the farm. Only then did they slow.

* * *

Stopping by the back of the stables, Juliette heaved in deep breaths, looking to Joel, behind them, and then back to Joel again, terror gripping her. 'Are they gone?' The voice, twisted with fear, didn't sound like her. 'Please tell me they are.'

With a quick glance into the darkness, Joel nodded. 'I think so.' He turned back to her. 'I don't think they'd be game enough to follow us here.' Sadness and fear shadowed his eyes as he considered her. 'Oh, Jules. I'm so sorry.'

She shook her head, a big part of her not wanting to admit something so horrifying had just happened. 'I'm okay.' It was a lie. She wasn't. All of her hurt. She craved for Joel to take her into his arms, to soothe away her fear and disgust as he made her feel safe and loved. But his wrists were still bound.

As if sensing her need, he looked to the doorway. 'I'll go and grab something to cut these off.'

She nodded, her bottom lip clamped between her teeth as he stepped into the darkness and flicked on the overhead light. She stuck to his side like glue, her breathing shallow, unable to take a full, free breath.

Joel grabbed a Stanley knife and freed her. 'Can you do mine now, Jules?'

There was so much concern and pity in his gaze that a rush of anger surged through her. She didn't want to be pitied. She wanted this to somehow never have happened, and if she couldn't have that, to forget this ever happened.

With trembling hands, she freed him, operating on autopilot, as if having an out of body experience. She wrapped her arms around herself, as if she could hold her shattered pieces together.

Joel looked to the bright red bloodstain on her torn and tattered dress. 'How bad is the cut on your stomach?'

Her knife-bitten flesh stung, but she brought her hand to cover it. 'Not bad enough for stitches.' There was no way she could go to the hospital.

Joel pulled her to him and her resolve broke. She sobbed against his shoulder, arms wrapped tightly around him. He combed his hand through her tangled, dirt-matted hair, rubbed her back, kissed her forehead. 'I'm so sorry, Jules.' He sniffled, as if holding his tears at bay. 'We'll call the police and tell them what's happened.'

No, no, nooo, a voice in her head screamed. They couldn't tell the police. They couldn't tell anyone. It would be a sure way for her parents to find out she'd snuck out. Then the atonement for her sin would begin. She couldn't risk being banned from going to uni, or worse. She pulled back and looked him straight in the eyes, shaking her head. 'Nobody can know about this, Joel. Not ever. Do you understand me?'

He looked at her as if she'd lost her mind. If only he knew the depth of her battles. 'What? Why?' he breathed, eyes wide.

'My father is why, Joel. He'll blame me, for all of it.' She choked back more sobs and sucked in a shuddering breath as she dropped her arms from him. She needed to get a grip before she said more than she should.

'No, he wouldn't. He's your father, he'd understand and want justice,' Joel said soothingly, but she stepped free of his touch.

'Stepfather, Joel. Malcolm will most certainly blame me. I snuck out to meet you tonight, remember?' She wrapped her arms back around her waist. 'I don't want anyone to know about this. What Levi did to me, it's shameful. Filthy. Repulsive. I will not allow myself to be gossip for the whole town, and I'm not going to let the Muller boys make an impact like that on my life, or on yours.'

'But, Jules, the Muller boys can't get away with this. Levi almost raped you.'

'*Almost*. Thanks to Ben, he didn't.'

Joel regarded her with sad eyes. 'I'll check in on Ben soon, to make sure he's okay, but … Jules …'

Joel tried to close the distance she'd created between them, but she stepped back, and he faltered. 'Surely Malcolm would want a man who did that to his stepdaughter behind bars?'

'Stop, Joel, please. I can't deal with all this pressure right now,' she cried, pulling together the torn parts of her dress. How would she explain it to her mother? 'I just want to pretend tonight never happened.'

Hurt seized Joel's already tense features. 'All of tonight?'

'Yes, all of it,' she snapped back, regretting her harsh tone instantly but unable to rein in her turbulent emotions.

Joel closed his eyes, shook his head. 'I'm sorry, Juliette, but you seriously can't expect me to stand back and let Levi think he's gotten away with something so disgusting. The arsehole has to pay for doing this to you and so do his brothers.'

She felt a flash of dark emotion, fear and anger mingling. 'Don't push this, Joel. You can't do anything about it.' She fought to gather every bit of strength she had left to stop from crumbling to the floor. If only Joel could understand the truth of her life at home. 'Not if you want us to be together.'

After a moment's contemplation, Joel heaved a frustrated breath. 'Fine then. We don't have to go to the police. I'll just take matters into my own hands.'

'What's that supposed to mean?' she demanded, watching him swallow down hard.

'I don't think I need to elaborate, Jules. It's best you don't know.'

'Oh no you don't.' She pointed at him. 'You won't go and do anything so stupid, Joel Hunter, and if you do, we are well and truly over.' The words fell from her trembling lips before she'd thought them through or even understood what they might mean. She hated not being able to tell Joel everything, but for his sake, and hers, it was imperative she didn't.

Joel threw his hands up in the air. 'Jules, you can't be serious. You're not thinking straight right now.'

He didn't understand. He couldn't. She was doing this to protect him, to protect herself, to protect her mother ... one day, he might understand, when she was free to tell him the truth.

But not now. 'I'm thinking real straight, so try me.' Refolding her arms, she stared at him fiercely. 'I'm not going to have you hurt them and then go to jail for years, or even worse. They hurt you really bad. Just imagine my life then, without you. It's not worth it, Joel. The Muller boys aren't worth ruining our lives over.'

Joel looked down at his muddy boots for a long moment before nodding. 'Okay.'

Juliette exhaled the breath she'd been holding. 'Promise me that you won't tell anyone, or go to the police, or do anything stupid?'

He looked at her, his mouth in a tight line. 'I promise.'

'Thank you.' She tipped her head, assessing him, the authenticity written all over his face. She could believe him. She trusted him. 'What was Ben doing down there?'

He hesitated before replying. 'I asked him to hide in the bushes and film me asking you to marry me.'

'Oh.' She softened now, her heart reaching for Joel's as she closed the gap, falling back into his arms – she wasn't in the right frame of mind, nor was it the right time, to tell him she would have said yes. 'We'll have to make sure Ben keeps his mouth shut too.'

'I don't think we'll have any problem with that.' Joel held her tight.

Gathering comfort from him, Juliette clung to the hope that they were going to make it through this, but she had to go. She needed to get back home. Now. Before this night got any worse.

CHAPTER
3

Rosalee Station, Central Australia
Eleven years later

It had taken only two weeks to break his promise.

Exactly fourteen days later, Joel lost his cool after trying to drown his sorrow and guilt. He'd never been a drinker until that day, but the amount of hatred and rage brewing after watching his beautiful Jules suffering in silence had made it impossible to stop himself, no matter how hard he'd tried to keep it at bay. In an all-out pub brawl, after being baited by the three Muller boys, he'd got a few good punches in and broken Levi's nose and, in turn, the agreement he'd made with Juliette. He hadn't fared too well either, staggering away with his fair share of injuries.

The town's senior sergeant, Wombat, off-duty at the time, was the one that broke up the fight and persuaded Levi not to press charges – Joel had thrown the first punch. Everyone thought

Levi was the better man, but Joel knew it was because Levi didn't want the motivation for the fight to be mentioned in a statement.

Battered and bruised, nursing a couple of broken fingers and a busted lip, and with his ego copping a pounding, Joel had gone and lost the best thing that had ever happened to him. Juliette had stuck to her promise, and no amount of apologising had changed her mind. Broken-hearted and with nowhere and nobody to turn to – even his own family – he'd done the only thing he could at the time and left Little Heart, their secret, and the only life he'd ever known behind.

Warding off the familiar heartache the painful memories evoked, Joel shoved the last of his buttery damper into his mouth and willed the whitewash of another hangover away. Washing it down with the last of his sweet billy tea, he huffed and eased out his aching neck. Becoming the black sheep of the family in the blink of an eye hadn't been easy, but he'd grown used to it. He'd had to, even though he'd never got over the fact his father had basically turned his back on him. He'd been deeply disappointed his son had succumbed to violence, and Joel, unable to tell him the real reason why he'd lashed out at Levi, had apparently broken his heart and his wholesome reputation even more when he'd upped and left town the night his father kicked him out.

No matter which way he turned, he just couldn't win.

In his dear mother's words, his father believed Joel was the one who had gone and turned his back on them and the church by not owning his crime of violence by apologising to Levi. Over his dead body would he ever give Levi the satisfaction, or humiliate Juliette by doing so. When he'd asked his mum if she felt the same way, stone-cold silence had been her reply. At least she still spoke to him and told him how much she loved him and missed him when he called about once a month. His little sister, Zoe, was piggy-in-the-middle. His father behaved as if he were dead.

He had to admit that, in a way, his mum was right. His faith in the church, and his father, had wavered a hell of a lot. What kind of god allowed such a horrendous thing to happen and the culprits to get away with it? What kind of father didn't have his son's back no matter what? It stung like buggery, had him questioning everything he'd been raised to believe, and made him even more determined never to step foot in Little Heart again, despite the fact he missed the farm and his family like drought-affected land missed the rain. As for Juliette Kern, as much as he missed her and reminisced about their good times, and as much as he wished he could give her the engagement ring he'd luckily found down by the river the day after the attack and for her to accept his proposal to be his wife, he knew without a shadow of a doubt that she'd never be his again. She'd moved on. Married her rich, snobby-nosed neighbour – her father would be tickled pink. According to Zoe, they were trying to have children. Juliette would make a wonderful mother, and he wanted to be happy for her, but was struggling to push past his grief and heartache. So that's as much as he needed to hear, from Zoe or anyone else. Any more information and his already snapped heart might shatter irretrievably.

Life went painfully on.

With his head pounding, the bellows of mustered cattle brought his attention back to the here and now. Wanting to avert his depressive, antagonising thoughts – he knew they did him no good, sometimes even drove him to the bottle – he focused on the untainted land surrounding him. It was hard to feel lonesome when filled with so much wonder for Mother Nature's heart.

Against a never-ending outback sky, the rising sun pierced the extensive stretches of hard-baked treeless earth with pewter light, igniting it to blinding brilliance. Despite the promised warmth the golden orb would bring, he stood shivering by the holding-yard gate as he watched two fellow stockmen, Bluey and Nugget, saddling up their horses, their throaty laughter compelling. His wide-brimmed hat pulled low over his shaggy brown hair, and his bearded chin tucked into his Driza-Bone, he chuckled quietly as Nugget tripped over thin air – the younger of the two was a true klutz.

This right here was what made him step from his swag every morning. As hard as it could sometimes be – the extreme weather, days on end in the saddle, no hot showers, and the lack of fresh food – it was all in a day's work as a stockman, and he loved the challenge. A place where lightning could strike for nights on end, Central Australia could go from one extreme to the other in a matter of just twenty-four hours. At night, the wind seared his lungs with bitter cold, and during the day it covered him in dust and sweat and incessant flies. The unforgiving countryside called for those who could fight the battle of isolation and drought. For Joel, it was a cinch to survive it compared to the dark cloud of grief and shame he was surrounded by every waking day, both for not being able to save Juliette and then for breaking her heart. Still plagued by nightmares of that night by the river, and tortured by endless thoughts of what-ifs and how-comes, bone-tired didn't even begin to explain how he felt. Hollow, destitute, desolate … every day spent in survival mode. That was the way of his life now. It was his kind of purgatory.

His lower back aching, he moseyed towards his trusty old horse, Ratbag, satisfied with the past week and a half spent in the saddle, but also looking forward to a long hot shower when they got back to the main camp this afternoon. Then, tomorrow, they'd all scrub up and head into the big smoke of Mount Isa for some well-earned time off. About nine kilometres from the main part of the station now, they'd been lucky enough yesterday to herd another twenty head just before dusk, with the help of the mustering chopper. The Rosalee Station owners, Georgia and Patrick Walsh, were going to be mighty happy with their mob of market-worthy cattle.

Two of the wild micky bulls that had proved to be absolute handfuls along the muster stomped and snorted impatiently as he passed them. 'Bit grumpy this morning, aren't we, fellas?' he said. 'You might want to pull your heads in if you want to be sent back out to pasture, my friends.'

Hoof pick in hand, he got to work checking his gelding's feet. He tapped lightly above each of Ratbag's pastern joints, his horse lifting each hoof for him in turn as he worked from heel to toe, paying special attention to the cleft around the frog. It was a job that didn't help his already aching back, but it had to be done every day. Ratbag, an aptly named old-timer, took the opportunity to nick Joel's hat, a game the horse often liked to play.

'Oi!' Joel snatched it back and Ratbag snorted. Joel eyed him, grinning, as he tugged it back on. 'You know what your trouble is, buddy? You've gone and lost your manners over the years. It's no wonder no other bastard wants to ride you. You're just lucky I love your guts otherwise you'd be retired, and god knows what that'd mean for you.'

Ratbag threw his head up, blowing air through his lips as though laughing. He was a cranky swayback with a nasty habit of nipping those who were less than wary around him, but Joel had come to love the old brute, even if he'd spent the first year trying his best to stay in the saddle. The horse had a habit of grinding to an abrupt halt if he'd had enough, or pig-rooting when he was fed up with weight on his back. But plenty of time spent together, following the dusty tracks and stock routes, rounding up the cattle on the stations that contracted them year after year, had warmed him to his grumpy mate, and the horse to him. Ratbag wouldn't let anyone else on his back. For Joel, it felt good to feel wanted, respected, loved – even if it was only by his horse.

Wandering towards him after a quick dash to the bushes, last night's dinner of leftover stew playing havoc with all of them, Curly, Joel's boss and bald-as-a-badger best mate, tossed a braided rope over his broad shoulder and sidestepped a nip to the butt from Ratbag. 'Ready to hit the road when you are, bud.' A barrel-chested man with arms that could wrestle the life out of most, Curly was gentle at heart, and the only person Joel felt he could really rely on, and, most importantly, trust. Family wasn't blood, like he'd once been led to believe. He was born alone and he would die alone – end of story.

'Righto, Curly.' Joel tightened Ratbag's girth strap. 'We're coming.'

With a cheeky smirk, Curly paused and pulled a bent rollie out of a crumpled tobacco packet. 'Yeah, and so is bloody Christmas.' He followed up his customary banter with a throaty chuckle before lighting his half-demolished cigarette and drawing in so deeply that the smoke came back out in a coughing fit.

Joel shook his head. 'Those things are gonna kill you one of these days, buddy.'

'Yeah, well, something has to. I might as well enjoy whatever it is.' Curly sauntered off, his bow-legged gait a tell-tale sign of his years spent in the saddle. He was talking to himself again – a habit Joel had grown used to over the years. Retrieving his broody mare, Dolly, from where he'd tethered her, Curly led her on a loose lead, which experience had proven to be a bad idea. Joel watched on, amused, as the mare waltzed behind her owner, tossing her head and yanking Curly's burly arm. Turning, Curly growled and gave her a light tap on the muzzle, stopping the misbehaviour in its tracks. Dolly stared back at him, wide-eyed and offended. Joel couldn't help but laugh at the pair of them. They loved to hate each other – and vice versa.

'That's enough malarkey from you, *Huntsman*,' Curly said, emphasising Joel's nickname lightheartedly as he climbed into the saddle.

'There can never be enough malarkey in this world,' Joel responded, faking shock-horror as he heaved himself onto Ratbag.

'Too right, mate, too right.' Curly gave his horse a light jab and they rode off to where Bluey and Nugget were already waiting on their antsy mounts.

The whipping of the chopper blades slicing through the crisp morning air grabbed their attention, and they glanced skywards. Right on cue, Curly's two-way crackled to life. 'Ready to hit it, boys?'

Curly held his thumb up to the chopper pilot looking down on them. 'Roger that.'

The five hundred head of livestock were methodically led out of the holding yard. It was a smooth transition as they bunched together, following their leader cattle, and moved towards the next, and last, watering hole. Bluey and Nugget rode at the edges of the flight zones, keeping the mob in check and applying a little pressure as needed, while Curly and Joel worked from the back, making sure to keep out of the cattle's blind spots. It was imperative to keep the mob as calm as they could. Sudden fright meant a world of absolute mayhem. So, like a well-oiled machine, they moved along at an easy pace, all of them knowing their job like the backs of their hands. With everything going to plan, Bluey and Nugget yarned casually while Curly smoked like a chimney.

Although Curly had more horse-savvy in his hands than most horsemen possessed in their entire bodies, after almost two weeks on this particular mustering contract, Joel could see his boss didn't have his mind on the job. Probably more on the women he'd be trying to bed in the big smoke of Mount Isa. All Joel wanted was a decent counter meal with a couple of icy cold beers to wash it all down, followed by a few games of pool before crawling into a real bed and sleeping for an eternity in a dark, air-conditioned room.

Times had most certainly changed.

When he'd first left Little Heart, an angry and damaged eighteen-year-old boy, he'd spent the first few years breaking more hearts than horses – his Casanova ways earned him a reputation amongst his fellow stockmen that he was none too proud of now. He'd stupidly thought wooing every woman who batted an eyelid at him would help him forget Juliette Kern, but all it did was make him yearn for her even more. Now he was a man, he knew better.

He was snapped from his thoughts when a rogue bull broke from the mob. With fire in his eyes, the one-tonne monster headed towards a patch of scrub. Some of the cattle spooked and broke ranks too, creating a knock-on effect that the men knew they needed to get a hold on quick smart. Shouting rang out, vehement, urgent. The chopper overhead snapped to action, dipping and diving. With Nugget, Bluey and Curly working to keep the mob from scattering in every direction, Joel turned Ratbag on a threepenny bit and took off after the belligerent beast. The chopper was hot on the bull's heels – it would be needed to push the bull out of the cluster of trees if the bugger got that far. Joel was hell-bent on not letting it get its way. And so was Ratbag. His head pushed forwards, mane flowing in the wind, the gelding mixed long powerful strides with thunderous bursts of speed.

Glued to the saddle, Joel homed in on the bull and lapped around him. Ratbag's pounding hooves seemed to shake the very ground. Man and horse were close to swinging the four-legged hooligan in the right direction when the chopper came in from the other side. The bull skidded to an almighty stop and spun, his menacing sights now on Joel and Ratbag. A wild-born killer with wide shoulders and rippling muscles, the bull was as cunning as he was savage. Joel's blood froze. Head down, tail up, deadly horns at the ready, the bull rushed forwards, charging.

With only seconds to think, Joel pulled at the reins to try to avoid the incoming missile, and even though Ratbag's head came up, the horse's body didn't swivel as fast. As time seemed to slow, Joel steeled himself, ready for the inevitable.

They were in the firing line.

There was a loud, sharp crack as Ratbag reared, whinnying in pain from the lightning jab of the pointed horns, before crashing to the ground, taking Joel with him. Agony struck as his legs and torso jammed beneath the horse, but he couldn't stop, desperately trying to free himself as the bull circled them, snorting and pawing at the ground. It wanted more. It wanted to kill both of them. Blood dripped from its horns and ran in rivulets down its face. Ratbag's blood. In a world of pain himself, Joel didn't dare to look to see if his old mate was dead. He didn't want to know. Couldn't handle the heartache.

Freeing himself from beneath Ratbag, whirling dizzily, he pushed himself onto shaky legs, terrified of facing his fate. The bull snorted, flicking saliva over its shoulder as it flung its head about … and then charged. Joel leapt away, and the bull skidded by, just barely missing him. Spinning back, he faced Joel again, wilder, fiercer. The world spinning, Joel almost met the ground once more, but he held himself steady. He didn't have the luxury to stop and think. He had to try to run to something, anything that would help to shield him. The chopper zoomed in on them, mercifully preoccupying the bull, giving him the time he needed to stumble towards the trees, gasping for breath. He could hear the loud bellows of his fellow stockmen from behind the cluster of trees and within seconds Curly was in front of him, diving from the saddle, his face grave with concern.

'Holy shit, Joel, are you all right?'

'I'm not sure, buddy.' Buckling over, Joel heaved up his breakfast. Blood trickled from his nose and dripped onto the ground. Straightening, he wiped it away with his sleeve. Arms aching and legs as heavy as stone, he knelt and tried to ease the dizziness. Curly was beside him, saying something he couldn't decipher. The whopping of the chopper blades sounded a million light years away. His thoughts turned to Ratbag, and he wanted to ask if his horse was okay, but his mouth was too dry to speak. His strength ebbed and the world around him swirled, twirled, twisted. Falling against Curly, he felt the world give way as everything went black.

* * *

There was the murmur of distant voices. Joel could sense himself floating between realms, but he had nothing to grab hold of, to bring himself to the surface. Was he still in grave danger? Frantically clawing his way to consciousness, he eventually blinked open lead-heavy eyes. His head pounding and his vision blurry, all he could make out were soft blue walls, although he could feel the crispness of the sheets he was lying on and hear the methodical beeping of machines, steady with his heartbeat. He was safe. The realisation gave him peace. His jumbled thoughts began to fuse together. The last thing he remembered was collapsing to the ground – he had no idea how in the hell he'd gotten to a hospital.

Someone clearing their throat had him turning his head. Curly's face came into blurry focus. 'Hey, bud.' Two words, yet his mouth felt as if it were filled with cottonwool, it took so much effort for him to address his boss.

There was a relieved whoosh of breath. 'Oh, thank Christ, Huntsman. I thought you were a bloody goner.' Curly straightened in his chair and scratched at his crotch. 'Scared the bloody bejesus outta the boys and me, you did, mate. We were capping it when we saw how much you were bleeding.'

'Which hospital?' Joel could feel the effects of painkillers stealing his words, pushing him into the mattress. He fought to regain his senses, wanting to know everything.

'Mount Isa.' Curly sucked in a breath and sighed it away. 'The flying docs had to get you here.'

'Really?' Joel shook his head slowly. 'I don't remember a thing.'

'Yeah, you were mumbling gibberish and in a load of pain, so they gave you something to completely knock you out. Worked a bloody treat, I tell ya.'

'Ratbag?' Joel's eyes stung, and he wasn't sure if it was from the bright light overhead or if tears had sprung.

His slight smile giving way, Curly shook his head. 'I'm sorry, mate. He was in a real bad way. We had to put him out of his misery.'

Joel nodded, feeling as if he'd just been king hit in the chest. Ratbag was his comrade, his workmate, his family … and just like that, he was gone. He didn't even get to thank him for saving him, or to say a last goodbye.

'I know it's a tough pill to swallow, mate, but it was for the best.' Curly placed a hand on his arm, giving Joel a few moments. 'And how are you feeling?'

Joel bit back his tears and pressed to find his voice. 'I feel like I've been hit by a truck, but yeah, I'm breathing, so I'm okay, I suppose.'

Curly nodded. 'No doubt.'

'What happened to me?'

'Luckily, no broken bones, but you hit your head a doozy.'

Joel breathed a sigh of relief. There was no way he could stay cooped up in hospital for long, the four walls would drive him round the bend. 'No biggy, then. How long before I can get back to work?' Joel had a good nest egg after saving almost every penny he'd earned over the years, but he didn't want to chip away at it. Besides, mustering alongside Curly was his life – he didn't know what he'd do otherwise. Hard work and distraction were his only way to survive.

Curly slumped back down, eyeing him almost sympathetically. 'You're not coming back to work for a while, Joel.'

'What's "a while", Curly?'

'A couple of months at least, Huntsman.'

Joel tried to sit up, but a wave of dizziness stopped him. 'Oh, come on. Don't make a mountain out of a molehill, she'll be right.' He begrudgingly eased back into the pillow.

'Sorry, mate, but it's the doc's orders. And mine.' Curly sighed, closing his eyes, and shook his head. 'You really need to get off the booze, Joel, and on the straight and narrow. You think I can't smell the stench of it hanging from you every day? Not good when we're meant to be a dry camp.'

Joel's defences fired. A couple of nips from his hip flask at night to help him sleep wasn't anything to write home about. And so what if he took a sneaky swig occasionally during the day, to break up the monotony of billy tea and water? 'You saying I have a drinking problem?'

'You're definitely no alcoholic, but you might end up that way if you don't figure your life out.' With Joel glaring at him, Curly offered him a slight smile. 'I've got your back, even though it might not feel like it right now. I don't want you to be worse off next time round.'

'There won't be a next time round.' Joel grit his teeth through both the pain of the conversation and the agony of his throbbing head.

Curly shrugged his massive shoulders. 'Maybe, but we're not going to risk finding that out.'

Joel heaved a sigh, wincing from the pain of doing so. 'So, tell me, what the bloody hell am I meant to do for two months?'

Curly stood, hands planted at the base of his bowed back. 'I've booked you a plane ticket home.'

'You what?' Without thinking, Joel went to sit up again, but the discomfort and wooziness sent him crashing back to his pillow.

'You heard me, mate. It's about time you faced up to whatever it is you're running from.' Curly leant on the side of the bed, looking Joel right in the eyes. 'I know you love and miss your folks and your sister. Maybe this is god's way of giving you no option but to go home.'

'Maybe, maybe not,' Joel bit back, hard and sharp.

'Look, I know you're pissed, but like I said, I'm just looking after ya.' Curly grabbed his hat from the back of his chair and tugged it on. 'I'll give you a bit of space to let it all sink in. I'm going to head downstairs and grab myself a toasted sandwich and a drink. Do you want anything? A can of Coke, a coffee?'

'No, thanks.' Stubbornly, Joel turned his head and stared out the window at a sapphire-blue sky.

'You sure? It might help to wet the whistle.'

His throat as dry as sandpaper, an icy cold sweet drink suddenly sounded real good. 'Okay, grab me a can of something, if it's not too much trouble.'

'No trouble at all.' Curly half-chuckled. 'Be back in two shakes of a lamb's tail.' He paused before stepping out the door, and Joel begrudgingly met his gaze. 'I'll let the good-looking nurse know you're awake, tell her you need a full-body bath.' He winked, chuckled, and off he went, his heavy footsteps fading down the hall.

Unamused by the banter that would usually have cracked him up, Joel lay staring at the ceiling, clenching and unclenching his hands. Was Curly right? Could this be god getting even? Or, at the very least, grappling for his attention after the speedy loss of his faith since leaving the township of Little Heart? Was his near-death a sign to make things right, to finally follow through with what had sat heavy in his heart and soul all these years? He hadn't parted on good terms with his dad or Juliette. He and Jules, and he and his father, had both said some hurtful things. He'd taken off for what was supposed to be a few days to clear his head. The few days had turned into weeks, then months and had gradually bled into eleven long years.

Gutless came to mind, followed by *coward*.

He mentally tried to shake away the thoughts.

Maybe it *was* time he ventured back to where it all happened.

Back to his family.

Back to her.

Home.

CHAPTER
4

Little Heart

For January, it was a little cooler than normal, the recent rain having washed away the humidity for now. The warm light of her lamp washing over her, Juliette paused and stared at her reflection. She looked old, exhausted. Done. Her life had turned out like nothing she'd imagined it to be. Loveless. Childless. Lonely. Her marriage had been wrought with complications at every turn, and having reached her limit, she wanted to know why her husband was home less and less. Even though he blamed it on his campaign to become town mayor, Juliette was struggling to ignore the possibility that he was seeing someone else.

Jumping into another relationship way too quickly to try to rid herself of the broken heart from Joel's untimely departure, as well as wanting to move out of her parents' home to make a life of her own between her weeks spent at university in Cairns, had been a huge mistake. But she'd made her bed. Now she had to find a way to lie in it if she wanted to avoid the dreaded D-word. She didn't want the stigma of being a divorcee, especially at her parents' church. She could only imagine how they would react. Surely, she and Lachlan could find a way to be happy again? That was if he wasn't cheating on her.

Lachlan was rarely home these days, and when he was, he was so distant he might as well not have even been there. He rarely touched her outside of when she was ovulating, never kissed her like he meant it, and had been sleeping in the spare room for the past six months because apparently he didn't want to annoy her by tossing and turning all night with his sore back.

Blinking back tears, she slipped the silky black robe from her shoulders and it fluttered to her feet. Her gaze snagged on the faint scar across her stomach, the one left by Levi's knife, and she trailed her fingers, featherlike, over it. After seven years at a university down south, Levi Muller had returned to nab the position as Little Heart's resident doctor four years ago. She always crossed the street if she saw the vile man heading towards her, and would rather die than seek out his medical assistance. Thank god he lived in the neighbouring town of Grander. Avoidance of him was the only saving grace, her way to pretend that he didn't exist. But try as she might to block it out, the haunting memory of that horrific night jolted her breath when, just beyond the door, footfalls sounded. She snapped back to the moment and grabbed her robe, tugging it back on.

Her husband swung the door open, but it didn't stop her racing heart. Lachlan silently closed the distance between them, his hands going straight to his relentless focal point: her breasts. The stench of booze clung to him, as did the overpowering scent of spicy aftershave.

Juliette fought not to recoil from him – she detested when he was drunk. 'Did your dinner meeting run later than expected again?' she asked a little scornfully.

'Yup, it did, Sherlock.' Without offering any further explanation, he parted her robe and shoved it from her shoulders, took one breast in each hand and squeezed. 'It's about that time of the month again, isn't it?'

'It is, but I got my period early,' she lied, disgusted with the thought of touching him, of him touching her, especially when he was inebriated. It seemed to be the only time he came near her. Was she so repulsive?

He flashed her a scolding glance. 'Oh, for god's sake.' He sighed, swore beneath his breath. 'So now we have to wait another month to try?' He looked at her as if this was all her fault.

Feeling exposed, Juliette snatched up her robe from the floor. 'Afraid so.' She blinked back hot tears as she pulled it on, the desire to pound his chest with her clenched fists almost overwhelming her. She longed for a child but wasn't about to try when Lachlan was so drunk. 'I'm sorry.' Her tone was artificially subdued – a fight would do her no good at all. She turned, tugged her robe in so tight the neckline had a stranglehold on her throat, and then busied herself by rearranging the bottles of perfume on her dresser. 'Why did the meeting run so late?'

'I was closing a deal with one of the councillors and got caught up having drinks to celebrate.' He unbuttoned his shirt and shrugged it off. 'Not that it's really any of your business what I do when I'm working.'

'If you haven't gone and forgotten, I am your wife, Lachlan.' Although wanting it to sound forceful, her voice was distant, hollow – the way she felt around him.

'Oh, here we go again. Nagging, bitching and moaning.' He glared at her before storming towards the half-open door. 'I'm too tired for this. I'm going to sleep in the spare room.'

'Don't you mean *your* room,' she cried after him. The slam of the door down the hall was his only response.

Juliette bit back a sob. She got nothing from him, none of what every woman deserved – no respect, no kindness, no love. Staring at her reflection once again, she shook her head. She kept longing for a shift in his attitude, for him to notice her, to care for her like he had right back at the beginning, when he'd chased her, wooed her, wanted her. When had he stopped wanting her? Had he ever truly loved her?

Maybe not ...

She'd fallen back to earth with a jolt. It wasn't going to happen. He wasn't going to be the husband she longed for, a man to share her life with. Not now. Not ever. Unless some kind of miracle happened – and she wasn't holding her breath for that. She needed to find out, once and for all, what was going on with him. But how? Slumping to the edge of the bed, she dropped her head in her hands and allowed the sobs she'd been holding back all day to surface.

* * *

Juliette glanced at Zoe Hunter, her best friend since they'd sat beside each other in church, concentrating behind the wheel. This was crazy. A snap decision spurred on by one too many wines over their last weekly catch-up before Zoe left to go overseas. But ... could Zoe's hunch be right? Was her world about to be turned upside down?

Struggling to hold herself together, she closed her eyes for the shortest of moments and drew in a deep breath. If the drive down the winding Kuranda Range hadn't been hairy enough, with Zoe taking the corners as if rally driving, they were now in the thick of rush hour. The traffic lights just up ahead turned amber. Would they make it before the red light? With Lachlan a few cars ahead, if Zoe stopped, they were going to lose sight of him. Juliette couldn't bear the thought.

'Hang on tight, hun, I'm going to risk it.' Fuelled by adrenaline, Zoe floored it, barely making it through before the traffic behind them came to a standstill.

A tattoo-covered bloke on a motorbike in the lane beside them gave them the thumbs up, and Zoe, cheeky gal, grinned brazenly back at him. The more cautious one of their duo as they were getting older, Juliette bit her tongue – now wasn't the time to lecture Zoe for her notoriously wild driving. Instead, she braced her feet into the floor and gripped her seat with both hands. It would be really bad luck if they found themselves involved in an accident, not just because the car was on loan from a friend so they could remain incognito but because they couldn't afford to be waylaid.

'You doing okay over there?' Zoe asked as she turned down the radio, the announcer's annoyingly nasally and overly happy voice fading.

'Uh-huh. At least, I think so,' she lied, forcing a wobbly half-smile. 'This really sucks.'

'I know, hun, but at least you can put your mind to rest, either way.'

'Yeah, I suppose so.' Juliette knew she couldn't go through this kind of caper again, and she needed to know the truth behind her failing marriage, once and for all. Her fingers tense in her lap, she stared at the back of her husband's brand spanking new four-wheel drive – a perk of his government job – now five car-lengths ahead of them. Lachlan appeared to be in a rush, as if he was late for a very important date. She prayed she was wrong.

They quickly reached the first of five roundabouts that kept the traffic flowing along the highway leading into the main hub of Cairns. Lachlan briefly vanished out of sight as he navigated around the bend, and Juliette craned her neck to keep him within her sight. Her stomach tumbled again with the thought of where his final destination might be.

'Call him, hun.' Zoe's authoritative voice snapped her from her internal chatter.

Juliette turned to catch Zoe's compassionate look. 'You mean now?' she stuttered.

Zoe nodded. 'Yes, right now.'

'What do I say if he answers?' Eyes wide, she looked to Zoe's hands gripping the steering wheel, her knuckles white. She was so very lucky to have a friend who cared so much about her.

'Just keep it simple. Ask him if he'll be home for dinner.'

Juliette's pulse took off like a bull at a gate. 'I can't.' She shook her head as she wrung her hands tighter.

'Why not? You call him all the time. Why's this time any different?'

'Apart from the obvious fact we're tailing him? I don't know if I can pull it off.' Her voice drifted in a hushed whisper as she thought about it for a moment. 'I've never been too good at telling lies.' Even though she'd kept two huge secrets from everyone – for good reason. And secrets were different to lies.

'You're not lying by asking him when he'll be home for dinner, babes.' Keeping one eye on the road, Zoe's tone was reassuring, comforting. 'Trust me, you're way tougher than you give yourself credit for. You got this.'

Juliette sniffled and centred herself. Zoe was right. She could do this. 'Yup, okay. I'll do it.' She grabbed her mobile from her handbag, dialled her husband's phone number, and pressed it to her ear.

Zoe switched off the radio. 'Put it on loudspeaker so I can hear it too.'

Juliette did as Zoe asked. It rang four times. One more ring and then it'd go to message bank. She held her breath …

'Hey.' Lachlan's voice made her jump.

'Hey, yourself. How's your day going?' A hornet's nest of alarm buzzed inside of her.

'Yeah, not too bad, I suppose. Just busy, as always.' He sounded a million miles away.

Her mouth feeling as if it were filled with cottonwool, she looked to Zoe for a shot of courage and got it in spades. 'Sorry to bother you at work, I was just calling to see if you'd be home for dinner tonight. I thought I'd cook your favourite – lamb chops, honey carrots and a potato bake.'

Zoe gave her the thumbs up and mouthed, *Good one*.

'Oh, sorry, Jules. I'm stuck behind this damn desk, and by the looks of the pile of paperwork I have to get through before the weekend is over, I'm not going to be able to make it home in time. Can I take a raincheck?' he added smoothly.

Oh, he was good. He was very, *very* good, at least when he was sober.

Bitter disappointment coursed through her. 'Of course.' The full implications of his words sinking in painfully, Juliette steeled herself, sucking in a quick, calming breath. 'Will you be home later, or are you going to crash at the office again?' A faint thread of hysteria almost stole her voice but a quick squeeze of her arm from Zoe gave her all she needed to stick with it.

'To be honest, I reckon I might be here all night, otherwise I don't know how I'm going to get it all done.' He cleared his throat. 'With election day only two months away, I can't go dragging the chain. As you know, every vote counts.'

She narrowed her eyes. 'Yup, I know the drill real well.' Anger churned in her stomach and she forcibly had to stop herself calling him out on his deceitfulness. 'I guess I'll just see you when I see you then.' She didn't need to *try* to sound upset – she was, deeply. All the plans she'd made for their future, the ones that had kept her pushing through every day for so long, were suddenly gone.

'Yeah, sorry, Juliette, but it's out of my hands.'

Juliette swallowed down hard, refusing to let her emotions overwhelm her. 'Uh-huh. I understand. Love you,' she choked out, her cheeks heating with both humiliation and anger. She did still love him. How could she not after being his wife for the past ten years?

'Yup, love you too.' There wasn't an ounce of emotion in the words, and it hit her that there hadn't been for a long, *long* time.

Unable to say another word, she grabbed the chance to end the call before she called him out on his bullshit. Tossing her phone back into her handbag, she took a few long moments to gather herself enough to speak. 'You're right, Zoe. He's a lying, cheating, callous bastard.'

'Oh, hun, I'm so sorry. You don't deserve this crap.' Soft and compassionate, Zoe's tone made her want to burst into tears even more. 'Damn men. All they seem to do is break our hearts. I don't know why we bother with them. They're nothing but bloody trouble.'

'Because we need them to have children.' Juliette almost laughed but, fearful of what she might be about to discover, released a muffled sob. 'But a fat lot of good that's doing for me.'

'We don't need a man to have children these days, you know. There is such a thing as sperm donation clinics.'

Juliette grimaced. 'Each to their own, but that's not an option for me, Zoe. I don't want to be a single mother.' Looking down at her wedding ring, she shook her head. 'I want my children to have a loving father. I want to be in a loving family. If Lachlan could find it in himself to go back to what we had when we were happy … maybe we'd have a chance to make this marriage work?'

'I know you do. It's been your dream for as long as I can remember. My brother made a big mistake, taking off like he did. He should have stayed and fought for you,' she grumbled, shaking her head. 'You would've made such beautiful babies together.'

'Ha, yeah, we probably would have,' Juliette said with a little chuckle, even as that old familiar sense of loss and hurt resurfaced.

Zoe kept one hand on the steering wheel and reached the other out to comfort her. 'You just hang in there, hun, okay? I've got your back.'

'Thanks. I'm trying to,' she replied, squeezing back the tears and then digging her fingertips into the points above her eyes where her head felt as if it was about to implode. 'I just hope my instincts are wrong and we're clutching at straws. Maybe he has a really good excuse for lying through his damn teeth.'

Zoe offered her a sad smile, her extended silence saying everything Juliette didn't want to hear. Juliette had been watching things fall apart for longer than she cared to remember, and she was tired of making excuses for her husband's actions, of driving herself around the bend trying to figure him out. And she was absolutely sick of placing all the blame on herself, and of trying to change everything she said or did in the hopes that he might pay her some genuine attention. Along the way, she'd lost who she really was – she knew that now. She needed to know the truth, as cold and as hard as it might be.

Hitting the brakes, Zoe took a sharp left off the Captain Cook Highway. 'Far out, talk about not giving us much notice. Looks like he's headed into the city.'

Lachlan was only three cars ahead now. Juliette nodded. 'Just make sure you don't get too close, hey? We don't want to go blowing our cover.'

'Don't worry, I'll hang back.' The traffic slowing, Zoe eased off the accelerator for what felt to Juliette like the first time in the hour and a half they'd been trailing him. Two more turns and they were cruising along the Cairns Esplanade. The crystal water lapped at the edges of lush green gardens, and the joggers and dog-walkers dotted the footpaths, all backdropped by a beautiful summer's day. How could such a peaceful scene exist when Juliette felt such turmoil? The oceanfront two-bedroom apartment she and Lachlan had bought a year before as an investment, renting it out to holidaymakers, was just up ahead. Surely he wouldn't be going to spend the weekend there without her … would he?

Just as she suspected, the brake lights lit up on his four-wheel drive and Lachlan indicated to turn into Crystalrock, one of Cairns' swankiest new holiday apartment buildings. She clutched at the possibility he was here on business. But why would he not tell her that? Zoe's grave expression matched the negative thoughts racing through Juliette's mind. She tried hard to not jump to any conclusions as they turned into the building's parking lot, making sure to keep a comfortable distance between them and Lachlan.

With shallow, panicked breaths, she watched her husband disappear into the underground parking lot. 'Don't follow him, Zoe. Just park out here, please.'

'What now, hun?' Zoe asked as she parked and switched off the engine.

'I've got every right to be here, so I'm going to go in. It's probably best you wait here.' Juliette's voice trembled, as did her hands as she grabbed her handbag and stepped out.

Zoe dipped her head and peered out at her through the passenger window. 'You sure you don't want me to come?'

'I wish you could, but it'll be easier to stay incognito if it's just me.' She leant on the windowsill. 'And as much as I appreciate you doing this with me, I feel like I need to do this bit on my own.'

Zoe nodded. 'Okay, but only if you're certain. Just make sure you stay out of sight and call me if you need me. I'll be right here.'

'I will.' So she couldn't chicken out, or burst into tears, Juliette spun on her heel and strode towards where a concierge was standing by the automatic doors. 'Thank you,' she said, as he ushered her inside with a smile.

As soon as she stepped into the impressive lobby, she spotted Lachlan through a crowd of Japanese tourists at the check-in desk. Pen poised, his back to her, he was signing something. She pretended to be checking out a stand of travel brochures, staying just out of his line of sight, but keeping him in hers. Her heart was beating so hard she could almost swear every man, woman and child in the near vicinity could hear it. She honestly had no idea what she was going to do if Lachlan caught her following him. Less than a minute later, and after a quick nod to the receptionist, he tucked some paperwork into his trouser pocket and made for the lifts, his head buried in his phone, the smile on his face one she hadn't seen in a very long time.

She watched him disappear into the lift and waited. She didn't need to follow him – she knew the apartment number he'd be headed to. Ten long minutes passed by as she paced the lobby, eyeing every attractive woman in the process, assessing whether they'd be heading upstairs to screw her husband. She teased the time out until she could wait no longer. Heading over to the front desk, she smiled to the friendly receptionist, taking note of her name badge.

'Hello, Regan. I've come to spend the weekend with my husband in our apartment, and I just need to pick up a room key.'

'Yes, sure. Your name?' Standing at a computer, the young woman had her hands at the ready.

'Juliette Davis.' Every one of her nerve ends shuddered as she held her breath.

'Ah, here we are.' Regan peered up. 'Have you got some ID for me?'

Juliette released the breath silently. 'Yes, sorry. It's been a long day.' She fumbled in her handbag, grabbed her purse, and plucked out her licence.

The young lady graciously took it from her. 'Well, thankfully, it's a Friday. And you've got the apartment for the entire weekend. How lovely.' She beamed a white-toothed smile.

'Yes, I'm looking forward to putting my feet up, with a nice glass of wine or two,' Juliette said, smiling through gritted teeth.

Regan handed the licence back, along with a digital key. 'Here we are. Enjoy that glass of wine or two.' She offered another friendly smile.

Juliette returned it forcefully. 'I will, thank you.' And off she strode, a woman on a mission.

The lift sounded and the waiting crowd filed in. Crammed into the back corner, Juliette stretched her arm out and pressed level fifteen. She bit her bottom lip, half to stop herself from crying, half to stop herself from screaming, as the ride upwards felt like an epic journey. Her heart thudded like bombs dropping as she stepped into the hall. Their apartment was only metres away, although every step she took felt leaden. She hated herself for doing this. Hated him for making it so she had to. But what other choice did she have? Carefully, she flashed the key over the reader, then eased the door open. The apartment was dark, but she could hear muffled voices coming from the main bedroom. He had someone in here, with him, in *their* bedroom. Her heart slipped and dropped, and she had to use every bit of resolve not to crumble to the floor with it.

Tiptoeing towards the half-open bedroom door, she followed a trail of clothing, relieved to see none of it was lewd lingerie. But pushing open the door, she was confronted by something she'd never have believed without seeing it with her own eyes. The air rushed from her. 'What in the hell,' whooshed from her trembling lips.

Two equally shocked faces stared back at her, and she was torn between fury, humiliation and utter heartbreak.

'Oh my god, Juliette. What in Christ's name are you doing here?'

She folded her arms tightly, glaring. 'I just thought I'd pop into your work meeting and say hi.' Fury won out, unleashing inside of her, raw and black and intense.

Lachlan's mouth opened and closed as he blinked owlishly. 'This isn't what it looks like.' He scrambled from the bed, as naked as the day he'd been born, taking the sheet with him and leaving a very naked, very handsome, young man behind.

'Enough of the lies. I've caught you red-handed, Lachlan.' She held up her hands, blinking back tears. 'Please give me some sort of respect and save it.' Swallowing down the flood of emotions, she shook her head. 'Don't treat me like some damn fool. You've been doing that for long enough now.'

'We ... um ... he ...' He looked to the red-faced, speechless bloke now sitting bolt upright in the bed, his hands covering his nether regions.

'Save it, Lachlan. I never would have believed it if I hadn't just seen it. And here I'd been blaming myself for your lack of attention and love.' She flashed him one last filthy, disappointed look before striding out the door, back down the hall, and towards the lift.

She had been expecting to be heartbroken, but this was even worse than she'd imagined. Feeling as if she was trapped in a nightmare, adrenaline drove her forwards, fresh pain washing over her again and again, but as crushing as it was, it was also laced with a certain kind of relief. At the very least, now she knew she wasn't the problem – it was Lachlan. And as shocking and overwhelming as it had been to see her husband with another man, it explained absolutely everything.

CHAPTER
5

It was a scorching Far North Queensland summer day; the only respite for the many country fair goers were the occasional cottony clouds drifting across the wide expanse of blue, shielding them from the harsh rays of brilliant sunshine, along with the fifty-cent icy cups that were flying from the freezer of the Country Women's Association stall.

From behind the counter of the cake stand, Juliette waved to a few of her students, smiling at their happy faces. She was overjoyed with the massive turnout for the fair, even as she was preoccupied with her own thoughts. She wished she could somehow block out the images that were playing like a broken record in her head, taunting her, driving the dagger deeper into her heart with each repetition. It was doing her no good, reliving it again and again. Lachlan had left for Brisbane three days ago for a week's worth of meetings, giving her a little reprieve. At the very least, the arguments had stopped. Now he was giving her stone-cold silence.

Almost a week after learning the shocking truth of why her marriage was failing, she was shattered, mentally and emotionally. And keeping it to herself, apart from confiding in Zoe and her Aunt Janey, was exhausting. She wanted to stop rewinding and pausing, to stop berating herself for not seeing it, to stop blaming herself for it having happened. Yet, try as she might, her mind always drifted back to those old rebukes and new images. She knew time would heal. After experiencing her fair share of wrongdoings over the years, she was well aware of that. But this, of all things, to drive a wedge between her and her husband? This would change everything. How was she ever meant to move past such a thing? The vows she'd stated at their church were something she took seriously, but how were she and Lachlan ever meant to work through something like this? Infidelity was the lowest of things to do to a spouse. She knew she should leave him. But what would that mean?

Rubbing salt into the wound was the familiar sensation of cramps beginning to seize her uterus like a clenched fist. According to her meticulously kept ovulation calendar, it was that awful time of the month again. Even though she'd prayed every day, as she had for the past couple of years, it looked as though it still wasn't her time to fulfil that dream. She was beginning to lose faith that it ever would be. Maybe becoming a mother wasn't in god's plans for her. She hated the thought. Even though it was for the best, for now. After what she'd witnessed, and now having looked back on their life together, she could see it as clear as day – Lachlan had only wanted her so he could have a child to keep his parents happy with an heir. He'd used her to hide the fact he was homosexual from them – there was no way they'd accept that, with their strict religious beliefs. Nor would their church while under Malcolm's strict leadership, and Lachlan was relying on them to vote him in as town mayor.

Blinking back unwanted tears, and with the grip of needing something sweet overcoming her, she fought the urge to eat an entire carrot cake and wash it down with a can of soft drink. Instead, she turned her thoughts outwards and observed the goings-on. The bouncing castle and chair swing ride had line-ups, and excited squeals could be heard all around. Children with painted faces enjoyed fairy floss, Dagwood dogs and hot chips, smothered in tomato sauce, as they roamed from stall to stall, ride to ride, and the scent of barbeque sausages and onions hung mouth-wateringly upon the air. In the middle of the field, the school principal stood with clipboard and megaphone in hand, ready to send eager kids and their parents, now tucked inside large hessian bags, racing to the finishing line. The donated prize was a family dinner at the local pizza shop. The kids looked enthusiastic, the parents squished up beside them, deadly serious. With a free dinner on the cards, the stakes were high.

In a world of her own, she jumped when Zoe lightly jabbed her in the ribs with her elbow. 'Look out at three o'clock, hun. You might want to take cover.' There was a playful expression lurking in Zoe's jade-green eyes, and the corners of her sassy mouth curled ever so slightly.

Switching her focus from the pretty face that often reminded her of what she'd lost all those years ago – Joel Hunter, a man she still fought not to give any thought to – to the cluster of women beneath the blooming jacaranda tree over yonder, enjoying their tea and scones, Juliette spotted her insufferable mother-in-law, the school's biggest financial contributor, departing the cackling group and hobbling straight for her. Jostling her walking stick, her long silver-grey hair up in its usual bun and her make-up piled on, and wearing an impeccably ironed crisp white linen number, the sixty-two-year-old stood out like a sore thumb amongst the casually dressed locals.

'Oh, fu … *fudge* it,' she muttered beneath her breath while unconsciously straightening her favourite summery dress. Margery Davis seemed to have an undesirable effect on her. Always had, from day dot. And forever would. Being a humble girl from an underprivileged family, Juliette had learnt she'd never live up to Margery's expectations, and she'd given up trying. Why the woman had supported her marriage to Lachlan in the first place, she hadn't a damn clue.

'Fudge it? Seriously?' Her blonde ponytail swinging over her shoulder, Zoe shook her head and laughed. 'I think it's safe to say you've been around young children way too long, my dear friend.' She wrapped an arm around Juliette's shoulder and gave her a squeeze. 'You need to get yourself out more so you can have adult conversations.'

'I have adult conversations.' It was said a little defensively, but she couldn't help herself. Grabbing her water bottle, Juliette took a swig.

'Oh, you do, do you?' Tipping her head to the side, Zoe lifted her sunnies and eyeballed her. 'With who, exactly?'

Cornered, Juliette huffed. Damn Zoe being able to always see straight through her – she could never pull the wool over her eyes. But she'd go down swinging all the same. 'My workmates, and you …' Brows rising, she straightened her shoulders as though winning the debate. '… and Brute.' She silently breathed a sigh of relief when the town gossip, the owner of the post office, halted Margery on her trek to the cake stand.

'Me, yes. Your workmates, yes. But our little Brutus? Seriously, how can you have an adult conversation with your dog?' Her tone soft, sympathetically so, Zoe shoved her hands into the pockets of her cute denim shorts and leant against the corner of the foldout table, almost empty now thanks to all the cake sales they'd made throughout the afternoon.

'Brute may not be able to answer me, but he sure does do a lot of listening.' Juliette knew she was digging herself in deeper but, as Zoe quite often pointed out, defensiveness was her coping mechanism. As was denial of the obvious.

'I know you don't want to talk about it today, but after what you caught Lachlan doing, and how he's giving you the silent treatment, like it's somehow your fault? You should take some of your power back. Go out and have some fun. And while you're at it, that wild and free zest for life he squashed out of you might just re-emerge.'

Juliette tried not to wince as Zoe hit that raw nerve. Her friend was not one for diplomacy, but she loved her, was always there for her, had seen and heard what she went through with Lachlan on a daily basis, before and after the shocking revelation at the apartment. Her comment was warranted, even if not well timed with Margery inbound. 'Please, Zoe, not here. Not now.' She blinked back the threat of fresh tears. 'I'm honestly at the end of my tether with it all.'

'Shit, don't cry. I'm so sorry. Damn me and my mouth.' Zoe's expression softened. She reached out and grabbed both Juliette's hands. 'It's just … I love you to bits, and I hate seeing you so sad all the time. It breaks my heart.' Looking down, as if warding off her own tears, she gave Juliette's hands a tender squeeze. 'You deserve way better than him. You know that, right?'

Like your brother, Juliette thought as she nodded. Zoe had never gotten over the fact she and Joel had never got hitched. If only she could tell Zoe the real reason why Joel had punched Levi that fateful night.

'I know you're trying to see a way around it all, because you take your wedding vows so seriously, but ...' Zoe came in real close, her voice dropping to an absolute whisper. '... you innocently married a liar who is using you to fool everyone in this town for his own selfish reasons. Therefore, your vows are null and void, in my honest opinion.' Zoe pulled her into a quick hug, and Juliette nodded against her friend's shoulder. 'I wouldn't worry about what anyone else will think, or how the people at church might judge you. Just make sure you look after yourself in all of this, okay?'

'I'll try. Thanks for always having my back,' Juliette murmured, her heart even heavier knowing Zoe would be leaving for her big overseas adventure tomorrow.

'Of course I do.'

'And thanks for keeping what I saw a secret,' she sniffled, straightening.

'My lips are sealed, hun.' She gave Juliette's back a pat. 'Anyhoos, the wicked witch of the west is almost upon us, so time to toughen up, my little buttercup. Deep breath, and like that penguin said in *Madagascar*, smile and wave.'

Clearing her throat, and making sure her sunglasses were covering any sign of teary eyes, Juliette plastered a forced smile on her face and turned, only to be met by an equally tight, fake smile, one she'd grown very used to over the years of being married to Lachlan.

'Hello, Juliette. Fancy this.' Margery clucked her tongue as she waved manicured fingernails across the table. 'I didn't expect you to be anywhere near the home-baking stand, especially when you don't bake at home anymore.'

'I don't bake because I have nobody home to bake for.' Juliette rose to the bait, and immediately hated herself for it.

'Lachlan lives under the same roof as you, Juliette, does he not?' Margery's smug expression was infuriating.

'Does he? Because I barely see him,' Juliette retorted.

Zoe's hand went to the base of Juliette's back in support. 'We're lending a helping hand today, Margery. You know, doing a good deed for the school, so how about you see the good in that instead of finding a way to chastise Jules, yet again?' she said with the brightest of smiles. 'Now, what would you like to buy?'

Margery threw daggers at Zoe, her lips tight. Zoe remained unperturbed. Juliette envied her friend's nonchalance. Margery sucked in a breath. 'Well then, how *noble* of you both.' It was said in a monotone as Margery flitted her gaze over what was left on the table, thankfully missing the leer Zoe gave her. She pointed to a chocolate cake and a tray of melting moments filled with passionfruit buttercream. 'I'll take both of these.' Slipping her hand into her pocket, she pulled out her purse. 'How much do I owe the school?'

'That'll be eight dollars.' Juliette popped both into a brown paper bag.

Margery handed over a ten-dollar note. 'Keep the change. That'll be *my* good deed for today.'

'Well, how noble of you,' Zoe said, so cheerily it was unashamedly obvious she was mocking the older woman.

Margery shot Zoe another glare.

Juliette bit back a smirk as she tucked the note into the change tin. 'Thanks for that.'

Taking the paper bag from Juliette, she leant forwards, resting a hand on the cane she didn't need but used to earn sympathy votes. 'So, when are you going to give me that grandbaby I've been waiting years for?'

'Soon, hopefully.' Juliette pushed back her heartache and spoke softly, measuredly. Margery wasn't privy to what had happened last weekend and Juliette wasn't about to take her mother-in-law's bait again. The self-absorbed gene seemed to run in the family, so it would be a waste of her breath to even try to defend herself.

'Oh, codswallop.' Margery emphasised her annoyance with a sharp rap of her cane. 'I don't intend on living forever, you know, so time is of the absolute essence.' Her thin lips tightened even more, making it appear as if she had none, and her grey eyes burned with irritation. 'Lachlan has told me how much he wants children, Juliette. If your stressful lifestyle is making you barren, you should stop worrying about your career and focus on doing what god blessed a woman to do.' She tutted with a shake of her head. 'You young people today, you're all so self-centred.'

With rage filling her entirely, Juliette kept her gritty focus on the slice of black forest she was going to inhale tonight for her dinner. She had nothing to say to her mother-in-law's blatant callousness. She could see Zoe was biting her lip so hard she was surprised she hadn't chewed it right off.

Moments passed. Long ones. Silence hung uncomfortably between the three women.

Margery finally broke it. 'This weather is insufferable, isn't it?' The haughty woman dabbed at her cheeks with a lace handkerchief. 'I'd best go and get some water before I pass out.'

Juliette smiled thinly. 'Sounds like a good idea. They have an abundance of cold water back at the CWA stall.'

'Right you are.' Her usually pale complexion aglow with the heat, Margery nodded. 'Bye for now.'

Juliette secured a piece of wispy hair behind her ear. 'Bye, Margery. Enjoy your cakes.' Juliette wanted to kill the woman with kindness, a trait taught to her by her own dear mother.

'Ciao, Mrs Davis,' Zoe said with a huge smile and an exaggerated wave.

Turning away with a roll of her eyes, Margery brushed the air with her fingertips, dismissing Zoe without even a word.

'It's no wonder hardly anyone likes her, except for the handful of people who crawl up her arse because she has money. I don't know how in the heck you put up with her, Jules.' Margery was barely out of earshot, but Zoe made sure to keep her voice hushed. 'You honestly deserve a medal, staying civil to the horrid old bat.'

Watching Margery hobble away, every over-pronounced step irking her to no end, Juliette nodded. 'Tell me about it.' She shrugged, sighing as she stepped out of the sunshine now creeping beneath the pop-up gazebo. 'But what good is it going to do me, being nasty back to her? It's only going to make me stoop to her level, and I refuse to do that.'

'You're a good person, hun, one of the many reasons I love you so much.' Zoe fixed her twisted bra strap and straightened her boobs beneath her singlet. 'And that son of a bitch! Pointing the finger at you for not having any children. If I could give him a piece of my mind ...'

Juliette half-smiled. 'I know, you'd let it rip.' Although she enjoyed every second with her grade-four students, Juliette yearned for a child of her own. 'I shouldn't expect anything less from him, though, I suppose. Once a liar and a cheat, always a liar and a cheat.'

'He's certainly shown you his true colours, which is why you seriously need to get the hell away from him and his horrible mother.' Not receiving a reply, Zoe rested a hand on Juliette's shoulder. 'Are you okay?'

Thinking about it for a few short moments, Juliette nodded. 'Yup, all good.' It was a lie. She felt like absolute shit, but she didn't want to add to Zoe's concern for her, especially when Zoe was due to leave Aussie shores in less than twenty-four hours to fulfil her dream of helping orphaned children in Cambodia, a dream funded by money raised by the Little Heart Church congregation.

After a slow, questioning glance, Zoe eventually leant in and brushed a kiss over her cheek. 'If only she knew the real reason she hasn't got any grandchildren, hey? She might just change her tune.'

'If only,' Juliette agreed. 'I think it could possibly send her to an early grave.'

'Hmmm, food for thought.' Zoe smirked as she glanced to the heavens. 'Kidding, not kidding.' She eyed Juliette for a few moments longer and then checked her watch. 'Shit, hun, I've got to run soon. I've got a Skype meeting with the head honcho in Cambodia at five, just to go over the final few details of the trip before I jump on the plane tomorrow night.'

Juliette forced a smile she was far from feeling. She was going to miss Zoe like crazy, and then some. 'Of course, you go now. I can pack up here.'

'You sure?'

'Yes, go.' She ushered Zoe out of the stall. 'Thanks for coming to help out.'

'I don't know if I'll have time to catch up tomorrow, to say bye.' Zoe's smile all but disappeared. 'So, should we hug it out now and get our farewells over with?'

Juliette sucked in a big breath, nodding. She'd been dreading this very moment for months now. 'I'm going to miss you so much, Zoe.' She squeezed her tight. 'Make sure you have heaps of fun, and ring me whenever you can.'

'I promise I will.' Zoe squeezed her back. 'We only get phone service in limited places, though, so don't stress if it's not for a couple of weeks.' She stepped back and wiped tears from Juliette's face. 'Stop it or you're going to make me cry. I'll be back before you know it.'

Juliette sniffled. 'Six months is a long time.'

Zoe tossed a hand through the air. 'Pfft. It'll fly by.'

'Yeah, maybe.' Juliette smiled through her tears. 'I love you heaps, hey.'

Zoe smiled back at her. 'Love you too. Catch you on the flip side, hun.' And off she went.

Watching Zoe leg it over to the car park, Juliette grabbed her mobile from her handbag and dialled Lachlan's number, her breath laboured and her pulse racing. She impatiently drummed the tabletop while watching kids and parents lob gumboots across the field to see who could get them the furthest. Six rings and, as usual, it went to message bank.

'You've reached Lachlan Davis. Your business is important, so please leave your message and I will return your call as soon as possible.' Even his voicemail message was mechanical, cold.

She gritted her teeth. 'Hey, Lachie, it's me. Can you call me back as soon as you get this message.' She went to hang up but added, 'It's actually important.'

Ending the call and tossing her mobile back into the depths of her handbag, she blinked back exasperated tears, her already broken heart splitting that little bit further. Not only because she knew he was ignoring her calls – his mobile phone was basically a part of his arm – but because he'd gone and thrown her into the firing line with his mother to save himself, once again. Who did he think he was, saying it was all her fault they didn't have any children? What a load of garbage. How many other people was he telling that to? Maybe a visit to church tomorrow was what she needed to guide her through. It would be a sure way to catch up with her mum, too, whose days were always filled with doing what her stepfather called god's work. Juliette saw it very differently.

She was deep in her bleak thoughts when someone cleared their throat from behind her. She snapped to, put on a happy face and spun around, ready to apologise for being a million miles away. Her breath hitched in her throat as she tried to blink away the image of the six-foot bundle of muscle and manliness. Dressed head to toe in everything she loved to see a bloke in – boots, jeans, button-up shirt, Akubra – and as if materialised from nowhere while silhouetted by the bright sunshine, she momentarily questioned if she was seeing things. She'd given up on this day ever arriving, and had always envisioned that, if it miraculously did, she'd have so much to say. Silence hanging heavily between them, he offered a hesitant smile and, as though she'd just been whacked with a cattle prod, her heart jolted as she froze.

The sudden weakness in her knees had her gripping the foldout table for support. 'Joel?' she whispered as she drank in his towering frame and strong physique – one she imagined powerful enough to wrestle a wild bull to the ground, and gathered he would have, many times over. No longer the teenage boy she tried to forget yet dared to remember more often than not, he'd matured into one hell of a masculine man.

He removed his sunglasses and perched them on the tattered rim of his hat, his intense sea-green gaze locking with hers. 'Hey, Jules. Long time, no see.' His voice was deeper, rougher, more commanding of her attention than she recalled.

Her heart and soul ruthlessly reaching for his, she fought a reply from her dry mouth. 'Yeah, it sure has been a *very* long time.' She'd always wondered how she'd feel if she laid her eyes on him again, what she would say to him in that moment. It wasn't this.

'Mmhhmm,' was his casual reply as he continued staring at her, as if drinking all of her in.

As much as she'd tried, she'd never forgotten him, the promises they'd made to one another, the intense way he made her feel, the way he unconditionally loved her, nor the way he'd wanted to protect her, to fight her fight, and how everything he'd done was always for her. Their love had been real, true – one she'd never been able to replace, as hard as she'd tried.

Her head spinning, she desperately tried to find something to say to put a stop to the way he was stealing her every breath. 'Where in the hell did you come from?' He was so close that she could smell the leather and earth that always clung to a stockman.

One thumb hooked through his belt loop, he wandered to the end of her barricade – the foldout table – and jerked the other thumb over his shoulder. 'Out yonder.' His breath-stealing smile connected to his dimples, broadened his chiselled cheeks, and sent her already racing heart into a frenzied gallop.

She gritted her teeth as she flashed him a dark look, filled with frustration. His charming, playful smile did nothing to curb her annoyance as every single bit of heartache he'd left her with the day he'd disappeared returned, full force. She lifted her sunglasses, finally finding her voice. 'That's not funny, Joel.' The fact he seemed so cool, calm and collected when she was so giddy she was afraid she might just pass out irked her to no end. 'I seriously can't believe you're acting so blasé.'

'Sorry, Jules. I just …' His smile disappeared as he looked down at his boots, hesitated, and then back at her with nothing but apprehension written all over his handsome face. 'I know there's a lot of water under the bridge. I just honestly don't know what to say or how to act right now.'

Even with the table between them, she took a little step back, not because she despised him, but because she was terrified of falling right into those big strong arms if he came anywhere near her. 'Does your family know you're here?' If Zoe had been privy to his arrival, she was going to give her an earful.

'Nope.'

He was telling her the truth. He always had. She didn't stop to catch a breath. 'Don't you think they should know?'

His jaw tightened before he cleared his throat. 'Yes, and they will. But you're the first person I wanted to see, which is why I waited until I saw Zoe drive off.'

Juliette spotted her mother-in-law glaring directly at her, the gaping mouths of the women sitting near her speaking volumes. The gossip had already started – the bush telegraph at its finest. It wouldn't take long for the entire town to know Joel Hunter was back, and his first stop had been to her cake stand. 'And why's that? Seeing as I'm the person you didn't bother to say goodbye to or keep in touch with.'

'That's exactly why I felt I should make the effort to put you first.'

Juliette tried to gauge his response, but his hat was shadowing his expression. 'Don't you think it's a little late to put me first?' As soon as the statement left her lips, she wished she could take it back. He had always sparked so much emotion in her, and she knew it was because she cared too much for him. Even so, it had come out wrong, especially when he'd done nothing but put her first back in the days when they'd been boyfriend and girlfriend. Besides, she was married now, although very unhappily, and she should have moved on from the memory of Joel and her together by now.

Joel's shoulders slumped, as if the weight of the world had just been dropped upon them. 'You have every right to hate me, Jules.'

The words stung, even if he hadn't meant them to. 'I don't hate you.'

Grimacing, he sighed. 'You could've fooled me.'

Juliette softened, almost smiled. 'I could never hate you, Joel Hunter. I'm just really, *really* mad at you for leaving without telling me where you were going or when you'd be back.'

He inhaled a sharp breath. 'I didn't know where I was going. Or when I'd be back.'

Lost in his eyes, Juliette found herself at a loss for words. She sensed something within him now that hadn't been there before, a loneliness and desolation deep inside. All she wanted to do was hold him and tell him what was hidden in her heart. But she couldn't. Wouldn't. Even though things were rocky between her and Lachlan, she would never stoop to his level and violate their vows. No matter how unhappy she was in her marriage, it would be extremely wrong of her. She was a Christian woman with good morals, and she was going to keep it that way.

'Look, I don't blame you for being pissed at me.' Joel shrugged, half-grinned. 'Hell, Jules, even *I'm* pissed at me for taking off like I did. Now I'm older and wiser, I know it wasn't a great decision.' He rocked back and forth on his heels, shaking his head as though totally disappointed in himself. 'I don't really want to get into it all, especially here, but the long and short of it is, I suppose … I was just hoping we could move past the past.'

Move past the past? Just like that? She went to fire a response, but he sensed it, stopping her by holding up a hand. 'Please, just hear me out. I know you're married and trying to have a family, and as much as I wish it could have been with me, I'm real happy for you. I just want us to at least try and be mates. It would mean a lot if we could be.'

His gaze pleaded with her to give in and let go. Juliette could feel the icy parts of her countenance melting. Folding her arms, she eyed him for a few lengthy seconds. The fact he was being so honest, so exposed about how he felt – traits she'd always loved about him – stirred something in her heart. 'We can try, Joel, but I can't promise you anything.' She swallowed back a rising lump of emotion.

Joel's smile was slow and sexy. 'Well, that's a good start.' The atmosphere around them settled, blended a little better. 'So, how about we try and start off on another foot, hey?'

Juliette nodded, sniffling. 'Sounds good to me.'

Joel seized her eyes with his once more. This time, a hint of happiness glowed in them. 'It's real nice to see you.'

'It's real nice to see you too, Joel Hunter,' Juliette said with a small smile. And she meant it. How was she meant to forget she loved him, with him being back in town in all that glorious flesh and blood? It was going to be tough, but if she wanted to keep her marriage and keep Joel in her life, she was going to have to find a way.

CHAPTER
6

Rubbing where his beard used to be, now replaced with a day's worth of stubble, Joel bit back his hurt that Juliette wasn't happy to see him. But what had he expected, after the way he'd left things? After the way he'd left her, he couldn't blame her one little bit for holding it against him. He'd screwed up, big time, and it was time he made things right.

For a few long moments, there was nothing but silence again. He smiled a little wider, not knowing what to say to ease the palpable tension as he stared into eyes that were hard. He hadn't been ready to face the ghosts of his past, yet here he stood, doing just that. He'd known it would be hard-hitting, seeing the love of his life after all these years, but this was beyond that – it was excruciating. The angles of her face were sharper, the creases at the corners of her eyes and lips deeper. She looked … fragile, and yet even more beautiful than he remembered, and it tugged on the few strings still attached to his broken heart.

Standing here, so close to her, knowing he'd never again take her into his arms and kiss her like his life depended on it, made something deep inside him collapse. After spending eleven years running over and over in his head what he was going to say to her if they ever had the chance to be face-to-face again, he'd gone and found himself at a complete loss for the right words the minute he'd laid eyes upon her. The bittersweet smile on her full, kissable lips, coupled with her broken-hearted expression when she'd spun around, shook him, and made him feel completely out of place just by being here. He shouldn't have arrived unannounced, although, thankfully, she seemed to be coming around.

'So, other than you becoming a teacher here, and getting hitched, have I missed much around Little Heart?' He offered her a gentle smile, then glanced towards the sporting oval he'd run around more times than he cared to count, watching the egg-and-spoon race in full swing.

She moistened her lips and exhaled slowly. 'Other than a few people leaving for the big smoke and a couple of the wrinklies passing away … not really.' Her words were stilted, as if she still wasn't sure she wanted to speak to him.

Joel laughed. He'd always called the older townsfolk wrinklies, and he liked the fact Juliette still did. 'Yeah, apart from a few of the shopfronts getting a lick of paint, and Domino's opening up, it still looks the same.' He felt her step in beside him and stole a sideways glance. It was hard to keep his eyes from her.

She nodded, her gaze to the front. 'You know small towns. The only thing that changes is the gossip, really.'

'Yeah, true.' He chuckled, liking the way she was easing into his company.

They shared another silence, more of a companionable one, one that would be impossible for most after walking in their shoes. With her so very near to him, his heart galloped faster in his aching chest. He had to do something, anything, other than stand here covertly staring at her. The ice needed to be broken further. So, without a second thought, he closed the small distance between them and pulled her into a hug that surprised him almost as much as it clearly surprised her.

'Oh, okay then. Let's hug it out, hey.' She laughed a little uncomfortably as she gave him a tight cuddle back, ending it with a few hearty slaps before stepping a foot away. 'We'd better be careful …' She glanced to the tables beneath the jacaranda tree, where many sets of eyes were glued on them. 'The spies are watching, and Lord only knows what they'll say if we get too chummy.'

'Who cares what they think?' Joel shrugged off her concern. 'We know there's nothing to it, and it gives them something to chatter about.'

'I care, Joel. I don't want people getting the wrong impression.' Her gaze, met and held by his, was filled with unspoken questions and profound heartache. He wasn't sure it was all aimed at, and because of, him. 'I honestly don't have the time or patience for the drama it'll cause me,' she ended with a huff.

Clearly, he'd gone and stepped over a boundary. He mentally slapped himself. 'You're right. Sorry, Jules, I shouldn't have hugged you.' If only she knew how controlled that had been of him, when all he wanted to do was strip her down and make love to her for the very first time, until the sun went down and came back up again.

'Don't apologise. Friends *can* hug.' As if she knew what he was thinking, her cheeks blushed. She averted her eyes, looking past him and towards the winners of the egg-and-spoon race now being handed their prize.

He looked to the hundreds of excited kids, the smiles on their faces endearing. 'Oh, to be young and carefree again, hey?'

Coming back to look at him, she seemed to have regathered herself. Somewhat. 'Yeah, it'd be nice.'

'It surely would.' He rubbed a hand over his stubble again. Watching fathers and their children sharing memorable moments made him pine for what he'd always wanted so badly. 'I can't wait to be a dad one day, so I can come to things like this with my kids. I just hope it happens, because ...' He half-chuckled. '... let's face it, I'm not getting any younger.'

'I'm sure it will.' Jules's voice quivered and she drew in a deep breath. 'You'll make a really great dad.'

'Thanks, Jules.' He heaved a slow, drawn-out sigh. 'I can't believe you actually did it, you went and made your dream of becoming a teacher a reality.' He was damn proud of her, so much so his chest filled with contentment for her.

She smiled softly, turned to him. 'Is it that much of a surprise to you that I'd follow through with it all after you left?'

'Not at all, you were always a go-getter.' There was hidden meaning in her words, and Joel heard it, loud and crystal clear.

She considered him and then turned back to the goings-on in the centre of the field. 'University was tough, but it helped me to get through things and diverted my attention from you.' Her dangly silver earrings swung as she shook her head. 'You broke my heart, leaving like you did, Joel. It took a long time to get past it all.' Her voice trembled and she cleared her throat.

Her declaration of heartache sliced his deepest parts to shreds, and Joel stole a few moments to regroup. 'I'm real sorry for hurting you, Jules. It was honestly the last thing I wanted. But you have to understand, after you told me you never wanted to see me again, I was in survival mode. The only way I could get through it, the best way for me to respect your wishes, was to get as far away from you as possible.'

Her beautiful eyes darkened. 'I know I made a mistake, breaking it off after the fight at the pub, but you didn't even give me a chance to explain myself or to take it back,' she replied, her tone icy. 'I was angry when I broke up with you, Joel Hunter. It was said in the heat of the moment. I didn't mean it for a second. You of all people should have known that.' Accusation rang in her words.

'I was an inexperienced eighteen-year-old boy. How was I supposed to know that?' He sighed, closing his eyes for the briefest of moments. God, how he wished he could turn back time so he could make things right.

She huffed. 'Fair point.' There was a pause before she added, 'It's done now. Like you said, we need to move past the past if we're going to be mates.'

There was a touch of sadness in her voice and he spotted a hint of sorrow in her eyes. Although no longer the sweet girl he'd fallen in love with, he could still see her, hiding beneath the hard facade. 'We *can* get past it, together, Jules.'

She nodded, smiling, although her lips still trembled. 'Yeah. I think you're right.'

The very thing that had brought him back here hung at the tip of his tongue. 'Have you ever thought about making them pay for what they did to you? To us?'

'No.' She bit her lip and glanced away. Her jaw clenching, she shoved fisted hands into the pockets of her pretty summer dress.

It was said so quickly, so harshly, that he knew she was lying. With the abrupt change of her disposition, he almost regretted speaking his thoughts, but he pushed on. He had to. 'They need to pay, Jules.'

'No, they don't.' She faced him now, her expression stormy. She raked him over with freezing contempt. 'If you want to work on being mates, you need to forget it ever happened.'

'I tried. I can't.' Simple. Honest. He'd never lied to her and he wasn't about to start.

'Well, I tried, and I did forget about it so I could move on in my life.' She blinked faster. Coughed. Briefly looked skywards.

She'd managed a deadpan expression, but her body language spoke otherwise. 'Have you really?' he asked as gently as he could.

'Yes, I have.' She fired this at him, her tone sharp. 'You know Desmond Muller died in a car accident four years ago, don't you?'

'Yeah, I do.' Not that he'd been sorry when he heard.

'So, in a way, don't you think Levi got his justice, losing his brother?'

'At the risk of sounding heartless, no, I don't.' And he meant it. She shook her head at him.

Joel drew in a long breath as he pondered his next move and then slowly blew it away. 'So it's a definitive no.'

'Yes, it's a definitive no.' She straightened and wandered back behind the foldout table.

He'd gone too far, too fast. Damn his need to fix everything as soon as he got here. He turned his back to the many eyes upon them to face her. 'You okay?'

'Not really.' She sucked in a breath. 'This is a lot for me to take in right now. Besides, it's not going to look good to everyone, with us hanging out like old friends.'

'But, Jules, we are old friends.'

'No, we're old flames.' She closed her eyes, shook her head. 'Please, Joel. Just go. We can catch up another time.' She opened her eyes but looked everywhere other than at him.

'Okay. I'm sorry. Please know I didn't come here to intentionally upset you.'

Silently, she nodded.

Seeing her so torn, Joel's reserve was giving way, really fast. He spun on his heel and walked away before he broke in front of her. He could feel her hard stare burning a hole in his back, could feel the strong pull of his heart back towards hers. He could understand her shield, protecting her from the harsh, bitter reality of what had happened to her that night by the river. She would've needed it to find the strength to move on, to move forwards. Without him.

He plucked his sunglasses from the brim of his hat and shoved them on. He never should have left. But he did, and now he had to make things right.

CHAPTER

7

Back behind the wheel of the second-hand LandCruiser he'd bought for a steal when he'd stepped off the plane in Cairns two days before, Joel headed out of the primary school car park and turned towards his next stop. His next big step – his childhood home, Hunter Farmstead. He wished it could be his home once more, if only for a little while, until he found his feet and decided if he'd be heading back out to muster with Curly again or staying to make a go of it here. That all depended on the coming weeks and how his father reacted to his arrival. He couldn't stay here, leaving things the way they were between them, or between him and Jules. He had to somehow get her to change her mind. Levi and Jackson had to pay for what they did to her. And his father ... well, in Joel's opinion, he needed to heed his own advice and show forgiveness, which would be a much easier task for his dad if he knew the truth.

After not speaking for the past several years, the very thought of being in the same room as his father sent his stomach somersaulting. But it had to be done – there was no more burying his head in the sand. And he wasn't going to drink to cover up his turbulent feelings. Staying dry was a given now. His hands sweaty and his mind racing, Joel tried to turn his focus outwards. He didn't want to lose his nerve. It was time to face his dad, to bear witness to the bitter disappointment in his eyes. And although it was going to cut deep, it was just something that had to be done if he was to consider moving back here for good. His mum would have his back, just like she always did, but ultimately, his dad had always been the boss of the house, and what he said went.

A flash of something in the sky caught his attention, and he glanced up to see Australia's largest bird of prey. Awestruck, he watched the wedge-tailed eagle circle the expanse of blue, its wingspan almost two metres across, as it caught the draught of warm air rising between the mountain ridges that surrounded Little Heart. The majestic bird's keen eyes examined the landscape below. Joel knew it was searching for its next meal – a wallaby, snake, lizard, or even a small kangaroo – not much was off limits for its lethal claws. He recalled the time he'd watched one swoop in and grab one of his mum's prized chickens from the yard, carrying it back up to its nest atop the mountains as if light as a feather. As a five-year-old boy, it had been a sight to behold. For his poor mum, it had been devastating.

As he pulled onto the main road through town, a road train whizzed past and he breathed in the earthy scent of the cattle onboard. It made him feel at home and calmed him somewhat. Focusing back on the rolling white lines stretching into the hazy horizon, he drank in the picturesque surrounds. The sense of freedom that permeated the wide-open space was inescapable, and although not the expanse of the outback he'd called home for eleven long years, Little Heart still encompassed the exhilarating feeling of being unrestricted, alive, content. If only he could clear out the skeletons in his closet and find a lady to love and cherish, a good-hearted woman to settle down with and make a family of his own. If only he could rewind the past and never leave, and make Jules his wife … but that was a fantasy, one he had to let go of.

Resting his forearm on the open window, he gazed out at the park that housed the annual picnics, ceremonies and concerts, ones that almost every man, woman and child would turn out for, given not much happened around here. Then came Juliette's Aunt Janey's famous bakery that sold the best meat-and-pea pies he'd ever sunk his teeth into, a couple of pubs, a butcher, stockfeed and rural shop, post office, a few banks, a handful of cafes, the new Domino's pizza shop smack-bang in the middle of it all. Little Heart was like almost every other country town he'd been through, appearing sweet and wholesome on the outside, but with its fair share of unsavoury people lurking in the shadows. He could name one such person who still lived near here right off the bat. Jackson Muller might have moved south, but Levi, the main culprit of that horrific night, still called the wider area home.

He had to talk Juliette around. She was the one that had to agree to go to the police. He wasn't about to upend her world if she wasn't ready to face the demons of her past. That didn't mean he couldn't give her a few gentle nudges, though. He knew how she worked. She needed to make the decision to do so herself, so he had to tread very carefully if he didn't want to fall through the thin ice they were walking on right now. Her friendship meant everything to him.

He rumbled over the familiar plank bridge over Little Heart River, so old and rickety he was shocked it still stood. Twelve clicks outside of the township, he gripped the steering wheel tighter. He was almost there. He was almost home. Blowing out a shaky breath, he did his best to rein in his uneasiness. Even though he'd done the wrong thing in their eyes, especially his father's, they were still his parents. He'd decided not to tell them he was going to be turning up on their doorstep, because he wanted his father to be unprepared, and their conversation, if any, to be off the cuff.

As his wheels touched unsealed road, he tried to take his mind off his arrival, and instead turned his thoughts to the day he'd left. Remembering how broken he'd been, and how scared he'd felt about leaving his safe haven of Hunter Farmstead, his heart sank even further. It had been a spur of the moment decision made in anger and heartache, one he was none too proud of. Then pride had kept him from returning until fate had made it so. Pondering this, he wrestled the steering wheel into a sharp left-hand turn. He passed Juliette's parents' property, the humble home a blur in the hazy distance, trying to ignore the memories the long dirt drive that led to it brought back – some good, some bad. Then, just ahead, the wrought-iron gates of his parents' property welcomed him. Rust had demanded its space. He shot a glance in his rear-vision mirror as gravel kicked up from his tyres, momentarily considering turning around. But he kept moving forwards, pushed by the need to fix his past, to stop running from the pain of it. There had to be light at the end of the tunnel. And if not, he was going to do his best to light it up himself.

He pulled to a stop but left the LandCruiser idling. Squinting into the late-afternoon sunshine, he undid his seatbelt and climbed out. The hinges of the gate squeaked as he pushed it open. Sweat creased his brow and trickled down his back as he moved the four-wheel drive forwards a few metres, climbed back out, shut the gate, then settled himself behind the wheel once more. The few clouds that had been lingering throughout the day had vanished, leaving no hope for a cooling tropical shower. Sunlight baked the driveway and glimmered off the horizon, making it appear as if water was up ahead, although Joel knew it was only a mirage. He sucked in a breath and smacked the steering wheel. Readied himself. It was now or never.

Rattling over a cattle grid and down the dirt track only wide enough for one vehicle, he fought to stay calm. The silent agreement of bush roads was the bigger the vehicle, the more obliged one was to move on over. If his father came from the other direction, he hadn't a damn clue what would happen.

The seemingly endless paddocks with swaying grasses stretched out before him, the breeze making it appear as if the long blades were dancing beneath the dazzling sunshine. The old windmill, set on tall metal scaffolds that he and Zoe used to climb, caught his attention, followed by the glint of the faded red tin roof of the low-set verandah-wrapped homestead. Beside it stood the old Bowen mango tree – it had certainly grown a heck of a lot taller in his absence. Behind it was the old tobacco barn his parents had renovated for his eighteenth birthday – it was the place he'd envisioned he and Juliette calling home and raising their family in.

Little had he known how much their lives could be turned upside down, and all because of a heartless group of bullies.

Justice needed to be served, but this time, the right way.

As he drank in the scenic surrounds, filled with untainted nothingness, something deep inside of him stirred back to life. This was not only the place he'd been raised, where his heart had remained the day he'd left – the heartbeat of it all was entrenched in his soul. This was where he'd wanted to make his life and to live it out. He couldn't do that with Juliette now, but hopefully, he'd follow through with his dream to be the fourth generation to tend to this land, and to then pass it on to his children. Zoe wasn't interested in doing so, and never had been. She'd made it quite clear she'd be happy with a payout when the time came.

But he could dream all he liked. That ball was in his father's court.

Set halfway up the side of a broad hill in the middle of open grassland, the colonial style homestead he knew every single inch of stood before him. Charming and welcoming, it was just like his beautiful mum, the flourishing gardens surrounding it all thanks to her green thumb. Admiring how big the multi-coloured bougainvillea at the side of the house had grown, he eased off the gravel drive and parked beneath the softly dappled light filtering through the big old gum tree, the very one he'd fallen out of as a ten-year-old and fractured his collarbone – all to Zoe's mortification – the summer stillness and nostalgia engulfed him. He wondered if his sister was home. Her cottage was out of sight, over the other side of the horse yards.

The sweetness of mango and lychee blossoms drifted upon the gentle breeze, as did the soft call of his father's prize cattle and the whinny of horses. Stepping from the driver's seat, the distant drone of a tractor caught his attention. He looked past the chook pen and over to the shed. His father's John Deere was gone – he must be out slashing, or fertilising the small Chokodam mango crop – the unique mangoes were worth prime dollars. His father had always been business savvy.

On autopilot, he slung the worn leather bag over his shoulder, relieved he'd have time with his mum before his father arrived home.

Striding with purpose, he eased open the sagging wooden gate, admiring a pair of vibrant blue Ulysses butterflies flittering amongst his mother's roses as he took a shortcut across the perfectly manicured front lawn, avoiding where the sprinkler was spinning a spiral of water droplets. The siren of summer was in full swing as cicadas harped from the row of golden wattles that lined the back fence. The insects' love ballad was an almost deafening soundtrack – one he'd almost forgotten while in the outback. Clearing the front six steps two at a time, he halted on the welcome mat before removing his boots and placing them neatly beside his mother's gumboots. He took a deep breath. Both nervous and excited, he couldn't wait to wrap his arms around her.

As usual, the front door was unlocked. Hesitating, wondering if he should knock, he shook off the idea and stepped inside. The scent of home – air-dried sheets, cedar, potpourri, and the faint lingering of cinnamon and coffee – hit him hard, and he had to fight back an overwhelming flood of emotions. Down the hall, a radio played gospel hymns and the clatter of someone stirring a pot interwove with the heavenly tune. Wandering down the passage, he could hear his mum humming from the direction of her head domain, the heart of the house – the kitchen.

The ache in his chest increased as she came into sight, her short auburn hair now turned silvery-white from the years, and her five-foot-nothing frame appearing even shorter. Her back to him, she was at the sink, swaying to the music, an apron tied around her hips. The mouth-watering scent was now even more prominent. Cinnamon scrolls, his favourite pastry, were baking. And something hearty was bubbling away on the stove. Her famous lamb stew, he guessed, the dish she cooked when she was expecting more than a few mouths to feed. The town gossips had done their job – she'd heard he was back.

Quietly, he rested against the archway of the homey space, the view out the bay window above the sink as jaw-dropping as he remembered. 'Mum?'

Starting, she spun, her hands coming to cover her open mouth. 'Oh my goodness. Joel!' It was said with an almighty whoosh. She rushed forwards, tears springing and falling beneath her glasses. 'It's true, you're really back.' She fell into his open arms and hugged him so tightly he could barely take a breath. 'I've waited for this day for so long, prayed for it every morning and every night.' She sniffled against him. 'Margery Davis and Zoe both called, but I didn't want to believe it until I saw you with my own eyes.'

Struggling to push words past the emotion lodged in his throat, Joel forced a chuckle. 'Gee whiz, Mum, talk about being tougher than you look. You're like a little boa constrictor.'

Chortling softly, she hugged him a little longer before untangling her arms from him. Stepping back, she pressed a weathered hand up against his cheek. Heavy tears still fell from her blue-green eyes. 'Oh, my beautiful son, look how handsome you are.' She blinked then sniffled. 'I'm so happy to see you.'

'I'm real happy to see you too, Mum.' Joel grinned from the inside out. 'But I don't know about the handsome bit. I think you're a little bit biased.'

'Oh, codswallop, Joel. You're as handsome as they come, and with a kind heart too.' She took off her glasses and plucked a tissue from the box on the kitchen bench. 'I told William you'd come back one day, when you were good and ready.' She blew her nose. 'And as I predicted, here you are.'

'And did he believe you when you told him?'

She shrugged, sighing as she tossed the scrunched-up tissue in the bin before she grabbed another two. 'You know your father. Stubborn as a damn ox.'

He nodded as dread stole his smile. 'I most certainly do.'

His mum regarded him for a few short moments, offering him a compassionate smile. 'So you should, because that's where you get it from.'

He flashed her a lopsided smile. 'I'm not stubborn.' He knew he was kidding himself.

'Uh-huh. The pope isn't Catholic either.' She rolled her eyes. 'It's no wonder you two butt heads like a pair of wild bulls. You're more alike than either of you probably care to admit.' She dabbed beneath her eyes and then motioned to bar stools at the breakfast bench. 'Sit. I'll make you a cuppa.' She looked to the oven. 'I made your favourite, to welcome you home.'

'I can smell that. Thanks, Mum.' He pulled up a stool, turned it around, and sat as if mounting a saddle, his forearms resting on the chair back.

'So … are you planning on staying home for good, or are you just visiting?' Her tone was a little wary. She didn't turn to face him, as if not wanting to hear his response.

Joel didn't know whether she was worried about his father and didn't want him to stay for the upheaval it would cause, or was worried about him leaving again. Maybe a bit of both. 'I'm going to give it a couple of months, see how things pan out.' He didn't want to put her under any pressure. 'And then take it from there.'

She turned to look at him now, smiling. 'That makes me very happy to hear.'

'So how do you think the old man's going to take it?'

Hustling to make them both a coffee, she looked over her shoulder. 'What do you mean, love?'

'That I'm home.'

She turned away again, her tiny shoulders slumping as she drew in a slow, steady breath. 'I honestly don't know.' Her reply was slow, careful even. The jug boiled, she poured the water into the mugs and, after carefully measuring out two sugars and a splash of milk in each, clanked the teaspoon around both. 'What I do know, without a shadow of doubt, is that he loves you. Give him time and he'll come round.' She wandered over and placed the steaming cups down. 'You'll see.'

'I hope so, Mum, because I'm not going to feel too comfortable being here if he's not happy about it. You know he'll make his feelings known.'

'Yes. Like I said, stubborn as an ox.'

'Mmhhmm.' He watched her grab the tray of cinnamon scrolls from the warming oven with chequered mitts, and his mouth watered. 'Wow. They look amazing, Mum.'

She eased the tray onto the sink. 'Good. I'll give you two then.' She plonked them onto a plate, along with one for herself, and toddled over to him. Standing, he pulled out the stool for her.

'Thank you. It's nice to see you're still the gentleman I raised.' She smiled and, with a little bit of an effort, got herself comfortable.

'You trained me well.' He settled in beside her and tucked into the most delicious thing he'd ever tasted in all his life, still warm from the oven. 'Holy dooly. This right here could stop wars.' He was grinning like mad now, the buttery taste taking him back to his childhood.

'I know.' His mum grinned like she couldn't quite believe he was next to her, eating her cooking. Crow's feet had appeared, as had laughter lines around her thin lips. Elbows poised on the table, she rested her head into her hands, studying him in turn. 'You look ...'

'Older.' He saved her having to speak the obvious.

'I was going to say tired.' She took a sip from her coffee, eyeing him over the rim of the cup. 'So, are you going to be staying here?'

One cinnamon scroll down, one to go. He could easily eat the whole tray.

'I'd love to, but I don't want to put you and Dad out, so I'm happy to rent a room at the motel in town, if ...'

She cut him off, placing her hand over his atop the bench. 'Nonsense, you'll stay here with us,' she said, patting his hand. 'For as long as you like.' She sniffled, straightened. 'This is your home, Joel. You shouldn't have been kicked out of it in the first place.'

'I think Dad might disagree with you on that one, Mum.'

'Well, let him.' She huffed. 'It wasn't your fault, what happened that night. I know the likes of Levi Muller and his brothers. They haven't got a decent bone in any of their bodies. Bloody troublemakers if I ever saw them. Desmond crashed his car because he was drink driving, and …' She tutted. '… I honestly have no idea how Levi was blessed enough to become a doctor.' She made the sign of the cross, muttering an apology to god for being unpleasant. 'Anyway, now I've got you back here, your father is going to have to like you staying, or he can move into the doghouse.'

'Wow, Mum.' His eyes widened as he slowly shook his head. 'That's a change of tune.'

'Is it?' The look on her face spoke of just how wrong he was.

He chewed thoughtfully. 'Dad's always ruled the roost here.'

'Is that so?' A mischievous grin surfaced and there was a twinkle in her eyes. 'Oh, Joel. Of course I allow him to think he does, so he feels like the king of the castle, but I know how to gently persuade him to do most things I'd like him to do. And, unlike last time, I am putting my foot down.'

'Thanks, Mum,' Joel said, feeling a swell of emotion. His mother had his back. 'I'm not too sure your tactics will work when it comes to me, though.' He shoved his last mouthful of scrumptiousness in.

'We'll see about that, won't we?' she said sweetly. 'You can make use of your eighteenth birthday present now.'

Joel smiled, nodding. 'Is the old barn still liveable?'

'It sure is.' She beamed from ear to ear. 'I've kept it ready.'

'You did?'

She nodded briskly. 'For when you decided to come back home. I told you, I knew you would.' His heart both swooned and ached. His poor mum, holding hope that he would return, for all these years.

'I'm so lucky to have a mum who looks after me, and out for me.' Joel leant in and planted a kiss on her cheek. 'Thank you.'

'Of course. You're my son, it's my job to look after you.'

A diesel engine neared and was cut. A door slammed and gravel crunched underfoot. Joel and his mum exchanged a look, breaths held. The squeaking of the back flyscreen door was followed by heavy footfalls.

'Whose LandCruiser is that outside, Sherrie?' His father's booming voice carried into the kitchen. 'They're parked in my spot.'

His mum clamped her lips shut. Joel's heart stopped beating as he prepared himself for the worst – he was already doing things wrong.

'And that damn rooster has crapped all over my shed floor again. If he's not careful, I'm going to put him out of my misery and add him to the freezer for Christmas lunch.' William walked in his socks into the kitchen, head down as he sorted through a pile of mail. 'Sherrie, did you hear me?' he called again.

'Yes, I heard you. How could I not, with you ranting and raving at the top of your lungs?' Her reply didn't hold back that she was annoyed.

Sliding to a stop just shy of Joel, William appeared as if he'd just seen a ghost. 'Well, strike me down.' Very slowly, he lowered his glasses to the end of his nose, staring at Joel over the top of them. His face paled and he took one deep, anguished breath. 'The prodigal son has returned.'

'Hey, Dad.' Joel watched his father blink faster but, within seconds, recompose himself as he marched past him and tossed the mail onto the bench. 'So, what are you doing back in town?' Folding his arms, he stared Joel down. 'You need money?'

'My goodness, William.' His mum's tone was harsh. 'Could you at least *try* and be civil to your son.'

Joel decided to be the bigger person. 'No, it's okay, Mum. He's allowed to feel however he needs to.' He stood, took a few steps towards his dad, who was muttering about being very warranted in how he felt, and offered out his hand.

Clamping his folded arms even tighter, William looked at Joel's gesture as if it was the most absurd thing he'd ever laid his eyes on. His jaw tightening, he arched a bushy brow in question.

Hurt, but not wanting to show it, Joel shoved both hands into his pockets. His father's reaction wasn't as bad as it could have been, but it was clearly going to take some effort to smooth things out. The ox he most certainly was, his father wasn't going to budge. Silence hung between them all, the ticking of the clock above the stove sounding like a bomb was about to detonate.

'I came off one of the horses on the last muster …' Joel said finally. 'I concussed myself, real bad. The doc says I need some time off before I can think about getting back to it, so I thought I'd come home and visit you all, seeing as I've finally got some time off.'

'You did, did you?' His father remained poker-faced.

'Yes, I did.' Joel tried to take his father's lack of concern on the chin as he diverted his attention out the kitchen window to where he felt free, unjudged. Understood. 'I thought it was time we tried to patch things up,' he added.

William remained silent.

His mum clambered from the stool and rushed for him. 'Good heavens, Joel, why didn't you tell me you'd hurt yourself?' She looked him up and down, as if searching for cuts she could cover with a band-aid. Satisfied there were none, she took his hand and tugged him back towards the stool. 'Come and sit. Rest.'

'Oh, for goodness sake, Sherrie, would you stop fussing over him,' his father grumbled. 'He's a grown man, not a ten-year-old boy.'

His mum shot a fiery glance at her husband as she dragged Joel back to his stool. Relieved for the distance between him and his dad, Joel sat.

'So where is he staying? Because I don't want him under my roof,' William grumbled, glaring at his wife, his nostrils flaring and his face reddening.

Even though he'd expected discord, Joel felt a pang of sadness at his father's open rejection.

'This place is beneath my roof, too,' she replied, closing her eyes for a moment, as if drawing strength, and sighed. 'I know you two have a lot of unresolved issues, but I've told Joel he can stay in the barn, especially seeing as it's his to begin with.'

'That barn is on my land, so that makes it mine.' William's harsh tone cut like a knife.

'It makes it *ours*, William,' his mum replied curtly. 'We gave it to him for his eighteenth birthday, don't forget. And I don't stand for taking back a gift.' Mimicking her husband's defensive stance, Sherrie folded her arms, and both of them looked at each other as if about to quick-draw.

Joel's heart sank. This wasn't good. The last thing he wanted was to cause friction between his parents. 'It's okay. I'll just go and stay in town.'

'Oh no you won't, Joel.' It was said through his mother's clenched teeth, without her looking away from his father. 'William?' One word, but it was said with so much gravity.

His dad remained tight-lipped. The stalemate continued.

Joel felt uncomfortable, but dared not move or speak. He'd never seen his mother like this, standing her ground. It was a sight to behold – she clearly felt very strongly about keeping him home. It made him feel extremely loved.

With a massive huff, William threw his hands up in the air. 'Oh okay, all bloody right. You win.' He glanced towards Joel. 'Just keep the barn clean, no bloody strange people coming to visit, and stay out of my way.'

Joel gave one curt nod. 'You got it.'

'Good.' With that, William brushed a cranky kiss over Sherrie's cheek and stormed out of the kitchen. 'I'm going to check on the cattle,' he grumbled over his shoulder. 'I'll be back in time for supper.'

Sherrie waited until the slam of the back flyscreen door before she ran to Joel and wrapped her arms around him, dancing on the spot. 'See? I told you.'

'Yes, you did.' He grimaced. 'That was magic to watch.'

'Even though he's like a grumpy old brute, and only getting more stubborn with age, your father is a big softy underneath that hard exterior.' She clapped her hands together. 'This is going to be so wonderful, having you home.'

'It's going to be real nice spending time with you, Mum, that's for sure.'

Cupping his cheeks, his mother regarded him with kind eyes. 'You're a good boy, Joel, with your father's determination and my soft heart. You'll get there with your father, I promise.'

'I hope so, Mum.'

'I know so.' Wandering to the stove, she took the lid off the huge pot. 'Your sister is coming for dinner too.'

Joel sculled the last of his coffee. 'Grouse. I can't wait to give her a hug. I'm glad I get to see her before she takes off on her overseas adventure.'

'She can't wait to see you, too, Joel,' she said over her shoulder.

Two hours later, Joel was still sitting at the kitchen bench, chatting to his mum as she rolled dumplings and plopped them into the bubbling stew, when he heard a car door slam, quickly followed by hurried footsteps across the verandah and down the hallway.

'Sounds like your sister is here,' Sherrie said, smiling.

'Couldn't miss her. Sounds like a herd of cattle coming this way,' Joel replied with a chuckle as he jumped up to meet her.

'Oh my gosh, you're really here!' Rounding the corner, her long bohemian skirt swaying around her ankles, Zoe leapt into his arms, wrapping hers around his shoulders.

Joel found himself choked up with emotion – she'd grown up so much. He'd missed so much. 'Far out, little sis. You're like an incoming missile.' He lifted her from the floor and spun her round. 'I've missed you so much.' His heart was singing a happy tune as he was drawn back to better days, with Zoe as his shadow.

He eased her down until Zoe's bare feet touched the floor and she beamed up at him. 'I'm so happy you're home, bro. About bloody time too.' She flashed a wayward grin and gave his biceps a squeeze. 'Gee whiz, you got some guns there, too. You been working out?'

'Nope, I'm not the gym type,' replied Joel. 'All hard work and no play, that's all.'

'Fair enough,' she said, turning to acknowledge their mum, who was tearing up as she watched her children together.

'Just when I've got you both home, one of you is leaving again,' Sherrie said, sniffling.

'Oh, Mum, don't cry.' Zoe reached out and wiped a stray tear from her mother's cheek. 'You'll get me started if you don't stop.'

Joel swallowed against the emotion rising in his throat. 'Yeah, trust me, you don't want to see me cry. I look horrific.' He pulled an over-the-top face to mimic it, and both women burst into laughter.

'Forever the larrikin, you are,' Sherrie said, giving him a playful slap on the arm.

Joel gently pulled her and Zoe into a group hug. 'Let's just try and be happy that we're all together for tonight.'

Both nodding into his chest, Zoe and his mum garbled their agreement. They didn't have Joel's view out the window. He watched as his father stomped across the driveway, his frown so deep it looked as if it had been etched into his weathered face.

Yes, they were all together. Now, if only they could all be happy.

CHAPTER
8

The candle flickered on the ledge of the shower cubicle, emitting the comforting scent of musk and vanilla. Resting her forehead against the coolness of the tiles while her aching back relaxed beneath the scalding water, Juliette couldn't help but add to her pain and imagine the complete opposite to her reality. She envisioned racing from the toilet, a positive pregnancy test in hand, to tell her doting husband the good news. He would then cry out with joy and take her into his arms as their life took its next perfect step. It was a ridiculous thought. Never, ever, would it unfold in such a magnificent way, especially not now. She allowed the tears she'd been holding back to fall in racking sobs as she wrapped her arms around herself, like she could hold all of her broken pieces together. As she'd suspected, her monthlies had arrived, and with a vengeance. The cramps were now almost unbearable, the hormones overwhelming, and her head aching as if a jackhammer were trying to smash its way out.

The distinct ringtone of her mobile sounded distantly, the Led Zeppelin tune 'Whole Lotta Love' shattering the ear-ringing silence of the rambling two-storey homestead. Begrudgingly, she turned the taps off and stepped from the steam of the shower. Snatching up her towel, she dried herself, wondering who'd called. Maybe, hopefully, it was Lachlan finally returning her call, almost four hours later. Or perhaps she was just kidding herself.

Glancing at the array of misleadingly happy wedding snaps, professionally framed and gathering dust on the hallway walls, she swore beneath her breath as she headed past what was now classed as Lachlan's bedroom and on to hers. Now she knew the cold, hard truth, she could see it in Lachlan's eyes in every single shot, and even wondered how she'd missed it. Although, apparently no one in town was any the wiser to his secret, or so he'd told her. The images of her, wrapped up in her new husband's arms, were a different story. She was very clearly floating amongst the clouds. She'd been a young woman back then, full of exhilaration and hope for a future that was nothing like she'd imagined or been promised.

If only things had been the way she'd imagined way back when she'd truly been head over heels in love – with Joel. She towelled her hair, pondering what her life would be like now if he'd stayed – married to a doting husband, with beautiful children, and undoubtedly very happy and very much in love. Even though she felt guilty, thinking about *him* when she was still a married woman, it had been a contemplation that had plagued her over the years, had left her tossing and turning all the nights she'd spent alone while silently questioning where Lachlan was and who he was with. Wishing she could rewind time so she could stop them going to the river that horrific night, Joel's handsome chiselled face preoccupied her mind and sent a quiver through her body. Just knowing he was back in Little Heart, virtually only minutes down the road from her, made her even more edgy. She tossed her towel over the corner of her bedroom door and got dressed. After working a faded pair of jeans up her damp legs, she opted for no bra and pulled her favourite comfy singlet over her head as she made her way towards the spiral staircase with her tiny, four-legged shadow, now off the end of her bed and by her bare feet.

'Finally decided to join the land of the living, hey, Brute?' she said, smiling down at her Jack Chi – a Chihuahua crossed with a Jack Russell. 'Correct me if I'm jumping the gun, but I reckon it's only because it's dinnertime, hmm?'

Brute stared up at her as he yapped a sharp reply. Zoe was wrong – Brute totally counted as conversation. To save him descending the stairs, a bit of a feat with his short legs, she picked him up, cuddling him to her. He rewarded the kind gesture with a sneaky lick to her face. 'Oi, you cheeky little bugger. You know better than that.' Grinning, she wiped at her cheek with the back of her hand, then kissed the top of his head. 'Thank god I have you for company. I love you so much, my little buddy.'

She passed the shelves, overflowing with her books, and ran her fingers along the spines as she wandered towards the kitchen. It had been so long since she'd found a moment to stop and do what she loved to do to wind down. She really needed to learn to make more time for herself instead of filling every spare moment with work, too afraid to stop and see what her life had essentially become – solitary. Unhappy. Padding into the kitchen, she flicked on the light, popped Brute on the floor, and contemplated her limited choices for dinner: a frozen meal or a can of baked beans on toast. She delayed the depressing choice and grabbed her phone from where she'd tossed it onto the bench. She sighed sadly at seeing the missed call wasn't from Lachlan, but at the same time felt blessed she had such a wonderful best mate. She listened to the voicemail. Zoe wanted to check in. Her brother was back in town and she wanted to make sure Juliette was okay. Juliette was grateful for the fact.

Plucking a can of dog food from the pantry, she tried not to tread on Brute, who wasn't leaving an inch between them, as she served some into his bowl. Before she'd even had time to rinse the spoon, he was sitting back at her feet, licking his chops. 'Far out, Brute, talk about inhaling your food.' She laughed softly to herself as she flung open the freezer. Pushing the frozen meals aside, she plucked a tub of salted caramel macadamia ice-cream from the depths, then a spoon from the cutlery drawer. Stuff the savoury food, this was exactly what she needed, along with a glass or two of red to drown her sorrows. Stopping at the wine rack, she purposely selected a pinot noir from the top shelf – usually Lachlan's special out-of-bounds area – picked up her glass from where she'd left it upended on the draining rack last night, and headed towards the comfort of the couch. She felt like an absolute rebel. Getting herself settled, she tossed Brute's ball, which had been buried beneath one of the cushions, chuckling at his eagerness to retrieve it as she dialled Zoe's number.

She answered in less than two rings. 'Hey, hun, thank god. I was so worried about you.' Zoe's anxious voice carried down the line. 'I was just about to drive over and check on you.'

'Hey, Zoe.' Brute deposited the spittle-covered ball at her feet and she tossed it again – and so the nightly ritual of exercising her ten-year-old doggy mate had begun. 'There's honestly nothing to worry about. I'm all good.' Juliette feigned an assuredness she was far from feeling before shoving a mouthful of delectable creaminess in, accomplishing instant brain-freeze.

'I know you're lying through your perfectly white teeth, Juliette. There's no way on this earth this won't be affecting you, especially after what your arsehole husband just did.'

Juliette groaned. 'I don't want to think about it right now.'

'Denial is not going to help you this time round. You need to get out of there.' Zoe, as always, was directly to the point.

'Please, Zoe. Just let me do this at my own pace.' Juliette sniffled, but refused to cry. 'With Lachlan away for work, it's giving me time here, by myself, to figure it all out.'

'Nothing to figure out, my beautiful friend. Other than once a cheater, always a cheater.' Ice chinked on the other end. Zoe was drinking. 'Oh yes, that's just what I needed,' she breathed.

'Rum and Coke?'

'The one and only,' Zoe replied.

Rarely a drinker, Zoe was clearly as rattled as she was about Joel's return. 'How'd the reunion go?' Not that she wanted to discuss Joel, but Juliette was desperate to steer the conversation away from her marital woes. She and Zoe had talked about it for countless hours and, in her opinion, there was nothing left to say about it all. She had a decision to make, one that nobody could make for her.

'Uncomfortable at first, but it didn't take long for me and him to feel like we'd never been apart.'

'Well, that's good, isn't it?' Juliette offered.

'Yeah, I suppose it is. It just sucks he comes home when I'm about to leave,' Zoe said. 'Life is a weird, muddled-up thing at times.' She exhaled a weighty breath. 'Even though I have just seen him with my own eyes, I still can't believe he's really back here.'

'Yeah, me neither,' Juliette said. Seeing Joel had felt unreal, even if the turbulent feelings he'd stirred up in her were all too real. 'How's your father feeling about it all?'

'He's not real happy about it. The stubborn old bugger barely said two words at dinner, and as soon as he'd eaten, he was up and outta there. But Mum's over the moon.'

Juliette tried to swallow down her guilt. Joel had only lashed out because of what they'd been through that horrible night. 'I thought that might be the case with your dad. He wasn't backwards in letting the entire town know he was disappointed with Joel hitting Levi, then taking off like he did, but at least your mum is happy about it.'

'Yeah, true. He always was her baby boy. Still is even though he's thirty.' Zoe half-chuckled, half-groaned. 'She's dancing around the house like Mary bloody Poppins, I tell you.'

Juliette couldn't help but laugh softly as she visualised exactly that. Sherrie Hunter was a sweet, loveable woman. William Hunter, as moralistic as he was, was a very hard man. She wouldn't like to be in Joel's shoes right now, trying to win him over. 'I can't believe you're leaving soon, Zoe.'

There was a short silence and Zoe sucked in a slow, steady breath. 'Me too. I'm excited and crapping my dacks all at once.'

Her glass already empty, Juliette filled it to the brim once more. She wanted a decent night's sleep for once. 'You're going to love it over there, helping all those kids. I just know it.'

'I hope they love me just as much.'

'Oh, they most certainly will,' Juliette said with a warm smile.

There was a pause as Zoe's ice rattled again before she said, 'So … Jules, tell me … how do you *really* feel about my brother being back here?'

Nerves ignited in Juliette's belly and butterflies flittered through her heart. Heaving a sigh, she closed her eyes. 'Honestly, other than shocked, I don't know how I feel,' she admitted glumly, flickering her lids open to find Brute staring at her. Fed up with the ball and now bored with chasing his tail, he'd scooted back to her and sidled up beside her on the couch, begging for a scratch. She indulged him. 'It kind of just exaggerates how messy my life is,' she added.

'Oh, hun.' Zoe sighed. 'I wish there was something I could do or say to take your mind off it all, but honestly, I don't think anything will.'

Juliette shrugged. 'A ride might help.'

'Touché, my friend.' Zoe laughed wickedly.

'Oh, for goodness sake, you and your dirty mind.' Juliette rolled her eyes. 'Not that kind of ride, Zoe Hunter.'

'Ha ha, sorry, couldn't help myself.' She sucked in a breath. 'Look, Jules, you know me, I can't keep my opinions to myself, and you're my best friend, so I feel I really have to have your back and make you see sense.'

Juliette's breath stuttered. Had Joel told Zoe about *that* night? She was going to kill him. 'I'm listening,' she said hesitantly.

'I know you're embarrassed that your husband slept around on you, and with another man for Pete's sake, but you're going to have to come clean about Lachlan at some point, at the very least to your parents so they don't condemn you for wanting a divorce, which I pray to god you will.' She said it all very fast, like she had to get it all out in one go.

'And just what's that going to achieve?' With Brute fast asleep, Juliette stopped rubbing his head. The thought of telling her stepdad terrified her, not that Zoe would understand it.

'You mean a divorce, or telling people the truth?' Zoe sounded a little annoyed.

Juliette shrugged. 'Both, I suppose.'

'Well, let me see …' Zoe said a little tersely. 'It'll give you a clean slate, with no blame on your shoulders, so you can get on with your life, living it on your terms, eventually with a man who will love you for the amazing woman you are, so you can fulfil your dream of having children.'

'Malcolm will never believe me if I tell him Lachlan's homosexual.' She could see her stepfather's reaction now.

'That's his choice.' Zoe's voice quivered, and she cleared her throat. 'The most important thing is that you know the truth of it all.'

'Yeah, maybe.' Juliette blinked faster.

'Well, it is the truth, Jules. And the truth hurts. Malcolm will just have to deal with the fact his holier-than-thou son-in-law is not what he thinks he is.'

'Yeah, I know you're right.' Juliette shrugged again, blinking back tears. 'But the thought of letting the cat out of the bag scares me to death in so many ways.' She thought of her dear mum copping the brunt of it and shuddered.

Zoe heaved a sigh. 'Look, I get that you're worried, but we only get one life and one shot at a happily-ever-after. For once in your life, Juliette, you have to do what's right for you. It's not like you're going to leave there empty-handed. You've been married to the guy for years, so you'll be entitled to half of everything.'

Juliette took a swallow of her wine. 'I wish leaving was that easy, hun, but it's not – I don't even want to think about dividing everything up right now. What a damn mess.'

'You just have to take the first step, my darling friend, and everything will fall into place. You'll see.'

'You really think so?'

'Yup, I do,' Zoe said with absolute conviction.

'And how's it going to look to everyone, up and leaving Lachlan the same time as Joel arriving back here?'

'Who cares how it looks? You have to learn to live for the moment, Jules. You shouldn't ignore the doors that open for you or the opportunities that are staring you right in the face just because of what someone else will think.'

Juliette sensed what Zoe was getting at. 'As much as you might think you know everything about me ...' Cradling the phone between her shoulder and her cheek, she reached for an almost empty tube of lip-gloss on the coffee table and spread some on. '... I don't want Joel back.' She rubbed her lips together. 'Not now. Not ever.'

'Uh-huh. I didn't say anything about Joel, but funny how he's the first thing that came to mind after my little pep talk, don't you think?'

Juliette rolled her eyes as she flopped back. 'I just played right into your hands, didn't I?'

'Guilty as charged, girlfriend.'

Juliette was about to defend herself by rattling off why she and Joel should never get back together but saved her breath. 'You're *good*,' she said with a smile.

'Yes, I am, and don't you forget it.' A deafening beeping noise sounded in the background. 'Oh shit, that's the smoke alarm. I forgot about the cake. Work is having a quick little going away party for me tomorrow morning and I thought I'd contribute to the BYO table. God help them all. I better run, Jules.'

Juliette enjoyed a bit of a chuckle at her friend's expense. Zoe had always been a terrible cook. 'Okay. Give me a call from the airport, let me know when you're about to leave?'

'For sure. Night, hun. Love ya.'

'Love you right back. Bye, Zoe.'

Juliette stared at the phone in her hand, thinking about what Zoe had said. At the back of her mind, a thought prodded, vying to be heard, but like a child, she fiercely ignored it. She couldn't allow herself to go down that path, for fear she'd never find her way back.

She only had hazy recollections of that night by the river, putting her fogginess down to the trauma of it all, her mind's clever way of blocking it all out. The pain and shame she'd felt for months afterwards had been debilitating, but she'd pushed through it. As hard as it had been, she had tried to make a life for herself. Now, that night just felt like a nightmare, a blur of images where she wasn't the victim. How dare Joel Hunter come waltzing back into her life, making her relive it all.

He'd had his chance and although she'd played a part in their break-up, he'd left her high and dry, with no option but to move on in her life without him. And so, she had. Joel Hunter was not going to own a piece of her mind. Not today, or tomorrow, or any other day for that matter.

CHAPTER
9

Seated in the front pew of the packed Sunday church, her mother at her side, Juliette looked up at the man who'd ruled her childhood with an iron fist and the length of his belt. How her stepfather could stand up there, in his religious garb, and preach about being a good Christian, was beyond her. However, she loved her mother to death and wanted to do nothing to provoke his wrath onto her, nor to cause her mother any unnecessary shame. So, she remained tight-lipped and kept their secret behind lock and key – not even Joel or Zoe knew that one. The scars on her heart, and the tiny ones on her knees from where Malcolm used to make her kneel and pray for hours on the cold, cement floor of the shed, were reminders, as were the haunting memories of being locked in the cupboard under the stairs just for saying 'oh god' or forgetting to clean her teeth before bed. She could only imagine what he would have done to her, and her mother, if he'd found out about her sneaking out the night Levi and his brothers had attacked her and Joel. And if he found out now, after all these years? The rage he'd have at being lied to? She hated to think of how he'd make her mother atone for her daughter's apparent sins. Now Juliette was beyond the reach of his unjust rules, he'd most certainly take it out on her mother.

Twenty minutes later, the service came to an end and she and her mum made their way outside with the rest of the congregation. Tables of home-baked goodies were waiting, alongside the usual refreshments of coffee, tea and juice. 'I feel like I haven't seen you in forever, Mum,' she said, waving to William and Sherrie Hunter before passing her mum a cuppa. She couldn't help but wonder if Joel was here too, and kept an eye out for him. 'Over a week, to be exact,' she added.

'I know, sweetheart. I'm sorry, I've been so busy.' Her short grey hair as impeccably neat as her crisply ironed blouse and slacks, Joan Kern straightened her white cardigan and offered a tender smile. 'I'll be at the saleyards tomorrow, along with your Aunt Janey, raising money for the extensions on the community hall with a bakery stand, if you'd like to come and help out?'

Reaching out, she rubbed her mum's arm, so thin and frail beneath her fingers. She was smiling, but Juliette could see the years of heartbreak etched into her mother's eyes. 'That sounds perfect, count me in.' She smiled at the ladies flocking to her mother's side, most of them sweet, though one in particular irking her. Juliette had never seen eye to eye with Kathryn Jensen on anything. Even so, she made an effort to be pleasant to the hoity-toity woman, for her mother's sake. 'Hi, Mrs Jensen.'

'Hello, Juliette. We haven't seen you here in a while.' She regarded her haughtily.

Clearing her throat, Juliette bit back unkind words. 'Yes, I've been meaning to make it each Sunday, but I keep getting caught up.'

'Really? Well, you of all people should know, dear, after being brought up in such a devoted Christian home, that god should come first.' She eyed her over the rim of her teacup, and with Juliette remaining silent, continued. 'So, how's Lachlan?'

'He's good, keeping busy too. How's Harold?' She glanced over to where Kathryn's husband stood beside Margery and Ronald Davis – her father-in-law was home for two nights before flying out on business again, and all three of them were listening intently to her stepfather. Malcolm Kern was honoured by many. Little did they all know the man who lurked behind closed doors.

'Oh, you know Harold. He's getting more forgetful in his old age, Lord help me.' She cackled like a strangled chicken, the sound grating on Juliette's already frayed nerves. Desperate to excuse herself so she could head home and go for a ride, she brushed a kiss on her mother's cheek. 'I'm off, Mum. I'll call you to organise helping out at the stand.'

'Okay, sweetheart.' She gestured over to her husband. 'Are you going to go and say hi to your father before you go?'

Juliette followed her mother's gaze, chewing the inside of her cheek. 'Oh, he's busy sharing god's word. Just say hi for me.'

Joan nodded, her lips tightly pressed together. 'Okay, I'll pass it on.'

They shared a fleeting moment in recognition of the common bond of what they'd been through with him. 'Love you, Mum,' Juliette said with a gentle smile.

Her mum placed a hand on Juliette's cheek. 'Love you too. With all my heart, my sweet Juliette.'

Before walking away, she took her mother's hands and gave them a gentle squeeze. 'Look after yourself.'

'I will. Stop worrying about me all the time.'

'Easier said than done, Mum.' She kissed her again. 'Bye for now.'

'Bye, sweetheart.'

Half an hour later, Juliette was home, out of her church attire, and in her jeans and a T-shirt. After her horrific week, she was determined to make it a great afternoon. Heading out to spend what was left of the day in the glorious sunshine, she made a slight detour to the kitchen, where she grabbed a couple of carrots and shoved them into her pockets. Her buckskin, Warrior, would love her even more for the treat. It was the least she could do in return for the uncomplicated, unconditional and fiercely loyal connection they'd had since she'd saved him from the meatworks almost ten years before. His owner had labelled him unruly and insubordinate, a complete waste of space. Juliette had labelled Warrior's previous owner a bully, and a man not fit to own horses when he felt it fair to train them with a piece of PVC pipe. Bastard. All Warrior had needed was understanding and a little love.

Pausing at the sink, she grabbed her upended wine glass from the night before, filled it with water and sculled it. She'd woken feeling a little under the weather and massively dehydrated – too much vino. She was glad she'd made an effort to go to church though. It was one of the only places she got to see her mother these days. Fresh air and Mother Nature were going to do her the world of good. The beauty of the bushland would help to take her mind off the fact that Lachlan had sent her a very short text late last night, saying he was caught up with work and would talk to her when he arrived home from Brisbane. Furious, she'd tried to call him as soon as she'd read it, but it went straight to message bank. He'd always been the master of ignoring the elephant in the room, but this wasn't going away. Sighing from the weight of her worries, she cursed his name beneath her breath when, speak of the devil, the rattle of the back door brought her gaze to that of her cheating husband.

'Hello, Juliette.' Lachlan stepped inside, suitcase and briefcase in hand, looking impeccable in his tailored suit. 'I didn't expect to find you here.' It was no secret he wasn't thrilled to see her. 'On a day like today, I thought you'd be out riding your big oaf by now,' he added, his tone icy.

His low blow at her horse made her blood boil. Anger, hurt and rejection swirled in nauseating circles. He'd wanted to sneak in and avoid her again. 'Why haven't you been answering my calls?'

'It's not like I ignored you.' His expression remained poker-faced. 'Like I explained in my text, I've been busy.'

'Too busy to take five minutes to call your wife back?' she huffed. 'For goodness sake, Lachlan, with what we're going through, I'd have thought you'd make more of an effort.'

He plonked his bag down and placed his briefcase on the kitchen countertop. 'I'm sure whatever it is you had to say would have taken longer than five minutes, and that's all I had in between meetings and the like.'

His nonchalance grated. 'I'm not even worth your time, Lachlan?'

'Please, Juliette. Don't start again. I can't deal with all of this on top of the upcoming election.' He closed his eyes, shook his head, and sighed. 'You know how much it means to me, running for mayor. I've wanted it since I can remember.'

The verbal arrow shot straight through her already broken heart. '*You* don't want to deal with *this*?' Her words were measured yet breathless. '*You're* the one who caused *this*, remember?'

'How could I forget when you keep reminding me?' His eyes were still shut. Groaning, he massaged his temples.

A rush of renewed fury fuelled her already racing pulse. She bit back the expletives she so wanted to fire at him like bullets so he could hurt like she was hurting. She didn't want to stoop to that level, and didn't want an argument, if she could help it. Harsh words and accusations weren't going to get them anywhere. Been there, done that. He finally opened his eyes, only to be met by hers, and they remained like that for a few long, uncomfortable moments.

He really seemed like he didn't care, and that hurt so much more. Before she burst into inconsolable tears, she drew in a steadying breath. Swallowing down her rising emotions, she folded her arms, and even though a part of her wanted to pretend this wasn't happening, and a very small part wished she could tumble into his arms and be told how in love he was with her, she stayed put. Long gone were the days she would welcome him home, excited to hear about his day. How wrong had she been to think her life could be right with a man like Lachlan Davis?

'I didn't think you were home until tomorrow,' she finally said.

After a long, drawn-out breath, he responded. 'My meeting for today cancelled last minute, so I hopped on the first flight home this morning.' His hands went to his lower back. 'I need a decent sleep in my own bloody bed. My back's killing me.'

In the past, she would have offered a massage and a heat pack, would have told him to put his feet up while she tended to his every whim. Now, it was impossible to be her usually empathetic self. There was way too much resentment for that. 'I would have thought a five-star hotel had decent enough beds.'

'Yeah, tell me about it.'

'I just did.' There was a fleeting moment of familiarity, of alliance through humour. He almost smiled. She almost did too. But she stopped herself from dipping her toes into that fake moment of bliss with a huff. Their marriage was a damn mess, and she had no idea how they were going to work through it, or if they even could. And as Zoe had pointed out, did she even want to?

He turned from her and, after checking there was sufficient water in the kettle, flicked it on. 'So, what did you call me about, other than to remind me what a bastard I am?' He busied himself, avoiding her eyes now.

Juliette hated his detachment, especially when it wasn't her who had gone and done the wrong thing. 'Please, Lachie. I'm not the bad guy, so stop treating me like one.' She was the victim here, not him. She gritted her teeth, making a conscious effort to remain as calm as she could. They'd argued until they were blue in the face the night before he'd headed off to Brisbane, and it hadn't got them anywhere. Fighting would not change the fact he was the way he was. 'Why does your mother think it's all my fault that we don't have any children?'

Lachlan glanced over his shoulder. 'What are you on about?'

'She said you told her it was *me* holding everything up, because I'm too stressed from work, and that was affecting my ability to fall pregnant.'

'Oh, that,' he said, chuckling as if it warranted such a flippant response. 'Does it really matter what she thinks when you don't like her anyway?'

'Yes, Lachlan, it does matter.'

'Why?' he huffed, shaking his head.

'Because it's a blatant lie, that's why, and your mother being the town gossip she is, she'll be telling anyone and everyone your BS.' She glared at his back, his ignorance adding more fuel to the fire. 'You're the one who refuses to go to the doctor and get checked so we can work out why we're having trouble, not me.'

'Damn straight I don't want to go. There's nothing wrong with me.'

'How are you so damn sure?' she demanded, knowing full well he was stating *her* body must be the defective one. Nothing was ever his fault.

His shoulders lifted a little. 'I just know, Juliette.' He blew a breath. 'So, what do you want me to do about my mother?' Still not looking at her, his spoon clanged loudly as he stirred his coffee. Black, no sugar. Hard and bitter, just like him.

'How about you do the right thing and tell her and your father the truth? And not only the half-truth, Lachlan. I think you should tell them *all* of it.'

'My parents know,' Lachlan replied simply. 'They were the ones who made a pact with your stepfather to get you to marry me, for the sake of the family name and to curb my *immoral ways*.' She could hear the smirk in his voice. 'You know how Mum and Dad live by the word of the Bible. They've warned they'll disinherit me if word ever gets out.'

His words punched her in the chest so hard it stole her breath. 'You're lying.'

'If only,' he replied. 'The house your mother and Malcolm live in and the land they call home? That was an enticement from my father. Malcolm promised your hand in marriage. All you needed to do was be a good wife and give me an heir. Looks like that's not going to happen now you decided to snoop where you shouldn't have been snooping.' He turned to face her now, spite written across his face.

She considered him, eyes wide, her mind reeling out of control. 'Does my mother know?' She almost fell to her knees, the hatred she already harboured towards her stepfather growing exponentially.

He shrugged again. 'Not sure.'

Oh god, no. If her mother knew, she wouldn't survive, it would crush her … Juliette bit back a flood of tears. She was not going to cry in front of Lachlan. The cold-hearted bastard didn't deserve to witness her heartache. 'I want a divorce.'

His expression spoke of how unreasonable he thought she was being. 'You're really going to ask me to do this now, right on the cusp of the election?' It was said without emotion.

'Yes, I am.' She dropped her head into her hands and took a moment to gather herself. The thought of divorce *was* terrifying, as much as she wanted out of this sham marriage. 'You can't expect me to stick around and live this lie, Lachlan. I deserve better.'

'With the cushy life you get to live being Mrs Davis, you're just being damn ungrateful and selfish.' His steely eyes bore into her, digging the dagger deeper.

Juliette couldn't believe what she was hearing. Slowly, she shook her head, choking back one sob after another. Never in her wildest dreams had she ever thought she'd be in a situation like this.

He regarded her with narrowing eyes. 'Does this sudden change of heart have anything to do with the fact your ex is back in town?'

'What?' She shook her head determinedly. 'No, of course it doesn't.'

'I don't believe you.' He sneered. 'I'm not going to be made a mockery of by my wife running off with some stupid childhood crush and blaming our failed marriage on me.'

Gobsmacked, Juliette regarded him. 'It *is* your fault our marriage has failed.'

He kept his resolute gaze locked onto hers. 'Maybe, but that part is going to be our dirty little secret, Juliette, because if you ruin my inheritance by blabbing, I'll be sure to make your life very difficult.'

With nowhere to turn, Juliette gave up the fight. She didn't love this man anymore. How could she? 'It's so typical of you to not take responsibility for your actions.' She thanked god he didn't know that Zoe had been waiting in the car for her that day. 'Everyone around you has to suffer just so you get to live your lie.'

'If you want to get out of this marriage, do it silently. That's all I have to say to you.'

Her disappointment in him, as a man and as her husband, overshadowed her anger. He clearly was never going to change, and she wasn't going to waste her time trying to force him to. 'I honestly don't know who you are anymore.'

'I don't think you ever did,' Lachlan replied in a monotone before raising his cup to his lips. 'Nobody does, except Roberto.'

'Please don't speak your boyfriend's name in front of me.' The tears tumbled now and she let them fall freely. 'All I ever wanted was to settle down and have a family. It isn't my fault that this hasn't worked out.'

'I know that. You know that. But not everyone else has to.' With not an ounce of repentance or compassion in his voice, it was all business for him. 'I can't change who I am, nor do I want to. I stupidly thought I could, when I married you, which was my parents' and your stepfather's plan, but this has proved otherwise. It's up to you. If you want to stay, we can try to make it work. In separate rooms, of course.' He finally took a step towards her, his expression softening just a little. 'I'll even stick with the ovulation days and try and give you what you want, Juliette. You could have a child. You could be happy. And I'll make sure you're paid a weekly allowance for sticking by me.'

Juliette reflexively took a step back. 'Have you totally lost your mind?'

'No. I'm just trying to make the best of an awful situation.'

What he was asking of her was a jail sentence. A life to suit him, where he could pretend to be someone he wasn't, to save face, to become the mayor of Little Heart, to inherit? She'd been a hopeless romantic ever since she could remember – a life without true love was not on her agenda. Clearing her throat, she looked to the ceiling, taking a few moments to wipe at her tears. She had no words, no words at all.

'Look, I know you loathe me right now, but will you at least consider my generous offer?'

Lachlan had sold himself out for the love of money and power, so it was no wonder he expected her to play a part in this too. But she wasn't about to sell her soul to the devil, especially for Lachlan's lies. She felt so much hatred for him right now that she couldn't even stand to look at him. 'I'm going for a ride,' she growled, then turned and headed out of the homestead.

CHAPTER
10

Her heart as heavy as stone, Juliette drove her trusty Holden Ute at snail's pace down the earthen track. She couldn't believe Malcolm had basically sold her for a house. But, then again, she shouldn't be surprised – he'd always been a selfish bastard. As for Ron and Margery, she wasn't shocked at their knowledge, or the part they'd played in covering up who their son really was. She just prayed to god her mother was none the wiser. It would kill her if she found out she'd been in on the sick plan too. Her instincts told her she hadn't been, and she had to trust in that. There was no way to ask without revealing what Lachlan had done. Just another secret she was going to have to lumber through her life.

Ignoring the monstrosity that was her in-laws' recently built seven-bedroom house, she passed the huge training arena before reaching the agistment paddocks. Gazing out her window at pristine white fences surrounding each of the neatly divided paddocks, a wistful sigh escaped her. As much as she loathed the greediness bred by money in the hands of the wrong kind of people, she had to admit, this place was her kind of heaven. Prized buckskins, chestnuts, bays, paints, palominos, and an Arabian stallion that was way too bossy for his boots, raised their heads to watch her amble past before dropping their muzzles back to the lush grass. Her horse, Warrior, was nothing like these expensive horses, all sleek and glossy like movie stars. Warrior was rough around the edges, a bit of a klutz at times, and had only cost her three hundred bucks, but he was worth more than gold.

After parking in front of the impressive stables, the door of the ute creaked as she pushed it open with the toe of her boot. Gravel crunching underfoot, she headed to where she kept her beloved horse, one Lachlan was none too keen on because Warrior wasn't bred from a proven bloodline. She didn't give two hoots, preferring the underdog to pretentiousness any day. Especially today. Horses in the stalls swivelled their ears in interest as she wandered past, and she nodded to the stable hands, busy mucking stalls, cleaning tack and grooming horses. She knew them all by name and made sure to say a quick g'day to each as she passed.

'Hey, Juliette, how goes it?' A familiar voice had her pausing at the second-last stall and gazing at a lanky bloke dressed in his favourite outfit – jeans, a Bonds singlet, a flanny and timeworn Blundstone boots.

'Hey there, Jimbo.' She smiled at the middle-aged guy brushing down her father-in-law's prized stallion. She hoped Ron Davis wasn't planning on going for a ride soon. She didn't feel like playing nice if she ran into him. 'I haven't seen you in a few weeks, have you been on holidays?'

'Nah, I had to have an emergency op to get some gallstones out. The bastards hurt like hell, I tell you. I'm usually a tough old bastard, but I thought I was on the way out when the pain started.' He flashed her a gappy smile, his two front teeth knocked out by a rogue wild horse a few years back. Claiming it gave him character, he hadn't been bothered with a trip to the dentist. 'I was dead-set fishing in the tinnie out in the middle of Woop Woop, minding my own business, when the pain hit me like a tonne of bricks.' He grabbed his side and grimaced, as if the torture was still there. 'I've never hoiked it to the hospital as fast as I did that night. I didn't know my old truck had it in her to drive like a bat outta hell.'

Juliette matched his grimace. 'Oh, ouch, you poor bugger.'

'Ah, I'm all good now. It'll take more than that to stop this old bloke.' He shrugged, chuckling. 'Anyways, enough about me. How are you going, pretty little lady?'

'Oh, you know, Jimbo, getting there.'

'Yeah, I know all about getting there. Would be good to get to wherever we're supposed to be getting to, though, one of these days.' He chuckled even louder this time.

Juliette grinned. It was nice to be in genuine, friendly company. 'You got that right, mate.'

A fly buzzing in his face, Jimbo performed the Aussie salute. 'Bugger off, you little bastard.'

'Fair enough, then. No need to get snappy,' she said cheekily.

'Ha ha, as if I'd talk to a lady like that, especially one as fine and beautiful as you.'

Juliette couldn't help but laugh. 'You're a charmer, Jimbo, I'll give you that.'

'Why thank ya, I try to be on my best behaviour with the ladyfolk,' he said, grinning playfully as he bent and picked up the horse's back leg, checking its shoes. 'And speaking of charming, is that husband of yours making more of an effort to spend a bit more time with you?'

Frustration and hurt crinkled her eyes. 'Things are still pretty much the same. Too busy focusing on the election to focus on me.' Jimbo didn't know the half of it, and Juliette wasn't about to fill him in, but she appreciated his concern.

With a loud huff, Jimbo paused and offered her a look of sympathy. 'I'm sorry to hear that, Juliette. He needs his head read, not wanting to spend as much time with you as he can.' He pointed the hoof pick in her direction. 'You deserve much better, but you know that, right?'

She'd heard that one quite a few times this past week, from Zoe, and in her own head. 'Shush.' She held a finger to her lips. Margery and Ronald Davis were not the most kind-hearted of employers. 'You never know who's listening.'

'Yeah, true, hey?' Jimbo looked left to right, scowling. 'It just gets me so worked up, seeing you so sad all the time.'

She blinked owlishly. 'I'm not sad all the time.'

'Yeah, you are.'

Letting Jimbo's words sink in, Juliette sucked in a breath. 'It's that obvious, huh?'

'Yup, at least to the people who care about you.' His bushy brows met in the middle, and he took steps towards her.

'And here I'd been thinking I was doing a pretty good job of hiding it,' she choked out.

From the other side of the railings, Jimbo gave the arm she had resting on the top railing a reassuring tap. 'Try and keep your chin up, okay? You may not be able to see the forest for the trees right now, but things will work out. They always do, one way or another. Sometimes even better than we ever thought they could.'

Moved by Jimbo's reassurance, she teared up, her vision momentarily blurry before she blinked her emotions back. She forced a smile. 'Thanks, Jimbo. I really appreciate you being here for me.'

'Any time, hey.'

Juliette cleared her throat and gave the railing a light slap. 'Righto, I'd better get a move on, or the day will be over before I know it.'

'Right you are.' Jimbo wandered back to the patiently waiting stallion. 'Enjoy your gallivant out yonder.'

'Will do. Catch you later.' She padded off, passing a few more stalls before reaching Warrior's.

'Hey there, my boy.' Her heart welled at the sight of him, as always. Warrior's liquid brown eyes took her in as he turned, nickering softly. He plodded over and, pressing his velvety nose to her, sniffed and then brought his attention to her pockets.

She gave a slight shake of her head as she pushed him back. 'Hey, where've your manners gone, buddy?' Pulling out a carrot, she offered it to him.

Warrior took it from her, careful not to nip her in the process. So big, and so gentle and kind, he was. He'd arrived on her doorstep as wild and broken as horses could come, but one long look in his big brown fearful eyes and she'd known she could earn his trust and, in turn, reclaim and heal his heart and spirit. As she'd placed a hand upon his withers that very first day, feeling the shudders of his wound-up nerves beneath her fingertips, she'd whispered to him, vowing to take good care of him and to never turn her back on him because he was proving too hard to handle. And she hadn't reneged on her promise, not even when Lachlan had demanded she get rid of the horse because his presence was an embarrassment to his family's stud farm. She swore beneath her breath with the recollection of the argument they'd had over her refusing to do such a thing, and the week of silence she'd copped from him. Lachlan Davis could be one cold son of a bitch.

She took a few moments to check Warrior's feet, cleaning out bits of mud and muck. Straightening, she scooped her hair back into submission, tugged her hat on, and flung herself into the saddle like a gymnast vaulting. It was time to forget about everything and to focus on the rhythmic beat of hooves and the bustle of the wind flying past her. She needed, just for a few blissful hours, to feel free.

With magnificent sunshine beating down upon her back and lighting up the specks of gold dusted through Warrior's coat, they walked until the thick scrub gave way to open grassland where wildflowers nodded their heads in the breeze, and then, with her gentle cue, Warrior opened his stride. They galloped for gold, the rolling landscape seeming endless as the gelding's drumming hooves raced against the wind. Pulling up near the river, they came to a stop at its edge. Sliding off, Juliette raised a small cloud of dust with her boots. She allowed Warrior a much-deserved drink as she knelt beside him, upriver, and cupped her hands to do the same. Rehydrated, Warrior flickered his lips and played a little with the water. Then, stomping in the shallows, he sprayed water in her direction, droplets now dripping from his muzzle.

'Oi! You cheeky bugger.' Crouched on her haunches, she smiled up at him. 'I seriously couldn't imagine my life without you in it, Warrior.' She patted his neck as she stood. 'At least I know I can always count on you to cheer me up.'

Swinging back into the saddle, she gently turned him around, allowing him free rein to open his stride. This was what she lived for – the country, her horse, and the freedom that riding brought to her heart and her soul. She needed to do more of this, more of what brought happiness to her life – and she resolved that from that moment forth, that was exactly what she was going to do. Levi Muller and his thug brothers had stripped her of her innocence that fateful night, and Lachlan Davis had trapped her spirit and sucked out her zest for life. It was time she grabbed hold of the reins of her life. To hell with keeping everyone else happy all the time. She only had one life, and she was going to make it hers.

* * *

After a night spent tossing and turning, Joel felt like death warmed up. Clearing his empty plate and coffee mug from his four-seater dining table and taking them to the sink, Joel washed them up and left them to drain. His mobile phone rang from his back pocket, startling him. After years without one, he was still getting used to it. Snatching it out, he took the call.

'Hello.' Stepping into the sunshine bathing the front of the barn, Joel braced himself against the verandah banister, one leg bent up against it.

'Hi, Mr Grant. You left a message this morning, asking for an appointment with the doctor sometime this week?'

'Oh, yes, I did.' He'd given a false name for a very good reason. 'Is it urgent?'

My bloody oath it is, he wanted to say, but refrained. 'Not at all. Just when you can fit me in will be fine.'

'Okay, great. Have you seen us before?'

The receptionist's voice was cheery and she sounded very young. 'No, first time.'

'How about next week, on Monday, four o'clock?'

Joel's heart took off at a gallop – he was really doing this. 'Okay, yup, that sounds perfect, thank you.'

'Great, all booked in. Can you please come five minutes earlier, just to fill in some paperwork?'

'Yeah, sure, no worries.'

'See you then, Mr Grant.'

'Yup, will do. Thanks.'

Joel hung up, pushed the phone back into his pocket and, with a deep inhalation, started to prepare himself for the face-to-face visit he'd been dreaming of ever since he'd broken the son of a bitch's nose. He just hoped he wasn't jumping the gun, doing this before Juliette had agreed to go to the police. All he wanted was for her to trust him and to know he was doing all of this for her.

CHAPTER
11

With cooling racks of mammoth scones and her famous double chocolate chip cookies taking up every square inch of bench space, the galley-style kitchen looked like a girl guide's bake-off. Aunt Janey was providing a lot of the gourmet goodies through her shop, but Juliette wanted to contribute to the great cause too. She'd got up early to start and was still in her pyjamas.

Cooking had always been her second love, with reading and horses coming in equal first place. Now she had almost seven weeks off for the school holidays, it felt great to be back in the kitchen as well as the saddle. Not only did it give her purpose, but it also helped to take her mind off her train wreck of a life. She felt good lending a hand for the fundraiser today. It had been a long uphill battle for her mum and aunt, but they were getting there. The government was only providing half of what was needed for the extensions on the community hall, to run a program for troubled youth. Her mum and aunt wanted to give those kids constructive activities so they wouldn't cause havoc for the community or themselves. The project was relying on the big hearts of locals to get them over the finishing line. Juliette didn't hold out much hope that a humble bakery stand would raise the remaining hundred thousand dollars they still needed, but it was a little step forwards.

Slipping the final tray of pumpkin scones into the oven, a firm rap at the front door fetched her from the kitchen in a flurry. Glancing at her watch as she hurried down the hallway, she breathed a sigh of relief. Her mum and aunt were early, so she still had time to look half-decent before heading off with them. Crying herself to sleep last night hadn't done her any favours in the looks department.

Tossing the tea towel still in her hands over her shoulder, she stifled a groan when she spotted who was on the other side of the door. That'd teach her for not peeking out the curtain first. 'Hi, Margery.' Overwhelming perfume combined with an air of overbearing arrogance.

Margery peered past her. 'Is Lachlan home?'

'No, he's gone to town to …'

'Good.' Margery cut her off. 'With Ronald flying out to Sydney again today, I've been left to deal with this mess on my own.' Her lips were pressed into a thin line, her gaze fierce. She took a step forwards, shoving her way past with her walking stick. 'Therefore, we need to have a little chat, you and I.'

Juliette's hackles rose. Margery was the most obnoxious woman she'd ever met, but she'd learnt over the years to never argue with a fool, if she could help it. 'About what, exactly?' Her arms folded defensively.

Margery jutted her chin out and peered down her nose. 'About what you *apparently* saw Lachlan doing.'

'There was nothing *apparent* about it.' Furious, Juliette fought back the urge to tell Margery where she could go.

The elderly woman stared back at her with pure venom in her eyes. 'In any case, you need to keep it to yourself, if you want your darling mother to continue to have a roof over her head.'

'I beg your pardon?' Juliette breathed.

Margery sneered. 'Lord knows your stepfather is good for nothing other than preaching god's word. He'd be still living in that dumpy old apartment behind the church if it wasn't for my and Ronald's generous offer of the house you grew up in. Besides all of that, you need to remember your vows, to Lachlan, and to this family.'

Juliette was stunned into silence. Remember *her* vows? She glared at her mother-in-law. 'Really? Well, I don't think abiding by my vows is an option when Lachlan hasn't taken *his* vows seriously.'

'Oh, come on, girly. Stop being a sook. You have a good life. An easy life, in fact, because you've married into this family. You'll just have to come to your senses and find a way to get over yourself and move past all of this.' She gave a sickening, fake, smile. 'We need a grandbaby, to carry on the family name.'

'I will not have a baby with a heartless man like Lachlan,' she retorted before sucking in a shaky breath. 'And as for keeping my mouth shut about his secret, I will, for my mother's sake.'

Margery stiffened. 'You're still going to leave my son?'

'Bloody oath I am.' With Lachlan's indifference and now this, Juliette had never been so sure of anything in all her life.

'Be very careful, Juliette, with how you go about all of this or you might lose your job at the school too. You know how much money Ronald and I give the committee, so I'm sure the principal would be favourable to a small request from me regarding your employment.'

A woman unaccustomed to not getting what she wanted, Margery's face had turned so furiously red she looked as if she was about to explode. Juliette took great satisfaction in the fact she was finally getting under her skin after all the years of being looked down on by this horrid woman. 'You don't scare me anymore, Margery,' Juliette lied. The loss of her job terrified her, but it was something she'd deal with later, if it came to that. She was over all the bullying.

'You should be petrified, girly.' Margery's chin quivered as she prodded a finger into Juliette's chest. 'You're going to regret this. I'll make sure of it.'

'The whispers around this town are so true. You really do have a heart made of ice.' Juliette stepped aside and pointed to the door. 'Just leave. I don't want you in my house.'

'Your house? Ha! This place is no more your house than the church your father preaches in is his,' Margery scoffed, casting her a disdainful frown and not moving an inch. She then huffed an impatient breath. 'Look, Juliette, I don't want us to be adversaries when we could be working together on this. How about if I offer you a healthy sum to help your mother and aunt with their senseless idea of a refuge?'

Her face heating, Juliette tucked wisps of hair behind her ears and then folded her arms once more. 'It's not senseless.'

Margery rolled her eyes to the heavens. 'Oh, dearie me, you really are stupid, aren't you?' She tutted and shook her head. 'Some people are born into this world to be nothing but trouble. The inferior are on the lower rungs of the social ladder, and no amount of helping them will change that. They're cursed with mediocrity from birth, and that's god's will. Trying to help them by offering activities to do so they don't get up to mischief is a waste of time and money.'

'As tempting as your offer would be under different circumstances, I will not let you bribe me into staying with your son,' Juliette said through gritted teeth – she'd hold a million bake sales to raise the money for her mum and aunt's cause if she had to. 'You've already got enough over me. I'm not allowing you any more control of my life.'

'I'm firmly suggesting you reconsider, Juliette, because bad things happen to good people all the time.' Lifting her head, Margery peered down her nose at her.

'Are you threatening me?'

'No, I'm merely offering you a word of warning. I wouldn't want to see anything untoward happen to you or one of your loved ones.' Margery said it so flippantly, Juliette fought the urge to slap her across the face.

'Get. Out,' Juliette growled. 'Now.'

With one last stern glare, Margery did as she was asked, and once she was across the threshold, Juliette did something she'd been dying to do for as long as she could remember and slammed the door in her mother-in-law's face. She was sick of dealing with her, of being the one to play nice, of this vile family's lies and manipulation. Margery Davis thought she could bribe or bully Juliette into being a Stepford wife? She had a fight on her hands.

* * *

Cruising along the outskirts of town, Joel clattered over the old railway line that divided the township into suburban and industrial perfectly, as if someone had drawn a straight line down the middle of Little Heart. Grabbing another Chicos baby from the almost empty packet beside him, he popped the sugar hit into his mouth before tugging his Akubra down a little lower to ward off the sunshine beating through his windscreen. It was just shy of ten in the morning and it was already so hot he swore he could almost fry an egg on his LandCruiser's bonnet. It was similar to the heat of the outback, although the humidity here packed an almighty punch. He wiped the beading sweat from his forehead as he shifted uncomfortably in the driver's seat. After a night of tossing and turning, he felt like death warmed up. And with his air-conditioner on the blink, it was either roll up the windows and swelter in the mobile metal oven or roll them down and eat dust. He'd chosen the latter.

But the stinking weather wasn't the only cause of his discomfort.

As if on autopilot, he drove to where he was fairly certain she'd be – he wanted to somehow, someway, talk her around on seeking justice. The twice-yearly livestock sale was the talk of the town, as was the fact it was doubling as a fundraiser for the extensions on the community hall. It was all his mum and dad had talked about this morning – his mother trying to fill the uncomfortable silence, and his father doing his very best to ignore Joel was even in the room. If only Zoe hadn't left as soon as he'd arrived back – he missed her friendly face. Always having been one to lend a hand for a good cause, especially when it had to do with her stepfather's church, he knew Juliette would be amongst the action. As would his parents, although, at his father's stern request, they were heading to it in his dad's going-to-town car, without Joel tagging along. Joel was more than happy to head there on his own. He just prayed his mother was right and that his father would come around, because he couldn't grit his teeth and bear it for too long. He'd rather go back to mustering with Curly.

As he turned down the familiar long dirt road, a small smile claimed his lips when he pictured Juliette, all countrified and ready for a day amongst bellows and shouting and dust and cattlemen. He liked the thought of seeing her in her element – she'd always loved the excitement of the saleyards. Not that he expected she wanted to lay her eyes on him. She wasn't answering any of his calls or returning them. But they had to talk. He had to make her see sense. He knew, after her reaction at the fete, that he was going to be met with dogged refusal. But he wasn't going to give up. This wasn't something she could go on pretending never happened. It had broken both of them. She seemed to be forgetting that. They'd made the wrong decision, remaining quiet. It was high time they made things right.

Just up ahead, a cattle truck stirred up a river of dust. Joel slowed, giving it time to settle so it didn't cover the interior of his four-wheel drive. Behind him, a few vehicles lagged back too. This was probably more traffic than the dirt track had seen in six months. Now the drought had broken, cattlemen would be keen to re-stock their herds, holding onto renewed hope.

Reaching the parking area, he slowed to walking pace. Cars and four-wheel drives were packed in like sardines and he wasn't about to drive around for half an hour to find a suitable spot. Bumping over a curb, through a bit of scrub, and then up a slight embankment, he ignored the No Parking sign and pulled up beneath the shade of a big old gum tree. Rules shmules – that's what a four-wheel drive was made for. Windows wound up, he jumped out and strolled over to the gates. Saying a quick g'day to a few familiar faces along the way, he went to where the racket of a good old-fashioned cattle and horse sale was taking place.

Sun-bleached posts and rails surrounded the yards, and a cloud of dust hovered above the bellows and whinnies. Passing a pen filled with prime Angus steers, he shot a sideways glance down a muddy alley where stock contractors hustled their cattle into order just as someone caught his eye. It hadn't taken long for him to spot her insanely beautiful face amongst the sea of people. Her black hair pulled tightly into a bun, and the faintest make-up on – just enough to still see the fine dusting of freckles across her well-pronounced cheekbones – she was wearing skin-tight jeans and a simple black shirt with the church's logo on it. Striding towards her with more of a spring in his step now, Joel was powerless to stop his gaze travelling from the tips of her boots to the top of her head.

She offered him a half-smile. 'Hey, you.'

'Hey, yourself.' He looked to her aunt beside her. 'Hey, Janey. Long time, no see.'

'Oh my goodness, Joel!' Janey pulled him into a warm hug. 'Juliette said you were back in town. It's so good to see you.' She gave him a few firm pats on the back before she released him. 'You staying or just passing through?'

The sun in his eyes, he tugged his hat brim a little lower. 'That depends.'

She eyed him curiously. 'On what?'

'My father.'

Janey's brows rose. 'Ah, yes. He can be a bit of a stubborn old bugger.'

Joel chuckled. 'He sure can.'

Juliette was fidgeting with her belt buckle as she looked from Janey to Joel and back again.

'Anyhow, I'd best get back to it,' Janey offered with a smile. 'Catch you later, Joel.'

'Yup, will do. I'll come and grab some treats before I head off.' He looked to the wide expanse of bright blue sky as Janey disappeared into the thick of the crowd. 'Nice day for it.' Shoving his hands into his pockets, he flashed Juliette the most charming smile he could muster.

'Sure is.' A hint of a smile twitched at the corners of her glossy lips, but she didn't let it spread. 'You come to buy some livestock or just to have a mosey about?'

His heart hammered in gratification for this stunning woman. 'Neither. I came to see you, actually.' Lifting his sunnies, his gaze collided with hers just a fraction too long. An unspoken exchange between them, raw and intense and oh so breathtakingly real.

As if lost for words, she cleared her throat and shifted from one boot to the other. Her silence hung, brash and heavy, and he could see the racing of her pulse at the side of her neck as she looked away from him. Was her quickened heartbeat because she still had feelings for him? Or was it because she couldn't stand the sight of him?

'You haven't been returning my calls, Jules.' Why beat around the bush when he could just get straight to the point? She'd always liked that about him.

'I know.' Shooting her steely eyes back to him, she studied him with unsettling candour. 'I've had a lot going on.'

'I thought you were on holidays, with school out?' He raised his voice a little to be heard above the crescendo of the auctioneer's calls. 'Anyone would think you're trying to avoid me.'

'What do you want, Joel?' She switched her weight from one foot to the other, looking at him as if she was debating driving the heel of her boot into the toe of his.

It did nothing to perturb him. He'd always loved her feistiness. *I want you.* He wanted to say it, but he bit his tongue. 'I want you to come to your senses.'

She blew a breath and shook her head. 'Oh my god, I can't believe you're going to try and pull that BS on me too?' she groaned, her arms folding. 'Why can't everyone just back the hell off and leave me be?'

'Sorry, Jules. I didn't mean to upset you.' Something was clearly bugging her, other than him. He wished he knew what it was, or who it was, so he could either comfort her or go and pull whoever it was into line. 'Are you okay?'

'Yup, all good.' She straightened. 'I'm sorry I haven't called you back, but I know what you're going to ask me to do, and the answer is still no.'

He offered her a mischievous smirk. 'Well, we're at a stalemate then, because I'm not going to take no for an answer.'

'Stop it, Joel, please.' She stomped towards the action, the anger in her steps making her hips sashay desirably.

Joel followed her, keeping his cool as he matched her posture and leant against the fence, both of them now watching the goings-on in the saleyards. He liked the way she didn't move away as her breath escaped her in a forceful exhale.

'I don't want to talk about this here,' she said, hushed but firm.

'Okay. Well, call me then and we can talk in private,' he replied. She threw him a sideways glance, and he knew he'd better heed the warning in it. 'Okay, I'll shut up.'

'About time,' she fired back.

'For now,' he added.

The shake of her head couldn't hide the hint of a smirk, and he felt a rush. He was making headway.

Dusty trucks rumbled behind where the auctioneer paced along the catwalk suspended above the yards, rattling off at a hundred miles an hour – only a trained ear could understand everything he was saying. After spending countless days here with his father, Joel could make out every single word. Bids were thrown into the ring in rapid succession. The hype of it was addictive and he quickly found himself drawn in.

He watched a frisky horse being dragged into the centre of the action. 'Blimey, that's one fine horse if I've ever seen one.' He tried his damnedest to ignore Juliette's perfume, drifting towards him amidst the stench of mud, manure and cattle.

'Yeah, he is, hey.' Juliette popped her sunglasses atop her head and took a better look. 'He'll be a tough one to get under the saddle, though.'

Smirking, Joel lazily lifted a brow. 'I'm not one to shy away from a challenge, Jules.'

'Oh, trust me, I know.' She cracked a small smile. The horse reared up, whinnying. 'But that's one keg of dynamite right there, Joel.'

With Ratbag galloping through his mind, his heart squeezed painfully tight. He missed his horsey mate and while he couldn't ever replace him, he needed another. He just hadn't realised it until this very second. 'Just my kinda horse, by the looks.' He flashed her a gallant grin as he raised a hand, placing himself in the bidding circle. The auctioneer pointed at him, and the bidding war was on.

'You're a sucker for punishment, Mr Hunter.' She sounded mighty impressed.

And he loved it.

Back and forth it went, between himself and two other determined blokes – they clearly saw what he did. But in the end, he acquired ownership of the wild horse at top dollar.

Unmistakably as wound up in the excitement of it all as he was, Juliette gave him a slap on the back. 'Good going, Joel, you're now the proud owner of a bucking bronco.' Her smile was wide, playfully so. 'So get yourself ready for some wild rides.'

'Yeah, tell me about it. I better make sure my health cover is up to date,' he said with an equally playful smile.

'Uh-huh.' She nodded before glancing over his shoulder and giving someone a wave. 'I better get back and give Mum and Aunt Janey a hand and let you go and organise how you're getting your new four-legged friend home.'

'Yeah, I hadn't really considered that part of it seeing as I didn't come here to buy a horse.' He shrugged.

'What are you going to call him?' she asked.

'Dynamite.' He didn't need to think about it.

'You are?'

'Uh-huh. That's what you called him, a keg of dynamite. So that's what he'll be.'

She smiled now, so warmly that it reached out and heated his heart. 'I like that. It really suits him.' She looked to the horse now being ushered down a pass.

'Yeah, it does.' Joel followed her gaze.

'Catch you round,' she said over her shoulder as she strode off in the general direction of the stalls.

'Yup, catch ya.' He watched her walk away and disappear into the thick of the lunch crowd, wishing he could run after her.

CHAPTER
12

Joel woke with a start to the crowing of a rooster, the resounding racket followed by the rustling of wings. Bolting upright as he blinked sleep-heavy eyes, he glanced up just in time to catch his mother's very spoilt Rhode Island rooster, Red, flap down from the rafter he'd evidently called home for the night. Then, clawed feet planted firmly on the floor, the egotistical fowl waddled off towards the door, sat ajar to allow the breeze in, to meet his flock of ladies clucking just outside.

Joel smiled to himself as he rested back and clasped his hands behind his head. Ribbons of sunlight filtered through the cracks of the old barn roof, bouncing off the walls, lighting up dust particles like specks of diamonds. The scent of tobacco still lingered, as if ingrained in the very foundations even after all these years. The familiar sights, smells and sounds – despite the cold welcome from his father – helped him to feel at home, as did his mother's love. The converted barn was perfect, kept immaculate by her. It had a functional kitchen and a decent sized bathroom, and a living area that was decorated with cowskin rugs covering parts of the scuffed hardwood floors, and paisley-patterned throws and cushions brightening the wear and tear of the comfy old couch – all visible from the mezzanine bedroom that looked over downstairs. He wholeheartedly loved the rustic charm of his new home. Give him this humble abode, with its majestic views and country charisma, over some posh mansion in the swanky burbs of the big smoke any day.

Climbing from the tousled sheets, he adjusted his boxers as he wandered over to the window and rolled up the bamboo shade. Golden sunshine streamed in and he blinked into it, keen to breathe in the view. The high peaks of the surrounding mountains dominated the skyline behind the barn, and a patchwork of lush green paddocks, marked by timber fencing, stretched out for as far as the eye could see. His parents loved this place, and it showed. Everything from the homestead and the outbuildings to the livestock and the fruit trees was maintained and cared for to the highest of standards. If only he'd been able to stay on here. If only his father knew the real reason he'd lashed out at Levi Muller that night, things might have turned out very differently. Levi had taken so much from him and from those he loved – Juliette, his parents, even Zoe. They'd all suffered at the hands of a man who didn't deserve to be walking free, let alone practising medicine.

Something had to give. Juliette had to realise it. He wasn't going to give up until she did, even though it was going to be an uphill struggle. She meant more to him than he'd ever be able to let her know, being a married woman. Losing her to Lachlan Davis of all men was his cross to bear – not hers. Although Joel couldn't stand the man, he just hoped Lachlan made her as happy as she deserved to be.

With a heavy sigh, he tried to divert his thoughts elsewhere. He was tired of wasting all his energy on something that was, for the moment, out of his hands. His belly rumbling, he headed down the spiral staircase and wandered over to the overstocked fridge. His pit-stop at the local grocery store yesterday had ended up costing an arm and a leg – he shouldn't have gone in hungry. On the flip side of the coin, he had enough food to last him a couple of weeks, and plenty to choose from – a luxury after living in the outback, where fresh food was a rarity and a can of baked beans was his go-to meal when the camp cook was nowhere to be seen. Laying his gaze on the bacon and the bowl of fresh eggs his mother had given him, he decided on a bacon and egg sanga, washed down with a cuppa. That was until he realised he'd forgotten to buy coffee – of all the damn things to forget. A strong cup of tea would have to suffice.

Half an hour later, showered, shaved and belly full, he tugged on his boots and Akubra and stepped outside, making sure to close the door behind him so Red didn't make himself at home again. It had taken him ten minutes to clean up the rooster's butt missiles fired to the floor from the rafters. His father and he now had one thing in common – annoyance with the dirty little bugger.

Beside the barn, clusters of bougainvillea had taken over the fence, the multitude of bright colours popping amongst the greenery of shrubs and bushes. Wandering past the old Fiat tractor, now overcome with dust and cobwebs after being put to rest when his father had invested in his new John Deere, he went into the shed and towards the tack room.

Shoving the door open with a creaky yawn, he stepped inside, his eyes taking a few moments to adjust to the dimness. Two saddles – Zoe's old dressage saddle and his old western – were shoved into a corner atop dusty saddle stands. Off to his right, his father's much-loved Syd Hill western saddle was on a rung below oiled stockwhips, harnesses and saddle blankets on hooks. The tack table, neat and orderly, housed currycombs, hook picks and the odd tool. His father's old hat hung from a rusty nail, dusty and sweat stained, along with the leather chaps he'd always worn when coaching a green horse. Wandering over to it, he took the hat from the nail, recalling all the times he'd had to recover it while his father was busy breaking a horse. He'd spent many a day watching his father from the sides of the training yard, dreaming of doing the same thing as his hero one day. Sad how fate had other plans. Would there ever be a chance to undo the past? He hoped so.

'You looking for something?' His father's gruff tone dragged him from comforting memories to the harsh reality of their tattered relationship.

Knowing his father's stance on being a manly man, Joel quickly cleared the emotion from his throat. 'Just a couple of things to use with Dynamite today, that's all.'

Standing just inside the doorway, William kept his distance. 'Your mother said you went and bought a horse. I didn't believe it until I saw the petrified looking thing in the paddock.' Shoving his hands into his King Gee pockets, his gaze remained steely. 'You could have checked with me first, made sure it was okay to keep it here.'

Joel half-shrugged. 'I didn't think you'd mind.'

'Well, for the record, I do mind squatters making themselves at home on my property, without an invitation.' His stare was becoming more and more frosty by the second.

'Okay then. You want me to get rid of him?' Joel knew his tone was terse, but what did his father expect?

'It's a little too late for that now, don't you think? With the saleyards shut for another six months, the poor bugger will be on the meatworks floor.' He huffed and shook his head. 'Never think things through, do you? Just don't expect me to help you. I've got enough to do around here.'

'I don't expect you to.' Joel levelled his tone, keeping it low and steady. 'And I'm more than happy to help around the place. Anytime.'

'Sudden change of tune, isn't it?' William's expression was scornful.

'What do you mean?' Joel matched his father's defensive stance, hands in pockets, boots planted wide.

'It's a bit hard to believe you want to lend a hand when you took off faster than a bull at an open gate, chasing some half-arsed dream of becoming a stockman.' He arched a bushy brow. 'You left me here to do it all after I'd been teaching you the ropes all your damn life.'

'I never dreamt of being a stockman, Dad. I'd always wanted to leave school and be by your side, doing what you taught me to do.'

'Could have fooled me,' William shot back.

'I didn't just leave here of my own accord, Dad. You kicked me out.' The words tumbled from Joel before he could stop them. 'What was I meant to bloody well do?'

'You were supposed to go somewhere for the night and think about what you'd done, and then come home and apologise.' His father half-shrugged, like it was obvious.

'You must have forgotten to teach me that one,' Joel grumbled. 'It wasn't for selfish motivations that I left here,' he said, measuring his words carefully. 'And I had good reason to do what I did to Levi Muller. The man's a bloody lowlife.'

'Oh, come on, Joel,' his father said. 'I know you two had gripes at school, but it didn't warrant you doing what you did to him.'

Gritting his teeth, Joel bit back a curse. 'If you knew the truth, maybe you'd understand and stop judging me so harshly.'

Yanking his hands from his pockets, William folded his arms tightly. 'Well, go on then, now's your chance to clear the air once and for all.'

Joel met his father's stormy grey eyes, his heart punching his ribcage. He *could* tell him, it would be so easy to explain, to be forgiven … but until Juliette came round, he didn't have a choice. He'd already broken one promise to her, all those years ago. He wasn't about to go and break another. And so, frustratingly, he was forced to choose silence.

'Cat gone and got your tongue, hey?'

'No,' Joel shot back.

'I'm all ears, Joel, so tell me this *truth*.'

Joel dropped his gaze to his boots. 'I can't, not yet, anyway.'

William heaved a huff. 'I wasn't born yesterday. You don't have a bloody excuse, you're just making things up so you don't have to take responsibility for what you've done.'

'That's not true,' Joel snapped, before shaking his head. 'I'm sorry, but …'

'Save it. I'm not going to stand here being treated like some old fool.' Rubbing his face, William turned from him and stormed back out the door. 'And don't try and make peace with me in front of your mother, because it's not going to work, and I don't want to upset her any more than you already have.' His heavy footsteps and laboured breath faded quickly as he stomped away.

His father was infuriating. Joel would have preferred a one-to-one chat with the devil himself than deal with his bitter disappointment. If only he could tell him why he left, maybe, just maybe, his father would find forgiveness in his heart. Perhaps he should approach everything from that angle, explain to Juliette how he needed to bring it all out in the open so he could mend the broken bridge between him and his father. But would she see his side, or feel he was being selfish by asking her to reveal her deep dark secret for his sake?

It was a fine line.

He had to walk it.

He made a snap decision to go for a wander. He needed a little time out in nature, by himself, before working with Dynamite, to clear his head and calm down. There'd be no winning Dynamite over when he was in a frustrated mood – the horse would pick it up immediately. Not a good way to start training and bonding. Stepping out of the tack room, he strolled to the back of the outbuilding and looked to where a path circled through the scrub bordering the eastern side of the farm and then split. One way led up to the ridgeline, with jaw-dropping views of the small township. The other way, an ugly scar through picturesque countryside, was a shortcut to his worst nightmare – the banks of Little Heart River. He'd only been back there once, reluctantly, to find the engagement ring he'd been planning to slip on Juliette's finger. His grandmother's one-and-a-half carat diamond ring had been with him ever since, and now sat back in the velvet box tucked away in his sock drawer. He still hoped he'd get the chance to fall in love again, so he could get married and have a family. He so wished it could be with Juliette.

To hell with Levi Muller.

As if with urgent purpose, he took long, angry strides towards the place he'd avoided like the plague. Minutes later, he was pushing through overgrown shrubs and bushes, the twigs and branches scratching at his forearms. Fear filled him but, as if a soldier barging towards the enemy, he thundered forwards. Other than his heavy steps, silence rose from the sodden ground. All around him, the trees had grown upwards and outward since he'd last been here, and the trail he'd once known so well that he could have walked blindfolded was now unfamiliar.

Ignoring the ache in his heart, he pushed on, grunting and groaning as he heaved himself up steep embankments made by storm washouts over the years. Almost there, the path turned sharply, ducking through a thicket of trees, before arriving at the edge of the river. Years of floods had washed it out further, widened its banks, but it was almost still as he remembered it. His legs were shaking and his chest heaving when he finally reached it, the very place his and Juliette's entire world had been turned upside down. Everything hurtled back with crushing intensity – Levi's wicked eyes and sickening sneer, Juliette's screams, Ben's look of utter terror, his own overwhelming cold fear as he'd watched on helplessly – it all surged within him like crashing waves, mixing with an underlying sense of loss and grief.

And with it came an even greater necessity to bring justice to Levi and his surviving brother. What they'd done that night had been horrendous, criminal. Why should he and Juliette still be reeling in the after-effects, all these years later, when the two Muller boys were living their lives to the full, as if nothing had ever happened? As much as Juliette said she'd put it behind her, he knew she hadn't. Couldn't. He truly believed if she got the closure she deserved, it would help her to fully heal, as it would him. If only he knew a way to gently get her to see this. One thing was for certain: he needed to talk to the one person who might have their backs if the shit hit the fan. He'd been slack keeping in touch with anyone other than his mum and Zoe. He hoped his old mate would be able to understand why, and to see past it.

With renewed hope that he might be able to bring everything to light, he wandered to the tree he and Juliette had carved their initials into with his pocketknife. It took a few minutes of searching before he found them, much higher than they'd first been. Up on the toes of his boots, he ran his fingers over the letters, smiling from his soul. They'd been so in love, so optimistic for their future together. Two kids, maybe three, a house on his family farm, travelling in a caravan around Australia when they retired, matching robes and slippers – they'd talked and dreamt about all of it. All those daydreams were gone forever. And forever was a mighty long time to be without the one he loved with all his heart and soul.

* * *

It was almost three in the afternoon by the time Joel had wrapped things up with Dynamite, and he was starving. Juicy hamburger in hand, with a wad of napkins in his lap to catch the drips of beetroot and mayonnaise, he backed out of the parking spot he'd scored right out the front of Jacqui's Outback Cafe. Even after all these years away, it was still exactly as he'd remembered it, and Jacqui and Fred still owned it. The painted chairs were still mismatched and the facade was dated as was the corrugated-iron sign that hung just outside the entrance, but it was good old-fashioned homestyle cooking at its finest.

Heading down the highway with Garth Brooks keeping him company on the stereo, just thinking about his next stop made his stomach roll. As uncomfortable as it was going to be, turning up unannounced on his doorstep to talk about what happened all those years ago, it had to be done. He and Juliette needed a witness, someone who could back up their story, and who better than the man who'd seen everything unfold? If it wasn't for Ben hitting Levi over the head with the rock, Joel dared not think what might have transpired.

A little way out of town, he turned down an overgrown dirt road leading into bushlands. By the look of the GPS, it wouldn't take him much longer to get to the address his mum had given him. She hadn't batted an eyelid when he'd asked her for it, although she had warned him that Ben wasn't the nice young man he remembered. 'He's turned a little strange over the years,' she'd said. 'A bit of a hermit, shall we say.' She had a habit of overdramatising things sometimes, so he honestly didn't know what to expect.

At the end of the rutted road, a lone dwelling on a small clearing of land proved his mother was right. Joel's pulse quickened as he remembered his forever-smiling childhood mate, and Ben's big dreams of travelling the world as a biological scientist. This place was a far cry from that. Looked like none of their dreams had worked out.

The rundown cottage, coupled with the cobwebs lacing the front verandah and the timeworn settee in the middle of it all, spoke volumes of the number of damns given by whoever lived here. Out front, beneath a tired-looking poinsettia tree, a pair of weathered plastic chairs and a matching round table sat on a patchy piece of overgrown lawn. A few paces from the front steps, a Rottweiler sunbaked, his eyes steely and focused on Joel. A heap of rusty old cars surrounded the outskirts of the house, and a lean-to carport that was barely standing sat off to the side of it all. Joel's decision to get out of his LandCruiser wavered when the front door swung open and the shadow of the young man Joel remembered Ben to be stepped out with shotgun in hand, his expression unyielding.

Stepping from the driver's side, Joel called, 'Hey, Ben, long time no see, buddy.' Best to make himself known quickly. He offered a quick wave. 'How the heck are you?'

Ben squinted cautiously over the rim of his glasses. Smoke swirled from the cigarette clasped between his lips. 'Who the hell are you?' He started to raise the barrel of the gun. 'And what do you want?'

Joel instinctively raised his hands. 'It's me, Ben. Joel Hunter.'

'Joel?' The gun dropped back to Ben's side and a smile broke, revealing yellowing teeth. 'Well, bugger me dead.' He strode forwards, down the few steps. 'Shut up, Bully,' he groused at his dog. 'This visitor is a welcome one.' Reaching Joel, he held out a grotty hand.

The stench of stale alcohol hitting him, along with the unmistakable smell of someone who hadn't washed for god-only-knew how long, Joel hesitated before reaching out to clasp it. 'Geez, it's great to see you, Ben.' And he meant it, even though he was shocked at the state of Ben and his home. There'd be an explanation for it all, he was sure.

'Yeah, sure is, Joel,' Ben said with a chuckle. 'I'm glad I worked out who you were before I put a bullet in your arse.'

'Yeah, me too,' Joel said with a half-hearted grin.

'Wanna come in and I'll make us a drink?'

Joel wasn't keen on touching anything inside the house. 'Oh, nah, I'm just passing through.'

'Fair enough.'

Joel shoved his hands into his pockets, rocking back on his heels. 'So, how's life been treating you?'

'Yeah, pretty good. I just stick to myself, and that keeps me out of trouble.' Tossing the butt of his cigarette, he grinned. 'Haven't got much patience for people anymore. Can't trust the bastards.'

'It can get like that, hey,' Joel said with wholehearted agreement.

'Mmhhmm.' Inquisitive eyes travelled over Joel. 'So, what's brought you back into town, Hunter?'

'Honestly?'

'Yeah.'

'To bring justice to the Muller boys.'

Ben's face drained of all colour, but he recovered quickly. 'What the hell for?'

Shocked by the response, Joel shook his head. 'What do you mean, what for?' He regarded Ben shrewdly. 'Don't try and tell me you don't remember what they did to us that night.'

Ben stroked the hair on his chin, pulling it into his unkempt goatee, pretending to be in deep thought. 'It's been a long time, Joel,' he said finally. 'To be frank, I don't really remember much about anything you and I did together.' He laughed unconvincingly. 'Hell, I can't even remember what I did yesterday.'

Aghast, Joel had to fight from grabbing him by the collar and giving him a good shake. Ben had chosen the same path as Juliette and done his best to shut it all out, to pretend it never happened. 'I don't believe you don't remember anything, Ben.' He softened his anxious tone. 'Come on, mate. I'm here. I've got your back.' Guilt hammered Joel hard. He'd not only gone and left Juliette to deal with the horrors of that night, but Ben too.

'Is that so?' Ben turned his attention to the galahs squawking from the branches of the poinsettia tree, his jaw clenching. He cleared his throat and spat.

'Yeah, it is,' Joel said sincerely.

'The way you left without a word? You're no mate of mine.' Ben's grip tightened on the shotgun. 'Those Muller arseholes made my life a living hell for *years*. They bullied me every chance they had. They never forgot I was the one who hit Levi over the head with the rock. Where were you then, Hunter? I've had to watch my own back ever since that night,' he said, his voice trembling. No wonder he didn't bother bathing, Joel thought. No amount of soap or hard scrubbing could ever wash away that kind of trauma. 'I suggest you get the hell off my property and don't bother ever coming back here.'

'Shit, Ben, come on. I'm not the enemy here. My parents kicked me out, I didn't have anywhere to go. I wish I could have been here for you, but …'

Ben cut him off. 'Too little, too late, Hunter.' He glared at Joel, as if he were the devil himself.

'I get it, you hate me for leaving town, but don't you think they should pay for what they did, to you, to Juliette?'

Ben raised the gun a little. 'Didn't you hear me? Bugger the hell off.'

'Righto, I'm going.' Hands raised, Joel took backward steps, his gaze not leaving Ben's. 'I'm hopefully going to talk Juliette into going to the cops, so if you decide to speak up about it all, I'd appreciate it.'

Ben remained silent, his finger on the trigger and the low growl of his dog as it yanked at the constraint of the chain doing all the talking.

Slowly, Joel climbed back into his LandCruiser, revved it to life and drove away. That so easily could have been his fate if he hadn't packed his bags and crossed paths with Curly. Thank god his dear mum and sister had stuck by him, too. He watched Ben disappear in his rear-vision mirror. Joel was a lucky man.

CHAPTER

13

A stir of restless discontent had Joel climbing from his bed at an ungodly hour – dawn still only hinting its arrival. Having done a few chores around the place, including ushering Red out of his house again, and letting the chickens out of their coop, he decided to head over to see his mum so they could share a cuppa and a chat. Spotting her on the way over to the homestead, in her robe with curlers in her hair and her floral gumboots on, Joel detoured towards the training yard, where his father was atop a mammoth of a horse, skilfully getting it to walk slowly backwards.

Spying her son wandering up behind her, Sherrie turned and smiled. 'Hey, love.'

'Morning, Mum.' Wrapping an arm around her shoulder, he tugged her into his side. 'Don't you look mighty stunning this morning?'

'Oi, you cheeky bugger.' She gave him a playful slap. 'I only popped out to drop off some smoko for your dad, but then I got caught up watching him.' Reaching out, she placed a hand on his face and lightly tapped his cheek. 'Are you sleeping okay? You look tired.'

'Yeah, like a baby.' A little white lie never hurt anyone, and he didn't want to worry her any more than he already had the past eleven years.

'If you say so.' She eyed him a little sceptically. 'How'd your visit with Ben go yesterday?'

'Yeah, not too bad.' Another white lie – they were starting to add up. The events of yesterday still sent chills up his spine. 'But you were right. He has become a recluse.'

'Sad, really, to see him like that.' She sighed and shook her head. 'It wasn't long after you left town that he seemed to disappear from society altogether. It's very strange.'

Something scratched at Joel's awareness – what happened that night had changed the course of Ben's life too. 'Any idea what made him go like that?'

'Not sure, really. His mother says he has a bad drinking problem. The poor thing doesn't know what to do with him anymore, and his father … Well, he reckons Ben's idle hands are the devil's workshop.'

'His parents have both given up on him?'

'Yes, I suppose so,' she said softly, her eyes sad.

'Bit like Dad when it comes to me,' Joel said bitterly, with a tip of his head in his father's direction.

'Your father loves you more than life itself, Joel,' his mum returned sharply. 'If he didn't, he wouldn't be so hurt that you left in the first place.'

'Okay, fair enough, but when's he going to stop holding it against me? Next week, next month, or maybe next year?' Joel knew he was being tetchy, but his lack of sleep was making him a little more sensitive than usual. 'And what am I going to have to do to get him to see me differently?'

Blue-green eyes met his, considering him. 'When he's good and ready it will just happen, Joel. You've apologised countless times over the years. It's his turn to come round to you now.'

He couldn't help his dismissive sigh as he glanced away from her. 'Mmhhmm.' He wasn't going to be holding his breath for that to happen.

Bringing her hand to his back, his mum rubbed it as she watched her husband, the look of pride on her face unmistakable. 'It'll all be okay, love, you'll see. God works in mysterious ways.'

'He sure does.' Joel didn't want to get into a big religious debate right now – after everything that had happened, his faith had wavered considerably.

Leaning against the timber railings, he rested his elbows on another and turned his attention to where his mother's was. Prancing and tossing his head, the horse was quickly pulled into line with a firm yet respectful jerk on the reins. His father rode in giant sweeping circles, bringing them in tighter, until the horse knew his rider was the one in control. William Hunter was an amazing horseman, and all ill feelings aside, Joel couldn't help but be proud of him. Catching his father's eye, he nodded, but his father disregarded the gesture.

Joel gritted his teeth. It cut, deep. He couldn't stand here and be shunned any longer, not in the dark mood he was already in. 'I've got stuff to do and people to see, Mum.' He brushed a kiss over her cheek. 'Catch you later on.'

'Yes, okay, love. I'm off to play cards with the ladies down at the community hall.' Her warm smile outshone the sun. 'Have a nice day, won't you?'

'Will do,' he called over his shoulder as he sauntered away.

A low whinny welcomed him as he turned the corner of the stables – at least Dynamite was happy to see him. It had been five days since he'd coaxed the reluctant horse off the float and into the paddock closest to the barn, but he and his new buddy were making headway. His head held high, and with a newfound confidence that comfort and security bring, Dynamite pranced along the fence line, trying to impress the seemingly uninterested mare next door.

Today would be the day man and horse would bond. Joel could feel it in his aching, weary bones. The heel of his boot hooked over the lower railing, without a pair of spurs in sight – he'd never put steel to a horse's flanks – he rested his elbows on a rail of the round yard and squinted into the glorious sunrise, observing Dynamite eating his breakfast. Thankful the two painkillers he'd washed down with his morning coffee were starting to kick in, easing the pain from his lower back and neck, he was steeling himself for climbing into the saddle and being thrown out of it – quite possibly several times. It was more of a risk with his recent concussion, but it was one he was willing to take. He'd always had a good seat when on the back of a horse, but Dynamite also had a damn good buck, so anything could happen. It paid to be prepared. What had made Dynamite the way he was, so mistrusting of humans, he hadn't a clue, but it would have been by the hand of man. Joel would have to make up for some bastard's cruelty. And he would, no matter what.

His head half buried in the food trough, the horse never took his eyes off the six-foot man over the other side. Although he'd come along in leaps and bounds, the gelding still had a bit of a way to go. But they'd get there, together. Joel was optimistic.

The shrill ring of his mobile brought Joel's attention from his horse to his pocket. He snatched it out, shocked to see the caller's identity. He cleared his throat, steadied his voice, before answering. 'Howdy, Jules, how goes it?' Cool, calm, casual. That's what he needed to be with her.

'Hey, Joel, I'm good, thanks.' She sounded a little breathless. 'I haven't got you at a bad time, have I?'

'Nope. Just getting ready to spend another day with Dynamite.'

'Cool, that's why I'm calling. How's he going?' She grunted, groaned, and a loud thump followed.

'He's coming along in leaps and bounds.' Wandering around in a circle, he chuckled as he listened to her heavy breathing. 'You right, Jules? You sound like you're running a marathon.'

'Oh yeah, sorry. Just unloading some bales of hay.' She exhaled a heavy breath. 'I'll pull up for a minute so I can talk without puffing.'

He imagined her on the back of her ute, feeding the horses, and his pulse tripped. They used to do that together, here, at his family farm. Her country edge had appealed to him big time, amongst a million other traits of hers. 'You're at it nice and early. I thought you would've slept in a bit, given that you're on holidays and all.'

'My body clock won't let me sleep in. I'm too used to being up at sparrow's fart to spend some time with Warrior before I head off to work.' She chuckled softly and then sighed. 'No rest for the wicked, as they say.'

'Ha, yeah, true. Times have changed. I remember when you could've slept for Australia.' He laughed with the fond memories of tossing pebbles against her bedroom window to wake her up. 'I used to have a hard time getting you out of your house before ten on a weekend.'

'Ha, yeah, I remember that. Adulthood doesn't allow for such luxuries, though.' She groaned, pausing for a few short moments, as though back there, with him.

Allowing himself a moment of bliss, Joel closed his eyes, imagining being back there with her.

Juliette cleared her throat. 'Anyway, I just wanted to give you a call because I found out some interesting background info on Dynamite for you.'

'You did?' He was chuffed she'd gone out of her way for him. 'You rock, doing that for me, thanks heaps, Jules.'

'I did it more for Dynamite, but you're welcome.' A playful note shone through her voice.

'Ouch. I've got feelings, you know.' He made sure to emphasise the lightheartedness in his tone.

'Do you now? I hadn't noticed.' Her familiar banter was unmistakable, and he loved it.

They both chuckled as the grumble of the four-wheeler made Joel glance over his shoulder. His father ambled past, his old cattle dog, Bandit, perched on the back of the bike. Joel raised a hand in greeting. His father returned it with a short, sharp nod, and then looked the other way. At least he'd acknowledged Joel was there – a small step forwards, possibly.

'I don't know if you know of him …' Juliette's beautiful voice took the sting out of his father's aloofness. '… but old Bob Brown down at the servo told me that Charlie Falcone apparently bought

Dynamite for his teenage daughter to use at western pleasure classes, and for his wife to use for her lessons at the pony club she runs on the other side of town.'

'Oh, yeah, I think I've heard of Charlie and his missus. If it's the bloke I'm thinking of, I recall people saying he's not so good to his horses, or his wife, for that matter.'

'Yeah, that's the one. He's a bit of a bully. Old Bob reckons Dynamite was a superstar at first, a bombproof kind of horse, he said, but after a while he got sick of all the rigmarole of spending every weekend traipsing around the countryside for events, only to spend the entire week in between with inexperienced kids on his back.'

'I can understand Dynamite's frustration.' Joel nodded to himself as everything fell into place. 'I mean, who wouldn't get sick of that?'

'Yeah, right? Old Bob told me Dynamite started playing up at the shows initially, and then that carried on into every day. He began making it hard for anyone to catch him or clean his feet, and refused being mounted, let alone ridden. Charlie sent him to be straightened out with some bloke down in Cairns, who believes in being heavy-handed. It worked for a little while, but not long enough. A couple of weeks into it, Dynamite started bolting and biting, and Charlie gave up on him, saying he was a liability.'

'Shit, poor Dynamite.' Joel gazed at the horse in the corner of the yard, his back end to him as he looked out at the other horses grazing in their paddocks. 'It sounds to me like Dynamite gave up on Charlie a long time ago, and for bloody good reason.'

'Uh-huh. So, just a heads up, he's going to be a bit of a tough nut to crack, but once you show him that you'll take care of him, I'm guessing Dynamite will be putty in your hands.'

'Mmhhmm, I've kind of already gathered that. He's got a real good nature and kind eyes. He just needs someone to believe in him.'

'That's a really nice way to look at it, Joel,' she said gently. 'He's a lucky horse, scoring an owner like you.'

'Thanks, Jules.' He found himself speechless with her compliment.

She chuckled softly. 'It's the truth.' There was a thumping sound in the background and she huffed. 'Righto. Warrior is vying for my attention by throwing his feed bucket around the paddock, so I better get going before he starves to death.'

'Ha ha. God love him.' Joel felt lighter in his steps as he headed towards the small tack room beside the round yard. He needed a few tools before he started the day. 'Thanks so much, Jules, appreciate the help.'

'No probs, anytime. Catch you round sometime,' she said just before the call ended.

Smiling like a lovesick fool as he tucked his phone back into his pocket, Joel tried to bring his thoughts to the here and now – Dynamite needed his full attention. He *deserved* his full attention. And Joel needed to be *at* full attention or run the risk of getting hurt. The art of being a passive leader for a horse was a gift he'd always had, thanks to endless days spent by his father's side, and one he'd refined over the years he'd spent working alongside Curly. Earning respect from a horse, and being able to build on it, was all about leading by example, not by brutality, unlike what some forceful trainers wanted to believe. From the get-go, Joel's plan had been to allow Dynamite to make his own decisions and come to his own conclusions about whether his new owner could be trusted. As the trainer, he was simply going to let whatever was going to happen, happen, and then go from there. Just like humans, every horse was different – there were no hard and fast rules to follow, other than treating Dynamite with the respect and love he deserved. It was a simple approach, but extremely effective – one that worked, every time, perfectly.

He worked quickly now, his new understanding of what Dynamite had been through making him all the more determined to show the horse that most humans could be trusted and that he wasn't one of the minority who mistreated animals. Stepping back out of the stables with his freshly oiled stockwhip hung over his shoulder, a curry brush, and a bucket with a handful of oats drizzled with molasses, Joel made his way into the holding yard, where Dynamite eyed him cautiously, the gelding's ears pricked back so far they were almost flat to his head.

'Come on now, buddy, play nice today, huh?' he said soothingly as he stopped and carefully placed the bucket a few feet from him. 'Look, I even went and brought you a treat.'

Dynamite eyed the bucket suspiciously and took a little step forwards, sniffing like mad.

Joel squatted onto his heels, his back against the bottom rung of the railings, and waited, making sure not to look Dynamite directly in his big kind eyes. Dynamite remained glued to the spot, but blind Freddie could see the horse was being more stubborn than fearful. The standoff began. Patience was now his virtue. Joel wasn't going to be the one to make the first move, he knew that much, so he remained nonchalant. Almost five minutes passed. Dynamite's ears pricked forwards and back, thinking. Assessing if it was safe to see what was in the bucket. Joel smiled to himself. His plan was working. Clearly choosing it was worth the risk, Dynamite took some slow steps towards him, his nostrils flaring. He was almost there when the backfiring of a car in the far-flung distance rang out. Dynamite jumped, peering over towards the echo.

Joel swore beneath his breath but remained calm. 'Nothing to see over there, buddy. You just keep your eyes on the prize.' He kept his voice gentle yet authoritative.

Dynamite stole a few more moments before turning his full attention back to Joel and the bucket, less than a metre away from him now. He stretched out his neck, taking a quick sniff, his lips smacking together. As much as Joel wanted to respond, to reach out and stroke Dynamite's muzzle now he was so close, he remained stock-still. Although he'd made ground over the last couple of days, the horse needed to learn he could fully trust him. He observed Dynamite's tail beginning to swish – a sure sign the horse was becoming more relaxed – as he finally closed the last bit of distance, ducked his head into the bucket and munched on the sweet treat. Moments later, and with his lips covered in black sticky goo, Dynamite moved to within an arm's length of Joel as he sniffed at his hat, then suddenly, cheekily, took it from his head.

'Hey, you. Give that back,' Joel said, laughing as he recalled how Ratbag used to do the very same thing.

Dynamite flicked it up and down in his teeth, as if toying with him.

Grabbing hold of the magical moment, Joel slowly stood and, taking one smooth step, came to Dynamite's side, finally at ease to give the horse a well-deserved neck rub. The gelding stretched it out, enjoying the attention. Smiling from ear to ear, Joel took pride in the fact his approach had worked and the hardest part was over.

The connection was created. Dynamite now trusted him.

CHAPTER
14

The Davis estate, perched high up on a hill, dominated the view and Joel, for the life of him, couldn't bring himself to drive past it. Instead, he'd opted to go into town along bumpy old tracks that eventually led to the side gates of the estate, a stupid decision. Desperate to lay his eyes on her once more, just knowing Juliette was on the other side of the pristine fence line drove his pulse wild. Should he just drop on in to say g'day? Isn't that what friends and neighbours did? Isn't that what they were striving to be, typical mates in a small country community? Slowing before he could talk himself out of it, he turned and stopped at a set of gleaming white gates that worked on a sensor. Before they'd swung open all the way, he'd squeezed his LandCruiser through, rattled over a couple of cattle grids, and then started up the long tree-lined driveway that would lead him past Lachlan's parents' overstated home – his mother had filled him in on their latest display of extravagance – and then, hopefully, from what he'd gathered from what Zoe had told him, to Juliette and Lachlan's home.

He idled past immaculately kept paddocks, impressive outbuildings and manicured gardens and lawns, even more stately than he recalled. Not a cent had been spared on the upkeep of this place over the years. He'd stepped foot on the property only once before, many years ago, to drop off a parcel that had accidentally been left by the postman at the Hunter homestead's front door, and it was neither a friendly nor inviting kind of place – exactly like the arrogant Davis family. Old family plus old money equalled pompous attitudes that drove him up the wall and made his blood boil. Never one to care about materialistic things, or how much money a person had, just how Juliette had fallen for a man like Lachlan Davis was beyond him. Maybe she'd gone and changed while he'd been away. Damn, he'd changed, a hell of a lot, so it was possible, but still envisioning her as the sweet innocent girl he'd fallen deeply in love with, and had never fallen out of love with, he didn't want to believe for a second she'd become like the family she'd married into.

Cruising past the main homestead with his window down, he caught sight of a curtain moving aside upstairs, but couldn't see who was peeking out at him. It would be Margery, he suspected. Nothing went past that nosey, gossiping woman. Shortly after – way too shortly for someone to have to live beside their in-laws – another, smaller, two-storey homestead, with wide wraparound verandahs both downstairs and up, appeared. A small timber sign hung from the picket fence, with *Lachlan and Juliette Davis* written upon it. He was at the right place. His jaw dropped. This was a far cry from Juliette's humble childhood home. But what had he expected, given the endless supply of money this family had?

Pulling up beneath a gigantic paperbark, he killed the engine and jumped out. One boot in front of the other, he strode towards the front door, only now thinking about what he'd say if it were Lachlan who answered. He hadn't a damn clue. What had he been thinking, coming here? He'd look like an idiot turning around and hightailing it now. He'd just have to wing it. His footsteps clumping across the timber boards, he arrived at the leadlight-adorned front door. Nobody responded to the beating of his knuckles against it or the two presses of the doorbell. Maybe she was still with her horse, or out in the saddle. Shoving his hands in his pockets, he was considering leaving when a dog appeared from behind him. Skidding to a stop at his boots, the Chihuahua cross something-or-other bared its teeth, each shrill yap hurting Joel's ears. Amused at the dog's need to protect its home, he bent and scooped it up, doing his best to avoid nips. A quick massage to the back of its head, along with a few coos, and the dog was putty in his hands.

The sound of country music being played out back caught his attention. He made his way towards Brad Paisley's honky-tonk voice. As he rounded the corner, he spotted Juliette lazing on a foldout sunbed, her eyes shut, her well-tanned slender legs that seemed to go on forever and a day crossed at the ankles. With her silky raven hair and smooth olive skin, she was a vision to behold. The sight of her, now all womanly in her bright yellow string bikini, stole his breath.

'Now that's one hell of a woman,' he whispered under his breath as he placed the tiny pooch onto the ground, watching it run over to Juliette, as if to protect her. Taking steps, he felt the inevitable connection they'd always shared drag him closer to her until his shadow stole the sun from her pretty face.

Her eyes flung open and she gasped. Propping herself up on an elbow, she quickly pulled a sarong over her bare skin. 'Oh my goodness, Joel, I didn't even hear you pull up.' She pushed her sunglasses to the top of her head, her glossy black hair spilling over her shoulder and covering the little love heart tattoo he wasn't familiar with but liked very much. 'You should have let me know you were calling in.'

He smiled and touched the brim of his hat in greeting. 'Sorry, I wasn't planning to when I left home.' Sometimes sparkly, other times stormy, he knew from experience that the depth of her chocolate eyes depended on her mood. And they were somewhere in the middle right about now, leaving him unsure.

'Right.' She eyed him cautiously. 'So you've just called in on a whim, with no agenda?'

'Yup.' He shrugged. 'I just wanted to say g'day.'

'You said g'day on the phone a few hours ago, remember?'

'Did I?' He pretended to think about it and then laughed. 'Well then, I just wanted to say it in person.'

A wary smile surfaced on her lips. 'You know I'm a married woman, right? It's probably not the best idea to be dropping in on me at home. Because it won't look good at all.' The intrigue within her unwavering gaze was unmissable.

There was something about him being here that she liked. He could see it, sense it. He stole a few short seconds to recover, to play it cool. 'Yeah, I know you're married, how could I forget with the size of that bloody rock on your finger?' Half smiling, he glanced towards where it sparkled in the sunlight, her hand resting on her thigh.

She held her hand up, as if assessing the ring for the very first time, seemingly unimpressed. 'Yeah, it's pretty, but you know me. I'm not into all the glitz and glamour. I wear it because it's a symbol, not because I want to show it off.' She dropped her hand back to her side. 'I'd take the O-ring off a motor if the man giving it to me truly loved me.'

He swore he could see gathering tears in her eyes, but if they were there, she blinked them back. Picking up on some hidden undercurrent, and not knowing if it was directed at him or Lachlan or just men in general, he cocked his head to the side. 'Why'd you go and marry someone like Lachlan Davis if you don't care about the money? Because I've known him most of my life, and I haven't got a good word to say about the bloke.'

Her brows bumped together in a scowl. 'You left. He charmed me. I fell for him,' she said simply.

There was so much in what she didn't say. It slapped him hard, stung him deep down in his soul. 'Fair enough. How's it all going for you, being a married woman?'

'Fine.' She couldn't even look at him now.

'Just fine?'

'Yup, just fine.' She gave him a lacklustre smile. 'What's with the interrogation into my personal life, Joel?' Her gaze was fiercely challenging.

'I just want you to be happy,' he responded carefully, evaluating her defensive body language – lips pressed tight, arms folded, the pulse in her throat racing. He hated himself for liking the fact that everything didn't seem peachy perfect between her and Lachlan.

He really did mean it when he said he wanted her to be happy; he'd just failed to make mention that he wanted it to be with him.

She inhaled a sharp breath and blew it away, staring at him. 'So … this is just a friendly call, from a friend, who only wants to be friends?' She pressed a finger to her lips and tipped her head. 'Kinda doesn't feel that way.'

His hunger for her tender touch almost rendered him senseless. 'Yes, exactly,' he lied. 'Just friends, being friends, and doing friendly things. That's us.'

'Okay then. In that case …' She produced a half empty can of Pringles from beside her. 'You hungry?'

'Depends.' He was actually ravenous, and not only for food.

'On what?' Her lips curled into a slow and oh-so-sexy smile.

'On what flavour they are?' He matched it with a dimple-studded smile of his own.

She feigned a look of shock he would even ask such a question. 'Salt and vinegar, of course,' she replied, offering the can.

'Well, then. How could I say no?' He smacked his lips together.

She flashed him an extra-bright grin. 'I thought as much.' She patted the ground near her. 'Come, sit. You're making the place look untidy.'

He laughed and glanced around at the opulent surroundings. 'How's that even possible?'

'Yeah, good point.' Amused, she eyed her dog, now squished up against her foot. 'Just watch out for Brute here. He has a tendency to bite when he doesn't know someone and they're getting a little close to me.' She looked back to Joel, mischief in her eyes. 'He may be small, but he could quite possibly rip an arm or leg off with those almighty teeth of his.' Her teasing grin put Joel completely at ease.

'Oh, he and I have already bonded.' He sank down, dangerously close to her, her sweet perfume wrapping around him. Reaching out, he gave a very submissive Brute a good scratch behind the ears. 'Love the name, by the way, little buddy,' he said, liking how Juliette was looking from him to the dog and back again, clearly a little shocked. 'What? Can't I be friends with your dog?'

'It's not like him to take to someone straight away, especially a bloke.' She shook her head slowly, eyes wide. 'He's had years living under the same roof as Lachlan and still hasn't really taken a shine to him.'

'Can't blame the little fellow for being a good judge of character, can we?'

Juliette gave him a friendly slap. 'Now, now, that's enough of that.' She shook the Pringles at him. 'Eat, so you stop putting your foot in your mouth.'

'Good idea,' he said, stuffing his hand down the tube and skilfully grabbing a handful of the crispy morsels.

They both munched in comfortable silence for a few moments. Juliette was the first to break it. 'We used to eat mountain-loads of these things, then complain because our bellies hurt.' Draining the last of her drink, she crunched on the ice cubes.

'Those were the good old days, when the only thing we had to worry about was what we were going to eat, and do, for the day.' He sighed wistfully then licked the eye-squintingly sharp tang of vinegar and salt from his fingertips.

'Yeah, they were.' Hugging her knees to her chest, she tipped her head to the side, gazing at him as though trying to read his thoughts. 'Why didn't you take me with you?'

Joel garbled through a mouthful of Pringles, 'When?'

Juliette arched her eyebrows. 'When do you think, Einstein?'

'Oh.' Joel finally swallowed. 'Because I believed you wouldn't want me to. I truly did, Jules. I left because I had no place here anymore, and I couldn't be living in this town without you.'

'So … how does it feel now, living here, without me?' Very deliberately, she shifted her focus and took a huge interest in her bright pink toenails.

Joel never took his gaze from her. 'You want me to be honest?'

'Uh-huh.' She didn't seem to want to look at him.

The easy atmosphere changed, shifting to something deep and intense and impenetrable.

Joel heaved a sigh, closed his eyes momentarily. 'I don't like it, not one little bit. But I'm going to have to cop it on the chin because I take someone being married seriously. I'd never condone cheating, or stepping over the line, and I know you're not the kind of woman to take kindly to any of that either.'

'That's good to know.' She turned and smiled at him now, but it was a sad smile, one that spoke of how he felt in his heart. 'I'm glad we can be friends, Joel. I really am.'

'Me too. It means the world.' He desperately needed to change the subject before he forgot his morals and gave in to his feelings, his innermost desires. They never got to make love, and it hurt knowing he was never going to know how it felt to be so intimate with her.

A long intense moment passed where they just stared at each other, the magnetic pull tremendous. He quickly steered his thoughts away from the hopeless track. 'I went and spoke to Ben about what happened to us.' He spat it out, shocking himself in the process.

Juliette inhaled a razor-sharp breath. 'You did what?'

Joel zipped his stupid mouth shut. She'd heard him, crystal clear, and he wasn't about to repeat himself. The good vibe came to an abrupt stop.

She shot to her feet and stood ramrod straight, her stormy eyes burning a hole right through him. Then, she started to pace, fear etched across her petite features. 'I told you not to go and do anything like that, Joel! I don't want all this dragged up. It'll only make me have to relive it again, and cause so much heartache and drama for my family.'

'What about the heartache and drama it's already causing, Jules? Have you seen what the secret has done to Ben? I know it's not easy to face what happened, but honestly, Jules, you can't just hope it goes away. It never will. Not until you get justice.'

He could see the wild fury – hot and raw – rise up inside of her. 'How dare you try and tell me what I need to do to get over it. And how *dare* you go and do this kind of thing behind my back.'

'I simply went and asked him if he'd help us if we went to the police.' He gave a small shrug, trying to make light of a very dark situation. Bad move – it only made her angrier.

'I think you should go.' Her voice shook.

'Please, Jules. Don't shut me out.' He got to his feet. 'I'm only trying to help, to do what I should have done all those years ago.'

'And what's that, Joel?'

'Protect you. Get justice for you. Make them pay the right way, instead of with my fists.' He dropped his head now, ashamed.

'You couldn't go and do that when it happened because I asked you not to speak a word of it.' Softening now, she took a step towards him, but stopped just short. 'We were both young and terrified.' Cautiously, she reached out and placed a hand on his arm. 'Nothing we do is going to change the fact it happened. And dragging it up now is only going to cause tremendous grief, believe me.'

'I get that, I really do. But Jules ...'

'What the hell is this?' Lachlan appeared from the homestead, all golden-haired, tall and wearing a black muscle shirt with tailored, very neatly ironed slacks.

Snatching back her hand from Joel, as if she'd been touching a venomous snake, Juliette took a big step backwards and spun to greet her husband. 'Oh, Lachlan, hi. You're home early.'

'Yeah, I am. Surprise.' He eyed Joel lethally over the top of his sunglasses as he stormed past Juliette. 'What in the hell are you doing here, Hunter?' He ripped off his glasses, his accusing gaze going from Joel to Juliette and back again.

Just trying to woo your missus, he wanted to say. 'I just called in to say g'day.'

'Is that so?' With a sneer, Lachlan shook his head. 'Well, you're not welcome here, so I suggest you leave.'

Juliette shot to her husband's side, her gaze fierce. 'Lachlan, that's enough.'

Joel unclenched his hands and raised both in submission. Belting Lachlan would feel good, but it wouldn't change a damn thing – once a spoilt brat, always a spoilt brat. 'All good, Jules. I'm leaving now anyway.' He tipped his hat, swallowing the smirk begging to appear. 'Thanks for the Pringles. I'll catch you round.'

'Hopefully not,' Lachlan barked after him.

Unruffled, Joel just gave him a wave over his shoulder. He wasn't interested in arguing with a fool.

As he climbed back into his LandCruiser, something told him there was way more to Juliette and Lachlan's story and, if his instincts were right and he treaded carefully, he might find out just what was causing such shadows in her beautiful eyes.

CHAPTER
15

It was the morning after Joel's impromptu visit. Juliette stared at
Lachlan, the tension crackling between them so thick, it could be
cut with a knife. She'd joined him at the table to work out how
they were going to do things, fairly, without making too much
of a fuss, but he was behaving like an insubordinate child, as if
everything wrong in their lives was her fault. He didn't want
her to leave. She had to. Having reached a stalemate, he now
sat in silence, pretending she wasn't even there. Hit by another
overwhelming rush of hurt and anger, she tried to swallow past
the terrible constriction in her throat. Lachlan had created such a
vast crevice of pain inside her, she could barely stand it. And yet
he did nothing to help her or to make up for his actions. With
each and every breath she took, she was fighting to handle the
unfathomable ache clenching her heart.

Her leg bouncing anxiously beneath the table, she hauled
in another tight, unsteady breath. In a strange kind of way,

she honestly didn't know who she was anymore, other than an almost thirty-year-old, childless, imminent divorcee. A divorcee who was going to need somewhere to call home when she left here – a home that would accommodate a dog, a horse, and hopefully had the essential furniture included. Not an easy feat in a town with a shortage of rentals, and she certainly wasn't in a position to buy until their finances were sorted. And it was over her dead body that she would ask to live beneath her stepfather's roof again. She'd rather live in a tent.

Wishing Lachlan would at the very least say something, anything, to break the monotonous silence – the room was so quiet, she would hear a pin drop – she got up and switched the radio on for some background noise. Then, sitting back at the dining table, her favourite breakfast of poached eggs on sourdough toast she'd made now cold, she glared over her cup of tea at Lachlan seated at the opposite end of the eight-seater table. She couldn't bear his ignoring her any longer. 'Are you going to even acknowledge I'm still sitting here with you, trying to somehow work out what we are going to do about a divorce?'

Heaving in a deep breath, Lachlan remained staring at the newspaper clasped in his hands. 'Nope,' he finally replied.

She blinked, astonished. 'I beg your pardon?'

'You heard me,' he grumbled.

Juliette felt like she was about to scream. Deep breaths, she told herself over and over. 'Are you forgetting that *you* are the one who cheated, ruining any chance we ever had of making it?'

'Nope,' he retorted. 'But I haven't gone and had my lover visiting me here, at our marital home, like you just have, have I? So, same, same, really.' He didn't even bother to lift his eyes to her but continued to peruse the paper as if this wasn't an important, life-changing discussion.

Fury rendered her momentarily speechless. Her breath hitched and like a rubber band pulled taut, something inside her snapped. 'Stuff you, Lachlan.' She shot to her feet, her chair tumbling backwards with a loud clatter. 'I didn't ask Joel to visit me, he just turned up. It's not the same in the slightest. I would never have done anything to jeopardise this marriage. You know that.'

'Actually, that's where you're wrong, because …' He smirked. 'I don't know that for certain.'

Juliette ground her teeth while taking a moment to find some sense of calm amongst the inevitable storm. 'Did you actually come home early yesterday afternoon, or did someone give you the heads up that Joel was here? Were you hoping to find me in bed with him, so it would justify what you have done to me?'

He met her gaze then, his eyes distant, withdrawn. Entrenched frown lines proved that, although he appeared somewhat detached, he was extremely annoyed. 'Mum did the right thing when she rang me. Have you got a problem with that?'

His bluntness made her flinch. 'Yes, I do, Lachlan. I'm entitled to my privacy, and she's a nosey old cow. She should learn to keep out of my damn business,' she snarled.

'Here we go again, with you attacking my poor mother.' He closed his eyes for a moment, sighing. 'I'll be sure to pass your annoyance on to her.' The emptiness in his tone was unmistakable.

'Oh, I'm sure you will.' Her voice was strained to the limit. 'Enjoy your mother–son bitching session.'

He flicked the paper shut and smacked it down on the table. 'I don't want to do this right now, Juliette. I'm tired and I have a headache. I don't have the energy for another of your goddamn speeches.' He looked to his watch. 'And on top of all that, I have to be at a meeting in less than an hour. I don't need all this crap to contend with.' With eyes as cold as steel, he narrowed his gaze and stood. 'You need to grow up and realise life is never going to be this picture-perfect, picket-fenced existence you long for it to be. This isn't one of your romance novels. This is real life.'

Red-raw anguish stabbed through her and the pain of his betrayal seeped into her soul. Her vision blurring, she hauled in a tight unsteady breath. His indifference was killing her. 'You're a cold, selfish bastard, Lachlan Davis,' she rasped as she slipped the wedding band and matching engagement ring off her finger and smacked both down on top of the newspaper. 'I stupidly thought I could stay here and we could work this separation out like adults. Clearly not. I'll be out of your hair as soon as I find somewhere to move, and we can sort out our finances and the divorce with lawyers, seeing as you don't want to play fair.' As the words scraped past her lips, her voice trembled, and she went to make a quick exit before she broke down in front of him. He didn't deserve her tears.

'You'll be sorry if you speak a word of what you know, Juliette,' he called after her. 'And don't think for a second you'll be leaving here with a penny of my money.'

She skidded to a stop and, her heart in her throat, turned back to face him. 'What do you mean *your* money?'

'You married into money, dear Juliette, and you'll be divorcing out of it.' His smug expression, so like his mother's, was infuriating.

'I've worked for a lot of what we've got, too, including the apartment in Cairns.'

He folded his arms, staring at her with indifference. 'Do you recall signing anything when we bought the apartment?'

No, she didn't. Her heart stalled as she frantically tried to remain poker-faced. 'You're just trying to blackmail me with bullshit threats,' she said, calling his bluff while silently praying. There wasn't a way for him to strip her of everything she deserved to have half of, surely?

'No bullshit. All fact,' he said with a sly smirk before turning and slipping back into the kitchen.

'We'll see about that,' she called after him.

Racing down the hallway, she stormed outside, both for fresh air and to avoid saying anything more in the heat of the moment. Pressing her palms against her eyes, trying to regain some sort of grip on her spiralling life, she choked back one sob after another. She'd given this marriage her all, had given Lachlan everything she was, and for what? To be lied to, mistreated, cheated on, and now threatened and blackmailed. It was so hard to breathe, she felt as if she was underwater. Lachlan was no different to his parents, a Davis to the very core – immoral, self-seeking, cruel. As was her very own stepfather for putting her in this position, for pawning her off for the house and land he called home. A naive young girl with a broken heart, desperate to get out from beneath his roof, she'd gone and played right into their plan. And now, Lachlan had her by the throat, but she refused to be helpless. She would stop his stranglehold on her.

Racing like a bullet from where he'd been sunbaking on the lawn, Brute skidded to a halt at her feet, greeting her as if it had been a year since he'd seen her, his tail wagging like the clappers. Looking down into his kind, innocent eyes, a bit of her tension faded away. She bent over to pluck her loyal companion from the ground, cuddling him to her. His unconditional company was a godsend – she needed all the love and support she could get right now. As if sensing her anguish, Brute whined then swiped his tongue up her cheek, collecting some of her tears. His concern for her evident, she couldn't help but melt.

'Thank god for small mercies like you,' she said, kissing him on the head and placing him back down. After a few short yaps, he bolted off, chasing butterflies around the garden.

Turning towards the east, where Hunter Farmstead lay beyond the distant row of towering pine trees, she caught her reflection in the double-glazed window. Gasping, she covered her mouth. She looked like death warmed up, times ten. She needed to get a grip. But how, when it all seemed like too much for her to handle?

As if a sign from the heavens, the wind picked up and the old windmill up the hill circled creakily, drawing her attention away from her grim appearance and to the untainted beauty of the bush. It beckoned her, away from humanity, and away from Lachlan. Her nerves strung out like a worn guitar, she decided a run up the mountain might help. The view from the top might help give a little clarity, a little peace. She could use the time alone, surrounded by Mother Nature, to get her head straight. Things had just gone from bad to worse, making her feel all the more trapped in a life she hated, with a man she detested with every fibre of her being.

Slipping back inside, relieved to see the bathroom door shut, she raced to her bedroom, changed into her running gear and joggers, got Brute comfy in his bed at the foot of hers, and quickly made her way back outside. With long-legged strides, she headed towards the track she'd run many times before. Passing the long-forgotten barn leaning precariously to the side, as if it were about to slip into a pile of rotting timber, she settled into a jog that ate up the distance. The muffled thump of her running shoes on the soft earth became a rhythmic background to her racing thoughts, gradually slowing them, releasing the hold they had over her, if only for a little while. Pushing herself harder, striding wider, the physical exertion made her feel stronger, more capable of handling what was ahead. There had to be a way forwards, out of the mess.

A steady breeze blowing across the untainted countryside spoke to her soul, whispering sweet nothings and filling her with gentler thoughts. It brought forth heart-warming memories of her and Joel and Zoe racing across these flats on their horses, reckless and carefree. Of her and Joel climbing to the top of this mountain from the other side so they could feel on top of the world while sharing some tender kisses. Those had been the days. She'd been so happy back then. Joel's love for her, and hers for him, was something she now knew was a one-in-a-million kind of feeling. They'd been blessed to fall for each other. Then Levi Muller had gone and taken it all away in the blink of an eye. Not wanting to lose herself in the anguish of that night, as she had many times before, she pushed her body harder, forcing her thoughts to the present. There was nothing to be gained from going back to the past, to that night.

Up ahead, warm morning sunlight illuminated each stalk of grass, and the gentle wind shifted and moved it, revealing a plethora of wildflowers still to open their hearts to the warmth of the sunshine. Slipping her headphones in and choosing her Spotify list for jogging, she moved in time to the beat. Mounting the stone steps the council had put in when improving the hiking paths of the Crystal National Park, one foot after the other, she went upwards and onwards, her breathing laboured and beads of sweat cooling her skin. She pushed through scrub, ignoring the scrape of the branches and the whipping of leaves as she took a small shortcut. Legs burning and heart pounding, she could see the summit from here, not that far away now. Lost in the thrum of music, she quickened her pace, pushing through the pain of her muscles. And just when she was sure her legs were about to give out, the path levelled, and the scope of the 360-degree view absorbed her.

Slowing, she jogged to the edge and stopped, breathing deeply. A few pebbles tumbled the hundred metres to the bottom. Up here, in the serenity of the bush, she felt like the only person in the world. Being that little bit closer to the clear blue sky was just what she needed. Spreading her arms wide, she brought them above her and bent side to side at the waist. Plucking her headphones from her ears, she then leant to touch her toes, inhaling slow deep breaths as she stretched out her lower back. The air smelt that little bit fresher up here and that little bit cleaner. Exhilaration that she'd made it to the top in record time chased her irritation and concerns away, for now. Then, standing, she stretched out her quads and calf muscles. Other than the chirruping of crickets and the singsong of native birds, a mesmerising quiet blanketed the far-reaching landscape. Twisting from side to side, she continued to gaze out over her majestic surroundings. Little Heart was a beautiful place and she was blessed to call it home.

She was just about to get herself settled on an outcropping of rock, where she could feel as if she were flying while she let her legs dangle, when a deep rough voice made her almost jump out of her skin. 'S'cuse me.'

She spun to see Joel staring at her from beneath a banyan tree, his back resting against the mammoth trunk, smug amusement in his sky-blue eyes. He pulled the twig he was chewing on from his lips. 'You're blocking my view,' he drawled slowly, the cheeky smile playing on his lips enticing his dimples to deepen.

'Oh, well, excuse me, Mr Hunter.' She returned his wayward grin while trying to ignore the blaze of heat rushing through her at the sight of him. Hands on hips, she watched him stand and take sauntering steps towards her, the pocketknife in the sheath on his belt very familiar. She pointed to it. 'Is that the Leatherman I gave you for your eighteenth?'

'This little baby?' He glanced down, patted it, his slow, sexy smile spreading. 'Yup, sure is. It hasn't left my side since you gave it to me.' His voice was smooth, encompassing, like a heady concoction of whiskey and velvet on a cold winter's night.

'Wow, it's so cool you still have it,' she said, pushing flyaway wisps of hair from her face.

'Why wouldn't I? It's helped me a lot along my travels,' he said, sending her heavy heart soaring.

'That's great, glad to hear it's come in handy,' she replied. She had to admit, he looked real good in his faded jeans and well-worn boots, his button-up shirt rolled to the elbows, revealing tattoos she wasn't familiar with. She couldn't help but wonder if he had more ink in places she couldn't see.

He reached her but left a good few feet between them. 'We seriously have to stop meeting like this, or people are going to start talking,' he said with an arch of his brows, sending her heart into even more of a skitter. 'And you know what the whispers are like around these parts.'

Relief and comfort filled her with the sound of his voice. She hadn't realised until that moment how much of a calming effect he had on her. 'Yeah, true hey.' She chuckled. 'I'm sure they'd all love some juicy gossip to twist and turn into some elaborate story.' She rolled her eyes skywards. 'Lord help us if the CWA ladies get a hold of it.'

'Uh-huh, they sure would get a buzz out of us meeting up in the middle of nowhere. It'd be the bush telegraph at its finest.' He laughed, deep and throaty. 'Good run up the hill?'

'Yeah, needed to let off a bit of steam, and it always does the trick.' She tipped her head, assessing him. 'And what are you doing all the way up here?'

'Just thinking about stuff.'

'Stuff?' she asked, intrigued.

'Yeah, stuff,' he repeated casually.

'Righto then,' she said, not wanting to pry. His gaze travelled over her, making her acutely aware of how she probably resembled a cooked lobster – all bright red and drenched in sweat – and smelt a little sweaty too. On the contrary, he smelt yummy.

Needing to do something with her hands before she gave in to her yearning desire and reached out for this mammoth of manly man, she rolled up her earphones and went to shove them into her pocket, but they dropped to the ground.

Joel promptly bent to retrieve them. She couldn't help but watch how his sinewy muscles flexed beneath his shirt as he did, couldn't help but admire the broadness of his shoulders, or the way his butt looked in his low-slung jeans. He was a heartthrob – had been *her* heartthrob, once upon a time. If she was being honest with herself, he was the memory she sometimes hungered for when she was feeling lonely, which was often these days. Not that she had anything to go off when it came to being skin to skin with him. But, far out, she wanted to.

'Here you go.' He passed the headphones to her, his expression turning solemn. 'So how did it go yesterday, after I left?'

She shrugged, released a pent-up breath. 'Not great. Lachlan's really angry with me.'

'I'm so sorry, Jules.' He closed his eyes, shook his head. 'I didn't mean to start a shitstorm.'

'Trust me, the shitstorm started way before you got there. Don't apologise. We weren't doing anything wrong.' The words tumbled from her lips before she'd had time to think. With everything so raw, fresh tears sprang to her eyes and she quickly tried to blink them away.

Concern deepening his expression, Joel quickly closed the little bit of distance between them and rested his hand on her arm, so gently and tenderly, she almost collapsed into him and buried her head in his big broad chest. 'Has he done something to hurt you?' His reply was stern, protectively so.

She wiped the few tears that had fallen from her cheeks, sniffling. 'He's done lots of things to hurt me, but nothing physical, if that's what you're referring to.' She tried to blame the lack of coffee for the fact she felt shivery and a little tongue-tied in Joel's presence.

'Mmhhmm.' Joel's gaze became darker. 'So, what sort of things has he done to hurt you so much?'

She waited a few brief moments for her heartbeat to steady and her breathing to settle. 'Oh, just the usual relationship stuff,' she lied. 'Nothing to go and worry yourself with.'

He regarded her for a few long moments. 'You real sure about that?'

'Yup.' She ran nervous fingers through her mop of sweaty hair and tried to force a smile.

A muscle in his cheek twitched before he looked away and heaved an almighty sigh. 'Come on, Jules.' His gaze swept over her. 'I'm one of your oldest friends, apart from my sister, so you know if you tell me anything, it wouldn't go any further, right?'

'Yes, clearly, because you've kept our secret all these years.' A cold chill swept through her as she recalled that horrible night in sudden, blinding intensity.

'Good. Well, just so you know, I'm all ears if you want to talk about it,' he said as his expression softened, his eyes never leaving hers.

She felt a piece of her trip and tumble into him. Almost succumbing to his offer, she picked at her fingernails. 'That'd just be weird, talking to my ex about my marital problems.'

'Yeah, well.' He sighed a laugh. 'Don't look at me like an ex, look at me like I'm a mate who cares about you a hell of a lot. And one who can keep a secret very close to my chest.'

Tempted to pour her heart out to the one man who had respected it, she came to her senses and shook her head. Her childhood sweetheart was the last person she should be telling her marital woes to. 'I don't want to talk about it right now. But thank you.'

A wave of different emotions crossed his face. 'Righto, fair enough, but know I'm here, anytime, okay?' He looked at her with the utmost respect in his eyes.

She smiled, nodded, sincerely grateful for their renewed friendship. 'Thanks, Joel.' She gestured to the magical view with a tip of her head. 'You know what would be nice, though? Just hanging here together for a little while and catching up on the good old days.'

'Really?'

'Uh-huh.' She tucked her hands into the pockets of her running shorts, his intense gaze making her feel a little giddy. 'If you haven't got somewhere else you need to be, of course?'

'Not at all. To be honest, there's nowhere else I'd rather be.'

She laughed softly, shaking her head. 'You're still the charmer, aren't you?'

'I do my best.' Grinning, he gallantly offered her the crook of his arm. 'Now come, sit with me on the edge of the universe and we will chat about anything that will bring a smile to that pretty face of yours.'

'Ha ha. Like I said, always the charmer.' She accepted his arm, hooking hers within it.

They sat side by side, swinging their legs and chatting about this and that, like they'd done all those years ago. And as they did, time stalled, rewound, paused, leaving Juliette feeling like she was a seventeen-year-old girl again, with so much love in her heart it was full to bursting, and with her whole life ahead of her – all of it made all the more exciting with Joel by her side. The sensation of that comforting thought, coupled with the upbeat memories they were reliving, brought a smile to her heart. And for a split second, when their conversation hesitated contentedly, she wished with everything she had that they could go back there, to that place, where she felt loved and safe and free. What a wonderful world it would be if it were so simple.

CHAPTER
16

A distant crack of thunder pulled Joel from his dreamy siesta. Blinking heavy eyes, he stared into what had been a bright blue sky when he'd retired Dynamite from their daily training session. Looking to his watch, he was shocked to see it was almost three in the afternoon. The appointment he'd put off twice, waiting to bring Juliette around to his way of thinking, was in less than an hour. He wanted nothing more than for her to trust him, so he could make up for leaving her to deal with this all on her own for eleven long years. He hoped that, by getting the ball rolling, she would see he had her back and would be at her side if she went to the police. If only she'd believe he had her best interests at heart. He wasn't going to give up trying to prove that to her – she deserved his persistence, and then some.

Swinging out of the hammock, his bare feet hit the coolness of the timber floorboards of the verandah as he collected his empty cup and plate and headed back inside. A smile lingered as he returned to the contemplations that had helped him to drift off to another place – he hadn't stopped smiling since yesterday afternoon, the few hours he and Juliette had spent atop the mountain, chatting about how life used to be, and laughing about all the wild and stupid stuff they and Zoe had gotten up to, had been a massive step forwards.

Rinsing his plate and cup, he upended both on the draining rack, pausing to gaze out his kitchen window to where the tip of a roof glimmered in the far-flung distance. Juliette lived beneath it with her conceited husband, sharing her life and her love with a man who, in Joel's biased opinion, was not deserving of it. The very thought he'd never have a life with her by his side, nor the family they'd always dreamt about, stabbed him straight through his heart. But, despite everything, she still felt like an essential part of him. He still wanted her, ached for her. So near her yesterday, with everything and everyone else swept to the roadside, he'd watched her every move, every gesture, like she was air and he was a drowning man. He'd hoped that the time apart would've made it easier to forget the hold she'd always had over him. It hadn't, frustratingly. Closing his eyes, he took a long, steadying breath. Between Juliette, his father, and seeking the justice they all deserved, this was proving to be way tougher than he'd first expected.

Wandering upstairs to his bedroom, he tugged on a fresh T-shirt and grabbed a pair of socks – the jeans he was already wearing would do. Dressed, he checked his mobile for any calls or messages. As usual, there were none. He only wanted to hear from one person – Juliette. No matter what he did to deflect his thoughts, he couldn't get her from his mind. Maybe because, deep down, he really didn't want to. After all, there was no harm in harbouring romantic and sensual thoughts about the woman who still possessed his heart, was there? Other than to himself. Too bad if there was because, for the life of him, he couldn't stop picturing her sweet lips and the way they turned up at the corners to form the most radiant of smiles – one that warmed him to his very soul. He swore he could still smell the scent of her citrusy perfume upon his skin from the quick hug they'd shared when they'd realised time had gotten away. She'd snapped back to the present and raced off, back to her life, back to Lachlan. Their bubble burst, it had torn an even deeper hole in his heart, watching her disappear again after they'd just reconnected so beautifully. He huffed a weighty breath as he recalled the sensation. So help him god, if he didn't stop thinking about her, he was going to drive himself insane.

Squishing some toothpaste onto his brush, he paced as he scrubbed. Oh, he wanted so much more than camaraderie with her, but that ship sailed a long time ago. He had to be grateful for what they could have – a good friendship – and focus on that. It plagued him, how she'd broken down and then refused to tell him why she was so torn up. His gut had twisted seeing her so fragile, so vulnerable. Lachlan was possibly living up to the Davis reputation of being cold and callous, and he guessed Juliette might be struggling to live with that side of her husband. But, as much as he wanted to, he wasn't going to force her to tell him. If anything, he was glad he could cheer her up a little just by spending time with her.

Spitting the toothpaste into the sink, he rinsed his mouth, splashed his face with some water and then dried it on the hand towel. He wasn't delusional. He knew there was no going back, but for that one breathless second, that one unguarded moment of silent recognition between them when she'd simply stopped speaking and stared at him the way she had, like she used to do, and her walls had crumbled, he'd caught a glimpse of the emptiness and heartache she was feeling, along with a yearning for the love and refuge they'd shared as a couple. He'd had to fight against taking her into his arms and kissing her as if there were no tomorrow, so she knew just how valuable, how loved, she was. He just prayed she could see in his eyes all that was in his heart, because that one brief moment had been all he'd had to show her such things before her dark eyes had glistened, clouded, and she'd looked away, towards the horizon.

Juliette wasn't entirely the same person he'd fallen in love with all those years ago – she was apprehensive, defensive, guarded and broken. Exactly what had brought him and Juliette to the top of the mountain at the same time had been a force outside of them, and the bridge they'd mended by just being able to sit and talk like old friends was beyond his wildest imagination. He had to be thankful for small miracles – maybe his mother's beliefs were right, and god did have his back after all.

After stepping out the back door, he tugged on his hat and boots, followed by his Driza-Bone, just in case the rain caught him out. In true tropical fashion, the weather had gone from bright and cheerful first thing this morning, when he'd jumped from his bed dressed only in his jocks to chase a very belligerent Red from the rafters and outside, again, to blustery this afternoon. Gazing out at the land that had stolen his heart a lifetime ago, he cleared the back steps two at a time and traipsed across the gravel drive, towards Dynamite's paddock.

Wind teased across the paddocks, stirring the long wisps of vivid green grass into a wild dance. The horses all looked a little antsy on their feet. Thunderheads were quickly building in the smouldering western sky, and splinters of iridescent lightning transiently possessed it in lustrous flashes. He wanted to check in on Dynamite and make sure the gelding wasn't freaked out by the imminent storm before he headed off.

Nearing the paddock, he called out to his horsey mate. 'Hey there, buddy, how goes it?'

Turning, and then plodding towards him, Dynamite stuck his head through the rungs and frisked Joel's pockets for any sign of a treat – he seemed a little miffed when he came up empty. 'Fair play. You gotta work for treats round here, my friend.' Chuckling, Joel pushed Dynamite's head back a little. 'Sorry, but them's the breaks.'

Dynamite threw his head in the air and whinnied.

Amused, Joel shrugged. 'And it's no use complaining about it, because I'm not going to change my mind, no matter how much you sook. Tough love and all of that.'

With that, Dynamite turned his rump to him and clomped away, making his way back over to the other side of the paddock where he was closer to his new love interest, the broody mare in the neighbouring paddock.

'Catch you later on then,' Joel called out to him. 'You big stud, you,' he added with another chuckle.

Wandering over to his LandCruiser, he cast a wary glance towards the ominous clouds as he slid behind the wheel, fired up the old girl and then turned up the Adam Brand song playing on the radio. Window down, the cool wind whisked the inside of the cab into a frenzy, strewn Minties wrappers and brown paper bags from his many trips to the bakery and fish and chip shop blustering about. Chuckling to himself, he caught each one and shoved the scrunched-up bits of paper into an empty takeaway coffee cup.

The scent of rain lingered, strong and sharp, as the atmospheric pressure built. Halfway into town, the ever-darkening sky finally cracked open in an ovation-worthy spectacle. He quickly wound up his window and flicked his windscreen wipers to top speed. Unable to see two metres in front of him, he begrudgingly slowed to what felt like a crawl, arriving out the front of the medical centre with only minutes to spare. He was relieved to nab the last parking space and killed the engine, the wipers screeching to a halt in the middle of the windscreen. Grabbing his mobile from the dash, he opened the app he'd downloaded especially for this appointment, slipped it into his pocket, and grabbed his wallet from the glove compartment. The rain was coming down in torrents, bashing against buildings, cars and the few people clambering into them, some beneath umbrellas that the wind was trying to snatch from their grips. And here he was, just about to step out of his four-wheel drive and into it all – his life in a damn nutshell.

His Akubra pulled low, he made a mad dash for the front sliding door. He shivered as he basically dove into the air-conditioned waiting room, thankful to find it was empty. Slipping off his Driza-Bone and tugging off his hat, he wiped the rain from his face. Hardbacked chairs lined the wall, facing a coffee table with neatly stacked magazines. Glancing around, he tried to find somewhere nearby to leave his coat and hat, not wanting to traipse water across the linoleum floors.

'You can hang it on the hook behind the door.' The very young, very pretty receptionist welcomed him with a wide smile.

'It's horrid out there at the moment, isn't it?' she added, glancing past him and to the rain-obscured view outside.

'It sure is. Talk about bucketing down.' He did as she'd asked and then made his way to the counter. 'I've got an appointment at four, to see the doc.'

'Mr Grant, is it?'

'Yeah, that's me.'

She passed him a form attached to a binder. 'Can you just fill this out? The doctor won't be too long.'

'Righto.' Remaining at the desk, he began scribbling his false name, an out-of-town address and a botched-up Medicare number, feeling bad for having to continue his fabrication. All done, he handed it back. 'Here you go.' This young woman would know who he was soon enough.

'Great, thanks, just have a seat.' She turned to the computer and began punching in his details, humming to herself. Pausing, she peeked up and over the top of the counter. 'Can I grab your Medicare card? This number doesn't seem to be working.'

'Yeah, sure.' Joel pretended to flick through the cards in his wallet. 'Oh, crap.' He sighed weightily. 'I'm sorry, I've left it on the table at home.'

She waved a hand through the air. 'No worries, these things happen. You can call me tomorrow and read the number out to me.'

'I will, thanks.' Joel watched the doctor step into the waiting room, take his chart from the file holder and, without looking up, call Joel's bogus name. Doing his best not to dive across the room and grab Levi by the throat, Joel's stomach did a sick roll as he stood and took indomitable steps towards his nemesis. The last time he'd seen Levi's ugly mug had been the night of the brawl at the pub, when he'd broken his nose. He still looked the same, but older and far less intimidating.

Totally unaware of the incoming missile, Levi stood back to allow his patient in. It was only then the man finally lifted his attention from the file in hand and met Joel's eyes. Absolute shock was swiftly followed by a combination of fear and rage as his steely gaze narrowed. 'You.' All colour seemed to drain from his face as he stared over the top of his glasses.

'Yes, me,' Joel said, storming into his office before Levi had time to slam the door in his face. With the toe of his boot, he turned and kicked it shut behind him. It did so with a slam.

Levi folded his arms. 'What the hell do you want, Hunter?'

The battlelines were clearly drawn. 'I just called in to have a little chat, that's all.' He locked his fierce gaze to Levi's. 'You got a problem with that?'

Levi strode behind his desk – a clear sign he needed to make some distance and assert his authority. 'If you've come to cause trouble, I suggest you go head on back to under whatever rock you crawled out from under.' Pulling his chair out, he sat while raking condescending eyes over Joel.

'I'm not going anywhere.' Widening his stance, Joel stood his ground. 'We've got some unfinished business to attend to, you and I.'

'I have no business with the likes of you, Joel Hunter, and if you think you're going to force me to play whatever game this is, you've got another think coming.'

'This is no game, Levi. It never has been for me.' He sucked in a sharp breath, reining in his anger. 'You need to own up to what you've done and take responsibility for ruining people's lives.'

Levi shrugged offhandedly. 'Not going to happen.'

'Yes, it is. If you don't, I'll do it for you and go to the cops to tell them everything about the night you tried to rape Juliette with your thug brothers.'

'They're never going to believe you.' Levi was so cool, it drove Joel's fury up another notch.

'Why's that, Muller?' His hands inadvertently fisted, Joel began cracking his knuckles.

Levi cocked his head and smirked. 'Because I'm respected around here. Nobody's going to believe you of all people, the bloke who knocked me out at the pub and then ran from town with his tail between his legs to pursue a stockman's job.'

'I wouldn't be so sure of that,' Joel said through clenched teeth.

Levi's smirk became more of a leer. 'And why's that, Hunter?'

Joel wasn't giving anything away. 'Why don't you just do the right thing and own up to what you did that night, for all our sakes?'

'Are you insane?' Levi threw his head back and gave a half-strangled laugh. 'Hell will freeze over first. I've got a damn good life now, and I'm not doing anything to jeopardise it.'

'Don't you want to clear your conscience?' Joel's tone was icy cold. 'Especially now you have a wife?'

'I don't have a conscience.' Levi's gaze simmered with the darkness Joel only knew too well. 'And leave my wife out of this.'

'I'm just pointing out the fact you should harbour even more guilt now you have a woman to take care of, one to protect from monsters like yourself.' With Levi taking his bait, Joel leant across the desk, so he was just inches from Levi's face. 'Isn't it weird that Levi, when twisted around, spells evil. Mighty fitting, don't you think?'

Shocked, Levi took a moment to regather, glowering at him but remaining silent.

Clearly hitting a raw nerve, Joel stepped back and folded his arms. 'I honestly don't know how you sleep at night.'

'Easily.' Levi sneered as he gestured towards his door with a tip of his head. 'Now get the hell out of my office before I call the police.'

It was Joel's turn to snigger cynically. 'You wouldn't be so frigging stupid to go and do that?'

'Watch me.' Grabbing the phone at the corner of his desk, Levi began stabbing numbers and then pressed the phone to his ear, his breathing now heavy, laboured. 'Hey, Kelly, it's Doctor Muller. Can you put me through to Wombat please?' He paused for a moment. 'Yeah, sure, I don't mind waiting.'

'Forget it. I'm going.' Joel held his hands up, feigning defeat. He hadn't got what he wanted, what he needed, but he didn't want to risk any trouble with Wombat either. 'I'll leave.'

Measuredly, arrogantly, Levi hung up the phone. 'Wise choice.' He huffed. 'I suggest you don't tread where you're bound to lose your footing, Hunter, because the price you'll pay if you dredge up the past might not be worth the carnage it'll cause to those you love.'

Joel's heart seized and his blood froze solid. 'Is that a threat?' he snarled over his shoulder.

'If you mean, am I threatening you, Juliette and your families? Yes, indeed I am. The truth of what happened that night by the river is never going to see the light of day,' he said darkly. 'Although, just for the record, I'll never forget the fear in Juliette's eyes or the sweet softness of her pert little breasts when I pinned her to the ground.'

'Shut your damn mouth, Muller.' Joel had to fight every urge to strangle the life out of the mongrel. 'You sick, twisted bastard.'

'On that note.' Rising from his high-back leather chair with the broadest of fake smiles on his face, he stepped towards the door. 'I'll walk you out.'

'No need,' Joel growled as he tugged the door open. 'Stay the hell away from Juliette and my family, you got it?'

'Nice seeing you again, Hunter,' Levi said in a nauseating tone.

Joel refused to respond as he stepped out of the claustrophobic space. The door slammed shut behind him. He flashed the confused receptionist a fleeting smile as he strode over, grabbed his hat and coat, then stepped out onto the wet sidewalk, glad to see the rain had dissipated. Taking strides towards his four-wheel drive, he reached into his shirt pocket and pulled out his mobile phone, ending the recording.

He'd got what he'd come for – cold hard evidence.

CHAPTER

17

Her harsh reality now deeply sunken in, Juliette's emotions had churned into the darkest of storms. With the realisation that her life was never going to be the way she'd imagined it to be, she'd begun to feel nauseated for most of each day, anxious for what her future was going to hold and for where she, Warrior and Brute were going to live. Apart from her marital woes, and with her self-control shot from the sheer exhaustion of it all, she could do little but think of Joel, of how patient he'd always been with her, of how he'd always loved her so passionately. The one thing getting her out of bed each and every morning, other than helping out in Aunt Janey's bakery on the odd day, was lingering on the what-could-have-beens of her past. And along with this, guilt had become her constant companion – for being naive enough to have fallen for Lachlan's manipulation, and for breaking up with Joel when all he'd been doing was defending her honour. The weight of it all was just too much to bear.

Something needed to give before she fell into a dark hole, without any way of climbing out.

Her mobile chimed from her handbag and Juliette grabbed it out, smiling when she spotted who the caller was. 'Hi, Aunt Janey.'

'Hey, sweetheart, how'd the afternoon go?' Janey's singsong voice wrapped around Juliette's aching heart.

'Yeah, really good.' Juliette dunked her finger into the cream bun she'd kept for herself and licked it from her fingertip. 'It slowed down a little after you left for your appointment.'

'Oh, good.' Janey breathed with relief. 'I was worried you were going to be completely run off your feet.'

'Not at all.' Her tastebuds in overdrive, Juliette snuck a little bite.

'I asked my friend at the real estate if she had any properties on the books that would suit you, but she doesn't have anything, and she doesn't know of any places coming up either.' Janey sighed. 'I'm so sorry I couldn't be the bearer of better news.'

Juliette's heavy heart sank further. 'I thought as much, seeing as nothing has been advertised in the classifieds of the local paper, but thanks anyways.'

The line went to static for a few brief moments, Janey's voice inaudible. 'Sorry, I'm driving and in a bit of a black spot … can you hear me?'

'Yes, I can. You're not holding the phone, are you?' Juliette said, concerned.

'No, little miss detective,' Janey said with a playful chuckle. 'I've got you on loudspeaker.'

'Good.'

'Anyway, sweetheart, like I said, you're more than welcome to come and stay with me in my flat.'

'I know, Aunty, and thank you, but I have Warrior and Brute to think about too. I'm sure something will come along.' Juliette wasn't holding her breath, but she didn't want to worry her aunt.

'Okay then, sweetheart.' Janey honked her horn. 'Damn kangaroos. I swear they have a death wish sometimes.' She groaned. 'I better let you get back to closing up. I'll catch you tomorrow.'

'You will.' The cream bun she'd been saving for dessert now all but eaten, Juliette got back to tidying up, the phone clamped between her ear and shoulder. 'Love you heaps.'

'Ditto, my beautiful niece. To the moon and back.'

As she finished straightening things up for the night – the day's takings counted and put into the safe – more thunder rumbled over the mountains. Juliette switched off the last of the lights, the glow of the streetlamps just enough to let her see what she was doing. Undoing her apron, she shoved it into her bag to take home and wash, along with the tea towels and tablecloths. She couldn't wait to have a long, hot shower followed by a couple of glasses of wine to help her drift off to some kind of sleep. Just about to hang a closed sign on the front door, she spotted a familiar four-wheel drive pulling up and parking beside her ute. What Joel was doing here was anyone's guess, and as much as she shouldn't, she liked the fact she was about to see him again.

The wind had picked up noticeably as she stepped outside and locked the door behind her, feeling Joel's gaze upon her, warming her from the inside out. A car door slammed shut and footsteps came up behind her. His familiar smile greeted her as she turned to face him, as did the hunger he always seemed to conjure up inside of her without the slightest of efforts.

'Hey, you. Anyone would think you're stalking me,' she said, genuinely smiling for the first time today.

'Well, they'd be right, because I kinda am.' His dimples deepened.

'Is that so?' Her heart's tempo increased as the heat from their chemistry reached inside of her, scorching her heart. An electric sexual energy that hadn't been there a moment ago jolted through her. Fighting the urge to tear every inch of clothing from his muscular body, she lifted her chin. 'And why are you stalking me?'

'Because I need to tell you something important.' He paused, hesitating, his gaze intensifying. 'Something you're not going to be happy about.' His words were so uncompromisingly direct, for a short moment she had trouble drawing a breath.

'Okay.' Her heart in her throat, she eyed him cautiously. 'Spill.'

He heaved in a breath. 'I paid Levi a visit today.'

Her heart split wide open. 'Oh, for god's sake, Joel!' She glowered, shook her head, and then looked to the heavens as she warded off tears. She couldn't fall apart. And she couldn't cope with this. Not now. Not with everything else she had to deal with.

'I'm sorry I went behind your back, Jules, but it was the only way.'

'You're sorry?' Somewhat regathered, she flashed her steely gaze back at him. 'I told you I didn't want all of this dragged up again, and what did you go and do?' She didn't wait for a reply. 'Exactly what you bloody well wanted to, without any regard for how I feel about it, or the drama it's going to cause.'

Joel took a step towards her. 'You're so wrong, Jules. I'm doing this for you, for both of us.'

He looked so hurt that all she wanted to do for a fleeting moment was wrap him up in her arms. She wished she could tell him how her mother would suffer if her stepfather found out she'd snuck out that fateful night. But that would mean owning up to all the abuse she'd copped from the man over the years, and she wouldn't, couldn't, do that. 'I call bullshit, Joel.' Disappointment and betrayal struck her in the chest and tightened like iron claws, ridding her of any rationality. 'You're only doing this to settle some stupid score between you and Levi.' She pointed accusingly at him, feeding off the cold anger coiling inside of her. 'Aren't you?'

'Damn it, Jules, give me some credit. You know I'm not that bloody shallow.' He snapped every word, and then clearly realising his tone was sharp, he paused and took a breath. 'I know you're hurt and angry right now, and justifiably so, but please, just hear me out and you might understand why I did it.'

She considered telling him to get stuffed, but curiosity got the better of her. 'You've got two minutes before I get in my car.'

He pulled his mobile phone from his pocket, stabbed it a few times, and then held it up. Levi Muller's voice was unmistakable, every word leading to an admission of his guilt. The trauma inside of her begged for a release, but she held it at bay, only just. She went quiet as her thoughts went to the dark place inside of her, the empty place she'd shoved all the pain and humiliation from that horrific night, the very same place all the haunting memories of her stepfather's unfair treatment of both her and her mother had been stored.

Joel broke the lapse of silence between them with a gentle exhalation. 'Can't you see we've got him exactly where we want him?' He nailed her to the spot with the intensity in his eyes. 'You and I, and Ben, deserve justice. We deserve to truly leave all of this in the past, but there's only one way that's going to happen, and that's by going to the police. There's no way the son of a bitch can get away with it, not now we have this kind of evidence.'

Numb yet so acutely on edge, all Juliette could do was stare blankly at him. She felt as if she were on a rollercoaster without a harness – one wrong turn and she was going to slip, fall and shatter into a million tiny pieces. Joel had a fair point about needing to seek justice to really let it go – she'd bottled it all up, buried it deep down inside of her, and it had backfired, causing her final words to Joel all those years ago to be bitter – a typical case of taking it out on the one she loved the most. Maybe this was her second chance to make things right, to do the right thing by herself and by the only man she'd ever truly loved with all her heart and soul. It wasn't only her that had lost it all because of Levi; Joel had too.

She sucked in a settling breath. 'He's got connections, so I wouldn't bet on that recording being the be-all and end-all.'

Hope fired in Joel's gaze. 'It's worth a try, isn't it?'

'I honestly don't know,' she managed to say past the tightness of her throat. And in that moment, she almost broke her promise to her mother and told Joel why she was so hesitant in peeling back the band-aid.

'How about I let you have some time to think it over?'

Biting her trembling lip, she nodded. 'Yeah, okay.' It was a mere whisper.

Joel's hand brushed over her shoulder and down her arm. 'I've got your back, Jules. Never think you're alone in all of this.'

Balancing on the brink of breaking down, all she could do was nod.

'I'll let you get home.' He took a step back, studied her for a few more moments, and then turned away.

She exhaled a held breath as she watched him stroll back to his four-wheel drive. Even from the back, he was spectacular, all muscle and strength, carrying himself with such confidence it was unavoidable to be drawn further into him. Step by step, she walked away from him and ambled towards her ute. Unlocking it, she slid in behind the wheel.

Joel pulled to a stop beside her and she wound down her window, remaining silent. 'Promise me you won't just go home and put a hex on me.' There was a ghost of a smile playing upon his lips, but such sadness in his eyes.

'I'm not promising you anything of the sort.' As angry as she was with him, the instinctive awareness that bound them together pulled her in even tighter. 'But I do promise I'll touch base with you tomorrow, once I've had time to calm down and get my head around what you've gone and done.'

'Okay, Jules.' He considered her for a few more moments and then tipped his hat. 'Chat tomorrow, then.'

'Yup,' she replied.

She watched him drive away, and the reality of the situation completely overwhelmed her. He wouldn't understand her deep fear of her stepfather, nobody would. Malcolm Kern was such a saint in everyone's eyes. Gathering every last bit of resolve she could muster, she revved the ute to life and headed towards home, her mind in a spin and her heart breaking all the more.

* * *

Plump ruby-red lychees and fleshy golden mangoes were in abundance on the surrounding farmlands, the branches of the seemingly endless lines of trees heaving beneath the weight of the tropical fruit. The sweet scent, tantalisingly familiar at this time of the year, drifted upon the gentle afternoon breeze, reminding Juliette of all the times she'd sat with a bowl of her favourites plucked from one of Joel's family's trees, the sticky juice dripping down both their arms as they devoured way too many for their stomach's liking. Long gone were those days. Adulting really sucked.

Shovel in hand, she picked up the last of Warrior's manure and tossed it into the wheelbarrow. Pausing, she caught her breath, and then leant the shovel up against the railings. Wheeling it out of the paddock and over to the ever-growing pile kept for garden mulch, she tipped it, cursing when half of it ended up on her boots; she wasn't in the right frame of mind for this crap – no pun intended, she thought with a chuckle. Job done, she stretched out her aching back and sighed. Although arduous, her day of hard work had helped her somewhat. Just for a little while, she'd stopped obsessing over all her problems, even if she hadn't made any of them disappear. She could run and hide, but not for long. Her troubles had to be dealt with, one way or another.

It had been almost twenty-four hours since Joel had told her what he'd done and, as much as part of her wanted to go to the police, for her sake and for his, she was afraid of the price her mother would pay, and that if she stirred the murky waters of her past, the sludge she'd pushed to the bottom was going to rise, real fast. No matter how hard she tried, she couldn't shake the feeling that Joel had betrayed her by going to Levi and recording the conversation, as clever as it was. Would he go and use it anyway, despite her reluctance to go to the police? Part of her believed he would. And the more she thought about it, the more she envisioned the drama it was going to cause, and the more it made her even more frustrated and angry and hurt. But, although she felt all of this, she hadn't forgotten she'd promised she'd touch base with him today. A woman of her word, she wasn't about to break that agreement. She just needed a little bit of time to build up the nerve to say what she was going to – he needed to drop the subject if they were to remain friends.

Stepping from the stables with her stomach growling for sustenance, she looked to the dusky sky. Relief from the heat of the day was arriving with the last smoky embers of twilight, the southerly breeze not only tinged with the sweetness of tropical fruit, but also with nightfall's freshness. Not in a rush to arrive back at the house, where Lachlan was working in his office, she drew up for a moment, resting against the paddock fence. It had been a long day, spent considering her extremely limited options, but at least she'd taken the first step and made her choice to leave here. After years spent walking in shoes that weren't really her own – her false facade built up to survive each day – she could feel the cracks widening, deepening, waiting to engulf her. If she disappeared down the hole, she wasn't sure she'd ever resurface. There had to be a place for her, Brute and Warrior to call home around Little Heart, surely?

Arriving back at the homestead and spotting Lachlan's vehicle gone, she found the house quiet, hauntingly so. Wandering down the darkened hallway, she dropped her saddlebags to the kitchen floor and spotted a yellow envelope on the dining table. Her name was written across the front of it in bold black letters.

Her heart stalled, then raced. What in the hell was Lachlan up to now? Dragging out a chair, she slumped down into it and pulled off her boots and socks, glaring at his handwriting. It only seemed like yesterday that a nineteen-year-old Lachlan Davis had turned up at the front door of her parents' place looking dapper, flowers in hand, ready to take her to her end of high-school dance. His eagerness to be her chaperone when she'd mentioned she had nobody to take her after Joel had skipped town had helped melt her frozen, broken heart. As had his constant romantic gestures soon after, and his support through her years at university. At the time, she'd found his advances irresistible, his encouragement for her vocation endearing, but now she saw them for exactly what they were – a ploy to grab her at her weakest.

Tucking her hands behind her head and stretching her legs out, she exhaled a breath she hadn't even realised she'd been holding. Stubbornly, not wanting Lachlan to get beneath her skin, she tried to bide her time, tried her best not to tear the envelope open with greedy inquisitiveness, but with curiosity getting the better of her, she snatched it up and did just that. It was a pre-nuptial agreement with her signature on the bottom of it. She gasped, eyes wide as she read it. The room spun. She felt as if she were about to be sick. She didn't recall ever seeing it before, let alone signing it. She did, however, remember Lachlan getting her to sign a mountain-load of paperwork a few weeks before they'd married, late at night, after she'd had a couple of wines, reassuring her it was all just trivial stuff. She'd trusted him. Hadn't even bothered to read what she was signing. What a damn fool she'd been.

The reality of what it meant hit her like a tonne of bricks. She was going to leave here with exactly what she came with – basically nothing. All the money she'd put into the house, refurbishing it, all the bills she'd paid ... none of it mattered now. Lachlan and his parents were going to make damn sure she left broke, monetarily and emotionally. How was she ever going to be able to afford a place on her own, one that would accommodate a horse and a dog? Tears threatened in her eyes, yet she closed them and willed them away. She was not shedding another tear over him, or their failed marriage, or this piece of paper in her hands. Something would give, and she'd find a way out of this mess. She had to.

Something else was paperclipped to the pre-nup, a small white envelope. She reluctantly opened it. Her fingers trembled as two photos and a handwritten note tumbled to the floor. Her knees cracked as she knelt to retrieve them. There was no mistaking who it was in the photographs, their hands all over each other and their lips touching. It was her stepfather and Kathryn Jensen. Juliette was horrified. Just how Lachlan had got the pictures and what he intended to do with them, she didn't want to know. Her throat felt as if it were about to close over as she began to read the note.

> *Ironic, isn't it, that your revered stepfather is cheating too. Who would have thought he'd do such a horrendous thing to your mother, especially being a man of god? If you move while I'm away this week, make sure you only take what was yours to begin with, and nothing else, and make sure you keep your lips shut.*
>
> *Don't make me have to spill your father's secret, Juliette. If you expose my private business or try in any way to challenge*

the pre-nup, I'll be forced to expose these photos. Your dear
mother will be humiliated, your stepfather will lose his
position as a respected man in this town, and possibly even
his role as minister, and my parents will be left with no
choice but to ask him and your mother to move out of the
home they so generously gave them.

What happens now is up to you. Take care, Juliette.
Lachlan.

Tears falling, she covered her mouth as she felt her world crumbling. Lachlan was a bastard, but this was a whole new level of deceitfulness. He'd just stooped to the lowest of the low, once again, to get his own way.

Well, she wouldn't allow it. It was high time she spoke to her mother and tried to make her see sense. The photos were going to be an almighty shock, but her mum deserved to know the truth of the man she was married to. Just like she had deserved to find out what Lachlan was doing behind her back. Lachlan had no idea about the horrific childhood she'd had because of her malicious stepfather. These photos might actually be the icing on the cake, the final straw that would make her mother see Malcolm for the horrid man he really was and leave him. She could only hope and pray it would be so. Lachlan might have given her the best gift.

Desperately needing fresh air, she tossed the envelope and pre-nup on the table, told Brute to stay put, and then stormed from the house towards Warrior's paddock, the photos still clutched in her hands. Realising, she shoved them safely into her back pocket. It was a bit of a walk, but she needed to let off steam before she reached her horse. Once there, and not bothering to saddle up, she swung aboard, walked him through the gate and then ordered him into a canter. Warrior, always keen to get out of his confines, accommodated her cued changes, his gait widening as they headed towards the seclusion of the Crystal National Park with Juliette clinging to his mane.

At the end of her tether, she gave in to the freedom of the ride, mindful now wasn't the time to turn up on her mother's doorstep. She needed to calm down before she did or said anything. And she wanted to talk to her mother when Malcolm wasn't around. This time of the day, the creatures of habit they both were, they'd be sitting down to their five-o'clock-on-the-dot dinner. So, not knowing exactly where she was headed, she rode on in what felt like a dim bleak world. But before she knew it, she was at the Hunter Farmstead, staring at Joel's front door from Warrior's heaving, sweaty back, her breath catching in her throat and her horse blowing and stomping beneath her.

She snapped to. Her stomach somersaulted, backflipped.

What in the hell was she doing here?

She was about to make her escape when the door swung open and Joel emerged, barefoot and dishevelled, and looking handsome as ever. With his hair damp, his low-slung jeans accentuating his six-pack and the strength of his magnificent chest – the breadth of it adorned with a tattoo of an eagle, wings spread so the tips touched each of his collarbones – he was a sight to behold.

Trying to look away but unable to, she reminded herself to pull it together as she offered a hesitant wave. 'Howdy.'

He acknowledged her with a slight tip of his head. 'Hey there, Jules. Fancy running into you here of all places.' His teasing smile deepened. 'Did you take a wrong turn somewhere?' He wandered down the steps towards her.

'Smartarse,' she choked out, making sure to avoid his eyes as he neared because, right now, as vulnerable as she was, she would undoubtedly tumble right into them.

'Sorry, but you know me. Can't help myself.' His big shoulders moved in a faint shrug. 'I thought you were going to call, not call in, but I have to admit, this is way better.' He stopped just short of her and, glancing up, his warm smile gave way to creases of concern. 'Shit, Jules. Are you okay?'

So much for trying to act all cool, calm and relaxed – she must look exactly as she felt. Her chest was so tight, she was afraid to speak, but she forced herself to, still avoiding his gaze. 'I've been better,' she admitted as she dismounted with ease.

Joel took a step closer. 'What's happened?' He scanned her face, frowning.

Sudden, sweet relief swept through her, just by being near him. 'Lots.' Wishing she could close the small distance between them, that she could fall into his arms, her eyes suddenly swam with fresh tears, and try as she might to blink them away, they fell and rolled down her cheeks.

'Oh, Jules, please don't cry,' he said softly, doing what she longed for by coming even closer, then brushing a knuckle along her cheek. 'Do you want to talk about it?'

Caught within his gaze, she had no words right now. Being so dangerously close to the one man who had always been true to her heart, close enough to now fall into his arms, she ached to rest against him, to feel the warmth of his soul and the beat of his heart beneath her cheek – the rise and fall of it mesmerising her. The pair of them sharing a moment, filled with all the sentiments she didn't want to admit to herself, she quickly glanced down at her feet, shockingly as bare as his. She hadn't even noticed she'd run out of the house without shoes on.

'Jules.' His voice was raw and husky and low. 'I'm really worried about you. Please, talk to me.'

For his sake, she found her voice. 'I don't know where to start.'

He ran his hand down her arm and then tucked it into his jeans pocket. 'How about from the beginning.'

She bit back a sob. 'It's a really long story.'

'I've got all the time in the world for you.' His expression was overwhelmingly empathetic.

So grateful for this man right now, she was struck speechless by the passion in his eyes. All she could do was smile sadly and nod.

Hesitantly, he reached out and swept a wisp of hair from her face, tucking it behind her ear. Then, he rested his hand on her cheek. 'Sorry to say, even though you're rocking the dishevelled hair and smudged mascara, you look like hell.'

'Gee, thanks.' Her sad smile widened just a little, and she couldn't help but admire his rugged masculinity up close. Stubble darkened his chiselled jaw, and the fine line of hair descending from his navel to beneath his jeans … so help her, she longed to trace it, and his kissable lips, with her fingertips.

He reached out and wrapped an arm around her shoulder. 'You want to come in for a cuppa? I promise I'll make you a mean one.'

She wanted to accept his kind offer so badly. 'You got something a little stronger?' What little resolve she'd had dissolved in a flash of heat as her breath hinged in her throat. She was treading into dangerous territory, although she couldn't help but like it, couldn't help but love the feeling it gave her, couldn't help the fact that being in the presence of this magnificent man, one who had loved her like no other, made her feel so desired, so important, so shockingly carnal.

Joel nodded. 'Sure do.' The look he swept over her made her feel as if she were on fire from head to toe, and something deep inside her thawed in that magical moment. 'I've got American Wild Honey and some tawny port.'

'A glass of port sounds nice ...' She skidded to a verbal stop. Panicked, she looked to the distant mountains, her pulse pounding and her mouth dry. 'I don't think it's wise for me to come inside with you, Joel.'

'Well, we can hang out back, if that makes you more comfortable.' He gestured to the verandah with a sweep of his arm. 'It's a great spot to sit and watch the sunset and chat about what's going on, if you'd like to.'

She paused, chewing her lip. It would feel so good to open up to someone she could trust, someone she could depend on.

'Don't overthink it, Jules. We're just friends yakking, that's all.'

She released the breath and smiled. 'Yeah, okay. When you put it that way, I suppose there's no harm in us just hanging out.'

'Exactly,' Joel said, returning her smile. He looked to Warrior. 'He's an absolute beauty.'

Juliette glanced up at Warrior proudly. 'He sure is. He's my absolute world, apart from Brute.' She gave the horse a gentle pat. 'Aren't you, buddy?'

Joel gave him a scratch on the neck and Warrior pressed into his hand. 'Ha, he likes that.' He peered back at Juliette. 'What about Lachlan?'

'What about him?' she snapped a little too defensively.

Joel's brows shot up. 'Woah up, I'm not having a go, just thought he'd be part of your absolute world too?'

'He used to be. That's something we can talk about over that glass of port.' She watched a look of surprise, then almost relief, slip over Joel's face.

'I reckon we might need more than a glass by the sounds of it.' He eyed her thoughtfully.

'Maybe we might.' She watched Joel share a brief moment with Warrior, relating like only a true horseman could, and her dispirited heart swelled.

'Want to bring him out back too? It's fenced so he can just wander about.'

'Sounds like a plan.' She gave Warrior a pat on the neck. 'Come on then, buddy, you heard the man.'

With Joel's hand gently resting on the lower part of her back, he lightly steered her around the house with Warrior in tow. Getting Warrior settled, she looked to the very porch she and Joel had sat on all those years ago, sharing kisses and talking excitedly about one day making this place their home. Wistfulness overcame her. She really hadn't ever stopped loving him, not that she would ever admit it out loud.

'You can hang out here, drink in the serenity, and I'll go grab us that drink.'

Joel's husky voice snapped her from her racing thoughts. 'Okay, thanks.' In a few more heart-pounding steps, she was by the outdoor settee, the very one they'd snuggled on many times over, and settling into it. She offered Joel a small smile. He did the same before vanishing into the barn, the screen door slapping shut behind him.

Gazing out at the breathtaking sunset, with the sun shooting the last of its golden rays across the far-reaching sky and setting it ablaze, she floated into a blissful world as it began its descent behind the mountain ranges. Effortlessly, the majesty of it brought her into the present moment, taking her away from all her problems. She loved the sensation – wished she could bottle it. The sense of calm and centredness she felt was mind-blowing. She hadn't expected her spur of the moment arrival here to be so comfortable, so soothing. And that brought her to consider whether she should show Joel the photos, made her wonder if she should open up and tell him absolutely everything. Maybe then he would understand her reluctance to go to the police. Or maybe that would be putting him in a very awkward position, one where he had more of her secrets to keep. Whichever way she turned, she felt trapped, and all because of three selfish, conceited, arrogant, heartless men. Malcolm Kern, Levi Muller and Lachlan Davis.

The only man who'd ever been true to her, who had always had her best interests at heart, was Joel. Wrapping her arms around herself, she listened to him rattling about in the kitchen as the late afternoon got longer and shadows crept across the back lawn. With the sun gliding away and a cool breeze picking up, wind rustled branches against the side of the barn, the wooden floorboards creaking as if stretching and groaning. The distant whinnies of horses and brays of cattle carried with it. Everything about this place felt peaceful, enticing – it always had. It was a little strange, knowing Zoe wasn't here, and instead thousands of miles away. She hoped her friend was having the time of her life – she deserved to.

Pulling the blanket from the back of the settee, she tugged it over her curled-up legs, drawing in a deep breath. She imagined the rest of the world slipping away and, for the first time in as long as she could remember, she felt as if she were home.

CHAPTER
18

Placing the last of the prosciutto beside the slices of pear and apple, Joel tossed the deli paper into the bin and admired his work of foodie art. Wanting to make Juliette feel special, he'd gotten a little carried away and taken longer than anticipated, but she was going to love what he'd rustled up to eat. She'd always been a sucker for a good cheese platter – blue cheese drizzled with honey her all-time favourite, and his. Little gestures counted at a time like this, and she should be treasured. She was the sweetest, strongest woman he knew, and she didn't deserve to have been dealt such a shitty hand in life – clearly things weren't going very well for her. He really wanted to be the one to save her from her troubles, but for now, he'd settle for making sure she was cared for.

Switching on the stereo, he picked one of his favourite CDs – he was in the mood for some heartfelt tunes, and Chris Stapleton knew just how to belt them out. Then, nibble board in hand, an unopened bottle of tawny port pinned under his arm and two glasses balanced between his fingers, he made his way back outside.

'Sorry I took so long. I thought we might need a little bit of sustenance between drinks,' he said, rounding the corner. His breath hitched when he caught sight of her, curled up on the settee, covered in a blanket, a dreamy smile upon her lips and her eyes closed. With her long lashes resting on her cheeks and her hair fanned out over the back of the settee, she looked so peaceful, so breathtakingly beautiful. He paused beside her – he honestly could stand here and stare at her face all night long, but his presence stirred her.

She blinked open her sweet eyes, ones that pinned him to the spot – he couldn't, for the life of him, stop looking into them. 'Hey, you,' she said croakily.

'Hey, sleeping beauty. You're looking a lot better already,' he said, placing everything on the coffee table and then settling down beside her.

'I must have drifted off.' She yawned, stretched her arms high. 'But back to reality, huh?' She screwed her face up.

'You must have needed a power nap.' Grabbing the port, he poured them both a generous glass.

She wriggled up straighter and accepted hers. 'Thanks.' She surveyed the platter. 'Oh my goodness, look at all of this. Yum.' Her sleepy eyes widened, as did her smile. 'You didn't have to go to so much trouble, Joel.'

'No trouble at all.' He rested back, pleased with her reaction. 'I thought you might be hungry.'

'I wasn't, but I am now.' She leant forward and, grabbing the cheese knife, cut herself a lavish piece of cheese and plonked it onto a cracker. 'I haven't had blue cheese and honey in forever.'

'Why the heck not?' Joel helped himself to the same thing and the pair of them moaned as they chewed.

'Nobody else likes it,' she finally replied, licking the honey from her fingertips.

'Well, they're all weirdos,' he said lightheartedly.

She laughed now. 'And we're not?'

'Nope. They don't know what they're missing out on.' He cut some more, placed it on a biscuit, and passed it to her. 'I freaking love this stuff, all thanks to you getting me to try it, very reluctantly at first I must add.'

'I knew you'd like it. You're a foodie weirdo, just like me.' She shoved his offering into her mouth.

'You got that right,' he said with vigour.

They both tucked into the delicious deli goodies and a companionable silence hung as they devoured a few mouthfuls, then sat back with their glasses raised to their lips. Joel couldn't help but steal sideways glances. Juliette was simply stunning, in every single way.

'I'd forgotten how nice this is.' Juliette's voice was soft as she gazed up at the twilight sky and the twinkling stars.

Admiring it all too, Joel's smile spread into one of complete gratitude. 'Yeah, you can't beat a view like this.'

'I wasn't talking so much about the view, although it is beautiful.' She turned to him, and a flicker of emotion from deep within was fleetingly exposed. 'I meant ...' She paused, assessed him. '... being with you.' Her voice caught on her last word, her lip quivering.

'I'm glad to hear it because that's how I want you to feel around me. I know we've had a lot of hurt, but it doesn't mean we can't be great mates, Jules.' Every fibre of Joel's being pulsed with longing for this exquisite woman. 'I care about you, and that will never change.'

'Thanks, Joel. I care about you, too.' Closing her eyes, she sighed, and then looked back towards the sky. 'You have this effortless knack of making me feel as though all my problems aren't so unbearable, as though I can somehow find my way out of the darkness.' She bit her lip, the hint of a smile at odds with her gathering tears. 'And I need that right now, more than you know. Thank you for being here for me.'

'I'll always be here for you, no matter what,' he said, his heart reaching for hers. 'I hope you know that.'

She nodded, blinking faster. 'I know, and I'm so very thankful.'

He gave her hand a quick squeeze and they shared a meaningful glance before settling back, bellies pleasantly full and glass of port in hand.

They were sitting so close now, he could just make out the fine scattering of soft freckles dusted across her cheeks, and the place on her neck where he knew she liked to have kisses feathered over. It took every bit of his resolve not to lean in and do so. He wanted to pretend she didn't have such a hold over him, over his heart, but this magical moment with her was proving otherwise. He needed to get a damn grip.

'I'm all ears if you want to spill what's going on in your life,' he said after a few minutes.

She sighed and nodded. Then, with a deep inhalation, she began. From tailing Lachlan all the way to their apartment in Cairns, to how her stepfather palmed her off to the Davis family, to Margery's selfish efforts to manipulate her, to her own longing for children, to arriving home a few hours ago to the pre-nup she'd unknowingly signed, and then, finally, to the photos of her stepfather cheating on her mother with Kathryn, he found his anger rising notch after notch, and his heart breaking for her.

'Far out, Juliette. This is way worse than I'd imagined.' He tried to find the right words, anything to make her feel better, as fury raged through him. 'Lachlan Davis truly is one lowlife son of a bitch.'

Staring down at her hands wringing in her lap, she nodded.

'Are you going to show your mother the photos?'

'I think so.' She looked to him, fear storming across her face. 'There's something else I should tell you. It might help you understand why I don't want to go to the police.'

He took a breath. 'There's more?'

She nodded. Cleared her throat. Sucked in a few deep breaths while avoiding his gaze now. 'My stepfather ... Malcolm ...' She choked back one sob, followed by another.

Joel rested his hand on her bouncing leg, gently stopping it and silently urging her to go on.

She turned to him, her face contorted with distress. 'He mistreated me and my mother, Joel. For years. He still takes his belt to Mum when he thinks she's sinned. She loves him so much for some stupid reason, and she takes it without grievance.'

'Jesus.' He shot to his feet, the rage rushing through him seizing his breath, and clenched his fists at his sides. 'That evil son of a bitch.' He unfurled his fingers and rubbed his hands roughly over his face, then through his hair. Looking to the starry sky, his breathing laboured, he tried to pull himself together before turning back to Juliette. 'What kind of things did he do to you?' He was almost too scared to hear it in case he lost his mind completely, and went and taught Malcolm Kern a damn lesson, one that would send Malcolm to an early grave, and him to prison.

Juliette unclamped her bottom lip from between her teeth. 'He used to lock me in a cupboard and make me pray for hours for things I didn't even understand, or he'd get me to bend across the chair and he'd belt me until my bum was red-raw, and sometimes ...' She was talking through her sobs now. '... he'd make me and Mum kneel on the cement in the shed and pray from dusk to dawn, just for saying god or damn, all the while with him sitting on a chair, glaring at us with his belt ready in his hands if we tried to stand up.'

Joel swore. 'He's meant to be a man of god.' It came out in a rush. With the realisation of her dire circumstances crushing him, Joel fell to his knees at Juliette's feet and gently placed his hands on the knees of her jeans. His teary gaze met hers, and he did his best to choke back emotion. He needed to be strong for her, no matter what. 'I'm so sorry you had to go through such horrific treatment in silence, Jules. You didn't deserve it, and neither does your mum. No woman does.' He briefly closed his eyes, shaking his head. 'I can't believe she stays with him. He's a disgusting human being. I should've seen it, with how scared you were of upsetting him. I should have helped you get away from it, from him.'

She placed her hands over his, smiling gently through her tears. 'It's not your fault, Joel. You had no idea. Nobody does.'

'Now I understand why you didn't want to go to the police that night, and why you still don't want to. It's all for your mother's sake.' He drew in a slow steady breath. 'You should've told me all this way back then, Jules. I would have understood. I would have helped you.'

She nodded. 'Maybe I should have, but I promised my mum I wouldn't speak of it to anyone. Besides, I'm telling you now, and now is what matters.'

'Well, now I know, I'll protect you and your mother with my life if I have to. That bastard is not going to hurt either of you again.' He stood, taking her with him, and pulled her to where she belonged – in his arms. She broke, sobbed into his chest, and he did his best to soothe her with his touch.

'So, where are you going to move to, because I'm gathering it most certainly won't be back home?' he said once she'd calmed a little.

'Too right. Moving back home is not an option. To be honest, I have no idea where I'm going to go.' She untangled her arms from around him and brought her teary gaze back to his. 'All I know is I don't want to move out of Little Heart. My work is here, and this is my home and always will be.'

He noted the tension of her mouth and the tiredness around her eyes. After spilling everything, she was totally exhausted in every way, and all he wanted to do was love her the way she should be loved. 'What about staying at Zoe's place until she gets back from Cambodia? Six months will give you plenty of time to get yourself sorted, and I'm sure she won't mind you housesitting her bachelorette pad one little bit.'

She glanced across the way, past the horse yards, catching the slightest glimpse of the roof of Zoe's quaint little one-bedder. 'Oh, I don't know if that's a good idea.' She looked to him, apprehension written all over her pretty face. 'What will people say, with me leaving Lachlan only to come and live here?'

He shrugged. 'Who cares what people say? You know the truth, I know the truth, and that's all that bloody well matters.' He hinted a smile. 'And besides, you got a better idea, Firecracker?'

'I'd forgotten you used to call me that.' Pausing, as if recalling all the times he had, she then frowned and sighed. 'And no, I don't have a better idea of where I should live, and not for lack of trying. There's not a rental in sight, or even the hint of one becoming available in the near future. They're as rare as hen's teeth around here.'

'Well then, it's settled. You, Warrior and Brute are moving here for now.'

'But ... I ... um ...' She stammered to a stop.

He could see urgent words lock her throat. However, she sucked in a deep breath and nodded. 'I think it might be my only option, so thank you, I'd love to take you up on the offer.' She puckered her lips, as if in deep thought. 'But what about your parents?'

'What about them?' He shrugged, careful not to meet her gaze as the pain of his father's treatment momentarily gripped him, and instead looked to the dark sky, laden with stars swimming amongst the silvery glow of the moon.

'Don't you think we should run it past them first?' She spoke softly, but the concern in her voice was palpable. 'I mean, I'm not even sure your dad likes me anymore. He barely says boo whenever he sees me in town or at church, or when I call over to visit Zoe.'

'The cranky old bugger doesn't seem to like many people these days, but it's his own stuff, so don't take it personally.' He tried to smile. 'Of course I'll run it by Mum, but she'll say the same thing I'm saying, that this place is your home too. They've always loved you like one of their own, Jules.'

'I love them too, even when your dad is being a cranky arse,' she replied with a warm smile.

Words dangling from the tip of his tongue, Joel sucked in a steadying breath. He was about to veer the conversation to uncomfortable ground, but he had to – the timing felt right. 'So, does this mean we're going to go to the police about Levi?' She went to retort, but he barged on. 'After you show your mother the photos, and she hopefully leaves Malcolm, of course.'

Her shoulders stiffened and her back grew straighter. 'Please, Joel. Not again. This is all too much for me to think about right now.'

But he didn't stop. Couldn't stop. 'I'll protect you, and your mum, you have my word.' He regarded her earnestly, and she writhed beneath his stare.

Huffing, she looked to the silhouettes of the horses, backdropped by the moonlight. 'I thought you'd get it and stop hassling me.'

'I do get it, and totally understand why you're afraid, but it doesn't have to be like this, Jules. We can work our way around it all.' He blew a weighty breath. 'Please, think about it because, in a way, you're going against everything you believe in by not doing anything about the Mullers. You know that, right?'

She turned wild eyes his way, and he flinched at the hurt and anger within them. 'Joel, I have enough on my plate, as you well know now I've told you everything, without you constantly pressuring me as well.' Her expression blazed into one of defiance. 'Surely you can appreciate I've reached my limit, if you care about me as much as you say you do, *right?*'

Joel bit his tongue. If looks could kill, he'd be dead. The band of pain that sat constantly around his chest constricted even tighter. But despite his compassion for her situation, and the hostility in her eyes, he pushed on. He had to. He could see her balancing on the edge of coming around to his way of thinking. 'As frightened as you are, we have to do this, Jules. Please, I'm begging you.'

She shot to her feet and pointed at him. 'No, we damn well don't! And if you go and do this without my consent, I won't want anything to do with you, not ever.' Her eyes shimmered with unshed tears, and she didn't bother to hide the bitterness in her tone. Her hands went to her hips. 'As wrong as it was, what they did to you and Ben, it was *me* that was sexually molested that night, and it was *me* that was left to pick up the pieces when you took off the way you did.' She turned her back to him, arms folded.

Her words hit him in the gut, painful and final, as if she'd just fired bullets at him instead of her icy words. 'For god's sake, Jules, can't you see I'm trying to make things right, and trying to make up for not being able to protect you that night? I didn't want to leave you. You told me we were over, and I …'

'Stop! Just stop, okay?' She sucked in a shuddering breath, dropped her head into her hands. 'I know it's my fault too, it's just …' She finally turned back to him. 'Since you've been MIA, it's been easier to blame our break-up on you, but now you're back and I have to look into your eyes again and see all the …' She stalled, shook her head, and choked back a sob. 'We shouldn't be talking about this stuff.'

'Okay, I'm sorry.' Nodding, he closed his eyes, squeezed back his own tears, then dared to meet her determined gaze once more. 'But, Jules, please. Just take a breath, and try to see what they did that night, and what they stole from us, from my side too.' He was well aware he was pleading with her now, but it was something worth getting on his knees and begging for, so he ran with it.

'What do you mean?' She eyed him inquisitively.

'My father doesn't want a bar of me because he doesn't know why I laid into Levi that night at the pub.' He kept his voice even. 'I reckon if he did, he might find it in his heart to forgive me. And I lost the one true love of my life because of it.'

She raised a trembling hand to quieten him. 'Okay.' She hung her head and sighed, over and over. 'I get it, I really do, and I'm sorry I'm being selfish.' She stayed motionless, but then lifting her head and staring into space, she replied, very carefully, 'If I do change my mind, and we do this, do you honestly believe Levi will get what he deserves, or will he do a couple of months in prison and walk out a free man?'

Hope exploded in his chest. 'I can't say whether the law will make him do the time, but he *will* suffer for the crime for the rest of his life, Jules. There's no way in hell the medical board will let him keep practising if he's charged with attempted rape, and I'm sure his wife will think differently of her husband if she knows the truth of who he really is.' Her distress obvious, he silently cursed himself for putting her in this position. 'I'm sorry, it's just ...' He prevaricated, tripped over his words, swallowed them before he told her just how much he loved her and how much losing her broke him. He'd gone and said too much already. 'We've both had to live with this dark secret long enough, don't you think?'

She broke now, sobs rising and tears flowing. Mortified at bringing her to this point, he stood and pulled her to him once more. Resisting him at first, but then succumbing, she buried her face into his chest, her body shuddering as she wept. Fighting to hold himself together for her sake, he rested his cheek against her head, cradling her to him, wishing he could protect her like this forever. At the very least, as long as she followed through with moving into Zoe's place, he could keep an eye on her for now and help her through this. His hand soothing her back, her ragged breaths eventually evened out, and an intimate silence enveloped them. He bent and pressed a kiss to her forehead, and although meant to be completely innocent, there was no denying the intense sensation of his lips upon her skin.

As if feeling it too, she pulled back a little and eyed him cautiously. 'What was that?'

He fought for his next breath. 'Me telling you I'm here for you and I'll look after you. That's all.'

'I think I'd better head back home.' Sniffling, she untangled her arms from around him and wiped at her cheeks. 'Before …' She verbally stumbled. '… it gets any later.'

He swallowed, and then nodded. 'You going to be all right, riding home in the dark, and bareback?'

'Don't worry so much about me.' She smiled softly, although it didn't reach her puffy red eyes. 'I've got this.' She gave his arm a tap. 'Let me know when you've talked to your mum about me staying at Zoe's for a little bit.'

'Sure thing, I'll head over there soon, then I'll call you.'

'Okay. Thanks, Joel.' She couldn't meet his eyes now, looking anywhere but. 'Thank you for lending your ear, and the yummy food and port.'

'Of course. Anytime.'

An awkward moment passed as she turned to him and they stared at each other. Then she made her way down the steps and to Warrior chillaxing beneath the big old mango tree.

'Let me know when you're home safe, hey?' he called after her.

'Will do,' she said over her shoulder.

Watching her stride away, her horse loyally at her side, Joel felt the familiar knot in his stomach. Was he ever going to get a second chance with her?

CHAPTER
19

Gunshots rang out, echoed, the ping of the metal cans exploding resonating deep within Joel as he recalled the many tokens of love and pride his father had once shown him. With the cold steel of the rifle comforting in his hands, the days of his youth rose up in a vision as his gaze distorted with unshed tears. He gruffly blinked them away. As a nine-year-old boy, his dad had taught him to shoot while controlling every breath so he could keep his hands steady. As a thirteen-year-old, he'd finally allowed him to sit in the saddle of a young, green, half-broke gelding, and ride the bucks out like he'd taught him, Joel's butt firmly planted, his hands gripping the reins. At seventeen, his father had proudly handed over the keys to his beloved old LandCruiser, and at eighteen, he'd given him the keys to his very own kingdom – the refurbished barn and an equal share of the farm.

Now, his father couldn't even give him the time of day.

Heavy-hearted, Joel recalled the solemn moment he'd stood at the crossroads of his life, one way leading to a peaceful existence spent working alongside his father, with Juliette as his wife, and their children to love and cherish. The other way led into some of the darkest and hardest roads he'd ever travelled, a lonely, broken, grief-stricken man. He'd been forced to choose the latter, forced to give up his dreams, to walk away from his one true love and his family. Sharp arrows of remorse shot through him once more, reminding him of all that he'd lost, of all that he was helpless to remedy. He thought about the cruelty that Juliette had grown up with at the hands of her stepfather. He thought about how she'd lost her real father to cancer when she was only five years old. He thought about how Lachlan had treated her with such disrespect. The injustice of it all was unbearable.

The box of ammo he'd taken from his father's gun cabinet in the shed, along with the .22 rifle, was now almost empty. His dad was a man of habit, and Joel hadn't been surprised to find the key in exactly the same place it had always been hidden. On a roll, another round of shots echoed through the thicket of trees lining the side of the creek bank as he fired. All the targets he'd lined up, bar six empty cans, were now blown to smithereens. Making sure the safety was on, and then carefully placing the rifle down beside him, he flexed his fingers. His back resting against the trunk of the paperbark, he squeezed his eyes shut and shuddered with the pent-up rage coiling through him. Being right back where it had all happened was overwhelming. But he was determined to somehow push through the sensations. He'd been here since the blackness of night had started turning powdery blue, trying to distract himself, trying to heal, just … *trying*. When he was a teenager, target practice had always helped clear his head, so it was worth a shot. Anything to take his mind off everything.

Taking a deep breath, he picked the rifle back up and cocked it. Then, steadying himself, his gaze narrowed down the barrel of the gun as he lined up the last of the cans he'd placed along the creek bank. The gun kicked with each press of the trigger. Moving the muzzle left to right, each can in turn exploded until there was nothing left to shoot and he had nothing to distract him. What was he meant to do now?

His thoughts persistently dragging him backwards, he wished he could stop the cogs of his mind turning. It was downright exhausting, reliving everything over and over, and frustrating as hell, knowing he couldn't do what felt so innately right, to both Levi Muller and Malcolm Kern. He understood Juliette's concerns, respected them even, but there had to be a way. The ball was now essentially in her mother's court. It all depended on what she did once she saw the photographs of her husband cheating with her friend. He prayed to god she did the sane thing, the right thing, and left the repulsive man for good.

Cursing the muggy heat that the rising of the sun had brought with it, he grumbled beneath his breath as he stood, ready to make his way back home. A bad headache battering his already weary mind, he pressed thumbs into pounding temples. The lack of sleep and ceaseless worry was doing him no favours. Stepping from the dappled shade of the towering trees, he tugged the brim of his hat down low on his forehead, shielding his face from the blazing morning glare. The now cloudless sky was a far cry from the leaden clouds he'd observed swallowing up the stars for most of the night from his hammock, before they'd heaved bucketloads of rain over everything in sight. The downpour was a sure way to intensify the already stifling humidity Far North Queensland was renowned for, and to send the mosquitos into a frenzied buzz.

It was just shy of ten when he took a shortcut through the small fruit plantation his dad and he had planted all those years ago. The sun had already burnt the mist from the rows of thriving mango and lychee trees. Just up ahead, a wildflower-speckled paddock filled with sunshine stretched out, the roof of the barn glinting just beyond it, and Zoe's cottage just over the way. He hoped Juliette hadn't gone and changed her mind overnight about calling the place home, for now. He wanted her nearby, to love her, to protect her, to heal her broken heart.

Along the road that led to the farm, the distinctive sound of a vehicle zoomed past, way too fast. Nobody drove like that around here – something had to be wrong. Now back in mobile range, he reached into his pocket and checked his mobile for what felt like the umpteenth time. There was still no reply to his three calls or the two text messages he'd sent Juliette last night. She'd done as promised and texted him when she'd arrived home safe and sound, but since then, it had been radio silence. Eager to tell her his mum – concerned for Juliette when he explained her marriage was falling apart – had gone as far as to say she could stay as long as needed at Zoe's place, he was becoming increasingly concerned something even worse than what she'd already told him had happened. He didn't trust Lachlan as far as he could throw him. Wouldn't put anything past the selfish, egotistical bastard. If he hadn't heard from her by the time he'd put the gun away and checked in on Dynamite, he was going to head on over to the Davises' place and check in on her. He knew he wasn't welcome there, but to hell with the consequences.

Tired of bullies, he'd be glad to teach Lachlan Davis a lesson, if it came to it.

The gun locked safely away, he traipsed across the drive, towards Dynamite's paddock, his newfound buddy, Red, the cantankerous rooster, in tow. For some strange reason, the obnoxious bird had taken a liking to him, and for some equally strange reason, Joel was finding the boastful fowl exasperatingly likeable. Under the shade of the big old jacaranda tree, Red's chicks were busy foraging and, like a dog to a bone, the rooster took off at a gallant gallop towards them. With a smirk and a shake of his head, Joel watched Red skid to a stop, then strut, his red comb wobbling and his wings and chest puffed out. Their ways of courting and wooing weren't much different to humans. The thought amused him enough to bring a much-needed smile to his face.

Trying to ignore the sun belting down upon his back and the gnawing of hunger in his belly, he revelled in the fact there was no sound, save for the quiet whisper of the breeze through the grasslands, the comforting lowing of cattle, and the sweet singsong of the native birds resting in the branches of their chosen trees. Mother Nature's soothing ballad offered a little solace to his tired mind and tattered spirit. Well aware he'd pushed the limits about going to the cops, he was also acutely aware it was very possible that if he went against Juliette's wishes, she would never speak to him again. As desperate as he was to fix what should have been fixed all those years ago, he wasn't prepared to risk her friendship – not even for his father. He'd lost her once. He wasn't about to risk that again. Without being able to speak the truth, it was pointless trying to bring his father around, to make him see he was still the moralistic, god-fearing boy he'd raised – a man for him to be proud of, a son he'd easily love.

Speak of the devil, the silence was broken as the grunt of the four-wheeler quickly approached and his father tore past him – the only greeting he got was the dust spiralling out behind the quad bike. In a bad mood already, Joel grit his teeth. *Where's the damn fire?*, he wanted to call after him. Frustrated after spending the past few weeks trying to pretend his father's heartless actions didn't hurt him, he was fighting to hold it all together. If not for his mother, and wanting to keep the peace for her sake, he'd have had his say by now. Enough was enough.

After lying in the hammock all night long, wide-awake and mulling everything over, he'd made his decision. If Juliette's mother left Malcolm, and Juliette still forbade him from going to the police, he was going to hit the dusty trails once more, in search of the virtually impossible – contentment. Without Juliette, he knew he never would truly be happy. He couldn't stay here, pretending everything was going to be okay because, no matter how he spun the story in his head, it wasn't going to be.

He reached Dynamite's paddock, happy to see his horsey mate at ease. Resting his forearms on the railings, he smiled, proud of how far the stockhorse had come in such a short amount of time. 'How's life treating you today, buddy? Anything new and exciting happening?'

The big bay raised his head a few inches, looking a little goofy with grass jutting from the corners of his mouth. His tail swishing, he plodded over, still munching on his earthy goodness. Small puffs of dust rose from his feet as he crossed the part of the paddock he liked to roll in, especially after just being hosed down. But just before reaching Joel, the gelding stopped, ears pricked forwards, head high. Joel turned just in time to watch his father's four-wheel drive roar towards them and then skid to an almighty stop.

His father's expression solemn, he regarded him with concern – his mum was the first thing that came to Joel's mind. 'Everything okay?' He took steps forward, arms folded.

'No, it's bloody well not.' For once, his father didn't take his eyes off him. 'Someone's gone and cut the top fence and about thirty head are out and on their way to bloody town!'

Joel stopped short of the driver's side. 'Who in the hell would have gone and done that?' He recalled the noise of a car speeding along the road almost an hour ago, and two possible culprits came to mind.

'Christ only knows. I just spoke to Wombat, and he's trying to round them up in the cop car over near Ned's place. I can only imagine the state they'll be in if he's got the sirens blaring.'

Wombat was an absolute character who looked exactly like Rich Uncle Pennybags, with his short white hair and curly moustache. 'Oh Lord help us.'

'Tell me about it.' His father slapped the door. 'So, come on then, don't just stand there gawking at me like a bloody galah. Get in. I need your help.' Huffing, he shoved a hand through wind-beaten grey hair and left it standing almost on end. 'The truck will be here in less than two hours to load the cattle up for the meatworks, and that's gonna be a bit tricky if the four-legged buggers are nowhere in sight.'

Joel felt a surge of desperation to rush to his father's aid. It was good to finally feel needed, despite the crappy circumstances. Tearing around to the passenger side, he was about to jump in when he caught sight of Dynamite, watching him vigilantly, and a thought struck him. He peered through the window. 'I reckon I'd be more help on the back of a horse, Dad.'

Bushy brows momentarily furrowed, and then his father nodded. 'Yeah, righto, but hurry it up. If they get into the scrub, we'll be looking for them in the dark.' He revved the engine, his hand at the ready on the gear stick.

'You head off, I won't be too far behind you.'

'Righto. I'll meet you over on Graham Road.' He rolled his eyes and snorted and off he went, like a bull at a gate, the tail end of the LandCruiser swaying to and fro on the loose gravel, his trusty old blue heeler holding on for dear life in the tray, the chain safely holding the old dog in place.

Joel didn't waste any time catching Dynamite, saddling him up and climbing aboard. Not used to the urgency, Dynamite didn't have time to even think about playing up. Swinging into the saddle, Joel settled in, reins firmly in his hands, and heeled into the stirrups as tight as he could. This was what he was made for, and it was a side of him his father was yet to see, after refining his horseman skills the past eleven years. Once away from the outhouses, and taking a shortcut through the bushlands, he gave Dynamite the cue and, like lightning uncorked, the horse shot forwards, skilfully weaving his way through thickets and ravines, sure-footed and confident.

The wind tearing past them, he steered Dynamite in the general direction of Ned's place, right next door to the Davises'. Minutes later, he arrived to find somewhat controlled mayhem, with Ned on his four-wheeler, his dad at the rear of the meandering mob in the LandCruiser, Wombat doing circles in his police car, sirens on but not blaring, and a gorgeous woman on her magnificent horse keeping the cattle in line over yonder. Although she was at a distance, Juliette was unmistakable. Both shocked and ecstatic to find her here, his heart leapt into his throat. He choked it back into place as he galloped over to her, careful not to spook the cattle.

'Howdy,' he called out as he approached her, returning a wave to Wombat at the same time. 'Fancy seeing you here. This is becoming a habit.'

'Hey, Joel. Yeah, it is. About time you turned up,' she replied with a sassy grin, just before turning her horse as though pirouetting and pulling a wayward bull making a beeline for the scrub back into place. Job done, she turned her attention back to him.

'Oh, fair go, Jules, I saddled up as fast as I could.' He flashed her a lighthearted smirk, rising to her banter as they all worked together, proficiently applying gentle pressure from all sides and easing the cattle along.

A few hundred metres up the road, a cow spooked, quickly communicating to the rest of the herd there was possible danger, which set them all off at a brisk trot behind their trailblazer. The young bull grabbed his chance for freedom once more and broke from the middle of the mob, his eyes set on a thicket of trees.

With Juliette busy trying to return order, Joel called out to her. 'I got the bastard.'

With Joel's cue, Dynamite wheeled after the one-tonne beast, the pair averting the bull's breakaway just in time before it vanished into scrubland so dense it would have taken them an age to get the rogue brute back. Joel's accident, and Ratbag's untimely death, came rushing back to him, but he pushed the painful memory away. He didn't have the luxury of time right now. Dynamite needed him, he needed Dynamite, his father needed the pair of them – he had to be here, in both mind and body. Pushing the snorting brute back into place, he caught sight of his father behind the wheel, the expression on his face one of pride as he watched his son at work. Joel couldn't help but allow it to sink into his heart, the short-lived moment refuelling the hope that they could somehow reconcile.

With wayward cattle splitting in different directions, and Juliette doing her best to keep them together, Joel joined her plight, Dynamite effortlessly riding at her horse's heels. They raced to steer the cattle back onto the dirt road before they gained refuge in the scrub. Galloping at a wide half circle, her butt planted securely in the saddle, Juliette successfully turned the lead cow and it doubled back, bringing with it the rest of the herd. Seamlessly working together, he and Juliette fanned out in perfect formation, each on either side, with his father and Wombat at the rear and Ned at the front. Crisis averted, the somewhat restrained cattle fell back into a steady march along the winding dirt road, the lead cow now trotting along as if nothing had happened, and the fence line now stopping them from making a break for it.

Dynamite now lathered in sweat and blowing, Joel fell in beside Juliette once more. 'By the looks of it, you could have gotten all this under control without me, I reckon.'

'Of course I could have.' Her face was flushed and her eyes glittered with excitement, drawing him in like a magnet. 'I'm more capable than most think.'

'Uh-huh.' Joel's eyes widened. 'I wouldn't argue with that.' Whether it was from the heat, the rush of the chase, or his compliment, he wasn't sure, but he watched a blush rise to her cheeks.

'Thanks, but I have to say, you look a little surprised,' she said archly.

'Nope.' His heart leapt and then settled into a steady thudding beat in his chest. Pointing to his face, his smile widened. 'This here is a look of total admiration.'

She eyed him enquiringly and then grinned. 'Good save, Hunter.'

'No, I'm being serious.' The creak of the saddle and the clip-clop of the horses' hooves made him feel completely at home, or was it also from being in her company?

'Well, in that case, thank you.' She was silent for a few brief seconds and then turned to him, the shade of her Akubra now shadowing her eyes. 'I'm not used to getting compliments.'

'Well, that's not kosher.' The band of emotions tightened across his ribs. 'You should be getting them all the time.'

Wordlessly, she smiled softly as she turned her attention back to the mob.

'Did you get my messages last night?' He eventually found the right time to ask, the cattle now completely at ease and strolling back towards home.

'Oh, no, sorry. My phone went flat just after I texted you to say I was home and I can't find my charging cord.' She shrugged, sighed. 'I tore the place to bits this morning but came up empty. I'm sure it'll show up, it can't just have vanished into thin air.'

'Yeah, I'm sure it will.' He regarded her for a few moments, caught up in her exquisiteness. 'Mum said you could stay in the cottage as long as you needed.'

'Yes, I already know.'

'How?' Had he just caught her lying? Had she seen his messages and just ignored him? 'You got ESP or something?'

'Something like that.' Taking a sip from her water bottle, she placed it back in her saddlebag, a playful glint in her eyes. 'Don't worry, Joel, I wasn't ignoring your messages. Your father told me.'

He'd forgotten how easily she could read him. 'He did? When?'

'First thing this morning, he woke me up by knocking persistently at my front door.' She looked skywards at a flock of raucous cockatoos.

'Really?' Joel brought his gaze back to her and arched a brow. 'So he does have a heart somewhere beneath his armour?'

'He sure does.' She cleared her throat, straightened. 'He does love you, a lot, you know.'

'Coulda fooled me.' Deep down, Joel knew her words rang true, but he was over being treated so unfairly.

Juliette bit her bottom lip and blinked faster. 'It's all my fault, the rift between you two, isn't it?'

'No, it's not, Jules.' Joel sucked in a sharp breath and blew it away just as forcefully. 'He may not know the truth, but it's his fault for being so quick to judge then turning his back. I'd never do that to my son or daughter, if I'm blessed enough to have children one day.'

Her forehead puckered. 'But if he knew why you and Levi got into that fight at the pub, it would change everything, right?'

He shrugged. 'Possibly. Or maybe too much water has gone under the bridge for it to ever go back to the way it was.'

'Don't give up hope, Joel.'

'Bit hard not to.' He heaved a weighty sigh. 'All I know is that if he doesn't come round soon, I'm going to go mustering outback again, where I feel at home.'

'Don't go and leave again.' It was said quickly, anxiously.

'Why not?' He wanted her to say she didn't want him to leave because she loved him and she didn't want to live without him.

'Because it's not going to solve anything if you do.'

'We'll see,' he replied casually. 'When are you moving into Zoe's?'

'I'm going to pack up my stuff today and move tomorrow, before Lachlan gets home from Sydney.'

He was chuffed, knowing she'd be his neighbour very soon. 'Want a hand?'

'Thanks, but Aunt Janey is going to come around and help. I don't have that much.'

'Okay, well, if you change your mind, I'm more than happy to help.'

'Thanks, Joel, appreciate it.'

They reached the bridge and, pushing the cattle across, the mob began to split, but it didn't take them long to ease them back from where they'd come. Juliette rode her horse with such confidence and authority, none of the cattle were game enough to try to make a break now because it meant they had to pass her first. Less than an hour later, they had all the cattle back safely in the holding pen, just minutes before the truck turned up to load them.

After bidding Wombat and Ned goodbye, Joel slid out of the saddle, as did Juliette, and they led their horses to the trough for a well-deserved drink.

'You were mighty impressive in the saddle today, Hunter.' The suspicion of a smile played around her mouth. 'Anyone would think you're a pro.'

Her compliment took him by surprise, as did the fact it felt as if she was actually flirting with him. 'I've done it a couple of times before.' He choked back his pride, tugged his hat off, and ran his fingers through his hair. 'I could say the same about you.'

His father rounded the corner of the stables, stopping short of them. 'Thanks, you pair. You did a good job of it.' He took his hat off and slapped it against his leg, sending a cloud of dust into the air.

'No worries at all.' Joel could hear the smile in his old man's voice – it was a sound he hadn't heard since he was a teenager. 'I enjoyed helping out.'

'Yeah, me too, Mr Hunter. And it's the very least I could do, seeing as you and Mrs Hunter are being so kind as to offer me a place to stay until I get on my feet again.' Juliette's smile was as warm as the sun beating down upon Joel's back.

'Of course, Juliette, you're like a daughter to Sherrie and me.' William nodded brusquely, then disappeared the same way he'd come.

Joel waited until his father was out of earshot and then whistled through his teeth. 'Wow, that was unexpected.'

'See, miracles really do happen, especially when you least expect it.' Juliette climbed back into the saddle.

Joel peered up at her from beneath his hat. 'Yeah, you got that right.'

She tipped her hat to him. 'I'll catch you tomorrow, neighbour.'

'Sounds good.'

'Yeah, it does, doesn't it?' She offered him a gentle smile, one that transported him back in time to when they were completely head over heels in love, before turning her horse and heading off.

He watched her fade off into the distance, her long ponytail bouncing around her back – the difference was, this time round, his heart wasn't as heavy. She was coming back. Maybe not to him, but to be near him, and that in itself was worth more than he could have ever imagined.

She was right. Miracles did happen.

CHAPTER
20

A loud yelp alerted Juliette to the fact she'd almost stepped on Brute. Startled, and hesitating on her tippy toes, she paused and looked down at him. 'For goodness sake, buddy, get out from under my feet, would you? I promise I'm not going to leave you behind.'

'He's scared the pants off me a couple of times, too, scooting around my ankles.' Aunty Janey giggled. 'He certainly lets you know when you're about to tread on him.'

'Sure does. He's got a good set of lungs for a little bitty fella.' Peering over the top of the last box of her personal belongings, she smiled at her aunt. With her tongue amusingly curled in concentration as they carefully descended the front steps, it tenderly reminded Juliette of her mother. 'You know what, Aunt Janey, you and Mum are looking more and more alike as the years pass.'

'Thank you.' Janey smiled wistfully. 'With how gorgeous my big sister is, I'll take that as a huge compliment, my love.' She groaned as they reached the ute and they both strained to place the box in the last little bit of space left. Then, pausing to look over the contents, Janey shook her head. 'After all these years of marriage and this is all you're allowed to take?' Waving a hand over the tray of the ute, she tutted then huffed, looking at Juliette with sympathy written all over her face. 'It obviously runs in the family to be a total narcissist.'

With Janey not knowing the real reason behind everything falling apart, Juliette didn't know what to say but, after a moment's consideration, she nodded. 'Seems that way.' She ran her fingers through her tattered hair, snagging on the knots. 'Just wish I'd figured that bit out before I'd gone and married him. Would have saved me a load of heartache.'

'You can't go and blame yourself for that one, my love,' Janey said gently. 'He's a master of making people think he's the bee's knees, just to get what he wants. I still can't believe he had the audacity to rub the pre-nup you don't even recall signing in your face, the dirty lowlife.' She sucked in a sharp breath. 'I pray the lawyer I put you onto finds a way around it all and you get what you deserve.'

'Me too, Aunty.' A wave of emotion engulfed Juliette and she bit back a sob, but not quickly enough for her aunt not to notice.

'Oh, love.' Janey wiped her hands on her jeans and then reached out, pulling Juliette to her. 'I'm so sorry you're going through this. If I could, I'd take your pain away and make it mine.'

Unable to stop her heavy tears, Juliette wrapped her arms around her aunt and wept into her shoulder. For a few poignant moments, they remained entwined. Then Juliette found the strength to gently pull away. 'Sorry I'm such a blithering mess.' She wiped at her cheeks. 'I'm just so exhausted.'

'Don't you dare apologise, love. You have every right to feel as you do. A divorce isn't easy.' She cupped Juliette's cheeks, eyeing her tenderly, just like a mother would. 'Be easy on yourself, and take all the time you need to heal that big, beautiful heart of yours, okay?'

Juliette sucked in a shaky breath, nodding sadly. 'I'll try to.'

Placing her hand to Juliette's chest, atop where her heart was breaking beneath, Janey smiled knowingly. 'I hope and pray that, in time, you'll follow what's been in here all along. Then you might just find your happily-ever-after.'

Steeling herself, Juliette observed her inquisitively. 'And what might that actually be?' She tried to wipe her tears away, but they just kept on coming.

'I think you already know the answer to that one, my love.' Brows raised, Janey tapped the side of her nose, indicating she knew way more than she would say.

In a flash, Joel's handsome face rushed to the forefront of Juliette's mind, but she mentally slapped the image away. Now wasn't the time to be thinking of him in such a way, not when she was so vulnerable, so tangled up in her woes. 'I have no idea what you're on about,' she said, feigning absolute bafflement.

'Oh, but I know you do.' Taking Juliette's hands in hers, Janey tenderly squeezed them. 'But I'm not going to harp on about it. For now, you need to focus on yourself and just allow the universe to bring to you what it may, when the time is right.'

'You're full of inspirational advice, Aunt Janey. Thank you.'

'I try my best to be an optimist, but sometimes being a pessimist is called for too.' With a brazen grin, she looked to her watch. 'I best get a move on. I have to have a shower and spruce myself up before my hot date picks me up for dinner and a movie.'

'You have a date tonight?'

'I do.' A blush rose to Janey's cheeks as she fiddled with one of her dangly earrings.

'Sooo?' Juliette rocked on her heels, a smirk plastered on her lips. 'Who's the lucky guy?'

'Jimbo.'

'Oh my gosh! Jimbo? Really?'

'Yes, really. Why are you so shocked?' Grinning playfully, Janey tucked her hands into her pockets.

Juliette shrugged. 'I just didn't picture him as your type.'

'I don't really have a type.' Janey tipped her head as though pondering this.

'Oh yes, you do.' Juliette's nods were exaggerated.

Janey leant on the back of the ute, crossing her feet at the ankles. 'And what might my type be, exactly?'

'Well, you've always gone for the clean-cut office worker, whereas Jimbo is the typical Aussie larrikin.'

'You mean Aussie yobbo.'

Both women laughed.

'Yeah, in a roundabout kind of way.' Juliette bit her lip sheepishly. 'He is as Aussie as they come.'

'He sure is. Do you know he even went and had his two front teeth fixed so he could look, as he put it, *dapper* for our date?' Janey said with an awestruck grin.

'Wow, now that's commitment.' Juliette shook her head, just as amazed. 'Go Jimbo.'

'Well, you know what they say about opposites attracting. And with my run of bad luck, I thought I'd switch tactics and go for a bloke I wouldn't usually date. And besides ...' She rolled her eyes. '... the poor bugger has been asking me to go out for the past couple of months, and I finally caved in and agreed so he'd stop pestering me.'

'Liar, liar, pants on fire.' Juliette waggled a finger at her aunt. 'You really like him.'

'No, I do not.' Janey's eyes darted this way and that.

'It's okay to like someone, Aunty,' Juliette said. 'It's been almost five years since Uncle Kevin passed.' She touched Janey's chest in exactly the same tender way her aunt had just done to her. 'You need to heed some of your own advice and follow what's in here.'

'Oh, stop it.' Janey playfully slapped Juliette's hand away. 'We're friends, and that's that.'

'We'll see,' Juliette said in a gently taunting voice. 'Jimbo and Janey sitting in a tree, K.I.S.S.I.N.G.'

'You cheeky bugger,' Janey giggled, shaking her head. 'On that note, I'm off.' She brushed a kiss over Juliette's cheek. 'You make sure you call me tomorrow if you'd like a hand unpacking and settling in over there, okay?'

'I will, thanks. I love you.'

'I love you, too, Juliette. So very much.'

Watching her aunt drive away, Juliette tried to focus her thoughts on the future in a determined effort to put the hurts of the present out of her mind. The wheels set into motion, things were happening extremely quickly, so much so that she hadn't had time to think too much until now. A hollow pang hit her like a tonne of bricks as she turned and went to close the door of what had been her home for the past ten years. Her chest heaved with a deep sob, but she choked it back. Brute circled at her feet and she bent to pick him up, comforted by his doggy love. Then, gritting her teeth, she slammed the door for the final time and did her best to gather her wits. She was doing the right thing. A clean break was what she needed. It was easier said than done, but worthwhile things always were.

Reaching her ute, she dispatched a wriggling Brute through the window and, as he settled himself on the passenger seat, she got herself behind the wheel, turned the key, revved the old girl to life and then turned up the Country Music Greatest Party Hits CD she'd had on replay this past week, singing the lyrics out loud. She refused to reminisce like she quite often did when driving around, or drink in the picturesque view that had stolen her heart. This was no longer the place she would lay her head at night. Passing the main homestead, she spotted her soon-to-be ex-mother-in-law standing on the front verandah, arms folded. Still singing, Juliette ached to give her the finger, but chose instead to not even acknowledge her. That would *really* grate her. Keeping her eyes on the gravel driveway, she looked to the future. There'd be no more looking back. There'd be no more yearning over what wasn't going to be. Time to get a hold of the reins of her life.

Ten minutes later, and feeling somewhat lighter now that the packing-up part was over with, she was driving through the front gates of Hunter Farmstead. It was so satisfyingly different to the life she'd grown accustomed to over the years of being married to a Davis. Unpretentious and welcoming, the place gave her the warm comfort of a mother's embrace. This was exactly the kind of place she felt at home. Actually, it was the only place she'd ever truly felt at home.

Deep in thought, she jumped when her phone rang from the dash. She snatched it up before it went to message bank, putting the speakerphone on. 'Hi, Sherrie.'

'Hi, love.' Sherrie's warm smile shone through her gentle voice. 'Are you over at our place yet?'

'Almost. I'm heading down your driveway as we speak.' Horses stirred in the paddocks and heads popped up and looked in Juliette's general direction as she passed. 'I'll call into your place for a cuppa before I unpack, if you're not too busy, that is?'

'Oh, I would have loved that, but I've had to pop into town to run a few errands. Can I take a raincheck?'

Juliette smiled. 'Of course, how's tomorrow?'

'Perfect. I'm home all day.'

'Okay. Thanks again, Sherrie, for everything.'

Sherrie tutted. 'Don't speak of it. You're always welcome, love.'

Juliette blinked back grateful tears. 'You're lovely.'

'So are you.' Sherrie paused and Juliette fought to pull her turbulent emotions in check. 'Enjoy settling into your new home, love, and I'll see you sometime tomorrow, okay?'

'You sure will. Bye.'

'Bye, love.'

She slowed as she neared the paddock closest to her new home, for now. Warrior, the first of her prized possessions, she'd moved this morning. He was now over the other side of the enclosure, strutting his stuff while clearly trying to woo the pretty Appaloosa mare in the neighbouring paddock. Chuckling to herself, she shook her head. Men. They were all the bloody same.

Reaching Zoe's cottage, she pulled up beneath the open lean-to carport and hopped out. Staring at her life, stuffed into the back of her ute, she sighed resignedly. There was nothing like having to start from scratch, all over again. She hoped her lawyer would get what was justly hers, but for now, it was one step at a time. After settling in here, she was going to tackle the visit to her mother, with the photographs. She prayed that it would change her mother's life for the better. Then, if her mother made the right choice and left her berating, abusive husband, Juliette was going to face her fears and, with Joel by her side, go to the police station and make a statement about what Levi and Jackson Muller had done to her. It was a good plan, but one that wasn't entirely up to her.

Grabbing two bags filled with her clothes and toiletries, she circled the water tank at the side of the cottage and wearily made her way towards the front door, the soft tinkle of wind chimes welcoming her. Wandering down the pebbled pathway, she looked to the purple-blossomed creeper lining the lattice that edged the wraparound verandah, and then to the green oasis that gave privacy and shade to the front and back of the house. White-petaled, sun-centred jasmine flowers flourished on either side of the four front steps, the heady scent a little overpowering as she climbed them. Kicking her thongs off when she reached the welcome mat she'd bought Zoe for Christmas, which asked *Did you bring wine?*, a smile bubbled up from within. She shoved the door open with a creak and stepped inside. The air was several degrees cooler and, as always, the cute home was as neat as a pin.

Brute padded in beside her, his collar jangling, and headed to where he always sat when visiting – his special spot on Zoe's cowskin rug in front of the telly. The lingering scent of the many candles, combined with the hundreds, if not thousands, of sticks of incense Zoe had burnt here over the years, tantalised her senses. The three-seater couch, with a throw and matching cushions, was a place where she and Zoe had shared many a night over glasses of wine, chatting about men, life, and random subjects. The familiarity of it all gave her a sense of being welcome here.

Home.

Dumping her bags on the queen bed in Zoe's room, she decided she was done moving for the day. There was always tomorrow to tackle the task of unpacking. For now, all she wanted was a nice hot shower and to slip into her favourite PJs, before putting her feet up with a glass of wine and watching the sun go down on the day she'd changed her life.

Once she was freshened up and feeling a little more human, she went to feed her four-legged friend – it was past his dinnertime. Wandering into the quaint kitchen, with its white cupboards and pale blue walls, she tugged open the groovy sky-blue Smeg fridge, which matched the kettle and toaster, plucked out a ziplock bag with Brute's kangaroo mince, her bottle of sauvignon blanc, deli-wrapped pepperoni and a block of Cracker Barrel cheese – thank goodness she'd dashed into town earlier on to grab the essentials – and busied herself preparing a slap-dash dinner. Then, with Brute basically inhaling his food, she fetched the box of BBQ Shapes from the bench, grabbed a long-stemmed glass from the overhead cupboard and made her way outside.

The setting sun's rays lengthened across the backyard as she settled on the top step and rested her back against the banister. A huge poinsettia tree shaded the front of the home from the afternoon sun. Beyond the couple of horse paddocks, rows of fruit trees and rolling green pastures drew her attention. As a teenager, she'd spent many a day in the school holidays picking and packing fruit or helping to sort cattle for the markets. The echoes of the past gripped her, and the heaviness of memories slipped over her. A familiar ache crept across her chest as she recalled all the happy times she'd spent here, by Joel's side.

Squeezing her eyes shut, she tried to block out the utter heartbreak of the day she'd come here to say she didn't want to break up with him only to find Joel gone. To never speak to him again, to smooth things over had, in itself, broken her. Even now, allowing herself to rest in the feeling of it all, anger and resentment and hurt washed over her. She quickly shook the melancholy from her mind before she drowned in it.

Instead, she imagined what it would feel like to be free to follow her heart, like Aunt Janey had said, despite the warnings of her mind. She visualised sitting on the back of Joel's LandCruiser, wrapped up in his arms as they gazed at a star-studded night sky, at peace, in love. Safe. And as her fantasy progressed, she pictured kissing him, imagining what it would be like to feel his strong hands sliding over her naked skin. Never having made love to him, she wondered how it would feel, especially now they were adults. Her nerve endings firing to life, she was more than tempted, but reality broke through too soon and she came to her senses, although her body still lingered in the possibility of him and her being a them.

The mournful cry of a curlew carried upon the gentle breeze, pulling her attention into the here and now and sending the hair standing up on the back of her neck – the sound had always given her the heebie-jeebies. Brute pushed through the old cat door and joined her, curling up at her feet. Staring into the golden gloriousness of the setting sun, she wondered what was next on god's agenda for her. It felt strange, no longer identifying herself as Mrs Lachlan Davis, and stranger still to be back here, at Joel's place. Full circle. A harsh lesson learnt in not rushing into things. As messed up as she'd been after breaking up with Joel, she'd gone into the relationship with Lachlan determined to be a good wife, and she had been. At the very least, she could hold onto that.

Sipping her wine, she tried to foresee the whispers around town once word got out of her impending divorce and the fact she'd moved here. Like a match thrown to dry grass, the break-up was going to spread like wildfire, the story becoming more and more twisted as it passed down the line. And she knew for certain, one way or another, the blame would be all on her. She'd have to take it on the chin, because she wasn't about to put Lachlan under the bus to save herself. The only solution, right now, was to take one steady step at a time, by herself, for herself.

Stirring out of his food-induced coma, Brute wriggled up beside her, his kind eyes staring at her. 'So, do you like your new home, boy?' she said, as she scooped him up and held him close. He settled into her, his cold nose wet against her neck. 'I'll take that as a yes.' She smiled and added, 'So do I.'

The rumble of an engine pulled her attention down the drive. Raising a hand to shield her eyes, she squinted into the setting sun. Pulling the LandCruiser up, Joel stepped out, the sunlight silhouetting his strapping shoulders. In his T-shirt and jeans, he looked so fierce with his clipper-cut hair and angled jawline, Juliette didn't know which response she felt the strongest, the need to remain aloof from the animalistic attraction she'd always had around him or the desire to tumble into his burly arms.

'Howdy, neighbour,' he said, swaggering over then coming to a stop before her.

'Hey, Joel.' His hair was damp and he smelt like Imperial Leather soap. She ached to kiss him. 'How goes it?'

'Yeah, can't complain.' His cavalier smile widened. 'Well, I could, but I don't want to. How 'bout you?'

'It's been a long day, but I feel much better now I'm here.'

'I feel better now you're here, too.' His smile faltered. He turned it towards the ever-changing horizon, then back to her. His eyes seemed to glow like the fiery orb of the sun.

Involuntarily, her fingers went to her lips as she tore her gaze from his, her heart pounding and her cheeks hot. 'It's a beautiful sunset, hey?'

He looked to the warm-hued sky. 'Ain't it ever?'

Moments passed. Comfortable moments, with both of them lost in the rich shades of orange, purple and crimson. Juliette knew the tingling warmth deep inside of her had nothing to do with the lingering heat of the day. Lachlan and Joel were such polar opposites – white collar and man of the land, shallow and deep, hurtful and heartfelt. She knew she was susceptible to her childhood sweetheart's charming ways. She needed to get a damn grip before she went and did something recklessly selfish. She was barely out of a marriage and needed time to find her feet and who she was again. So as much as she craved to tear off his every inch of clothing, to feel his strong body bearing down upon her, she shifted to standing, the empty plate in hand, and sculled the last of her wine.

At her bare feet, Brute stood too, his head going from her to Joel and back again – he clearly knew the humans were acting a little weird around one another.

Turning his attention back to her, Joel hesitated at the foot of the steps. 'Anyway ...' He sucked in an uneasy breath. 'I hope you don't mind me just dropping in, but I brought you a little housewarming gift.' He held up the box of Lindt assorted chocolate balls. 'As I recall, these little beauties were your favourites.'

'They still are. And if I remember rightly, they were yours too.' She smiled with fond memories. 'Do you remember how we used to battle over the last one, but you were always chivalrous and gave it to me in the end, though you loved stirring me up.'

'That I did.' A touch of a smirk quivered on his lips. 'A woman should always get what she wants from her man.'

His brazen statement stole her breath, but she quickly retrieved her pulse and pulled it into line. 'Well, in that case …' Sweeping her gaze over the magnificence that was all of him, her heart begged to be closer to his. What would it hurt, just spending some time with him? '… you better get your Wrangler butt up here and share those chocolates with me.'

He beamed. 'I thought you'd never ask.' Joel clearly didn't need any more of an invitation, clearing the steps two at a time.

Juliette gestured to the swing chair. 'Pull up a seat.' She held up her glass. 'I'm just going to duck inside to get a refill. Would you like one while I'm at it?'

His shoulders lifted casually as he flashed her a roguish smile. 'I don't have anywhere else better to be, so why the hell not?'

She returned in minutes with the rest of the bottle and two glasses, only to find Brute curled up in Joel's lap. Juliette's heart melted. 'He's got you wrapped around his little paw already.' She settled down beside Joel, liking the feel of his thigh up against hers.

'It's not hard.' Joel smirked. 'He's insanely loveable.'

'Only to people he likes.' She chuckled, rolling her eyes. 'He's a right little turd to people he doesn't like.' She pointed to her doggy mate. 'Those teeth may seem tiny, but they hurt when he nips an unsuspecting ankle.'

Joel feigned absolute shock-horror. 'Oh, come on, look at him, all sweet and innocent. It's not possible he could be so unfriendly.' Joel stroked Brute's head so gently Juliette wished it were her that he was running his hands over.

His eyelids heavy, Brute looked as if he'd died and gone to heaven. Joel's genuine kindness to his new friend was endearing. Lachlan had never had the time of day for Brute, or Warrior, or her, for that matter.

As the sun began to slip behind the mountain ranges, Juliette poured them each a generous glass of wine. Accepting his with a dreamy dimpled smile, Joel one-handedly opened the box of chocolates, making sure to offer Juliette the first. She went straight for the white chocolate filled with creamy sweetness. Joel grabbed his preferred one, salted caramel. Time stalling and rewinding, they tucked in, laughing and playfully slapping each other's hands away from their chosen chocolates. Before she knew it, she'd gone and scoffed eight, and had lost count of Joel's heists.

Simple things gave such simple pleasure.

Sitting so intimately close, she watched him lick the chocolate from his fingertips, the gesture doing something insanely erogenous to her insides. 'Talk about knowing exactly how to make a gal feel better,' she said.

Joel peered at her over the rim of his long-stemmed glass, all too dainty for his manly hands. 'No probs. Anything to make you smile.'

'Aww, shucks.' She playfully batted her eyelashes. 'You're such a sweetheart.'

'Only with people I like.' He grinned like a bad boy about to do something terribly wrong. 'Like Brute, I'm a bit of a turd to those I don't.' He smacked his teeth together. 'I've got sharp fangs too.'

Juliette laughed at his antics. He'd always been able to make her laugh, even when she was sad – he clearly hadn't lost the knack. Although doing her best to keep the atmosphere light and friendly, she still gushed beneath his blue-eyed stare. If she was being completely honest, she wanted to feel his arms wrap around her so much that she could barely stand it. She took a gulp of her wine, followed by another, as he continued to look at her with those piercing eyes.

'You know what?' she finally said, breaking the slightly awkward silence.

'Nope, I'm afraid I don't. Tell me about this "what".' The curl of his lips became even more playful, almost a little suggestive.

Their glasses empty, she poured them another, draining the bottle. 'Don't worry,' she said, passing the glass back to him. 'I've got more wine inside.'

He took his glass from her and raised it before taking a sip. 'Good, because I reckon we might be on a roll here.'

The wine helping her relax, Juliette took a few moments to drink all of him in.

'I can hear your mind ticking away.' He turned and studied her with intense eyes. 'What are you thinking about?'

'I'm thinking that I can't believe a woman hasn't snapped you up yet.' Curling a leg up beneath her, she turned a little in her seat and considered him with equal curiosity.

His smile all but disappeared. 'I haven't wanted anyone to snap me up.' Looking away from her, he seemed to drift somewhere else. 'I haven't been interested in settling down, and I've been too busy working to bother with all the drama of a relationship.'

'Mmhhmm.' His answer was not overly convincing. Her gaze fell to his hard-worn hands. 'That's a shame. You'd make a good husband, and a good father, Joel.'

He flicked his gaze back to her and, unlike before, it was filled with so much depth she could hardly breathe. 'I can't go and let a woman fall in love with me when I'm already in love with someone else now, can I? That would just be selfish.'

She had to fight to control her breath, to keep it somewhat even. 'I suppose that would be unfair.'

He nodded, very, *very*, slowly. 'Mmhhmm.' Seizing her eyes with his, he refused to let her go.

Like a deer caught in headlights, she blurted out the first sentence she could hustle together. 'So, who's the lucky woman then?' She knew all too well that she was that lucky woman, but what was she meant to do with such information?

His smile was deliberately slow. 'That's for me to know and you to find out.'

'Righto then,' she said, fidgeting as if she were covered in fire ants.

'What the hell are we doing, Jules?' he sighed, shaking his head.

She froze, swallowed hard. 'What do you mean?' She felt heat rise to her cheeks as his leathery, manly scent drove her wild.

He half-chuckled and then sobered, his gaze intent. Reaching out, he gently cupped her face. 'I see you for the amazing woman you are, Firecracker. You know that, right?'

The hunger in his eyes rattled her, and the raw intimacy in his voice sent her heart into a fervent flutter. It felt really good to be cared for by a man like him, but equally terrifying and overwhelming. 'Thank you, Joel. That means a lot,' she choked out as she looked away, regarding the twilight sky.

Bracketing her face with his hands, he gently turned her back to him, his passionate gaze giving her the undeniable understanding of all he felt for her. And just like that, as though completely helpless, her soul tumbled. Before she could say anything, think anything, before she could talk herself out of what her heart craved, everything around them faded away, leaving just her and him, here, living in the moment together. Her voice of reason echoed in the back of her mind, but it was distant, incoherent.

Silently, he leant in and kissed the tip of her nose, so softly, so tenderly, her toes curled. Their magnetism was a force to be reckoned with, the flicker of old flames turning into an inferno of want and need. She captured his mouth with a hungry kiss, his lips feeling like a drug she'd been craving for an eternity. The clamour in her heart made it hard for her to think about anything other than making sweet love to him for the very first time. Grabbing hold of that profound irrefutable desire, she ran her hands beneath his shirt and up to his chest, loving how his muscles clenched beneath her fingertips, how his heartbeat quickened, and how his breathing grew heavier with her intimate touch.

Running his lips up the side of her neck and to her ear, he lingered. 'Are you sure about this?'

With his hesitation, her voice of reason stormed to the forefront of her mind. 'I really want to …' she breathed, and then pulled back just a little with a groan. 'But maybe it's not the best idea we've had.'

'Maybe not.' Leaving his hands on her hips, he made a soft sexy male sound from deep within his chest. 'You know, you're killing me right now.'

Juliette threw her head back and huffed. 'That makes two of us.' The fact they fit like they were made for each other was hard to ignore.

He pulled back but left his hands on her thighs. 'As much as every single part of me wants you, we really shouldn't be doing this.'

'Yeah, you're right.' She untwined her arms from around his neck and flashed him a bashful smile. 'But it's all your fault we got into this predicament in the first place,' she purred, her pulse wildly uneven.

'Mine?'

She nodded, smiling sassily. 'Yes, yours.'

He matched her wayward smile with a bad-boy one of his own. 'And why's that?'

'Because you're waaay too tempting.' She sat back and pulled her knees to her chest, peering at him coyly over the top of them. 'In every single way.'

'I like it when you look at me like that.'

'You might well do, but you're as frustrating as you are tempting.'

'Ditto, Jules.' He grinned when she gave him the forks. 'Just because we're not going to sleep together doesn't mean we can't snuggle up and stare at the stars for a little while, though. I don't really want to end the night here, at least not on this note.'

'You know what, I really like the sound of that.' She grabbed his arm, settled back, and draped it over her stomach. They cuddled up nice and tight for a little while, neither of them feeling the need to talk in their drowsy contentment. A chill had crept into the breeze and she shivered against him. Wordlessly, he pulled her closer, so there wasn't an inch between them.

After a long comfortable silence, he brushed a gentle kiss across her cheek. 'It's cold out here. Let's go to bed and snuggle. It might help you get a good night's sleep.'

She contemplated it. 'I don't know if that's a good idea.'

'Trust me.' Shifting to face her, he smiled. 'I have plenty of self-control.'

She laughed. 'I'm glad to hear one of us does.'

He stood, taking her by the hand, and she allowed him to lead her into the cottage, down the hall, and towards the bedroom.

'I usually sleep in my boxers, you okay with that?' Joel's fingers were at the ready to unzip his jeans.

She nodded, smiling. 'Perfectly okay, especially when I'm already in my PJs.'

'And they're very sexy PJs at that.'

Juliette looked down at her very daggy attire. 'If you say so,' she said lightheartedly.

'You'd look good in a hessian sack.' Taking off his shirt, then slipping off his jeans, he never took his eyes from her.

Juliette trembled at the sight of him. He was a hell of a lot of man, with ripples and tattoos, his skin sun-kissed, his towering height making her feel safe and protected. 'I don't know about that, but thank you.'

He pulled back the covers and they climbed in. She snuggled into him, and Joel hugged her tight. 'Night, Jules. Sweet dreams.'

'Night, Joel. Dream sweet.' The warm look in his eyes made her heart canter. As he cuddled her into him, she felt herself drift then float into the beginnings of a blissful sleep.

CHAPTER
21

Soft sunlight filtered through the curtains and glistened like glitter over the bedroom. Juliette woke slowly, taking a few moments to remember where she was before becoming aware that she was snuggled tightly into Joel, her head resting against his bare chest. The weight of his big strong arms warmed her, and the slow rise and fall of his chest was soothing, almost dragging her back to sleep. It felt so good, so *right*, just being here with him, as though they'd never been driven apart. What she'd give to stay like this forever, to pretend they were together, without a care in the world. So close, with his breath feathering across her cheek, the thought she could reach up just a little and place her lips upon his sent shivers of delight through her. But as much as she longed to do so, it would be a mistake.

The breeze shifted the curtains, sending sunlight flickering across his handsome features. Stirring, he opened his eyes, his warm smile all-encompassing. 'Hey there, you.' His voice was husky and his stubble had grown darker overnight, giving him more of an edge.

Her stomach fluttered and then plummeted like a rollercoaster. 'Hey there, yourself.' Six feet of absolute temptation, he was a magnificent example of what a man should be – rugged, protective, strong and courageous. She could only imagine what people would think, and say, if they were caught in bed together. Nobody would believe they hadn't made love. Should she really care if they didn't? Like Joel had said, they both knew the truth of things, and after being lied to for most of her life, she was learning that was all that really mattered. To hell with the gossips.

'How'd you sleep?' His voice washed over her, stilling her thoughts.

The heat in his eyes warmed her all the way to her toes. 'Better than I have in forever.' She untangled from him and stretched with the grace of a cat.

'Good.' His smile was sexy and sleepy. 'Mission accomplished then.'

'Too right.' Rolling onto her stomach, she pushed wisps of wayward bed hair out of her face before resting up on her elbows. 'Thank you for staying here with me, and being a decent man while you're at it.'

'No, thank *you* for letting me spend the night.' He sucked in a breath as he brought himself to sitting, resting his back against the bedhead. 'Sorry about kissing you, it's just …' He paused, regarding her, the burning light in his eyes one she was familiar with from all those years ago, although, now, it seemed richer, stronger.

She cut him off. 'Please, don't apologise. We honestly can forget it ever happened.'

He contemplated this. 'What about if I don't want to forget it happened?' His lips quirked, those lips she longed to kiss again, and again, *and* again. 'I know now isn't really the right time to be telling you this, but I still love you, Jules.' The raw emotion in his voice moved her unbearably and she blinked back a sudden onslaught of tears. 'No matter what, I always will. I just want you to know that,' he added earnestly.

She stopped breathing, unable to answer him for fear of what she wanted to say with all her heart and soul. 'Well, while we're being totally honest with each other …' She halted, trembled, wondered if she was doing the right thing, but the need to tell him the truth, so he knew how much he meant to her, drove her onwards. 'I still love you, too, Joel. Very much.'

'You do?' He gazed at her as if savouring her every word.

'Yes, I do. But that's not enough to make this work between us. There's a lot of water under the bridge, Joel.'

'I know.' He briefly closed his eyes, sucked in a slow, steady breath, and then gave her a rueful glance. 'I shouldn't have given in to how I feel, especially when you're going through a divorce. I'm sorry. I just couldn't help myself.'

'It wasn't entirely your fault, Joel. I kissed you too, and I wanted you too.' She took a few moments to catch her breath and steady her voice.

He drew in another deep breath and then smiled, though a sadness lingered in his gaze. 'So, where do we go from here?'

She thought about it. 'Let's just focus on today. Right now, I'm feeling very blessed to have you here, helping me through the mess I've got myself into.' She smiled. 'Especially seeing as your sister has decided to go gallivanting halfway across the world right when I needed her the most.'

'If she knew how messy it'd all gotten, she'd be back in a flash. You know that, right?'

'Yes, I do. Which is exactly why you can't tell her when you finally get to talk to her.' She sat up. 'I don't want her giving up her dream because of me.'

'Well, I'm glad I can be here for you.' He leant in and gripped her hands, looking at her like no other ever had – as if she was his breath, his reason to live. 'I know I hurt you when I left, Jules, but hopefully now you've spent some time with me, and you understand why I did what I did a little better, you can forgive me and we can move forwards with all that turbulent water under our bridge.'

Momentarily, Juliette found herself lost for words but, desperate to clear the air and make peace, she forced herself to say what she needed to. 'To be honest, to you and to myself, I forgave you a long time ago, Joel.'

'You did?' He looked at her with uncertainty.

She nodded and bit her lip, weighing up what she was about to say next. 'All these years, it's been easier putting all the blame onto you, seeing as you weren't around, but now you're back, and I'm going over everything again …' She sucked in a shuddering breath. '… it's me I'm finding it hard to forgive, for turning my back on you like your father did.'

There was nothing but love in his eyes as he regarded her. 'You had good reason to feel the way you did.'

She picked at the chipped paint on her fingernails. 'Your father thinks he has good reason too.'

'Yeah, I suppose he does, but that doesn't give a father the right to judge as harshly as he has.' Joel clasped his hands behind his head before resting back again. 'If I had a child and they went and did something I didn't condone or understand, I would never turn my back on them, no matter what.'

'I know you wouldn't.' She tried to curb the rising sense of guilt for hurting him, and for not wanting to report what Levi had done to her. 'I'm going to go and visit Mum today, while Malcolm is at his men's club meeting down at the church. I just hope she doesn't blame me for bringing everything to light about his affair with Kathryn.'

'Yeah, it's a common thing for people to want to shoot the messenger when they're confronted with something unpleasant.' He heaved a weighty breath. 'But I have to say, something tells me your mum is going to breathe a sigh of relief once it sinks in.'

'I really hope you're right.' The tears she'd been holding at bay gathered and fell. 'Because once I know she's not living under his roof, I've decided to go to the police with you and tell them everything that mongrel did to us that night.'

'Oh, Jules, are you serious?' He gathered her into his arms, holding her tight. 'I'm so relieved. This is the right thing to do.'

Sniffling, she nodded into his chest. 'I know it is.'

He stroked the back of her head. 'Where do you think your mum will go if she leaves him?'

'I'd say she'd move into the spare room at Aunt Janey's place, above the bakery. She offered it to me when I told her I was leaving Lachlan, but I couldn't move there, not when I have the animals to think of.'

'Yeah, makes it harder with them tagging along,' he replied lightly. 'I don't think Warrior would dig being kept indoors.'

She looked up at him and chuckled. 'It would be a little cramped.'

'Too right.' He raised his brows. 'How 'bout we go and have a cuppa with Mum? She'll love catching up with you, and it might help you take your mind off everything.'

'I'd really love that.' She disentangled from the comfort of his arms and stepped from the bed. 'Do I have time for a shower first, to freshen up?'

'Yeah, of course, go for it.'

Juliette grabbed her towel from where she'd slung it over the corner of the bedroom door. 'You want one too?' She paused in the doorway.

Joel's eyes glinted with mischief. 'With you?'

She tipped her head, grinning. 'No, you cheeky bugger. After me.'

His chuckle was deep and gravelly. 'Nah, I'm right. I'll have one later, when I get home.' He stretched out on the bed, his masculinity so very tempting. 'I'll be right here.'

'Righto, back soon.'

'Take your time,' he said, smiling at her in a way that made her stomach fill with butterflies.

She did, shaving her legs, washing her hair and even taking the time to apply a little tinted moisturiser, mascara and gloss before tugging on her favourite denim shorts and singlet and joining him back in her bedroom. He was a sight to behold, spread out with the sheet kicked off, the ripples of his burly chest donned with artistic ink, the romance novel that had been on her bedside table now in his big, strong hands. He was engrossed in the pages.

'You enjoying that?'

'Uh-huh.' He didn't turn to her, but the quirk of a cheeky smile played on his lips.

Tossing her towel back over the door, she wandered towards him and sat on the edge of the bed. 'What bit are you up to?'

He finally peered over the top of it, wiggling his eyebrows. 'The raunchy bit.' He sat up, closed the pages and placed the book into his lap. 'I reckon I need to start reading books like this. It's not as mushy as I thought it would be, and the main bloke is a real man who even wears an Akubra and rides a horse.'

'Sounds a bit like you, huh?' She toyed with the ends of her hair that she'd swept into a high ponytail.

'Yeah, I suppose so,' he said after a thoughtful moment.

'I know a few blokes that read them, and they're hooked.'

'Well, there you go.' He grinned. 'I feel better, knowing there's more of my kind that like reading them.' Sliding past her, he stood, grabbed his clothes from where he'd tossed them last night, and began getting dressed.

Juliette started making the bed but couldn't help peeking towards him as she did. Carnal images chased through her head, and she ached to shove him back on her bed and have her way with him.

Zipping up his jeans, he flashed her a knowing sideways glance before dragging his T-shirt over his head. 'Busted.' There was a thread of amusement in his tone as he tugged the shirt down over his rock-hard abs.

She grinned despite herself. She wasn't going to deny she was perving. 'Sorry. Can't help it.'

Dressed, he helped her straighten the doona. 'Right back at you.' He eyed her with consuming focus, the tilt of his lips teasing her.

But she wasn't giving in to his charm, or her desire to tear every shred of clothing from him. Even though she blushed from head to toe as the heat of his brazen, blazing stare pressed into her skin, even from the opposite side of the bed. His magnetism was lethal. She swallowed against the shocking surge of heat and quickly busied herself, grabbing her phone and whatever else she could distract herself with. Bed made and pillows fluffed, she slipped on her thongs and they made their way outside into the glorious summer's day.

* * *

Juliette shifted in her seat, folding then unfolding her legs. The way Joel kept glancing at her from where he was leaning up against the butcher's block in the centre of the impressive galley-style kitchen was making her insides crash and tumble.

'Well, I might leave you two lovely ladies to it and go and check in on Dynamite. I want to take him for a bit of a gallop to stretch his legs,' he said casually, draining the last of his coffee. 'You want a hand unpacking once I'm done, Jules?'

'Yeah, that'd be great, thanks, Joel.' The conversation felt unnatural, the undercurrents between them hopefully only noticeable to themselves. 'But make it later this arvo, when I get back from Mum's.'

'No probs, just give me a shout and I'll head over.' He brushed a kiss over his mother's cheek. 'Catch you later, Mum.'

Pausing, Sherrie tipped her head, assessing him like only a mother could. 'It's not like you to wander out without having a shower first thing in the morning, love.'

His mouth kicked up at the corner, but other than that, he remained impressively poker-faced. 'I just thought I'd better check in on Jules first thing, to make sure she was settling in okay.'

'Is that so?' Her lips quirked too, but she allowed the smile to spread as she turned to Juliette. 'Nice of him to think of you straightaway, isn't it, sweetheart?'

It took Juliette a moment to breathe before she could reply. 'Yes, it is. Lovely.' She offered a quivery smile in Joel's direction and, while his mother wasn't looking at him, he pulled an oh-shit-we've-been-busted face. Juliette had to fight from bursting into laughter.

'Anyhow, toodle-loo.' And off he went, his socked feet padding down the hallway followed by the slap of the door. Short moments later, his boots clomped across the verandah and faded as he walked away.

'I really appreciate you and Mr Hunter letting me stay here.' From her place at the dining table, Juliette watched Joel's mum at work. For a homestead with many rooms, this was the place people always gathered, to delight in her cooking.

'Of course, sweetheart. Anything to help out.' Surrounded by mixing bowls, with a smear of flour on her cheek, she was very clearly in her happy place. 'You've always been like a daughter to William and me.'

She smiled softly. 'Thank you, Sherrie. That means a lot.' The scent of the sourdough bread baking in the Aga made her stomach grumble.

'Good Lord, I heard that from here,' Sherrie said with a chuckle. 'Sounds to me like you need feeding.' Placing the last of the plates in the draining rack, she bustled over to the pantry and went up on her tippy toes, plucking her biscuit tin from the shelf. 'Would you like a jam drop cookie to dunk in your tea?'

'Oh, yes, please.' She smiled as Sherrie offered the biscuit tin to her, and she helped herself to two. 'I've really missed this, sitting here with you, drinking cups of tea and chatting. It's sad how time seems to get away from us.' Juliette felt silly, having avoided doing exactly this all these years because she felt guilty it hadn't worked out with Joel.

Sherrie turned and offered Juliette the warmest of smiles. 'Me too, love. More than you know.'

Juliette looked to where the huge bay windows brought the outdoors inside. 'Have you heard anything from Zoe yet?'

'No, but hopefully on the weekend. She did mention it would be a few weeks or so before she'd be able to get to a phone, so I'm not too concerned.'

Joel's father clomped in, bringing with him the lingering scent of grass and horse, with a tinge of manure. 'Oh, hi, Juliette.'

'Howdy, Mr Hunter,' Juliette garbled through a mouthful of jam drop.

'Gee whiz, it's dusty out there today. Just look at the state of me.' He banged his pants, to demonstrate just how dusty it was. 'Can you pop the kettle on, please, Sherrie, I need to wet my whistle before I head back out.'

'Oi, you bugger, I've just finished dusting and don't need the likes of you bringing it all back in with you,' Sherrie replied with a chuckle as she flicked the switch on the kettle.

Juliette loved seeing the two of them together, so compatible and so in love, even after thirty-odd years together. She wanted a love like theirs. A love like Joel gave her, and one she wanted to give him.

'I just had a phone call from Wombat about the fence that was cut.' William's bushy brows furrowed even further as he grabbed the canister of coffee. 'Apparently, someone reported seeing a silver Land Rover Discovery speeding down the road on the same day, around the same time.' He shook his head as he put two teaspoons of sugar in his cup. 'The weird thing is that the only person I know around these parts with a four-wheel drive like that is Levi Muller.'

Juliette's breath hitched in her throat at the name. She fought to remain composed as Joel's father continued. 'This better not have anything to do with Joel being back.'

Juliette was thankful the attention wasn't on her right now. She watched Sherrie, wide-eyed, quickly shake her head.

'Of course it doesn't, William.' Sherrie busied herself grabbing the milk from the fridge. 'Levi Muller is a well-respected man around town, and certainly not someone who would carry a grudge from eleven years ago.'

Juliette's pulse pounded in her ears as she listened. Taking the milk, William regarded his wife. 'You certain of that, Sherrie?'

'My word, I am,' Sherrie shot back, before offering Juliette an apologetic smile as she headed back to the table. 'Sorry, love, you don't need to hear all of that. Now, where were we?'

'Oh, no worries at all.' Juliette glanced at her watch. 'I'd best be off. I'm going to call over and see Mum.' Moving as if she'd been sitting on glass, she gathered her empty cup and went to the sink to rinse it out.

'Oh, okay, love. We'll catch you later on then?' Sherrie looked a little confused but tried to cover it up with a smile.

'Of course.' She brushed a kiss over Sherrie's cheek. 'Thanks for morning tea and the chat. Bye, Mr Hunter,' Juliette said, passing him as he was clanging his teaspoon noisily against his coffee cup, a habit he'd always had.

'Catch you round, Juliette,' he replied before slurping from his coffee, grimacing when he burnt his lip.

'Bye, love,' Sherrie said with a wave.

Her heart in her throat from what she'd just heard and what she was about to do, she headed outside, slipped her thongs back on, and wandered back to the cottage to collect her bag with the photos. Joel had gone and stirred up a hornet's nest. She was fairly certain it *was* Levi Muller who had cut the fence, not that she could prove it. Nor did she have the mindset, or time, to try.

Hopping into her ute, she revved the engine to life and drove on autopilot, the trek to her parents' house taking fifteen minutes because she was driving so slowly. Parking in the shade, she grabbed her handbag and hopped out, smiling when her mother appeared at the front door.

'Hi, sweetheart.'

'Hey, Mum. How are you?' She kissed her cheek.

'Yeah, you know, getting there.' Joan stepped to the side. 'Come in.'

Juliette cringed a little as she stepped inside, the scent of mothballs and Malcolm's pipe tobacco overwhelming her senses. She didn't come here often, as rarely as possible these days. The haunting memories that clung to every corner of the home were the ghosts that kept her away. Putting her imaginary blinkers on, she followed her mum into the kitchen, where two place settings were neatly arranged alongside a pot of tea and two matching cups. She pulled up a chair and sat, as did her mother. A warm, homemade bacon, leek and asparagus quiche – Juliette's favourite – sat at the centre of it all.

'You shouldn't have gone to so much trouble, Mum.'

'Don't be silly. It's not every day my girl comes home to have lunch with me.' Joan smiled, but there was sadness in her eyes.

'I'm sorry, Mum, but you know why that is.' She offered her a meaningful glance.

'Mmhhmm, I most certainly do. One day, I hope you and Malcolm can smooth things over so I don't have to be piggy-in-the-middle,' she said, pouring them both a cup of super strong black tea. She eyed her daughter across the table while cutting generous pieces of quiche. 'So, what do you need to talk to me about?'

Juliette spooned a couple of sugars into her cup. 'A couple of things.'

Joan took her fork and dug in. 'Okay then, go ahead. I'm all ears.'

'I've left Lachlan.' With it having dangled on the end of her tongue for days, Juliette spat it out. She cringed as she waited for her mother's reaction.

'You've done what?' As though only just hearing her, even though a few seconds had passed, Joan straightened, spilling a little of her tea. She grabbed a napkin, mopping it off the table. 'Why would you go and do something so silly, Juliette?'

'Because he wasn't treating me how I should be treated.'

'You know men. Most of the time they don't know how to treat women appropriately. Cut the man some slack.' She sighed, smiling as though that was all Juliette needed to hear to renege on her decision. 'You're financially set for life being there, Juliette. You don't want to throw that away. Believe me, struggle street isn't pretty. I've been there, after your father died, and it was tough. If it wasn't for Malcolm, I don't know what I would have done to make ends meet. We both have a lot to be thankful for in him.'

Juliette had heard this speech a thousand times before, and she was tired of it. 'Malcolm didn't save us, Mum. He made a life of unjustly ridiculing and tormenting us.'

'Juliette, don't start please, not today.' Her mother huffed. 'I just want to enjoy lunch with you, without fighting.'

Juliette swallowed down her hurt, nodding. 'Okay. I'm sorry.'

'So, tell me this. Does you leaving Lachlan have anything to do with Joel being back in town?'

'No, it most certainly does not.' Furious that her own mother would insinuate such a thing, Juliette bit back an eruption of expletives. This wasn't the direction she wanted this conversation to go. 'Did you know that Malcolm pawned me off to the Davises to be Lachlan's wife so you could get this house?'

'Oh, Juliette, what a thing to say.' Joan rolled her eyes. 'Malcolm would never do such a thing.'

Her mother was like an ostrich with its head in the sand when it came to Malcolm. Yet Juliette breathed a silent sigh of relief. It would have damn near killed her if her mother had known all this time. 'Mum, listen to me. It's the truth. He's not a man to be trusted.' Her irritation with her mother's ignorance rising, she plucked the photos from her handbag and pushed them across the table.

'What's this?' Joan sat forwards, placed her cup down, and slowly picked them up. The realisation of what she was looking at played across her face and she covered her mouth. 'Oh my goodness. Malcolm and Kathryn … but she wouldn't … couldn't. She's my friend. And as for Malcolm, I … he …' She glared back at Juliette, as though it was her fault. 'Where on earth did you get these?'

Juliette was dumbfounded, but then, with her mother's sense of obligation to Malcolm bred and fed by his control over her, what had she expected? 'From Lachlan. He's trying to use them to blackmail me, so I don't try to get what's rightfully mine in the divorce.'

Her mum's tear-filled gaze flickered from her, to the photos, to her again. 'I can't believe it. I thought he was happy with me, that he loved me.'

'Mum, a man doesn't inflict pain upon a person when he loves them.' She reached across the table and placed her hand over her mother's. 'You need to start seeing things for what they are, and how toxic your relationship with Malcolm really is.'

Visibly stung and shaken, Joan snatched her hand back and placed it in her lap. 'He doesn't inflict pain on me, he helps me repent my sins. He helped us both. There's a big difference.'

Something in Juliette cracked. 'For god's sake, Mum, snap the hell out of it!'

'Don't you use god's name in vain in this house, Juliette.'

'Sorry.' Juliette paused, drawing in a steadying breath. 'Malcolm's a bastard, and you're letting him unfairly hurt you. And you allowed him to unfairly hurt me, too, when I was beneath this roof.'

'No, I didn't.' Joan's shaky voice wasn't convincing, and neither was the heartfelt pain contorting her face.

Juliette could see she'd hit a raw nerve and, as much as she hated upsetting her mum, she had to run with it. 'Yes, you did. But I don't hold it against you, I hold it against him, for brainwashing you into believing it was okay, that his heavy-handedness is an act of god when it's nothing of the sort, Mum. It's abuse, hands down.' She heaved a desperate breath, allowing her hushed, pale-faced mother a few moments to take it all in. 'I honestly thought this would've made you see sense. You deserve better than him, way better. Just like I deserve better than Lachlan Davis.'

Tight-lipped, Joan turned the photos face down and pushed them back towards Juliette. 'I don't want to know about it.'

'Are you serious?' Juliette sat back, glaring at her mother.

'Yes, I am.' Joan straightened, sniffled, but quickly composed herself. 'Where am I going to go if I'm not here?'

'Go and stay with Aunt Janey for a little while.' At her mother's panic-stricken expression, Juliette felt bad being so forceful, and so hurt and angry, but she couldn't help herself. She had to make her see sense, once and for all. It was for the best, for her mum and for her. And then it hit her like a tonne of bricks. This must be what Joel had felt like, desperately trying to get her to go to the police. The sudden realisation that he had only been doing what he had to in order for her to heal, even in the face of her resistance, overcame her.

Her mother was looking away now, blinking fast. 'But this is the only life I've ever known.'

Juliette nodded gently. 'I know how you feel, Mum, because I've just gone through the very same thing. But you have to take a stand and finally tell Malcolm that you won't let him treat you the way he does.' She went for what she knew her mother would understand – the Ten Commandments. 'And besides all of that, infidelity is a sin.'

'Yes, I know.' A sob broke, and Joan dropped her head in her hands, weeping.

Knowing all too well what she was feeling, Juliette shot to her mother's side and took her into her arms. 'I'm so sorry, Mum. I know it hurts.' She rubbed her back. 'I'm here for you. If you want to leave this life, I will help you, every step of the way. I promise.'

Holding her tight, Joan nodded into her shoulder. They stayed like this for a few moments. Pulling back a little, Joan wiped at her eyes with a tissue she'd grabbed from her pocket. 'Let me go and pack a bag. You can drive me to Janey's before he gets home.'

'Oh, Mum. Thank goodness.' She looked into her mother's fearful gaze. 'You're doing the right thing. He's not going to hurt you anymore. I'm going to make damn sure of it.'

CHAPTER 22

Crickets and frogs chirruped, lured out by the late-afternoon shower. Staring at the star-studded night sky, Juliette ended the phone call with her mum and sucked in a shuddering breath. It had been a long and very emotional day getting her settled at Aunt Janey's. Hopefully time was going to make it easier for all of them. After a venomous phone call from Malcolm, demanding his wife come straight home at once, and her mother courageously standing her ground with Aunt Janey by her side, Juliette could only pray time would help them all heal.

Hearing someone behind her, she turned and looked up to find Joel staring back at her, a tender, adoring smile playing on his lips. 'Hey, you.' Pushing her concerns of the day away, as well as all that lay before her now that secrets were being revealed, she drank him in. 'How long have you been standing there?' she asked softly.

He looked at her for a moment longer, twisting her insides electrifyingly. 'Long enough to fall in love with you even more than I already am.' Settling down beside her on the step, he tucked stray hair behind her ears. 'I thought you could do with one of my famous mochachinos with a twist.' He passed her a steaming cup and wiggled his brows.

'A twist, hey? Cheers.' The warm mug felt good in her hands. She peered down into its frothiness and, taking caution not to burn her mouth, took a tentative sip. 'Wow, it *is* good, I'm impressed. What's the secret ingredient?'

'Lurve … and a little bit of rum.' He slid his arm around her shoulders. 'The least I could do after the stressful day you've had.' He moved his gaze over her like a sweet caress. 'How's your mum doing now?'

'She's an absolute mess, but Aunt Janey's comforting her as best she can.'

'That's good that Janey's there for her. She's a tough woman, your aunt, and your mum is going to need all the support she can get.' He rubbed Juliette's back. 'And how are you feeling?'

'Upset, angry, tired and relieved, in a weird way.' She sighed. 'It's going to be scary, opening up to what happened that night, and then having to stand up in court and say it in front of everyone, but with you by my side, I know I can get through it all.'

He nodded, then offered her a reassuring smile. 'I've got you, Jules.'

'You always have.' She smiled from the inside out. He hadn't shaved for two days, and the rough shadow across his jaw made him all the more rugged. Feeling the hum of electricity deep inside, she fought to control her breath. 'Thank you, for everything.'

'You, Juliette Kern, *are* my everything.' He placed a gentle kiss on the top of her head. 'So, no need to thank me.'

In that very moment, Juliette felt more loved than she ever had. She smiled up at him, and his eyes were like looking into the sun. Searing. Overpowering. For a moment, all she could do was stare, caught between each breathless moment.

'Would you like me to cook us some dinner?' His voice weaved over her, inside of her.

'No, thanks.' She shook her head. 'I'm not really hungry.'

'You have to eat something, Juliette.'

'Wow, Juliette hey? That's when I know you mean business,' she said with a soft chuckle.

'And don't you forget it,' he said with a grin that faded to a look of pure, unconditional, love. 'I wish I could take your heartache away, Firecracker.' He sighed deeply. 'I hate seeing you so torn and upset.'

His intense look lit fires along every inch of her skin. She gently placed a hand upon his chest and smiled through her tears. 'You do take my heartache away, just by being near me.'

'Ditto, beautiful,' he breathed. 'Now, come on back inside and let me whip you up something yummy.'

'Oh, okay then,' she said, standing, enjoying the way he led her, insistently but playfully, inside the cottage with Brute at their feet.

Five minutes later, the microwave beeped and he passed her a mug of pea and ham soup.

'This smells delish.' Her belly rumbled at the thought of tucking in.

'Told you I could cook, even if it's frozen leftovers from my sister's deep freeze.' His smile shivered through her, right down to her toes, as he popped his mug into the microwave and it beeped into action.

Half an hour later, their bellies full, and the pair of them relaxing on the couch watching telly, Juliette snuggled in closer to Joel, though she was more interested in him than the cooking show he seemed engrossed in. As though privy to her thoughts, he took her hand in his and casually brought her fingers to his lips, trailing a soft kiss over them. Then he brought his lingering gaze, filled with promise, closer until they were a mere breath apart, leaving his delectable mouth just shy of hers.

'We shouldn't.' Caught in the moment, her breath became ragged, as if she'd just run a mile.

'Yes, we should,' he breathed as he leant in, claiming her lips in a no-holds-barred kiss. A plethora of fireworks exploding inside of her, Juliette let herself tumble, so wrapped up in him, the world could have fallen apart around her and she wouldn't have even noticed.

* * *

Joel hardened in response to her quickened breath, to her demanding touch. Who had he been trying to fool, telling himself he could be her friend and be happy with so little of her? Her hair smelt of sunshine and flowers, her skin felt like silk. When she'd leant in and he'd kissed her, there'd been no going back. Her lips were soft and sweet against his and as she paused for breath, dizzy with their kiss, her eyes were hot on his. The passion within them aroused a primal need and he realised he'd rather die than not make love to her. His hunger for her was relentless. He wanted to touch her, taste her, all over, with adoring savagery.

Desire, warm and sweet, spread through him like wildfire. Her desperate touch was his undoing. Capturing her hips, he dragged her to him, his mouth meeting hers demandingly. She returned his kiss, quivering beneath his touch as he circled his tongue around hers. Pulling her from the couch, he slid her to the floor with him, upon the sheepskin rug. He positioned himself so they were side by side, her arms and legs entwined around him as he strained his body against hers. She curved into him so perfectly, as if made for him, and him for her. They were meant to be. Always had been.

Teasing where her nipples pushed beneath the thin cotton of her dress, he smiled. 'You have too many clothes on.' His voice was thick, raspy with desire.

'So do you,' she breathed while pulling his T-shirt from him. Then she helped him out of his jeans with a rapacious insistence.

Blazing hunger raged through him as he helped her wriggle out of her dress and she moaned low in her throat, driving him on, driving him wilder. But then, in unison, they slowed, lingered in their touches, and gazed at one another, unfathomable love passing wordlessly between them.

'My god, you're magnificent, Jules.'

'Ditto, Joel Hunter. In every single way.'

'I need to be one with you.' He urgently sought out her lips once more, and she arched into him as he slid his lips down her throat, over her breasts, pausing to savour her nipples, grazing his teeth over them before taking a downward trail.

Juliette writhed beneath him, moaning. 'Please, Joel. I want you. Now.'

Craving to give her what she wanted, what he wanted so badly, unhurriedly he slid within her, inch by glorious inch, until they finally became one. And then he was lost, drowning in her, their lovemaking beyond anything he'd imagined. Nothing else, except him and Juliette, existed. The entire world had faded away, leaving just him and her, here, loving one another in the way he'd craved for what felt like forever. Her cries of pleasure were like a spark to his soul, and a flood of heat swept through him as he matched her thrusts, and together they climbed the pinnacle and tumbled, blissfully, breathlessly, over the euphoric edge.

* * *

Bed hair extraordinaire and her sleeping eye-mask still in place, the suddenness of her alarm had Juliette leaping from the bed. Running blind, she stumbled over the pile of clothes on the floor, kicked her toe on god-only-knew what, and barely stopped herself from hitting the floor when she grabbed hold of the dressing table, knocking everything on top of it over in the process. A quick warning bark let her know Brute had been caught up in the mayhem.

'Sorry, buddy,' she said, his soft padding paws fading off down the hallway as he escaped the madness. She needed to let him out for toilet duties. Pronto.

Groaning while slipping her lavender scented eye-mask to the top of her head, she pulled her knickers from where they'd crept into her butt and straightened her skew-whiff tank top. A note from Joel sat upon the bedside table with a bright red hibiscus flower resting beside it. She tucked the flower behind her ear as she plucked the note up and, grinning like a lovesick teenager, read it.

Good morning, gorgeous. Sorry I had to slip out early, I
didn't want to wake you. I'll catch you a little later on and
we can pick up where we left off, before falling asleep. ;)
Love you, Joel. Xx

Wandering down the hallway, she drifted on the lingerings of
the erotic night. High on Joel, she let a very antsy Brute out to
relieve himself before she found herself in the shower with no real
idea how she'd gotten there. The tenderness of Joel's touch, the
hunger of his mouth, the ecstasy of his fierce yet gentle possession
of her – she'd been helpless against the powerful tide of passion
rushing back and forth between them. Humming to herself, she
grabbed the bar of soap and ran it over her body, recalling how
he'd kissed almost every inch of it.

Stepping from the shower, she towelled off, suddenly feeling
guilty for what Joel had gone through with his father, and all
because of her fear of Malcolm. She could see the pain in Joel's
eyes, the storms he'd raged against to keep her secret, but not for
much longer. She needed to make things right. For him. For them.
For herself. So she could be whole again, and so she didn't follow
in her mother's footsteps by ignoring what was right in front of
her all this time. Joel was right. Without answers or closure, the
deep wounds in her were still open, still bleeding. But before she
went to the police with him, she had to face her demons head-on.

Dressed in a few minutes, she was in her car before she knew it,
drenched almost through to the skin after having to run through
the rain. Her windscreen wipers thrashing madly, she wriggled
in the driver's seat as she sped along the highway, a woman on a
mission if she'd ever been one. It didn't take her long to get to her
first stop. Pulling up out front of the building, she cut the engine

and slowly exhaled. Her fingers gripped the steering wheel so tightly they cramped. The darkness in her stirred. Her blood boiled and her pulse raced out of control. She was furious and terrified. Even so, she stepped out, marched towards the door, and stepped inside.

Relieved the waiting room was empty, she tried to smile at the receptionist. 'Can I see Doctor Muller, please?'

'Sorry, but the doctor is a little busy right now. Is it urgent?'

'Yes, it is.' Juliette's chest tightened, as did the fists shoved into the pockets of her jacket. 'Does he have a patient with him?'

'No,' the receptionist answered warily.

'Good, then he's free to see me.' Juliette choked down the lump in her throat. She had this. She could do this. Without a second's hesitation, she shoved the door open and stormed into his office like a heat-seeking missile.

Levi Muller paled before her eyes. 'Juliette, what are …?'

The very sight of him sent a jolt through her so savage she almost stumbled as the small room closed in on her. 'Are you really going to ask me what I'm doing here?'

'Yes, I am,' he said through gritted teeth. 'I don't want you here, so that means you're trespassing.' Forceful and egotistical, he was infuriatingly sure of himself.

Shards of hostility crackled through the air. She sucked in a breath and dove, headfirst. 'Joel is right, you need to pay for what you've done to me, and to him.' Slamming her hands down on his desk, she levelled her stare into his muddy brown gaze, noticing with satisfaction the fear etched into it. 'And so help me god, I'm going to make you pay.'

'I wouldn't if I were you, Juliette.' His eyes narrowed and a thin, sly smile slashed across his face. Running hands through his fiery red hair, he rose and took steps towards her.

As spine-tinglingly fearful as she was of him, of the hands that had torn at her clothes and had tried to strip her of her virginity, she stood her ground. 'Don't try and intimidate me because I'm not scared of you.' She stood stock-still, tall and confident. She refused to give him the satisfaction of sensing her utter terror.

'As I said to Joel, the police aren't going to believe your story for a second.' He folded his arms and rested back against his desk. 'So save your breath and stop wasting your time, and mine, playing this stupid little game.'

'Oh yes they will believe us. We have evidence.' She instantly regretted saying so but ran with it. 'Damning evidence at that.'

'I don't believe you.' Although his shoulders lifted in a heavy shrug, something in his gaze shifted.

'I don't care if you don't believe me.' She swallowed down the fear threatening to close her windpipe. 'The police will.'

Levi rolled his eyes and sighed. 'It was so long ago, Juliette, when we were all young and stupid. Can't you just let it go and get on with your life?'

'Being young and stupid is no excuse for trying to rape me.' It was said with way more conviction than she felt right now. 'You lowlife son of a bitch.'

'I didn't rape you.' He almost laughed but stopped himself. 'You stupid girl.'

His indifference about something so tragic, so life-altering, blew her away, but what had she expected from a man like him? Before she burst into tears, or punched him in the face, or both, she spun in her boots and stormed out the open door, past the shocked receptionist, who she was sure as hell had just heard everything, and into the sunshine. And then, to her surprise and relief, she took the first deep breath in what felt like eleven long years.

One demon slayed, one to go.

She climbed back into her ute, reversed out, and headed towards another place she'd avoided like the plague. She drove on autopilot, not allowing herself the luxury of changing her mind. Ten minutes later, pulling around the side of the house, she spotted his car. Panic, fuelled by her living nightmare, fired her already racing pulse into a wild frenzy. But unlike every other time she'd thought she was courageous enough to do this, then chickened out, or used the fact she didn't want her mother to cop his wrath, she had no excuses. She wasn't running away. Just like facing up to Levi, she could do this – she had to. She wanted to be whole again, to be all of the woman she knew she could be, for herself, and for Joel.

Striding towards the patio, she stopped at the front door and raised her hand to knock, but was startled when it shot open and fierce eyes glared out at her.

'What in the hell are you doing here?' Her mammoth of a stepfather stepped out, leaving only a few inches between them. 'It's all because of you that Joan has left, sticking your nose where it isn't welcome.'

Intimidated but determined, Juliette swallowed down her fear and looked up into the eyes she hated. Her breathing laboured as she tried to piece together everything she'd rehearsed, but she was failing to open her dry mouth.

'Well?' he roared, making her jump. 'What have you got to say for yourself, girly?'

She took a little step back, considered making a run for her ute, but stopped herself, just. Hands fisted at her sides, she finally found her courage and her voice. 'How *dare* you pawn me off to Ronald and Margery Davis to get this house.'

He shrugged, smirking. 'Well, it worked a treat, didn't it?'

Juliette had to stop herself from slapping him across the face – it wouldn't end well if she did. Red rage washed over her, and she glared at him through slits, her teeth gritting hard and her fingernails digging into her palms. 'I hate you, Malcolm. For all that you've done to me, and to my mother. It's your own fault she left, and about time she did. You're an evil man, a cheater and a sinner, and she deserves better.'

His burly arms folding across his quickly rising and falling chest, he seemed to get bigger before her eyes. He leant into her space, an inch from her face. 'What did you just say to me?' Then, not waiting for a response, he straightened and began to pull his belt from the loops of his trousers.

Terror gripping her, Juliette turned and ran. Jumping into her ute, she locked the door, and only then did she dare to look back. He skidded to a stop at her door and bashed on her window, his contorted face the epitome of malevolence.

'Open this damn door, Juliette, or …'

She revved the ute to life and took off down the driveway, gravel flying out behind her and the tail end swaying. Sobbing, she glanced into her rear-vision mirror to watch him quickly fade away, the belt hanging from his fisted hand. He was a bully and a coward – a man who hid behind his cloak and the walls of that house. When she went to see Wombat at the police station with Joel this afternoon and told him what Levi had done that night, she was also going to tell him about Malcolm and the hell she and her mother had lived in for all her life. She wasn't sure anything could be done about it, but at the very least, Malcolm would be chased from the church, and this township, once word got out – and around here, that wouldn't take long.

CHAPTER

23

It was close to ten and Juliette was fighting to keep her eyes open. The four hours she and Joel had spent with Wombat down at the station, giving their statements, and sitting there while he'd listened to the recording Joel had got of Levi confessing, had been even more exhausting than she'd expected. Now, curled up on Joel's couch with a blanket tossed over her lap, and Brute rolled into a ball beside her, another yawn had her stretching her arms high. Through bleary eyes, she watched Joel pottering in the kitchen, making them toasted ham and cheese sandwiches and tea. She still found it hard to believe she was here, with him, feeling so loved, so cared for, so protected, while Levi Muller was spending his very first night behind bars. But it was only the beginning. Wombat counselled them to be ready for the next couple of weeks – the courtroom was going to be gruelling. It made her even more exhausted just thinking about it. Gently manoeuvring Brute, she stretched out and closed her eyes, just for a few moments …

'Jules, baby, wake up.'

'Hey?' she muttered, trying to force open sleep-heavy eyelids. Joel was kneeling down beside the couch, his hand resting on her hip. 'Dinner is served.' He gestured to the coffee table, where two toasted sandwiches and two steaming mugs waited.

Shaking the sleepy fog from her mind, she slowly sat up, swung her feet to the floor and eased over so Joel could sit beside her.

'You feeling okay?' Worry laced his tender tone.

She nodded. 'I feel like I've been run over by a truck, and then reversed over for good measure, but I also feel like a huge weight has been lifted from my shoulders and my heart now that everything is out in the open.' She raised her brows. 'Well, other than the fact Lachlan cheated on me with another man, that is. I don't think it's necessary to reveal that bit of the story. We'll leave that to fate to figure out.'

'You're a good person, Jules, keeping it to yourself for the sake of a man who doesn't deserve it. And I'm super proud of you, facing up to everything today, although …' Grim lines etched the sides of his mouth. '… you really should have taken me with you to see Levi and Malcolm. Anything could have happened to you,' he said in his strong, sure voice.

'Yes, you're right, but it didn't.' She offered him a gentle smile – he was only worried for her. 'Please don't take it personally. I just needed to do it on my own. And I knew if I told you, you would have tried to stop me.'

'Damn straight I would have. Okay, I'll try not to take it personally.' He shifted a little, his mouth twisting into the smallest of smiles. 'I can only imagine how you're feeling right now.'

When Joel passed her the plate with her toasted sandwich, Juliette's mouth watered. 'You're going through it all too, Joel. Don't forget.' She gave him a loving, thankful smile before tucking in.

'Yeah, in a way, but it's you that's living every second of it, and it's you that had to relive the fear of what Levi did to you.'

'I felt ...' She grimaced. '... I don't know if it's the right word, but ... a little *dirty*, telling Wombat what happened that night in such minuscule detail, but then I know, in time, by seeking the justice we deserve, it will help me heal.' She took a sip from her tea. 'And it's going to help your relationship heal with your father too.'

'Yeah, I hope so.' Joel swallowed his mouthful of food. 'Are you going to be okay, having to go over it all again with my parents tomorrow morning?'

'Of course. I'm actually keen to see how your father will react once he knows the truth of just how brave and protective his son really is.' She tenderly placed her hand on Joel's cheek. 'Everything's working out, for all of us.'

'It sure is.' He smiled from ear to ear. 'Who would have thought, when I came back here, that you and I would be together again?'

'It's a dream come true,' Juliette said with an equally big smile.

'Ain't it ever?' Placing their empty plates back on the table, Joel pulled her to him and kissed her. 'I don't ever want to live another day without you by my side.'

'Ditto, my beautiful man.' Needing to be closer still, Juliette straddled him and wrapped her arms around his neck. Her robe fell open a little, revealing her naked body beneath the silky fabric. His gaze drinking all of her in, Joel slid his hands beneath it and over her bare skin, igniting heat with the suggestive trail of his fingertips. Juliette ached to ravish him as she felt him harden beneath her.

He tilted his head up to look at her, smouldering fire in his eyes. 'I need to show you how much I love you.' He undid her hair from the careless twist at the nape of her neck.

'I'd like that very, very much.' She arched into him a little more and leant into his ear. 'You're my absolute everything, Joel Hunter,' she said in a breathless whisper.

His hands gripped her hips and, standing, he took her with him, across the lounge and up the stairs that spiralled to his bedroom. His eyes remained hard on hers as he eased them both onto the bed.

Pausing, Joel smiled. 'I have something I need to ask you.' His gaze blazed with the same fire she felt for him deep within her soul.

He looked worried, and she found herself holding her breath. 'What is it?'

Leaning across her, he tugged his bedside drawer open and then, pulling her up to sit with him, opened the tiny box, revealing the engagement ring he'd offered to her all those years ago. 'Juliette Kern, my little firecracker, my soul lover, my best friend, my world, will you be my wife?'

Tears sprang and she let them fall as she covered her gaping mouth. 'Oh my goodness, Joel. Yes, yes, yes!' She held her hand out and he slipped the ring onto her finger. Antique and filled with so much significance, this ring was much more beautiful to her than the one that used to rest there. She regarded him through her teary gaze, loving the way he looked the happiest she'd ever seen him. 'I love you, so much.'

'I love you too, Jules.' He took her hand in his, gazing at the ring, his thumb rubbing her hand. 'I completely understand you're not officially a divorced woman, but as soon as you are, my beautiful fiancée …' He raised his eyes to her. 'You and me are getting hitched.' He pulled her to him and kissed her like he could never get enough of her.

Juliette's heart sang the most beautiful of tunes. Joel had just made her the happiest woman alive. Her fingers itched to run through his hair while she kissed his generous mouth, long and deep. In the space of a heartbeat, she gave in to him, tumbling into his embrace, his hungry caresses making her heart skip and skitter. Her breathing out of control, she locked her arms tighter around him, his groan of pleasure driving her on, making her want him all the more. She reached down between them and released him from his jeans, revelling in his manliness. Stroking the silky smoothness of his longing for her made her ache for him all the more. She tipped him backwards, raised her hips, angled herself and sank down, driving him deep inside of her, unable to bite back a moan. He moved with her and she surrendered to him as his hands traced the curve of her hips and her back, before lacing into the loose hair at the nape of her neck.

He rose up and took a nipple into his mouth, teetering her on the edge between pain and pleasure. She could barely catch her breath as she arched further into him. Succumbing to her silent pleading, his thrusts became harder, hungrier, deeply satisfying. The madness of tumbling off the erotic abyss gripped her tighter and tighter as he took control, taking them to where they both needed to be. The blazing fire built between them as she trembled then grabbed him as she made a low sound of surrender, quivering and falling even further in love with him.

Sated, she collapsed into him, and he rolled her over, easing himself on top of her. The weight of him, warm and solid, made her softly sigh as happy tears stung her eyes – ones filled with relief and gratitude for this magnificent man. He held her close, loving her without a word needing to be spoken, more deeply than she'd ever felt. A tragedy had pulled them apart, and now fate had brought them back together, stronger and more in love than ever. She was never going to leave his side, and as she pondered this beautiful notion, she drifted and then slipped into a satisfied slumber.

It was pouring buckets when she woke hours later, close to midnight, the heavy drops crashing on the corrugated roofing of the barn like bullets. Finding Joel gone, she slipped from the bed, tugged her robe back on, and made her way down the staircase. She found him in his office nook. Watching him from the doorway, his feet up on the desk and his handsome face aglow from the brightness of his laptop, Juliette felt her heart and soul stir. He was a whole lotta man. And the best thing was, he was all hers. Her heart skipped a few beats with the very thought.

She padded in quietly and placed a hand upon his neck, massaging the knots with her fingers. Joel groaned and pressed back into her hand, his eyes closed.

'You like that?' she purred.

'Yes, I most certainly do.' Casting a dreamy look upwards, he smiled. 'You. Are. Amazing.'

'Ditto, Mr Hunter.' She leant over and gave him an upside-down kiss. 'And just for the record, I can't wait to become Mrs Hunter.'

'You're not the only one,' he said, flashing her his knee-buckling dimple-clad grin.

His mobile phone rang from the desk, making both of them jump.

Spotting the caller ID, he snatched it up. 'Hey, Mum, is everything okay?' Juliette watched his face grow grave with concern as he nodded. 'Okay. I'll be there real soon.' He ended the call and sucked in a shuddering breath.

Juliette moved to stand in front of him, fear gripping her insides. 'Joel, what's happened?'

'Dad's been rushed to hospital. He's had a minor stroke.' Joel was as pale as a ghost. 'He started slurring, and then he couldn't focus on anything. Mum wanted to call an ambulance, but you know my old man, he wouldn't let her and insisted she drive him to the hospital. By the time they got there, he was apparently real bad.'

'Oh my god. Is he going to be okay?'

He nodded, very slowly, as if unsure. 'Mum said they've got him on a drip with some clot-busting medication, and apparently he's out of danger for now, so that's a relief.' He grabbed his LandCruiser keys from beside his laptop. 'Talk about everything happening at once.'

'Murphy's law.' Juliette placed her hand on his back. 'Do you mind if I come in with you?'

He cupped her cheeks and held her gaze. 'Of course not. It would mean a lot to me, and to Mum and Dad, having you there.'

'I'll just go and throw some clothes on. Won't be a sec.' And she dashed back upstairs, as did he, both of them dressing in record time before rushing out the door and to Little Heart Hospital.

* * *

Reaching the hospital, Joel strode towards the front sliding doors with Juliette's fingers tightly interlaced within his. The scent of steriliser and the squeak of the linoleum floors beneath their shoes greeted them, as did his mother, near the reception desk.

'Hey, Mum.' He hugged her, kissing her cheek. His already laboured breath caught in his throat as he met her worried, red-rimmed gaze. 'How is he?'

'He's not getting any worse, so that's a positive.' She brushed a hand down Juliette's arm, a silent gesture of gratitude. 'I don't want either of you to be shocked when you see him.' She sucked in a sharp breath, her eyes teary. 'He looks pretty bad, love, with one side of his face a little droopy, but that's to be expected, the doctor said, and apparently, in time, it can improve.'

'Well, that's a good thing, right?' A huge lump formed in Joel's throat as the reality of the situation hit him, damn hard. He swallowed it back. He had to be strong for Juliette and his mother, as well as his father. 'Can I go in and see him?'

'Yes, of course.' Sherrie started walking down the deserted hallway. 'His room is just down the end of this corridor.'

Joel's breath caught in his throat as he and Juliette followed his mum. William Hunter was a proverbial shadow of himself, and even though his mother had tried to prepare him, it was a shock to the system. He'd never seen his father looking so weak, so vulnerable, as if all the life had been drained from him. A drip in his arm, machines beeping beside him, and his eyes closed, he almost looked dead. On the opposite side of the bed, Juliette's arm went comfortingly around his mum's shoulder. He blinked fast as he looked to them, and his mother gave him a sympathetic smile. He dropped his gaze to the floor, needing a few moments to gather himself. Nobody said a word as he took a few deep breaths.

His dad stirred, shifted a little in the bed. 'Sherrie.' He blinked open heavy eyelids. 'Are you here?'

'Yes, love.' Joel watched his mum step to his father's side, placing a gentle hand upon him. 'I'm here, and so are Joel and Juliette.'

He looked up at her with a soft, favouring smile. 'They are?' His gaze drifting over the room, William turned his face to Joel, Juliette now by him. A small smile curled his lips. 'Hi, son,' he said, slowly.

'Hey, Dad.' The droops of his father's lip and cheek were extremely confronting. Joel sank into the chair beside the bed for fear of buckling to his knees. 'How are you feeling?' Juliette was rubbing his back, and it was helping him stay somewhat centred and calm.

'I've been better,' his father said with a soft chuckle. 'But, on the plus side, god's kept me alive to fight another day.'

'Yes, yes he has,' Joel said with gratitude spilling from his heart. To lose his father before they'd made amends would have been devastating. 'I'm so glad you're going to be okay, Dad.' He choked back a sob, unable to hold it at bay as a few tears sprang. He sniffed and quickly wiped them away.

'Oh, Joel.' With gentle, caring eyes, his father lifted a hand, reaching for him, the gesture making it impossible for Joel to keep it together. More tears built and rolled down his cheeks as he took his father's hand within his.

'I love you, son,' William said, his voice croaky.

'I love you too, Dad. So much.' Joel watched his mum cover her heart with her hands, tears falling.

His father broke too, and wept. 'I'm so sorry for turning my back on you. I never should have done that.'

Joel couldn't believe what he was hearing and, although relieved to hear it, he didn't want his dad wasting energy on him. 'Don't worry about it now, Dad. Focus on getting better, okay? Because we all want you back home.'

William nodded and gave Joel's hand a squeeze. 'You're a good boy. I'm proud of you.'

'That means everything to me, Dad.' Joel felt a comforting hand on his shoulder and he turned around to see Juliette giving him a warm and encouraging smile through her tears.

To be forgiven and loved, even before his father knew the truth of it all, was more than Joel could have ever wished for. With his parents near him and Juliette by his side wearing the ring he'd longed to slip upon her finger, his dreams had come true.

CHAPTER

24

Four months later

Juliette woke with a start, her heart beating its way into her throat. Today was the day they'd been waiting for. Cuddled up beside her, Joel tenderly soothed her, his soft whispers all she needed to her racing pulse. Blinking heavy eyes, she looked to the glow of the bedside clock for what felt like the umpteenth time – exactly four hours and twenty-three minutes, and they'd be back in court to hear the verdict. She was losing herself in Joel's rhythmic breath as he drifted back to sleep when a flash of lightning through the crack in the curtains followed a boom of thunder. With Joel not stirring, she tried to stay still. He was absolutely exhausted after the events of the past few months; with day after day of court and helping with his father's recovery, he needed his sleep. It was wonderful to see William and Joel closer than they'd ever been, the knowledge of why Joel had done what he had to Levi only adding to William's desire to make things right between them.

The rain came stealthily at first, a drop here, a drop there, tapping on the leaves of the big old gum outside the window and popping off the corrugated roof over the back verandah. Slipping from Joel's arms and their bed, she wandered over to peer outside. A sudden gust of wind shook the shrubbery and blew the rain in slanted rivulets across the drive, sending a fine spray across her face. A deluge of rain, as if the storm was directly upon the barn, swiftly followed with another deafening clap of thunder, as if god had just upended a lake from the sky. She quietly shut the window and crept from the room and down the stairs, adoring the way Brute was curled up on his rug, with Red settled on his perch beside him. He was the most overconfident yet loveable rooster she'd ever met. It was endearing how the mismatched pair had become the best of friends.

Shutting herself in the bathroom, with a candle lit, she turned the tap and filled the bathtub. The water was deliciously hot and steaming, and she slipped beneath it while trying to empty her mind. As she'd predicted, it soothed her aching muscles and helped ease her worries. Nearly half an hour later, with the bathwater cooling, she slipped out, dried off and tugged Joel's fluffy robe around her, loving how his scent still lingered upon it. How she loved him so. She held up her hand and admired the symbol of their love, his grandmother's beautiful engagement ring, now hers.

Amongst the angst of their lives, there were so many blessings to be thankful for, and she pondered them as she dried her hair. Levi had been arrested for a long list of offences – assault, attempted rape, intimidation with intent to cause harm against Ben, along with the charge of tampering with William's fence.

It had taken an immense amount of courage for Ben to come forth with the video he'd kept all these years of that horrible night in all its graphic detail. The amount of bullying and intimidation the poor bloke had endured at the hands of the Muller boys had been heartbreaking to hear in court.

The way the townspeople had rallied around her and her mother, and Joel and Ben, gave Juliette immense peace and helped her sleep at night. The church community had essentially chased Malcolm from town after shunning and shaming him, and her mum was tentatively enjoying her newfound freedom as a single and very safe woman. And to top it all off, Juliette's lawyer had been able to find a loophole in the pre-nup, giving her exactly what she was entitled to from her marriage with Lachlan. Lachlan and his parents were none too happy about it, but there was nothing they could do – the law was the law. She had let people know he'd had an affair, and that was the reason she'd left, but nothing else. Not that his infidelity had hampered his cause – Lachlan was now the very proud town mayor and, with everything aside, he was doing a lot of good for the community, and Juliette had found it in her heart to be happy for him. All in all, things had worked out better than she'd hoped or expected the day she'd decided to leave him. And the icing on the cake was that she was going to marry her childhood sweetheart, the love of her life, and they were going to have the family they'd always dreamt of.

Emerging from the steam of the bathroom, she headed down the hall to the kitchen, where she planned to make herself a hot chocolate as well as a coffee and some scrambled eggs on toast for Joel. Breakfast in bed was one of his favourite things and he deserved to be spoilt. She flicked on the overhead light – sunshine should have been glittering through the bay window by now, but the ominous clouds had stolen the sky. With the rain still drumming upon the roof, it blurred the glass of the windows, the breeze pushing its way between the cracks. She hoped the storm cleared before they had to head back down to the Cairns District Court. The Kuranda Range was a shocker in the wet. Although nervous, she couldn't wait to hear what the jury had decided.

* * *

Joel woke with a start and stared at the shadows that crept about his walls and ceiling. Thunder grumbled in the far-flung distance and the scent of rain filled the air. With Juliette gone from their bed, and the smell of toast and coffee wafting up the stairs, his belly rumbled. That, and his longing to kiss her good morning, had him swinging his legs over the side of the bed. Images of the previous night swept through his mind, hardening him in an instant. A demanding, generous lover, Juliette was all he'd imagined her to be, and more. He was totally sated and, from her pleasure-filled cries, he gathered that she too was satisfied.

As he pulled on some boxers and a T-shirt, he contemplated the day ahead. Even though they had damning evidence, the legal system could still be a gamble – corruption and underhanded payouts were rife within what should have been a system for the victims, not the criminals. He didn't trust Levi or his scheming solicitor. Tension coiling like a spring within him, he said another silent prayer as he rubbed a hand over the rough stubble along his jaw. He'd have to make sure to shave this morning. But first, he wanted to go and shower his beautiful fiancée with the love she so deserved.

* * *

Almost seven hours later, they sat amongst their family and friends in the crowded courtroom. Television crews had come in hordes to hear the outcome of the highly publicised case. Offering her a look of support, he held Juliette's hand, and she squeezed his fingers tight, her anxious expression the epitome of what he was feeling inside. On the opposite side of him, his father rested a reassuring hand upon his back and his mum offered him a comforting glance. Ben and his parents sat in the seats behind them, and he turned to offer Ben a reassuring smile. Ben, now looking more like the man Joel remembered, nodded in return. His life was on the road to better things.

The judge looked to the prosecutor, Valerie Shaw. 'You may proceed to close.'

Valerie stood, straightening her skirt before stepping out from behind the desk and stopping two feet short of the jury box. 'Ladies and gentlemen. You've heard from the witnesses, and from Miss Kern. You have seen the irrefutable evidence, so please, do not allow your judgement to be clouded by the defence's very clever, and very misguided, declarations.' Valerie flashed Levi's lawyer a solemn glare as she marched past him in her skyscraper heels, her strides deliberately measured.

Joel felt a certain kind of relief with her on their side. It had been a gruelling few weeks, theirs and Ben's sworn testimonies being dragged over the coals. But the prosecutor's delivery was faultless, her pauses punctuating her declarations of guilt on all the charges, and her lengthy, meaningful looks to the jury holding their attention, each juror clearly hanging on her every word.

After a long pause, Valerie continued. 'I trust you are all going to do the right thing, the just thing.' Valerie's sharp eyes scanned over the men and women of the jury. 'Juliette Kern deserves justice, as does her fiancé, Joel Hunter.'

Watching her take her seat again, the sting of emotion almost overwhelmed Joel. Over the other side of the courtroom, a sly smile was itching to spread across Levi's face. Jackson Muller would be facing his charges of being an accomplice at a different time. Levi's shrewd lawyer tried to desensitise the jury to the horrendousness of the crime by repeating, over and over, how it was, in fact, an *attempted* rape, reminding them how much of an asset to the community Levi had been, and still was, how he'd repented after losing his brother, Desmond, in the car accident, and how he was no longer the senseless boy who'd committed the attack all those years ago.

The judge and Valerie shared a brisk nod, and he brought his gavel down. 'We will have a recess to allow the jury to reach their verdict. Court will adjourn until then.'

They'd been warned the verdict could take some time but, before Joel knew it, he and Juliette were back in their seats, breaths held, pulses racing, as they watched the lead juror stand, ready to deliver their verdict.

'Ladies and gentlemen of the jury.' The judge looked towards the middle-aged woman. 'I understand you have reached a verdict?'

She nodded. 'Yes, we have, your honour.'

The judge nodded. 'Would you please give the verdict to the court so it can be read out.'

The bailiff approached her, took the paper, and then handed it over to the judge.

The judge stared at Levi, his steely gaze unrelenting. 'The defendant will please rise.'

Levi did as he was told. Joel glanced over to where Bluey, Nugget and Curly were seated at the back of the courtroom. He was honoured the three of them had made the long trek here to support him and Juliette.

The judge took a moment to adjust his glasses, and then proceeded. 'We, the jury, find the defendant, Levi Rodger Muller, guilty of all charges.'

There was a collective gasp as Joel and Juliette shared a look of elation coupled with relief.

Joel took great satisfaction as he watched the shadow of defeat fall upon Levi's face as a murmur of voices quickly led to a loud commotion.

The judge forcefully gavelled the courtroom back into order. Then, addressing Levi, his face was unsympathetic. 'The defendant is bound over to sentencing, and will be remanded in custody until then, without the option for bail.' He smacked the gavel down. 'This court is adjourned.'

Now free to say and do as they wished, Juliette reached up on her tippy toes and met Joel's lips in a quick kiss. 'I'm so relieved it's over.' All strength had left her voice as her gaze pleaded with him to hold her.

And so he did. As he hugged Juliette to him, she sobbed tears of both joy and relief against his chest.

* * *

The blaring of the alarm clock she'd forgotten to turn off had Juliette bouncing from her bed, still half asleep. Slapping it into silence, she dragged a hand through her sexed-up bed hair. It had been a wild night between the sheets, a celebration of sorts. A coy smile grabbed her lips as she recalled Joel, atop her, doing things she'd never imagined. Oh god, how she loved this man of hers. She flung the curtains open, squinting into the glorious sunshine, admiring Warrior and Dynamite grazing in their paddock. Just like Brute and Red, the two horses had become the best of mates. She drew in a deep breath, smiling. Less than a week had passed since the guilty verdict and the sentence had been handed down. Levi was going to prison for seven years. The anguish of the court case, and of that fateful night, was no longer shadowing their footsteps.

She raced down the stairs and breezed into the kitchen, a spring in her step. 'Good morning, my sexy, yummy fiancé.'

Joel smiled at her over the rim of his Aquarius cup. 'Good morning, Firecracker. How'd you sleep?' He pushed his chair back, gesturing for her to straddle him.

She didn't need any more of an invitation. As she got comfortable, she wrapped her arms around his neck and kissed him. The skill of his mouth and his touch made her nipples grow hard and as she rested back a little, she couldn't help but notice he was having trouble keeping his eyes on hers.

'You right there, Mr Hunter?' She glanced down to where he was looking and back at him, grinning.

'I can't help it. You're captivating.' Mischief lurked within his gaze.

She melted into him, loving the feeling of his body pressed up against her own. His mouth captured hers again, the sweep of his tongue, hot and hungry, fanning the flames of her desire.

'I want to make love to you, Jules.'

Her senses quivered. 'Now?'

'Yes, now.' His fingers moved to the hem of her singlet, his gaze intensifying as he lifted it to reveal her breasts.

Searing passion gripped her as he lowered his head, and she found herself groaning in pleasure as his tongue slipped over her taut nipple, and his teeth teetered her on the border of pleasure and pain. Hungry for him, for the pleasures she knew he could bestow upon her, she pulled his shirt up and over his head. He lifted her and stood, and they tore at each other's clothes, leaving a trail as they headed back upstairs. Falling to the bed, he gripped her hips and took her with him. He positioned himself so she was beneath him and she wrapped her legs around him, tangling her fingers in his hair. Usually so teasingly slow, this time he slid into her greedily, and she matched him thrust for thrust, crying out as he brought her close, and then hovered her above cloud nine. With their gazes locked, and unable to hold back any longer, she lost herself in their carnal world, as did he, and they tumbled, together, into a sensory abyss.

Gasping for breath, Joel rolled to his side. Juliette snuggled into him, her heart swelling with love for this magnificent man. They took a few moments to come back to earth and to catch their breaths. To just be with each other.

'It's truly all over, isn't it?' she whispered into his chest as he stroked her hair.

'Yes, it is.' He bent and pressed a kiss onto her cheek.

'When you came back to Little Heart, I never thought I'd get to tell you how much I love you, but here we are, loving each other like crazy.' Snuggling in closer, she smiled from the inside out.

'Yup, and ain't it just the best?' Joel's voice was husky, dreamy.

'It sure is,' she said, squeezing him tighter.

Joel tipped her chin and captured her gaze. 'I never understood the true meaning of forever until I fell in love with you, Jules.'

'That's so beautiful.' She brought her hand to his cheek. 'I love you so much.'

Joel placed his hand over hers, smiling. 'I love you too, always have and always will.'

Juliette blinked back happy tears as she brought her cheek to his chest, savouring the sound of his big beautiful heart beating beneath it. This, right here, was all she'd ever truly wanted, or needed.

Finally, their life together could begin.

ACKNOWLEDGEMENTS

A colossal cheers to my incredible team at Harlequin Headquarters – from my wonderful publisher Rachael Donovan, who has pushed me to places I never imagined and keeps on pushing me to reach past my comfort zones, to my meticulous editors ... Libby Turner, I've thoroughly enjoyed working with you and look forward to doing so in the future, and Julia and Annabel – you're both the best! To the design wizards who've once again created a tremendously captivating cover with a hottie pattotti front and centre, and the rest of the inspiring and supportive team who've helped make The Stockman's Secret the very best it can be. I thank my lucky stars to have been part of the wonderfully supportive Harlequin family for many years now, and I look forward to many more to come.

To my beautiful, sweet girl, Chloe Rose. You're such an inspiration to me, my darling daughter. The way you see the world, the way you show endless love, keeps me on my path of kindness and gentleness. You're a blessing in my life, and I love seeing your smiling face each and every day. Thank you for being you, and for loving me the way you do. I'm one lucky mum! Xx

To my magnificent mum, Gaye, I honestly can't put into words just how much you mean to me. You've sacrificed so much for me, and love Chloe with all your heart, and then some. I feel extremely blessed and proud to call you my mum, and my best friend. You know me better than anyone else in this world and love me the most. Thank you, for the amazing human being you are. Love you heaps.

To my wonderful dad, John. You've taught me the importance of standing strong, and also humbling myself to forgive – for these two qualities, I will always be thankful. Both have gotten me through some of my toughest battles in life – and I've had my share. I love you for the amazingly wise and caring man you are. Xx

To my awesome sisters and sisters-in-law, Mia, Karla, Talia, Kristy, Rochelle, and Hayley.

What a strong bunch of women you are, in so many unique ways. I love you all dearly. Xx

To my beautiful friend, Ebony … we crossed paths and connected from the get-go. You're an awesome soul, in so many ways – I cherish every moment we get to hang out together. Love being a road rebel with you – stuff the leathers! And thanks for being a set of eyes, as well as a passionate reader of my books! Xx

To my beautiful Soul Sister, Fiona Stanford. We live so far apart, yet we are super close. You've been by my side from the beginning of my writing journey Fi, and I know you will remain by my side for the rest of the way. You rock, Sis! Love you heaps! Xx

To my gorgeous German forever friend, Katie! You may live thousands of miles away, over the other side of the world, but you're always close to my heart. We've shared some crazy adventures, ones that have inspired many of my stories. I've known you for almost half my lifetime now … and will know and love you for the rest of it. Come visit me in Australia! I miss you, oh dear Katie! Xx

And lastly, but most importantly of all, a huge, wholehearted cheers to YOU, the reader! I'm constantly humbled to have so many of you reaching out to me to tell me how much you love my books. I treasure how I can take you away from the stresses of life and fill your hearts with love and joy. Without each and every one of you, I wouldn't be doing what I love. So, a huge group hug for this! I honestly still have to pinch myself when I see a book with my name on the front on the shelf … it will never get old. I admire how many of you have been on my journey the past fourteen years, and I enjoy meeting my new readers along the way. Here's to me breathing life into more sexy heroes and strong country-blooded heroines in the future! I've got so many stories waiting to be told.

Until my next book has you hiding somewhere quiet, tucked away from the demands of life, keep smiling and dreaming!

Mandy xoxo

talk about it

Let's talk about books.

Join the conversation:

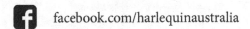 facebook.com/harlequinaustralia

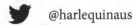 @harlequinaus

 @harlequinaus

harpercollins.com.au/hq

If you love reading and want to know about our
authors and titles, then let's talk about it.